Raves for Mark

UNQ

"Connor Grey is rapidly becoming one of my favorite fantasy detectives."
—*Locus*

"A tale filled with magic, mystery, and suspense . . . a well-written story with characters that will charm readers back for another visit to the Weird."
—*Darque Reviews*

"A solid adventure filled with unique characters and plenty of fast-paced suspense."
—*Pulp Fiction Reviews*

"Mark Del Franco is a master at combining modern fantasy with crime-detective mystery. Fans of either genre are sure to find a good read in *Unquiet Dreams*."
—*BookLoons*

"An urban fantasy wrapped around a police procedural that makes for a fast-paced, action-packed novel . . . This looks to be a great new urban fantasy series, judging by the first two books in the series."
—*Gumshoe*

"Del Franco's clear and textured voice ensures that readers vest instantly in characters and story. Waiting for the next installment will be tough."
—*Romantic Times*

"Readers who like a mystery as the prime plot of an outstanding fantasy will be thoroughly entertained and challenged. This is a great new series with the potential to be a long-lasting one."
—*Genre Go Round Reviews*

UNSHAPELY THINGS

"It will pull you along a corkscrew of twists and turns to a final, cataclysmic battle that could literally remake the world."
—Rob Thurman, national bestselling author of *Deathwish*

"[An] entertaining contemporary fantasy mystery with a hard-boiled druid detective . . . a promising start to a new series."
—*Locus*

continued . . .

"An engaging urban fantasy . . . a bravura finale."

—SF Reviews.net

"Masterfully blends detective thriller with fantasy . . . a fast-paced thrill ride . . . Del Franco never pauses the action . . . and Connor Grey is a very likable protagonist. The twisting action and engaging lead make *Unshapely Things* hard to put down."

—*BookLoons*

"The intriguing cast of characters keeps the readers involved with the mystery wrapped up in the fantasy . . . I look forward to spending more time with Connor in the future and learning more about him and his world."

—*Gumshoe*

"A wonderfully written, richly detailed, and complex fantasy novel with twists and turns that make it unputdownable . . . Mr. Del Franco's take on magic and paranormal elements is fresh and intriguing. Connor Grey's an appealing hero bound to delight fantasy and paranormal romance fans alike."

—*The Romance Readers Connection*

"Compelling and fast paced . . . The world building is superb . . . Fans of urban fantasy should get a kick out of book one in this new series."

—*Romantic Times*

"A very impressive start. The characters were engaging and believable, and the plot was intriguing. I found myself unable to put it down until I had devoured it completely, and I'm eagerly looking forward to the sequel."

—*Book Fetish*

"A wonderful, smart, and action-packed mystery involving dead fairies, political intrigue, and maybe a plot to destroy humanity . . . *Unshapely Things* has everything it takes to launch a long-running series, and I'm very excited to see what Del Franco has in store next for Connor Grey and his friends."

—*Bookslut*

Ace Books by Mark Del Franco

The Connor Grey Series
UNSHAPELY THINGS
UNQUIET DREAMS
UNFALLEN DEAD

The Laura Blackstone Series
SKIN DEEP

SKIN DEEP

Mark Del Franco

ACE BOOKS, NEW YORK

THE BERKLEY PUBLISHING GROUP
Published by the Penguin Group
Penguin Group (USA) Inc.
375 Hudson Street, New York, New York 10014, USA
Penguin Group (Canada), 90 Eglinton Avenue East, Suite 700, Toronto, Ontario M4P 2Y3, Canada
(a division of Pearson Penguin Canada Inc.)
Penguin Books Ltd., 80 Strand, London WC2R 0RL, England
Penguin Group Ireland, 25 St. Stephen's Green, Dublin 2, Ireland (a division of Penguin Books Ltd.)
Penguin Group (Australia), 250 Camberwell Road, Camberwell, Victoria 3124, Australia
(a division of Pearson Australia Group Pty. Ltd.)
Penguin Books India Pvt. Ltd., 11 Community Centre, Panchsheel Park, New Delhi—110 017, India
Penguin Group (NZ), 67 Apollo Drive, Rosedale, North Shore 0632, New Zealand
(a division of Pearson New Zealand Ltd.)
Penguin Books (South Africa) (Pty.) Ltd., 24 Sturdee Avenue, Rosebank, Johannesburg 2196,
South Africa

Penguin Books Ltd., Registered Offices: 80 Strand, London WC2R 0RL, England

This is a work of fiction. Names, characters, places, and incidents either are the product of the author's imagination or are used fictitiously, and any resemblance to actual persons, living or dead, business establishments, events, or locales is entirely coincidental. The publisher does not have any control over and does not assume any responsibility for author or third-party websites or their content.

SKIN DEEP

An Ace Book / published by arrangement with the author

PRINTING HISTORY
Ace mass-market edition / August 2009

Copyright © 2009 by Mark Del Franco.
Cover art by Chris Cocozza.
Cover design by Annette Fiore DeFex.
Interior text design by Laura K. Corless.

ISBN: 978-0-441-01743-0

ACE
Ace Books are published by The Berkley Publishing Group,
a division of Penguin Group (USA) Inc.,
375 Hudson Street, New York, New York 10014.
ACE and the "A" design are trademarks of Penguin Group (USA) Inc.

PRINTED IN THE UNITED STATES OF AMERICA

10 9 8 7 6 5 4 3 2 1

For Jack, who made this one possible

SKIN
DEEP

1
CHAPTER

AS SHE LEANED back in her seat, the van's motion vibrated against the base of Laura Blackstone's skull. She rocked her head, hoping it would soothe her tense muscles. It didn't. Odors tickled her nose—the scents of hot electronics, clean gun oil, and leather uniforms. If someone blindfolded her and spun her around, she'd still know immediately that she was inside a SWAT-team van.

She couldn't see outside the van, but she didn't need to sightsee in Anacostia. With years of law enforcement under her belt, she knew all of Washington, D.C.'s neighborhoods well. The historic Anacostia had its share of crime and urban blight mixed in with bland strip malls and expensive homes.

This time, the neighborhood had a drug lab that the local SWAT team wanted taken down. Nothing unusual about that—it was what SWAT teams did. And since Captain Aaron Foyle needed specialized backup, he called someone he could rely on: Laura Blackstone. Actually, he called "Janice Crawford." That was the persona Laura used when she worked with the local D.C. SWAT team.

Laura looked at the men in the van and, not for the first

time, wondered what humans thought of her, really thought of her. Did they see the person behind the ability? Or was she always perceived as this fey being who manipulated essence, some inhuman thing with the power to perform what they believed was magic?

After over a century of coexistence with humans, the fey were still feared and misunderstood. Unlike most fey, Laura wasn't technically from Faerie—she had been born and raised in the United States, an American citizen. That helped smooth the way in most social situations since she didn't have the same cultural baggage as the Old Ones—the fey originally from Faerie. Laura and the other here-born fey fit into the modern world, and what's more, they wanted to fit in. They could pass.

And Laura passed as human better than most fey. Druids didn't look different. They didn't have long, pointed ears like Teutonic elves or strange-colored skin like the solitary fey. They didn't fly like the Celtic fairy clans. They didn't have wings at all. The difference between druids and humans—between Laura and humans—was that she manipulated essence, and they didn't. Couldn't.

Tapping into the inherent energy around them, the fey used essence to fly or to fight or simply to turn on the lights. What was as natural to Laura as breathing, humans called magic. She couldn't understand their fear.

As they neared their target, the tension built in the van. Laura pulled at her flak jacket, trying to adjust it so it fit more comfortably. Again. They weren't made for women. Conversations muted or faded away as the other team members readied for the assault. Everyone dealt with those last few minutes differently. Laura was glad no one in the group was a talker. The less small talk she made, the fewer details she had to commit to memory for the Janice Crawford persona. Instead, she spent her time mentally reviewing her agenda for the next day's meeting at the Guildhouse.

When the public saw Laura Blackstone—the actual Laura Blackstone—it only ever saw a public-relations director for the Fey Guild. Her role was to put a good face on fey activities. Some people thought that meant making excuses for whatever trouble the fairies and elves and other fey got into. Laura liked to think it was a matter of perspective.

Sometime in the early part of the twentieth century, the realm of Faerie merged with modern reality. No one knew what had happened to cause what came to be known as Convergence, although it was clear it was something that had occurred in Faerie. Over the next hundred years, the fey moved out into the greater world and became part of the social and political landscape. In order to gain human allies and assure people that the fey meant no harm, the Seelie Court established the Guild to respond to concerns raised by both humans and the fey.

The Guild played many different roles. It served as the diplomatic embassy for High Queen Maeve of the Seelie Court at Tara, the fairy queen who rarely ventured outside her mist-shrouded home in Ireland. The Guild also worked as a policing force on the local level for magic-related crimes committed by the fey.

But for criminal activity on the international level, the Seelie Court, along with the governments of other nations, provided law-enforcement staff to the International Global Security Agency—InterSec—to investigate and resolve criminal activities wherever needed. And Laura Blackstone was one of InterSec's best operatives.

By day, Laura sent out press releases. But by night, she had another life as an agent with InterSec, which no one at the Guild knew about. Only a few outside InterSec knew Laura Blackstone worked undercover. She had spent years keeping it that way.

The SWAT team's intelligence had uncovered information that the drug lab had two brownies as security. Brownies were low-powered Celtic fey. From an essence point of view, they had enormous stamina, great organizational skills, and other rudimentary essence abilities. They were useful as security guards dealing with humans, but for someone with druidic training, brownies weren't much to worry about.

Laura overheard enough of Captain Foyle's radio conversation to know they were close to the mission target. Foyle rose from his seat as the van slowed and stopped. "Arrived."

The tactical team stood, guns ready, black helmet visors down. They hopped out on silent-soled shoes, adjusting gas masks into place as they moved into formation. Foyle grabbed Laura's arm at the door. "Where's your gun, Crawford?"

Laura turned her visored face to him. She knew the staff file Foyle had reviewed, one of several different résumés she maintained for different personas. It didn't tell her whole story. Foyle didn't need to know Laura was an expert marksman—which wasn't part of her Janice bio. That was not why she worked with SWAT teams. As far as Foyle was concerned, all Laura—Janice—did was work essence. As a druid, she had a long list of skills that came with her heritage. She could pull energy out of organic material—even people if circumstances were dire—and channel it into bolts of burning essence. Or she could use that same energy force to create a barrier of hardened essence to protect herself and others. If Foyle needed someone to shoot a gun, she wasn't going to waste her time doing it for him. Plenty of humans were expert marksmen. "I don't use one."

To his credit, Foyle didn't show any anger. "You have enough essence ability to overcome interference from metal. Take the Uzi pistol, at least."

Metal, particularly iron, complicated using essence. Unless, as Foyle said, someone had enough ability to overcome its effects, metal warped the aim of an essence-bolt or caused a spell to fail. Laura had no problem with metal at all. The Janice persona profile gave her enough ability to be competent against it. Laura didn't change the tone of her voice. "If you saw my file, you also saw I've never shot anyone. I don't intend to start tonight. We do our job right, I won't need a gun."

It was an equivocation on her part. Janice had never shot

anyone. Laura had, though. She wasn't keen to do it again. They stared at each other. Foyle released her arm. "Okay. Stay where I can see you."

Laura hopped to the pavement into the stark white light of a streetlamp. Other units moved in the shadows outside the pool of light, checking their weapons. Foyle had chosen a night-time assault to avoid the presence of civilians as much as possible. They stopped a block from the target—a brick apartment complex, run-down and mostly abandoned. Laura fell in behind the rest of the team while Foyle took the lead. He led them down the street at a hustling gait. Laura liked Aaron Foyle. He had the classic command résumé, a former Marine who had risen through the urban-assault ranks at an above-average rate, someone people looked up to.

Sweat trickled down her back. In addition to the standard SWAT-team gear, she wore her natural body shield. To the sharp-eyed, a slight air distortion shimmered around her body when light struck it from certain angles. Her body signature was strong, especially for a druid, and the shield drew enough energy from it to blunt the force of anything thrown at it.

Behind Foyle, Salvatore Gianni carried the battering ram, which looked like a toy in his large hands. Gianni was a big slab of a man and struck Laura as the type who was good at what he did and happy to leave it at that. Every unit needed leaders and followers. She saw Gianni taking the role of good soldier for Foyle, content to do his part and be that guy who waited for orders.

Her heart rate jumped as the street ran between close buildings. The narrow lane provided perfect cover for an ambush. As they scuttled along the cracked sidewalk, she scanned the rooflines. No movement anywhere. Her anxiety spiked at the emptiness. She noted it in a detached, professional way, years of experience having taught her to keep focused on the job at hand and not her emotions. After the mission was over, she could deal with feelings.

When Terryn macCullen, her superior at InterSec, mentioned in a meeting that he wanted more contacts in the D.C. police force, she volunteered to go undercover. As an InterSec freelancer for the SWAT team, the newly created Janice Crawford persona wouldn't take up much time, and Laura wouldn't have to travel. Despite some misgivings, armed missions spiced things up once in a while, though they were not something she wanted to do on a regular basis. She might be an expert shooter, but that didn't make her bulletproof.

The team threaded through a tired section of the neighborhood that had never seen gentrification and probably never would. Most buildings had graffiti or broken windows. Most streetlights were out. Most people who lived down there were armed as a routine precaution. It was a far cry from the more commercial districts that had the sheen of middle-class commerce.

Behind Gianni ran Gabrio Sanchez, a tough guy whom Laura pegged as someone who liked the adrenaline rush of confrontation, liked being point man as much as possible. His record impressed her, though she suspected a few too many achievements were based on luck. He flirted with her during the entire prelim meeting. She had seen it before, the macho swagger of someone who had earned a position in the elite squad. She did her best to ignore him. As long as he didn't pull the save-the-damsel-in-distress routine with her, she'd let him ogle her all he wanted.

An abandoned apartment complex came into view, several low-rise buildings three stories high. A few apartments on the street side of the property had been cleared of squatters, and a line of officers were stationed to keep bystanders out of the line of fire. Intelligence located the drug lab near the middle of the property. A central building on the edge of what might once have been a playground was the main target. Laura scanned for snipers and security cameras. Nothing. She had expected at least one person outside, but there were other ways to keep a lookout. The dealers probably thought the brownies were more than adequate. Still, the lack of outside scouts made her uneasy.

When she was a teen, she realized her essence-sensing

abilities were poor. Despite substantial power, she had limited range in sensing the body signatures of others, something druids usually were the most adept at. Laura had to practically be on top of someone before she could sense their species essence. She kept her deficiency a secret, worried it meant she would be perceived as weak and destined for an unexciting desk job. That fear made her more sensitive to visual cues and her own intuition. And her intuition kept warning her that the drug dealers should have had a lookout.

Jonathan Sinclair, the last of the entry unit, took position in front of her. He was the newest member of Foyle's squad. Where Gianni was stout and wide, Sinclair was tall and imposing. An underlying calm flowed off him that Laura thought could either make him sharp under pressure or overconfident. He had solid skills and good recommendations from well-placed people, so she decided to watch him in action before she made any judgments.

The Metropolitan Police barricaded the street a block in either direction to keep civilians out. SWAT-team members peeled away from the line to take up positions in doorways while others broke off down an alley to secure the rear of the building. The clock ticked off the last few minutes before the team made its move.

Of the squad from the van, only the five of them remained in motion to act as the entry unit. Foyle fell back as they neared the building entrance. Sanchez took point while Gianni moved up with the ram. Laura allowed Sinclair to shift into a protective posture beside her. While she could hold her own, having someone with a gun watch her back until the action started was prudent.

Laura focused on the spot in her mind that controlled essence. The desolate playground offered little but dirt and worn grass, which made the essence flow feeble, but she pulled enough from her surroundings to establish a good base charge. White light bathed her hands as essence flowed through her. She let the power build and held it primed for release.

Adrenaline surged through her in the last microseconds

before entry. As the team reached the entrance, everything seemed to speed up and slow down at the same time. Sanchez overshot the door and took the right flank while Foyle took the left. Gianni had the ram in motion as he slipped between them. She and Sinclair hung back to let them do their work.

Essence cluttered the doorway. Everyone and everything left essence behind on things they touched, even the air. It dissipated over time. At narrow entry points like doors, people crossed and recrossed their essence trails, leaving a jumble of signatures for anyone fey to sense. Even standing several feet away and with Sinclair blocking the way, Laura felt a flurry of species signatures. Illicit activity brought together diverse people, and here it was no different: humans, elves, druids, and odd sensations that meant solitaries—fairies who fit no general fey category. The trails were fresher than she would have liked, but she trusted Foyle had moved the team in at the right time.

With a single strike from the piston-action ram, Gianni took out the door. It jumped in its frame, curling outward in a puff of dust. In a synchronized dance, Gianni spun away as Sanchez grabbed an edge of the metal door and yanked. It slammed to the ground. Foyle tossed in a flash-bang grenade, and everyone ducked. Despite her visor, closed eyes, and turned head, Laura saw the flash. The wall vibrated against her back from the concussive force.

A fraction of a second after detonation, Sanchez led the entry team in while shouting identification. Three humans lay inside the door. Laura sensed they were dazed and dismissed them. The point team leaped over the prone bodies, leaving them for the sweep unit to secure.

They charged down a dark, narrow hall, Gianni and Sanchez running shoulder to shoulder. Laura moved in a crouch behind Sinclair and Foyle. Ignoring the shouts of "Police" and "Stand down," she opened herself to the surrounding essence, searching for the body signatures of her targets. Her job was to take the brownies out of commission. The rest of the team would secure the drug lab.

Tightening her focus, she found the distinct body signatures of two brownies. Intelligence on the mark, she thought. One signature felt stronger. The first brownie had been standing in the hall shortly before the door came down. Twenty feet in, she felt the second signature, then the cool static of a cast spell.

"Everybody down!" she shouted.

The team didn't hesitate. In unison, they stopped, ducked, and crouched to either side. A bolt of yellow lightning scorched the air above them. Laura gauged the trajectory, threw out her hand, and released her essence reserve in a wide flare. She smiled as, up ahead, a male voice gave a short scream. Someone on the team tossed a smoke grenade forward.

Human essence surrounded her. Except for the team, she didn't recognize any of it, which meant they were targets. She clicked on the microphone on her radio headset. "We've got three on the left, two straight ahead, all human. I'm getting metal essence warping on the left. We've got guns, people."

Foyle and Sanchez shifted positions as gunfire burst from the left. Concerned, urgent chatter crackled on Laura's headset as other units reacted, followed by Foyle's calm assurances that they were fine.

She felt the other brownie receding into the building. With little mental effort, she pulled a small node of essence into her head and imprinted her thoughts on it. The fey called the process "sending" because they used it to project mental messages and images to others. Laura liked using them because they were faster, and sometimes she didn't have the few moments to dial a phone number or click on a radio. She threw the sending to Foyle's mind. *The first brownie is down. The second is running to the rear. Second unit back there can't handle it. I need to go in.*

Foyle's voice came over her headset. "Sanchez with Crawford. Gianni and Sinclair, cover fire on my lead."

Straight ahead, Laura sent to Sanchez. She stepped around Sinclair to move in close with Sanchez. Foyle and the others opened fire as she and Sanchez charged past the open doorway. Stray reaction fire responded.

"What've we got?" Sanchez radioed.

Two at two o'clock. I'll smoke them. Keep going straight.
She pulled a canister from her vest and tossed it as two
humans appeared in a doorway on the right. They stumbled
back as acidic haze erupted around them. Sanchez released
a burst of suppression fire, and they rushed past. A bend in
the hallway blocked their line of sight. Sanchez laid more
fire into the opposite wall and rolled across the floor. He
signaled all clear, and Laura came in behind him.

An explosion rumbled farther up the hall. The reverberation made her stumble into Sanchez as the lights went out.
Sanchez cursed under his breath as radio chatter filled their
ears. "The drug lab is down there. Sounds like we lost it,"
he said.

The infrared in her goggles snapped on. A wave of nausea rolled through her as the night vision conflicted with
her essence vision. She turned off the infrared.

"Which way?" asked Sanchez.

*Ahead and left. The brownie's around the next corner, let
me . . . Hold on.* They froze in place, hugging the wall.
Laura blocked out the noise of shouts and gunfire and concentrated on the body signature. The brownie essence wavered in her senses. One moment it felt like a brownie should
feel, the next it intensified. She pushed at her essence-
sensing ability to sharpen its acuity. The brownie felt normal again. Brownies liked to work with wards—stones the
fey used to accompany spells. The brownie ahead of them
must have some kind of ward on him, an amplifier perhaps,
to boost his firepower.

*We're good. Lay down cover, then drop. I'll hit the tar-
get. You secure,* she sent to Sanchez.

"Got it," he said.

They reached a doorway at the turn. Sanchez went in
low, firing, and dropped to the floor. Laura followed him
and released a burst of essence into the room. The small,
dark shape of the brownie wheeled away from her with
surprising speed.

Dammit. I missed him, Sanchez. Be careful.

They huddled behind an overturned desk. The walls between several rooms had been torn open to make one large space. The odd sight of workstations of machinery cluttered the area—it seemed to be some type of abandoned illegal sweatshop. The metal warped Laura's essence perception, the only ability it tended to affect since it was her weakest. A strong brownie signature at the far end of the room read as living essence. That was all she cared about. Behind her, she sensed more body signatures building up in the hallway, unknown humans, not SWAT personnel. She kept them at the edge of her awareness, but focused on the brownie.

Get behind me and watch the door. Sanchez didn't question her, but let her—unarmed from the human perspective—take the point. She guessed he was used to working with fey folk, probably partnered with the team's regular druid, who was out on sick leave.

She drew essence into her hands, a charge large enough to knock the brownie unconscious. Taking a deep breath, she sprang up and fired, running the length of the room. The brownie appeared for a brief moment—almost as tall as she, medium brown skin, and rust-colored hair. His plain face twisted in annoyance as he raised his own hands and returned fire. Laura dodged it and caught him with a shot full in the chest. He fell behind a stack of packing crates.

Laura skidded to a stop. The brownie essence wavered and faded away, replaced by another species signature. Glamoured. He wasn't a brownie. She was chasing an Inverni fairy glamoured to appear as a brownie. He had been playing the same game she was—hiding his true nature behind an illusion, and a dangerous illusion at that. Janice Crawford, with her supposedly limited abilities, could handle a brownie. An Inverni fairy, though, was at least as powerful as Laura Blackstone's full abilities.

Trouble, she sent to Sanchez.

Gunfire erupted behind her.

"Here, too. Stay down," Sanchez radioed.

Laura sensed fear in the outer hall. Fear enhanced essence signatures, especially faint human ones, and helped her pick things up beyond her normal sensing range. *You've got three targets, Sanchez. The first is five feet to the left of the door, two more six feet behind him.*

"Got it." She liked his detached reaction, especially since, from the sound of things, the mission was spiraling out of control. She was hearing too much gunfire. These people were prepared, better prepared than the intel had indicated to say nothing of the unexpected challenge of an Inverni fairy. Behind her, Sanchez fired. By the screams in the hall, she judged it a good hit.

The Inverni wasn't moving. Laura imagined that he was doing the same thing she was—assessing the next move, trying to gauge the power of the opponent. Invernis were among the most powerful of the fairy clans. They had strong resilience against essence-fire, which made them challenging enough to face without the other huge advantage they had maneuvering against a druid: Invernis could fly.

She decided surprise and aggression were her best options. Because of their power, Invernis tended not to expect frontal assaults. She hardened her body shield and ran toward him. As she reached the crates, he rose with a fiercely determined face.

Laura ducked as he gestured, pale blue essence crackling from his fingers. The machinery nearby warped the strike, sending it off target. Laura reached out with her own ability and reflected the bolt back at him. It splintered in two, one branch arcing back to the crates, the other hitting the workstation next to Laura. The Inverni ducked. Laura's right side burned incandescent white as her body shield absorbed the backlash. She released her shield to deflect the overflow into the floor. In that moment of exposure, a stray essence-spark grazed her shoulder. Essence coursed through her, like an electrical shock of hot pain. Her essence-sensing ability flickered and vanished.

Dammit. I'm head-blind, Sanchez.

"Tie that up back there. I've got four more on me." Sanchez's voice sounded tight in her earpiece. More gunfire exploded and another flash-bang went off.

Laura shook her head, but the head-blindness stayed

with her. Something wasn't right. No one protected a drug lab this much. She hardened her body shield again and drew essence into her hands. She was strong enough to take down the Inverni but needed to be closer.

Aiming, she fired and charged forward. The crates burst, debris flying in all directions. The Inverni scrambled away and launched into the air as he returned fire, his blade-like wings ablaze with indigo light. Laura made a running slide under a nearby table as bolts of essence shot down.

She imprinted as many details as possible to her memory as the Inverni rose toward the ceiling. Short brownish hair, elongated body, sharp features. By the way he was dressed—an oddly tailored suit and a satchel strapped across his chest—he didn't look like he had been expecting a fight.

Short bursts of essence pinned her under the table. The Inverni fired at the ceiling with his other hand. Rolling from side to side, Laura followed his line of fire. He was targeting a soot-dark skylight to blow open an escape route. Between firing at her and the skylight and the satchel restricting his wings, he missed both targets. Laura paused, timed her move to his shots, and rolled onto her back.

She fired a lancing blow across the Inverni's chest. He tumbled backward and hit the wall. Recovering, he rose toward the skylight again. A smile crossed Laura's face. She wasn't going to let him get away. She blocked his path with a barrage of essence-bolts. With a frustrated cry, he changed tactics and bore down on her, hands outstretched and glowing.

The pile of crates next to her toppled. She rolled away as they thundered down, trapping her under the remains of the table. She heard glass breaking and shards hit the floor around her.

"Crawford?" Sanchez radioed.

I'm good, she sent. She lifted her head. Debris caged her in, splintered crates on all sides. Inches away from her face, incongruous, a USB thumb drive lay among chips and scraps of wood. It was cracked and hot when she picked it up, and she slipped it into her vest.

"Your target escaped. I could use you back here," Sanchez radioed.

Working on it, she sent. Laura swore under her breath. One part of her assessed the situation while another prepared a tirade for Foyle. Sanchez had been calling for backup since they entered the room, but no one was showing up. It was sloppy. If the damned Inverni hadn't escaped, she wasn't sure how long she could have held out against him.

She pushed and pulled at the crates until one that didn't threaten to collapse the entire pile on her moved. A burst of essence skittered several boxes away. She crawled through the opening.

Her stomach clenched as Sanchez abruptly gasped in her earpiece. *Sanchez?*

He didn't answer. Another flash-bang went off, then a smoke grenade. She exhaled in relief. *Sanchez, what's your status?*

Anxiety welled up as she heard a strangled sound. She crawled among the remains of the crates. Moonlight shone through the shattered skylight and gave the smoke in the room an eerie glow. She tried to open her essence-sensing ability, but her head still buzzed from the Inverni's hit.

No shooting sounded. Out in the hall, the firefight was dying down. Running in a crouch back to Sanchez, Laura powered essence into her hands. In the haze, she made out his uniformed body hunched behind the desk. Sanchez sat with his head tucked. His gun lay on the ground next to him. She put a hand on his shoulder. "Sanchez?"

He groaned and rolled to face her, his hands clutched at his neck. Laura sucked in a breath as blood seeped between his fingers. She hit her radio comm. "Man down! Man down! Back hall, first door on the left!"

She tried to pry his fingers away. Sanchez shook his head. He opened his mouth, exposing bright white teeth framed with blood. "Stop."

The rest of his words were lost in a gurgling rasp. "Stop what?" Laura asked.

When he tried to speak, he voiced a nauseating liquid

sound instead. Whatever happened to cause the mission to fall apart was beside the point now. She had to focus. Laura pressed her hands firmly against his to help staunch the wound. Closing her eyes, she summoned all the healing knowledge she had. She pushed aside the thought of her low-level medical skills and chanted. Essence flowed out of her, and their clasped hands glowed with its white light, tinged pink from Sanchez's blood.

He stared at her with intent eyes, willing her to succeed. The blood flow continued. They both applied pressure to the wound while Laura chanted.

Sanchez's eyelids fluttered, and his head lolled to the side.

"Dammit! I need a medic now!" Laura shouted into her radio.

Sanchez relaxed his grip. "Stop. Try," he managed to say.

Blood pulsed thick and dark from a deep gash. Laura pressed her hands into the wound. "I won't stop. Come on, Sanchez, hang on. They're coming. Hang on."

He grabbed her left wrist and pulled. Laura struggled against him. "No! Stop it. They're coming. Just a few more minutes."

Sanchez brought his other hand up and pulled her left arm away. She grappled with him, but his grip steadily pulled her hand away. He forced her arm back and thrust his hand into hers, scratching at her bloody palm. "Stop," he said.

Laura stared down at the marks he made. "A? What are trying to say? Aaron?"

Sanchez shook his head, the effort feeble. Not Aaron Foyle. He tried again. This time Laura thought it was a number. "Four?"

He started once more, but his head fell back. His eyes closed, and his arms dropped to his sides. Laura stared in horror as his essence faded. A noise from the doorway caught her attention. Everything slowed down again. The smoke receded from her as if the hallway had inhaled. A hazy silhouette appeared. Laura leaned forward, expecting a medic. The muzzle of a gun flashed. Something hit her head with the hardest punch she had ever felt. Red light filled her vision as she fell backward. Her head slammed against the floor, then everything went dark.

A moment—an eon—later she opened her eyes and heard shouting and confused voices chattering on her earpiece. Three men stood over her.

"Is she dead?" one asked.

Someone knelt. She recognized Sinclair, smelled rich, burnt gunpowder on him. "She's alive."

Darkness and silence descended, sounds receding first, then her vision becoming narrower and narrower. Foyle leaned in next to Sinclair. Laura fought against a faint. She dragged her right hand across her body, trailing a clumsy hand along her biceps. Under the sleeve of her uniform, she found the small, flat sending stone embedded under her flesh. She pressed it firmly before blacking out.

The stone pulsed with an emergency sending.

2
CHAPTER

IN HER FIRST moments of awareness, Laura realized three things in quick succession: she was propped up in a hospital bed, she had no idea where she was, and she had no idea what she looked like. Panicked, she lurched up and slammed her body shield on. The beeping rhythm of a heart monitor increased.

A soft hand touched her arm. "Relax. You're safe."

Relieved to hear Cress's voice, she dropped back against the pillows as she realized she was in the med clinic at the Guildhouse. Safe. Protected by the layers of security of the InterSec unit.

On a green vinyl armchair next to the bed, Cress perched with her usual stiff posture. The thin smile on her face softened her unsettling whiteless eyes. Laura thought most people would not be relieved to know they were being watched over by a *leanansidhe*. The *leanansidhe* survived by absorbing essence, and the greatest and easiest source was people. They had few, if any, moral qualms about draining living beings. Cress, though, had chosen a different path and turned to healing. Whatever anxieties Laura had about *leanansidhe* in general, she had no doubt Cress was one of the best healers she had ever met.

Laura rubbed her face. "How long have I been out?"

Cress checked her watch. "Eight and a half hours."

"Was I compromised?"

Cress smiled. "No, we responded to your signal in plenty of time. Janice Crawford lives on."

Laura exhaled to calm herself. The Crawford identity would have required a ton of paperwork to replace. "Did Sanchez make it?"

Cress shook her head. "Dead at the scene."

Anger burned in her chest. Sanchez's neck wound had been too severe. She had known that as soon as she saw it. He hadn't had a chance. She remembered trying to fuse the rip in his skin, but she hadn't had enough healing skill. She didn't think anybody would have in that situation. The image of him struggling with her rose in her mind, then vanished, leaving nothing but a vague sense of frustration and fear. Laura looked down at her hand. "Was I holding something when you found me?"

"We found a USB drive in your vest. Terryn has it. How do you feel?""

Laura regarded her hand a moment longer, then curled the fingers closed. "Slight headache. What happened? The last thing I remember was Sanchez bleeding."

Cress couldn't hide a smile. "You were shot in the head."

"What?" she said.

Cress leaned forward and placed a gentle hand on Laura's arm. "You're fine. It was a grazing shot. Your helmet took the brunt of it."

Laura gingerly touched the left side of her head. "I don't remember it."

Cress nodded. "You have a concussion. Some memory loss is typical, but you should regain it quickly."

As Cress spoke, Laura picked up the strong essence signature of an Inverni fairy approaching the room, which made her realize that she could sense Cress's body signature as well. She had been head-blind at the apartment-complex raid, that much she remembered. But the episode had been thankfully temporary. Her sensing ability had returned. A moment later, Terryn macCullen entered.

Despite a passive expression, the tall Inverni's translucent wings undulated in agitation, pinpoints of white and
blue flashing in the faint veining. Stray strands of his hair,
blacker than night, drifted in the essence flowing off him.
His eyes glittered a deep emerald against his unearthly pal-
lor. Cress stretched up and out of the chair with a sensual
shiver that drew Terryn's gaze. Even without an exchange
of words, Laura felt the emotional bond between the two.

He scanned Laura's face but spoke to Cress. "Can she
report for duty?"

Cress spoke to Laura instead of Terryn. "You should rest
a couple of days, but I don't think there's any damage."

Laura tried to smile. She clenched her hand again, wondering what she was not remembering. "I feel fine."

Terryn shifted his eyes to Laura. "Excuse us, Cress."

As she left, the essence field of Cress's body signature
interacted with Terryn's. He gave no sign of it, but Laura
sensed the satisfaction it gave him. Their relationship sus-
tained Cress and kept the predatory aspect of her *leanansidhe* nature in check. By willingly letting her siphon some
of his essence, Terryn helped her rise above what her biol-
ogy demanded. Laura wasn't sure what he got out of it.

"Did you have your shield up?" said Terryn.

Laura frowned. "I would be surprised if I didn't. I remember being head-blind, so the body shield could have
been affected, too."

"Tell me what happened."

She recounted the raid in a detached, formal manner as
she told him the events step-by-step, from the moment she
left the van until the moment she looked up from the
wounded body of Sanchez. Her memory failed there, a gap
she tried not to show frustration over. As a druid, she had a
natural talent for memory retention, and years of training
had honed it. Druids might not always recall instantly, but
they almost never forgot.

Terryn's eyes narrowed when she told him about the unexpected presence of the Inverni fairy, but he didn't interrupt. She wondered what he would say or do about it. The
Inverni fairies were powerful, and Terryn's family had ruled

over the largest clans for generations. An Inverni involved with a crime like drug dealing—to say nothing of trying to kill a police officer—was not something that would be taken lightly by the clans when they heard about it. Invernis had enough problems with their political image without adding lawbreaking to it.

"You remember nothing after summoning help for Sanchez?" he asked.

Laura pushed herself higher on the bed. "It went bad from the get-go, Terryn. Either the intelligence was wrong or there was a tip-off."

He pulled the damaged USB drive from the pocket of his tunic and handed it to her. "Does anyone else know about this?"

She pursed her lips. "I don't think I mentioned it on the comm. I saw it, thought it was odd, and picked it up. It had to have come from the Inverni. I got a good hit on a bag he was carrying. I was alone when I found it, that I'm sure of."

Terryn nodded. "Okay, write it up, then I'll decide what to tell upstairs."

Laura didn't respond. Working as part of InterSec was an exercise in cooperation and misdirection. She'd lost track of the number of law-enforcement agencies involved, and none trusted any of the others. She was proof of that. She'd gone undercover in most of the agencies at some point.

She threw off the bedsheet and swung her feet around to the floor. "Where's my gear?"

Terryn arched an eyebrow. "I imagine Cress would know. Where do you think you're going?"

She held the back of her hospital gown closed more for courtesy than any sense of embarrassment. "I have to go back. There's something I have to check before it's too late."

Terryn crossed his arms. "And if I don't allow it?"

Laura looked him in the eye. "I'll tell everyone you touched my ass."

She couldn't help the twitch of a smile, and neither could he. He bowed his head. "I'll tell Cress you have something to do. I want you back here as soon as possible, and if you feel at all ill, I want you to return immediately. That's an order."

"Thanks," she said.

She paced along the bed, her lack of memory gnawing at her. Her entire life was based on remembering—her name, her history, her work. One misstep could not only expose the Guild's or InterSec's unauthorized involvement in cases, it could get her killed. She didn't mind if the Guild or InterSec was embarrassed. Like all institutional organisms, they survived beyond the moment. She wouldn't.

Cress returned. Not bothering to hide a sour expression, she held Laura's SWAT-team uniform well away from herself. "I hate the smell of gunshot residue."

"Me, too," she said, lying a little. She liked the smell in a way she couldn't describe. It wasn't enjoyment, per se, but she did experience an element of pleasure in the thin rime of residue permeating her hair and clothing after a session at the range. It was an emotion that had to do with a sense of accomplishment. Washing it off had its own pleasure, too, like shedding a layer of skin associated with work.

Cress pulled the curtain around the bed as Laura removed her hospital gown. "Can you be less modest?"

Laura chuckled as she wrestled into her underwear and pulled the pants on. As a healer, Cress dealt with naked bodies on a regular basis in the context of her work. But because of the fear they engendered, *leanansidhe* were vigilant about issues of exposure. I would be, too, Laura thought, if being discovered as a *leanansidhe* meant being chased by an angry mob. As a druid, Laura spent too much time naked with her colleagues, both male and female, to think much about modesty. Something about baring her skin to the light of the moon, in a forest glade with her fellows, seemed natural and right. She didn't think about nudity as exposure, but as a means to an end—in so many ways.

Cress kept her face turned away. "I had to check your vest in after I inventoried it. You can pick it up downstairs," she said.

Laura slipped on her shirt. "Don't need it. Just have an errand to run."

With a glance to confirm that Laura was clothed, Cress faced her again. "An errand in your soiled uniform?"

Laura ignored the comment. "Do you have my stone?"

Cress held out the thick gold necklace. The green stone—an emerald Laura had had for years—glittered in the fluorescent light. Laura kissed the gemstone to honor its power and slipped the chain over her head. Residual essence draped a glamour over her. She charged the stone with an extra burst of body essence. A brief static tickled her entire body as the full Janice Crawford glamour settled over her.

Laura hadn't wanted the SWAT-team persona to be too attractive, so she had lengthened the nose just short of distraction and fleshed out the appearance of her body frame by an extra twenty pounds. She looked trim but solid. Janice's face was similar to her own, although she had dark red hair and light brown eyes instead of Laura's blond hair and wider-set green eyes. She pulled her hair up in a clip. "How's it look?"

Cress nodded. "Perfect, as usual. Are you going to tell me what you're doing?"

"No." Laura trusted Cress but made it a habit of treating everyone on a need-to-know basis. Cress handed her a small baggie. Laura emptied the contents into her pockets—cash, the Crawford badge and ID, car keys, and a cell phone.

She hugged Cress briefly. She did trust her. And cared for her. Cress understood trust like no one else. She had chosen Terryn, and he had returned her affection. When a *leanansidhe* committed to a relationship, she committed more than her heart. She'd walk in front of a bus if he told her it was safe. If a lover left, the *leanansidhe* could spend years in a madness of disbelief.

"No stunts, please. I want the rest of the night off," Cress said, as they left the room.

Laura followed her out of the med clinic as she tucked in her T-shirt. "Will do."

In the elevator lobby outside the InterSec offices, they went their separate ways. Down in the Guildhouse garage, Laura glanced wistfully at her Mercedes SL and jumped into Janice Crawford's Honda SUV. She exited the underground garage and cut across the National Mall to pick up the highway. Out on the bridge, the lights across the river came into view. Everything looks attractive at night in D.C., she thought. Even Anacostia.

She parked the SUV a block from the apartment complex. Car and pedestrian access had been restricted, which didn't endear the police to the troubled neighborhood. Laura looped her SWAT-team badge around her neck. At the nearest barricade, a police officer asked for photo ID, too, but she didn't hassle him for hassling her.

Crime-scene vehicles littered the street. Two ambulance vans sat on the worn lawn of the building where the drug lab had operated. Medical examiners surprised Laura as they brought out a body on a gurney. Twelve hours later, and they were still finding bodies? She lifted her badge for the officer at the door. People walked the hallway inside, the same hallway the entry unit had stormed. It looked nothing like she remembered. Of course, now it wasn't dark and smoke-filled. Bullet holes scarred the walls, white chalk circles around them. She avoided talking to anyone but moved deeper into the building.

She paused to examine the long hall. Crime-scene markers scattered across the floor like restaurant reservation tents. She passed the makeshift sweatshop, making her way around spent shell casings. On the left, her eyes trailed over the holes Sanchez had blown through the wall. Blood splattered the wall on her right. A long smear marked where someone had slid to the floor. She felt grim satisfaction that Sanchez had hit his final targets.

The adjoining walls had been hacked through a string of apartments to create one long hallway. The farther she went, the more bullet holes riddled the walls, more than elsewhere in the building. Another archway revealed a large room, not as big as the sweatshop, but still a sizable workspace. A lone investigator squatted a few feet from the arch, sweeping his flashlight beam across the floor. He shifted his gaze to her, then back to the floor. "This room isn't proc- essed."

She nodded. "Just looking."

The blackened front wall showed evidence of the explo- sion she had heard during the raid. Three tall, evenly spaced windows were blown out. Lab equipment trailed in disarray across the floor. Broken glass containers the vague shape of beakers and vials showed the soot stains of burning, whether from chemical processing or the explosion, Laura couldn't tell. Water from putting out the resulting fire satu- rated everything.

In the next room, a jumble of tables was shoved against a wall. Computers and cabling tangled within the pile and onto the floor. She paused. The room had a distinct lack of shell casings and bullet holes. It was the geographic center of the building, yet she saw no evidence of the fighting.

Opening her essence-sensing ability, she picked up sev- eral immediate hits, which was not unexpected near a door. What *was* unexpected was that the door had been warded, spell-blocked in some way. She pushed her awareness against it, studying the mode of warding. Door wards took many forms—sound or sight barriers, security shields that allowed certain people in or kept specific people out. They could be hardened to a substantial degree. Someone with enough ability could even create a barrier in the small area of the door that would slow a bullet almost to a stop. Not a brownie. They weren't strong enough. An Inverni fairy would be, though.

Laura sensed nothing dangerous and stepped through, the invisible ward sliding over her with the sensation of flowing water. At minimum, then, the ward was not an ac- cess barrier, but likely a sound deterrent. Once she was fully past the ward, essence flashed across her vision. The room had been a hub of activity, more so than the drug lab. Multiple species signatures in green, yellow, and pale white flickered everywhere, losing integrity without their original sources present to reinforce them. The dominant hits were human, but she also sensed an Inverni fairy, at least two

Teutonic elves, and several brownies and dwarves. Crime made strange bedfellows, but the collection of so many adversarial groups together was unusual.

Laura stayed on clear floor space, keen on not stepping on any potential evidence. If they were beginning to process the drug lab, they had not even initiated a walk-through in this room. The scene tech in the lab would be furious if he knew she had entered.

The computer equipment looked intentionally destroyed. A SWAT unit would not have smashed monitors, yanked cables, or mangled circuit boards. The outside wall had three windows like the lab. The middle one was open. She surmised it made an easy escape route for at least some of the people who had been there.

An essence signature moved behind her, at the edge of her range. Alarmed, Laura whirled to face the empty room, waiting several moments for the signature to return. Outside the window, the only people in sight were law-enforcement agents. Across the way stood another apartment building, its first-floor windows and entrance covered in graffiti-sprayed plywood.

A flash of light above caught her eye. Broken windows showed empty black squares. Her ability didn't extend far enough for her to be able to sense if anyone was there. The flash didn't return, but she couldn't shake the feeling that someone was watching her. The mysterious essence reappeared behind her, and she spun. By the time she reached the hallway, it had vanished altogether.

Alert from the odd occurrence, she retraced her steps to the sweatshop. Crime-scene investigators were spread throughout the room, videotaping. Standard investigative op would be to process the scene from the front of the building to the back, so Laura knew they hadn't begun to process the room for physical evidence either.

She gave the overturned desk a wide berth. She didn't need to see Sanchez's blood. At the far end of the room, a videographer recorded the jumble of crates that had fallen during her fight with the Inverni fairy. Once he started taping, he was required to keep the tape rolling. By habit from working undercover, she avoided being photographed as much as possible, so she stayed out of his range.

After he moved away, she approached the tumbled pile of crates and opened her essence-sensing ability. Around her, the body signature of the others in the room ghosted into her range. All weak, indicating human, which made it easier for her to dismiss them and focus on the space in front of her. She found her own essence from earlier, a concentration in and around the broken crates where she had been trapped, a thinner layer trailing up the aisle from her two runs during the shoot-out.

She circled the crates and found what she had returned for, a thick residue of Inverni essence. Anger and fear or stress had amplified his essence, enough for her to register not only his species, which Laura already knew, but also his unique body signature. The sensation filled her mind and settled into her preternatural memory. She wouldn't forget it.

As she finished, she sensed Aaron Foyle behind her. "Are you okay?" he asked.

She nodded. "Just came to look."

Laura felt anger coming off him in waves. "What happened?" he asked.

She resisted the urge to sigh. Being part of law enforcement meant constant repetition of information. Before the next twenty-four hours had passed, she'd have to have written two reports for Terryn—one a redacted official one, one for his eyes only—another report for Foyle, and probably others. She debated how much she should say without being debriefed by Terryn. "I'm not sure yet. I've got some memory loss from a concussion. The medics said coming back might jog something."

He glanced up the aisle, noting, she assumed, who was in earshot. "Well?"

She shrugged. "Not much. Right now, all I can recall is firing at the objective and calling for help."

Foyle shook his head. "I've got a dead officer, Crawford. I want to know what happened to Sanchez, and I want to know now."

She kept her face and voice neutral. "I told you I have memory loss. They said it will come back soon."

Foyle tilted his head back to look at the skylight. "How did a brownie get up there?"

Laura followed his gaze. "It wasn't a brownie. It was a fairy."

He looked at her sharply. "What do you mean?"

Laura kept her eyes on the shattered skylight. "The intelligence was wrong. It was an Inverni glamoured as a brownie."

He folded his arms across his chest, his voice sharp when he spoke. "No one else said anything about a fairy."

"I'm not sure I understand your meaning . . . sir," she said.

Foyle stepped closer. "Listen, Crawford. An officer is dead, and his killer escaped with you as the only witness."

Despite her anger, Laura remained cool. "What exactly are you implying?"

He set his jaw. "You aren't a team regular, and the only perpetrator who seems to have escaped was fey."

She felt a slow burn at the phrase "team regular." It was a loaded term usually used to imply someone fey was not regular, not human. She pitched her voice low and controlled. "I did you a favor, Foyle, and almost got killed for it. You have a lot of nerve race-baiting me."

He let his own anger edge into his voice. "Who do you think you're talking to, Officer?"

Laura stepped around him. "I left the med unit against doctor's advice. You need something from me, you call Terryn macCullen."

She had stalked all the way to the door when Foyle called out, "Crawford, I want a report in the morning. You can amend as you recall."

Laura stopped, ready to snap at him, when her eye caught the overturned desk. Whoever had shot her would have stood where she was. Sanchez would not have been visible, but she would have been. She shivered as she examined the essence on the threshold.

"Crawford?" His voice startled her.

"Will do, sir."

With an effort of will, she did not look over her shoulder as she left the building. Once past the barricade, she circled around the back of her SUV and let the moment sink in. Cursing under her breath, she yanked the door open and got in the car. Gripping the steering wheel, she forced her breathing to slow. A flash of uncharacteristic panic went through her. She locked the doors. With a forceful exhale, she started the SUV.

Driving along the winding parkway that led back to downtown, Laura allowed herself to acknowledge what she was thinking. Standing in the doorway, standing on the spot from where someone had shot at her, she had not sensed essence from unknown drug dealers or whatever the hell they were. She had registered and recognized three distinct signatures. She had no way to tell if all three people had been together when she was shot or if one had stood alone before the other two arrived.

She pulled out her cell phone. Terryn picked up on the first ring. "MacCullen."

"We've got a problem. I'm coming back in right now," she said.

He didn't speak right away. "You don't sound like yourself. What's wrong?"

Laura took a deep breath. "I think our side took out Sanchez. I think they tried to kill me, too."

3
CHAPTER

"DO YOU WANT backup?" Terryn asked.

Laura's eyes shifted to the rearview mirror. As she neared the Anacostia Bridge, more cars appeared on the parkway. "No. Let's keep this line open."

"Okay. Can you give me details?"

"Not now." Eavesdropping devices littered the District more than anywhere else in the world. Terryn probably thought the same thing because he didn't press her. She put down the phone and switched the call to the dashboard system.

"I'm getting Cress on the line," said Terryn.

The light changed, and she drove onto the ramp for the bridge. Traffic receded behind her. "No, wait. It's okay. No tail."

She was so focused behind her, she didn't see a van shoot up a side ramp until it was huge in her passenger window. She yanked the steering wheel left and stomped on the accelerator. The van caught her rear panel, spinning the SUV. Laura lurched forward, but her shoulder strap slammed her back against the seat.

"What was that?" Terryn said. Laura found herself smiling at how calm his voice sounded.

"Bad driver, I hope," she said. She spun the steering wheel back and pulled away across the bridge. Another van appeared on her left while the first van came up close on her right. "Okay, I definitely have a problem," she said.

"I'm on my way," he said. Over the car speakers, she heard the rustle of the phone on the other end moving.

"Will Terryn be enough?" Cress asked.

Laura reached into the foot well to get her magnet-mount light. She lowered her window, then slapped the light on the roof. "I don't know. Tell him I've got a roof light on."

On her left, the side door of the van rolled open. Laura's heart jumped as the barrel of an M16 slid into view. She could do many things with essence and a fast car, but she couldn't stop a bullet, and she didn't have a fast car. She swerved as the gun went off, her rear windows shattering in a spray of glass. She sideswiped the van. The larger vehicle had inertia on its side against the SUV, but the driver veered away. Laura smiled. Only a crazy woman tries to use a Honda as battering ram.

"Janice?" Cress said.

"I'm good," Laura replied. She hit the gas and pulled in front of the van, feinting left and right to keep it from passing her. The second van joined the first. They separated, widening the distance between them, while gaining on Laura. When they reached the bumper of her SUV, the M16 reappeared as a black-clad figure wearing a nondescript mask leaned out the door. He started firing.

Laura slammed on the brakes. The vans flew past, and she released a surge of essence through the windows. White lightning leaped from her hands and raked both vehicles, rocking them on their tires. The sniper fell inside as the van swerved away. She flew past the second van as it zigzagged wildly on blown tires.

"Report, please," Cress said, calm as ever.

"Still here."

The lead van pulled a U-turn. Laura shifted gears and accelerated the SUV in reverse to gain some space. The second van pulled across the road behind her, and she hit the brake. The door opened and another shooter jumped out. She was trapped. "Dammit. In case I don't make it, Cress, tell Terryn . . ."

Cress cut her off. "Tell him yourself. You always have options."

She was right. Laura knew that. She shoved the stick shift into drive and floored it. The SUV's tires screamed until they grabbed pavement. She shot forward as gunfire rang out behind. The van in front cut sideways and stopped. The first shooter stepped out.

The sky crackled with blue-white lightning. Laura ducked as her windshield exploded to the sound of the M16 firing. She kept her foot planted on the accelerator. Peering through the steering wheel, she saw a remote possibility of swerving around the van at the last moment. At speed, the SUV would either barrel-roll or fly off the bridge. Better that, she thought, than the odds of surviving a head-on collision. She dropped farther in the seat, hoping not to die when she hit the guardrails.

More lightning flashed, and this time Laura recognized it: a lethal surge of essence. The van in front of her exploded in a black-and-orange fireball. Terryn soared into view, his gossamer wings in full flare, burning with fierce white light, his body a dark shadow between them. He brought his arms down and aimed. Cobalt blue essence-bolts leaped from his hands, striking the van behind her.

Laura hit the brakes and jumped out, her hands ablaze with white essence. Terryn landed beside her, burning like a fuel cell, his eyes glowing a violent blue. Something detonated inside the lead van, and the roof shredded fire and metal. In a blur, Terryn lunged over Laura and discharged his essence into a covering shield. Metal debris pummeled them. They stumbled to the ground, Terryn's shield deflecting the shrapnel.

Laura found herself inches from Terryn's face and smiled. "Thanks, boss."

He held his hand out and pulled her up. "Was this your idea of an errand?"

Both vans billowed smoke. Laura stared a moment and shook her head. "No essence. They're all dead."

Terryn gazed toward the Anacostia side of the river. Lights flashed red and blue behind stalled traffic. "This was professional. I doubt we'll find anything in the vans once the fires are out. Let's go. I want to see how this plays out in channels."

They returned to her SUV, and Laura drove around the burning van.

"Report, please," Cress said.

Terryn settled himself back in the passenger seat. "The situation has been resolved. We're on our way back."

"Good," said Cress. "Pick up some ice cream, please."

Terryn smiled as she disconnected. Laura kept the police light on the roof. Wind whipped through the missing windows. Police cars and fire engines came at them the wrong way. Laura pulled to the right to let them pass, but she didn't stop.

A police car broke away from the contingent and followed them. The driver waved them down. Two Metropolitan police officers jumped out, both with their hands on their guns in open holsters. Neither drew his weapon. One stopped at the front of the SUV and kept his eyes on Terryn, while the other made a wide berth near the driver's side door. "ID, please?"

Laura held up her badge on its chain. She kept a straight face when Terryn flashed an air force ID from a billfold. The air force didn't allow fey staff. Terryn at least had the courtesy to glamour his wings so the officer wouldn't know he was fey and have to pretend he didn't notice. The officer took the IDs and handed them to his partner, who returned to the squad car. He peered toward the burning vans. "Air force and SWAT, huh? What's going down?"

Laura tilted her head to let Terryn take the question. He leaned forward. "We're not sure. A fender-bender, I think."

A thin smile streaked across the officer's face. He made a point of looking at the SUV's missing windows. "I see. Did you install this air-conditioning yourself?"

Laura chuckled. "Can you believe this? Can't park your car anywhere in this town."

The officer's partner stepped out of the car and called

him over. They conferred briefly, and the officer returned to the SUV. He handed the IDs back with an impressed look on his face. "Never saw a clean check come back so fast. I suppose it's pointless to ask for contact info."

Terryn nodded. "We're working on something."

The officer tapped the roof of the car. "Thanks for your time."

Laura drove away. "Fender-bender? Do you think he didn't notice the fireball?"

Terryn shrugged dismissively. Off the bridge, Laura pulled the police light in and slowed down. "I seem to have upset someone tonight."

"What happened at the apartment building?" he asked.

She glanced over at him. "I went back to get the Inverni signature before it faded. Someone was watching me. I found the angle I was shot from, and there were three signatures: Aaron Foyle, Salvatore Gianni, and Jonathan Sinclair."

"All SWAT personnel?" Terryn asked.

Laura nodded. "Foyle broke my balls about being the only person in the room when Sanchez died and letting the Inverni escape. I told him to talk to you if he was going that route."

Terryn arched an eyebrow. "Janice Crawford has balls?"

Laura laughed. "You bet your ass she does."

"So who was trying to kill you on the bridge?"

She had seen only Foyle at the drug lab, but that didn't mean Gianni and Sinclair weren't there as well. The vans showed up so quickly, she had the feeling that she hadn't imagined someone watching from the next apartment building. "Well, if any of the three of them doesn't show up for work tomorrow, I think we'll have a clue."

Terryn leaned forward. "Stop up here, please. Cress likes something called Chunky Monkey."

Terryn's lack of cultural knowledge amused her. She often had fun at his expense, more so because he didn't always pick up on it. "Is it made from real monkeys?"

He shrugged. "I asked her that, too, but she wouldn't answer."

While Terryn went inside a convenience store, she ignored the curious stares from pedestrians. He came out with a small bag and tossed a pack of gum to Laura through the remains of the windshield.

After arriving at the Guildhouse garage, Laura parked the SUV in Janice Crawford's usual space. She retrieved a duffel bag from the backseat, shaking off broken glass. One more glance around the interior confirmed that nothing else needed to be removed. She didn't take it for granted that parking at the Guild meant some idiot wouldn't rob her. The SUV held the bare minimum of equipment most of the time, so she needed only the duffel.

When they entered the elevator lobby, Laura stepped sideways along the wall. She dropped the duffel and unbuttoned her shirt.

Terryn paused. "You're changing here?"

Laura pulled off the shirt. "I don't want gunshot residue in the Mercedes." She kicked off her work boots and dropped her pants. She smiled at the amusement on Terryn's face.

"There are cameras, you know," he said.

She pulled a black, wrinkle-free skirt and a plain white T-shirt out of the duffel. "Do you think this is the first time I've done this?" She pointed up at the camera over her head. "It's angled for the elevator. It can't see me here. I checked."

"And you don't find stripping in front of me the least bit inappropriate?" he asked.

She pulled out a matching business jacket, followed by a pair of flat-heeled shoes. She hated the suit, but it survived being stuffed repeatedly into a bag. As she absorbed the essence out of the emerald on the chain around her neck, the Janice Crawford glamour evaporated. Instant Laura Blackstone, public-relations director. "For one thing, you've seen more at the beach. For another, you are in a relationship with a *leanansidhe*. If Cress suspected you had the least bit of interest in me, she'd tell me, and we'd both make your life miserable."

He chuckled. "True. I'd still prefer you at least ask me to turn away next time."

She stuffed her SWAT-team gear into the duffel bag. "Will do, boss. Tell Cress I'll see her in the morning."

Terryn pressed the elevator button. "I'd prefer to debrief you now."

Laura picked up the duffel and leaned against the wall. "Terryn, I have been in a police raid, watched an officer die, been attacked by an Inverni, shot at, and have a concussion and partial memory loss. Then I was chased by maniacal van drivers, shot at again, wrecked the Crawford SUV, and I'm really worried you and Cress are about to eat chunks of monkey. I'd like to go home and sleep."

Terryn stepped into the elevator. "It's ice cream with nuts. You need to get out more, Laura. All I can say is, be in early, please."

She nodded once. "Will do."

"Good night," he said, as the doors closed.

Laura slung the bag over her shoulder and returned to the garage. In one smooth move, she tossed the duffel in the back of the Mercedes and started the engine. She tilted her head back and inhaled deeply. It still smelled new. She loved her car.

She cranked up the volume on the satellite radio. She spent a lot of time in cars. Music was one cultural trend that she managed to keep tabs on. When she wasn't in an undercover persona, the stations she gravitated to were considered alternative—angsty boy bands singing about what a bummer life was. She didn't think they had any understanding of what that meant, but she liked the beat. She sang at the top of her lungs as she raced up the exit ramp, ignoring the pounding in her head. Turning onto Pennsylvania Avenue, she hoped the only problems on the final leg home would be long traffic lights. When she was Laura Blackstone, the only thing people shot at her were questions. Generally, it was easier to dodge those.

4
CHAPTER

AS LAURA ENTERED her apartment, she dropped her keys on the entry table and picked up the mail. She flipped through the envelopes, sorted the junk out from the bills, and put the two stacks on the kitchen counter. The refrigerator held little more than breakfast items and condiments. She pulled out the orange juice and mixed it into a healthy shot of vodka. Leaning on the counter, she stared into the living room and drank, not gulping, not sipping, but in a slow, measured manner, as if taking medicine before bed.

The housekeeper had been in. The only difference between before and after her visits was the dust quotient. Laura liked the living room in an intellectual, even aesthetic way, but she rarely used it for anything. She didn't entertain. The Alexandria apartment was supposed to be home, but she spent little time in it. Instead, it had become about keeping up appearances. A high-profile professional at the Fey Guild would live in such a place. Nicely appointed. Spacious. Expensive.

She wandered with her drink to the sliding glass door that led to the balcony and a view of the river. It was nice, in a city-nice kind of way. The area had history, quaint shops and boutiques and cafes. If she were only a Fey Guild director, she imagined she would love living there. But as it was, she had no connection to the place. She didn't associate with her neighbors or interact with the local neighborhood. That would mean keeping up contacts, establishing relationships, and having another aspect of her life that needed to be guarded against her undercover work and vice versa.

She rubbed her finger along the wet edge of her glass, thinking about the politics and strange winding path that had brought her to this point in her life, where she went home alone after two days of people trying to kill her.

When the world of Faerie inexplicably merged with modern reality, the factions were simple and clear-cut. On the one hand were the Celtic fey such as herself, ruled from Ireland by High Queen Maeve. On the other were the Teutonic fey, who answered to Donor Elfenkonig, the Elvenking of Germany. The two strains of fey had spent decades in open hostilities, each side blaming the other for the loss of Faerie. After a hundred years, still no one understood what had happened to cause Convergence.

Laura wondered where she would be if the merging hadn't happened, even who she would be. She was a child caught between the twilight of Faerie and the dawn of Convergence. Her parents raised her as a Faerie druid child would have been raised, not like other hereborn fey, who had been immersed in modern culture. Faerie meant something to her. Maeve meant something to her. Protecting and defending the Celtic fey—and, yes, the bewildered humans caught in the middle—against the aggressions of the Elvenking meant something to her. That was why she'd entered into the service of the Guild and, eventually, InterSec.

She finished her drink and returned to the kitchen, rinsed the glass, and placed it on the drainboard. In the bedroom, she removed her drab white T-shirt and the black business suit and laid them out on the bed. As she walked into the bathroom, she ran her fingers through her hair, scratching at her scalp. The scent of gunshot residue made her nostrils flare. Glamours could do many things, but filtering odors was difficult. When she stepped in the shower, the water sluiced the smell off her.

With the water pouring down on her head, soothing the pounding in her skull, Laura tried not to think, a skill she had mastered to an uncomfortable degree. But despite parking her car, having a drink to unwind, undressing, and showering, her mind would not rest. She had been shot at before with both bullets and essence. She had risked her life more often than she cared to remember. She always separated those things from herself, thought of them as part of the job. If she spent time stressing about it, she shouldn't be doing the job.

But tonight, doubt hovered in the corners of her mind. She had almost died and was not sure why. Did all her deeply held beliefs about Faerie and Maeve and justice really have anything to do with almost dying in a drug lab in a run-down building in a run-down neighborhood? Did all that mean anything anymore? she wondered.

She toweled off, checking herself for bruises and cuts. It was not unusual for her to come off an assignment at the end of the day only to realize she needed a bandage. She parted her hair on the side to examine the area where the bullet had slammed the helmet against her head. The simple act of moving the thick blond strands made her wince from subtle pain. A rich maroon-and-green bruise smeared across her scalp. She combed her hair straight to her shoulders, glad it covered the spot. She wouldn't have to create a minor glamour to hide it, though someone was bound to comment about the dark circles under her eyes. At least she could pass them off as insomnia.

She wrapped herself in an oversize white bathrobe. Cinching the robe closed, she took one more look at herself in the mirror, as if hoping her reflection might give her an encouraging nod. It didn't.

She cut through the kitchen to turn off the living-room lights and check that the security alarms were on. She trailed her free hand along the back of the tan sofa as she walked past it, its nubbed fabric tickling her fingertips. The maid had unwrapped and fanned magazines beside a vase of fresh flowers on the coffee table. Every couple of weeks new magazines arrived, the old ones vanished, but Laura never read them. She had subscribed to them long ago to give the illusion that she had interests in decorating and cooking. Every time she used the apartment, she messed up the layout so it would look like she read them. She wondered if the maid took the old ones home.

Without conscious thought, she retrieved the glass from the drainboard and had the vodka bottle in her hand. She stared at it, startled to see her own hand through the glass and clear fluid, as if someone else was holding this thing she had not meant to hold. She placed the bottle next to the empty glass on the counter.

Enough, she thought. The drink, the shower, the maid. She knew enough about her work and her life to know the dangers of the long, slow slide into a bottle. She had seen it happen time and again to others, but she wasn't going to let it happen to her. Flipping through the bills again, she glanced at the bottle and decided to make one more drink after all. One more, then, one more than usual, and that would be it. Getting shot in the head and almost run off a bridge warranted a little leeway.

She took the glass to bed with her and turned on the television. The news recycled the story about the failed raid. If an officer hadn't died, the coverage would have been a blip of a mention and on to the weather. Laura preferred when that happened. It meant an operation had gone off without a hitch, so much so that the media didn't think it was newsworthy.

Despite the exhaustion, the headache, and the bruises, she would step up and do what InterSec required her to do. It was important. Too important to risk failure. Maintaining multiple glamours was taxing, but she would manage it. That didn't mean she wanted to. It meant she knew what she was in for.

Tomorrow she would pretend she was plain Laura Blackstone, public-relations director for the Guild. She would get up in front of a meeting or a reporter or a strategy group and spin the Guild and the fey in the best light possible.

People would compliment her on her marketing talents, despite the fact that the skill was predicated on not telling the whole truth in order to get what she wanted. She was good at it. Too good, she thought lately, to the extent that she wondered if deep down she had started lying to herself.

She drained the remains of her drink and slid the glass onto the nightstand.

5
CHAPTER

TO AN OUTSIDE observer, which in a Guildhouse invariably meant a human one, a meeting at the D.C. Fey Guild attracted an assortment of people not encountered on a regular basis. Most everyone knew what a Celtic fairy or a Teutonic elf looked like. Dwarves were obvious and easy. Druids didn't raise an eyebrow, but the average person had a hard time telling the difference between a brownie and a kobold. The solitary fey were another matter altogether.

The solitaries claimed neither Maeve nor Donor Elfenkonig as their leader, though the various individuals and groups had natural affinities for one or the other. In truth, "solitary" was a bit of misnomer, because not all solitaries were single, lonely individuals. The name was more a recognition of their status apart from the more mainstream fey, who often despised and belittled them when they weren't dismissing them. After Convergence, the solitaries had found a new voice for themselves in a world where monarchies did not hold sway.

Laura shifted in her seat and glanced around the conference table as the public-relations staff meeting drew to a close. The department had more solitaries than any other at the Guild. Politics dictated that the group tasked with convincing humans that the fey should be treated inclusively employ the solitary fey even the Guild didn't love. Their high profile rarely translated into much authority. To the other fey, they still lived under a cloud of fear and suspicion.

A large contingent of brownies were part of the department. They weren't solitaries, and they had a tendency toward efficiency that the solitaries lacked. The other staffers ran a gamut of species that kept taxonomists awake at night. Blue-skinned nixies milled about the floor, too fidgety to remain in seats, while the odd wood fairy with its bark-skinned flesh sat as still as an oak. Several sleek selkies, almost human-looking when out of the water, gathered in a clique at one end of the table, as far as possible from the pale merrows at the other end. The two fey water species had an intense dislike for each other.

Laura used her body language to appear attentive to Resha Dunne. He was a merrow, a member of one of the most hostile types of sea fey. Where his brothers tended toward aggression and seduction, particularly with human women, Resha seemed insecure and tentative about everything. Of course, Laura had never seen him in his water aspect, which was when his species tended to be at its worst in temperament. Even so, Resha was someone she chose to spend little time with. He felt clammy and smelled damp to her.

Although he was the solitary representative on the Guild board of directors, Resha voted the Celtic party line as a matter of course. He never attended a meeting that he couldn't drag into overtime. What could be discussed in an hour took two when he was involved, with a monotonous litany of agenda items and committee forming at the end for the next meeting. Usually Laura delegated one of her staff to deal with him, but the fey exhibit being planned at the National Archives was too high-profile for her to avoid him without insulting him. She flipped through the memos in front of her to hide the fact that she was scanning her PDA to monitor email.

Keeping the lives of her competing personalities under control was difficult to do alone. Terryn helped enormously, either by direct intervention or propagating disinformation campaigns on her whereabouts. That need to juggle and balance was one of the reasons she avoided an independent personal life. It would add yet another layer of subterfuge and lies that she didn't think was worth it. At least, that was what she had convinced herself of.

Terryn was running interference for her with Foyle while she attended the Guild meeting. Every few minutes, Foyle would send an annoyed text message, demanding Janice Crawford report for duty. Duty, in this case, meant desk work while the fiasco of the raid was investigated. Terryn would respond with his usual calm and noncommittal reply.

No less than three congressional committees were demanding answers about the raid. She swore to herself when she saw Senator Hornbeck's Fey Relations Committee on the list of interested parties. Laura Blackstone was having enough trouble with him about the National Archives ceremony she was working on with the Guild. She didn't need to open another front of aggravation with him.

"Are there any other questions?" Resha asked.

His usual meeting-end question was met with an apprehensive silence. No one ever had another question once Resha had wrung dry every possible topic. Laura moved her attention back to the pale merrow. Everyone in the conference room shuffled their notes into folders and briefcases, unconcerned that Resha droned on, announcing the date and time of the next meeting. He would send an email about it and at least two reminders.

Laura picked up her folders and PDA. She had enough time to get a few hours' work in before Terryn couldn't put off Foyle any longer.

"Laura, do you have a minute?"

She paused at the door, too long to pretend she hadn't heard Resha. Fixing a smile on her face, she faced the conference room. "Sure, Resha, what's up?"

He gestured at the empty seat to his left. Against her better judgment, she sat, hoping against hope that he wouldn't keep her long. His eyes shifted beneath heavy lids as he waited for the room to empty, a pleasant smile plastered on

his face. At least, through Laura's years of familiarity with
his kind, she knew it indicated pleasure. To the uninitiated,
it had the cold tooth slash of a predator.

"I was hoping you could help me with something," he
said.

She popped the cap of her Waterman pen and held it
poised over a blank sheet of paper in her notepad. "Sure."

Resha reached out a long thin hand, the pale fingers too
long for comfort, the dull gray claws more so. As much
as she would have liked to, Laura did not recoil from the
cool, slick touch on her arm. Just because Resha was not as
lecherous as his brother merrows did not mean she wanted
him to touch her. "No, no, it's not something official. Well,
technically. I was wondering if you knew much about
glamours."

With exaggerated care, she replaced the cap, keeping her
eyes on the blank sheet of paper as she considered how to
answer him. Resha wasn't a political game player, at least
not a powerful one. The Guild board of directors let him
run programs that had little political impact, or at least impact that Resha couldn't screw up or interfere with. Why he
was asking such a loaded question made her start looking
for exits and doing a mental inventory of passports and
bank accounts. As a druid, she couldn't lie and say she
didn't know anything about glamours. All druids did. She
forced the smile back on her face. "Oh, I haven't used them
in years. I was much more fascinated by them when I was
young."

Resha nodded, dropping his hands on the table. "I was
wondering what you thought if I got one. Would it be difficult?"

She relaxed, but not completely. Not until she understood where this was going. "It would depend on what you
needed. They're easy to purchase. I can think of a few jew-
elry stores that might take custom orders."

He nodded, his lidded eyes narrowing. "Yes, but I'm un-
certain about discretion."

She smiled, more genuinely. "Everything has a price,
Resha."

"What would you think if I pinked my skin?" he asked.

The idea was so mundane, she almost let her jaw drop. Here she was fearing one of her undercover personas had been compromised, and Resha was being used to wheedle information from her, when he was only talking about cosmetics. "What do I think personally or professionally?"

"Both."

She shook her head. "I don't see a reason in either case."

He smiled again. "Yes, well, you have an aspect that humans find pleasing. You can pass as one of them. I can't."

He had a point. With his exaggerated features—the sharp peak in his forehead, those teeth and claws, the blade of a nose—humans knew he was fey, even if they might not know exactly what kind. Those physical traits didn't include what happened when a merrow hit the water. She didn't have the heart to tell him that making his pale white skin any other color would not change a thing about his appearance.

Steeling herself, she reached out and squeezed those cold, pale hands. "Don't take this as anything more than a compliment, Resha, but you're a perfectly handsome man of your species. Why are you worried about what humans think?"

He pressed his wide lips together. "Television, Laura. The National Archives ceremony is going to be televised. People in Washington are used to dealing with solitaries who don't fit the human mold. But outside the cities, particularly out West, it's a different story. Most of this country does not see the fey on a daily basis."

She tapped his hand for emphasis. "Which is precisely why you shouldn't change a thing. This ceremony is about alliances and cooperation. We're celebrating our diversity."

He shook his head and shrugged. "Yes, well, that's fine when you're not the one with the camera in your face because you're diverse."

Laura stood and retrieved her folders. "Resha, I'm hearing none of this. Be who you are. If we can't do that, then everything the fey have been fighting for here is pointless."

He smiled again, that strange merrow smile that demon-

strated exactly what he meant by other people not understanding. "You always put the best spin on things."

She grinned at him as she made for the door. "That's my
job, Resha. Wear your blue Hermès tie. It complements
your skin tone."

She cut through the service kitchen to the back stairs
to avoid the slow elevator. As she climbed the two flights
to her floor, she decided to be amused by the conversation
instead of annoyed. She was the last person to criticize
someone who wanted to change his looks. Keeping her
head down, she strode down the long hallway through the
accounting department, one of the few areas of the Guildhouse where she wasn't peppered with questions when she
appeared.

As she entered her office, her assistant, Saffin Corril,
followed her in. "Your zipper's in the front," she said.

Laura dropped her paperwork and spun her skirt around.
"Dammit, I wish I'd never bought this thing."

Saffin placed a stack of pink messages on the desk.
"Stop wearing it on days you have a meeting in the fifth-
floor conference room or start taking the elevator."

Laura looked up from the first message on the stack.
"What the heck does that have to do with my skirt?"

The brownie smiled. "You always take the stairs from
the fifth floor too fast, then you charge down the hallway to
avoid people. Poof. Your skirt spins."

They stared at each other. The corner of Saffin's mouth
twitched, and Laura laughed. She dropped into her desk
chair. "You're too observant for your own good."

"Can I have a raise?" she asked.

"No. You can have next Tuesday off. I'm out of the office, and you've put in a ton of time on the Archives ceremony," said Laura.

"Groovy. Thanks," she replied.

Laura nodded with a slight smile as she flipped through
the messages. Saffin was tall for a brownie. With her long,
wispy, blond hair and slender body, Laura could picture
Saffin with flowers in her hair on an ashram in the sixties,
which was where Saffin was then. Brownies gravitated to

hospitable situations that reflected their preferred demeanor and liked to take task-oriented positions that played to their industrious natures. People loved brownie assistants and financial managers. But if someone prevented one of them from performing his duties, a brownie might turn into a boggart. Their boggart nature ranged from annoying to downright dangerous. A brownie transformed from a passive, friendly person into a gangly aggressor with teeth and claws to back it up. No one wanted a maniacal boggart harassing them for a response to a memo. Saffin confessed to Laura she was asked to leave the ashram because she kept going boggie when others forgot to weed the soybeans. Saffin liked a tidy garden.

"Senator Hornbeck's office called three times," Saffin said.

Laura dropped her head back. "Good gods, why won't that man leave us alone? I am not going to put Tylo Blume at the podium. I don't care what favors he's done Hornbeck."

The senator was pressing her to include Tylo Blume as a speaker at the Archives' exhibit opening. Blume supported Hornbeck's ideas about mutual cooperation between humans and the fey, a sentiment Laura didn't disagree with. But Blume wasn't in the same league as the other speakers and had done little to support the cause until recently.

Laura suspected Blume would use the opportunity to promote his security firm. The U.S. government had become so stretched with its Homeland Security initiatives, they hired private security contractors like Blackwater and Titan—and Blume's own Triad Global—to support regular law enforcement. Triad was hired to maintain the building perimeter for the Archives' fey exhibit opening while regular government operatives handled the higher-profile guests, to say nothing of the documents, inside the Archives. Laura didn't think anyone needed to provide Blume with free advertising because Hornbeck wanted to score political points with the Teutonic elves.

Saffin placed another folder on her desk. "Speaking of which, Triad sent over a revised traffic ban around the Archives. The Capitol police didn't like some of the sight lines on the VIPs."

Laura tilted the charts toward the natural light from the window. Triad loved their color printer. They did good work. That didn't mean she owed them anything more than their fees. "This is fine. Any more changes on the Treaty display?"

The centerpiece of the Archives exhibit was the 1914 Treaty of London that recognized Maeve as High Queen of the Celtic fey and Tara as a sovereign territory within Ireland. Over a century later, the document, signed by Prime Minister H. H. Asquith of the United Kingdom, President Woodrow Wilson, and Maeve, continued to generate controversy. The National Archives was going to display it for the first time as part of its major fey exhibition, along with never-before-seen letters, documents, and film footage from the early days of the Guild. Threats against the exhibit had been made by militia groups that believed the Treaty was the first step in world domination by the fey over humans. It was an old story in the U.S. and Europe. The U.S. government responded with security improvements on the documents and the ceremony.

"No more changes today. It's still early," said Saffin.

Laura nodded understanding. "Can you check with the Guildmaster's Office and see if Rhys wants me to review his speech again?"

"I did. He does. They'll have something for you to look at tonight," she said.

Laura reached the bottom of the messages. The last two were from reporters. She recognized the names and knew they weren't calling about the ceremony. She sighed as she realized the raid was going to complicate more than one of her lives. "What are you hearing about this police raid in Anacostia, Saf? Anything I need to handle?"

She wrinkled her nose. "Don't think so. The District's SWAT team is being blamed for now. They took out a brownie, and the only other fey involved was a druid team member named Janice Crawford. She got hit by a bullet, but she's okay apparently. InterSec is stalling. Maybe you could call Terryn to see what's going on."

Laura did not raise her head but stayed focused on the messages. "Terryn macCullen? Why would I call him?"

Saffin shrugged. "You guys are friends, aren't you? He might return your call."

Her mind raced as she tried to recall mentioning Terryn at the office. They had routine Guild/InterSec interactions, but that was expected. Laura wondered what she had done to imply she knew Terryn as more than a colleague at another agency. Saffin was observant, and she had been with Laura a long, long time. She must have picked up on a pattern Laura hadn't noticed she was creating.

"I was thinking," said Saffin into Laura's silence. "This might be a good angle for the ceremony, a fey person getting wounded during a joint human-fey exercise. I can do a preliminary interview with this Janice Crawford if you like."

It's a great idea, Laura thought. It was why she valued Saffin so much. No one else could cover for her like Saf did, run things in a pinch, and have the intuition for the big picture all at the same time. "Let's wait and see what develops. We don't want egg on our faces if something screwy was going on there. Good thinking, though. Anything else?"

"There's a sale at Talbots," she said.

"I don't have time, Saf."

Saffin smirked over her shoulder as she left the office. "Oh, I know. I'll be back in forty-five minutes. Don't forget to eat lunch."

"I won't be here when you get back. Text me if you need anything," Laura called after her.

Laura did a mental inventory as she stared out the window. The ceremony was under control. Hornbeck was a problem. She debated bringing in Guildmaster Rhys to get the senator to back off, but the idea didn't sit well. It felt like conceding she couldn't handle him. On the other hand, she couldn't avoid Aaron Foyle much longer, and she had no idea how much time she would need to deal with the SWAT-team investigation. She considered tossing Hornbeck on Resha Dunne's lap. But the way the two of them liked to hear their own voices, the ceremony would be over before a decision had been made. She shook her head. She liked the Archives project and didn't want to see it ruined. She sighed and picked up the phone to call Hornbeck.

6
CHAPTER

IN THE PARKING garage beneath the Guildhouse, a new SUV was parked in Janice Crawford's spot. Laura opened the unlocked door, slid into the driver's seat, and popped the glove carpet. Keys, registration, insurance information—all in Janice Crawford's name—stacked in a neat pile. She started the engine, and the radio came on to Janice's favorite station—heavy metal. Whoever had taken care of the car had set all the radio selections for her. She adjusted the rearview mirror, barely noticing that the face that looked back was Janice's. When she wore a glamour, she was the glamour.

Exiting the garage, she turned in to light traffic, scanning back and forth from the side mirrors to the rearview for a full city block. She had been followed so many times, the behavior was automatic. No cars stood out, although several were black with tinted windows. In D.C., that was like saying a car had wheels.

The District police station house for Anacostia was a large and modern building, implying on the one hand that the neighborhood needed a heavy police presence while on the other hand indicating that the city cared enough about it to construct a forward-looking building. Laura skipped the parking lot and parked on the Irving Street side of the building in a space reserved for police vehicles.

She pulled her PDA out of her duffel bag and gave her email a quick check. Saffin was fielding press inquiries for both the drug raid and the Archives ceremony. Nothing she couldn't handle on her own. Saffin also sent a personal note that she had bought a sweater at the Talbots sale. A quick message from Resha thanking her for the advice. She shut the PDA down and slipped it in one of the larger cargo pockets on her pants. The duffel contained her handbag with her Laura identification and a pair of black dress slacks and a cream-colored blouse in case she had to go back to the Guildhouse before the end of the business day. Even though she doubted anyone would be audacious enough to rob a car in front of a police station, she slung the bag over her shoulder and entered the station house. No sense taking chances.

She had been in the District 7 house a couple of times and knew where Foyle's office was. After showing her badge, she skipped through security. Jonathan Sinclair was on the phone at a desk in the SWAT-team section. He flashed a pleasant smile and waved her to a vacant desk. Next to his. If he hadn't smiled, she wouldn't have given it a second thought, but given the tension they were all under, she couldn't help being suspicious. Despite years of gender integration on the force, it was still a male-dominated operation and women were tolerated only after they had spent twice as long as men gaining respect. If another desk had been open, she might have ignored him and taken it, but there was none. She gave him a tight smile and dropped the bag.

"Crawford," Foyle barked.

She looked over her shoulder at the open door to his office. Foyle sat at his desk reading, not looking at her. She went to the door. "Reporting for duty, boss."

He continued reading a file. "Sit."

She sat. And sat. So much anger surrounded Foyle, she didn't need her empathic ability to feel it. He went through four more pages, then pulled another file to the center of his desk. It was her report, delivered that morning as promised.

He stared at her. "There's nothing in here I don't already know." She didn't answer. "Why does that bother me?"

"It bothers me, too, sir. I'm told my memory will return."

He leaned back and put his hands behind his head, staring again. The casual pose tightened Foyle's shirt, showing off his biceps and chest. The regulation short haircut, sharp uniform, and piercing blue eyes were all meant to intimidate. Posturing was an old game, and Laura knew it. She played it herself, even now as she made a point of sitting upright and attentive.

"You didn't see who shot Sanchez, and you don't remember who shot you."

She shook her head. That was her role. Submit. Acquiesce. Demonstrate that she would take crap from a superior officer but no one else.

"Convenient," he said.

He was trying to provoke her, but she let it slide over her and didn't respond. She could play the silence game, too.

"Sanchez's headset was damaged, and we lost contact. Did he say anything?" he asked.

Another memory flash. Laura looked down at her hand. Sanchez had held it and pressed his finger into it. Why would he do that? Had he given her something that she'd lost and still couldn't remember? "He couldn't talk, I think. I seem to remember he couldn't talk because of the wound."

"After Sanchez asked for help, there was a six-minute gap in which you did not speak. When you did, it was to call for a medic," said Foyle.

"That was when I was trapped under the table."

"And you didn't radio for help?"

She concentrated on the moment. Even though she remembered being trapped, the memory was not clear. "Sanchez was under fire. We called for backup, but it didn't come. Help would have come from behind whoever was shooting at Sanchez. I thought I was on my own."

Foyle leaned forward and clasped his hands. "You can hear on the tape when Sanchez received his wound. At least that's what it sounds like to me. You must have heard it, yet you didn't react or say anything."

"I did. I . . ." She paused, remembering.

"What?"

She didn't meet his eyes. "I used a sending instead of the headset. It was instinctive."

"And against protocol. Do you still say he didn't speak?" Foyle said.

She shifted in her seat. Foyle was right. Mission protocol dictated that the fey vocalize in order for there to be an audio record. Sendings were frowned upon unless they were explicitly part of a mission plan. "I'm not comfortable where this is going, sir."

Foyle swiveled his chair and looked out the window. "He was dying, Crawford. He was a smart guy. He had to know. Last words are important. Whatever he said would have been important. I don't want to tell his family his last words were to ask for help and no one answered."

That part was true. On that point, he was sincere. The waves of essence Laura sensed confirmed how troubled he was. "As soon as I remember anything, you will be the first to know," she said. It was a lie, of course. It would depend on what she remembered.

"How long have you been with InterSec? Two years?" he asked.

"Nineteen months." She didn't add that she'd created Janice only after Foyle requested someone from InterSec with druidic and SWAT training. That first mission for him had been a low-key surveillance. Dull. He needed a female druid because the female target often went to the gym.

"Shit rolls downhill, Crawford. For an old swamp, D.C. has a lot of hills. Think about where you stand. Go find a desk. Dismissed."

She stood, feeling awkward. While it would have been a stretch to describe her relationship with Foyle as that of friends, they had been collegial with each other. His sudden aloofness again made her think she was being set up for something. It wasn't outside the realm of possibility. In the past, she had put in more time than nineteen months to set someone up for a fall. At least when she did it, she knew she was taking down a bad guy. If Foyle was setting her up for something, she couldn't fathom what it was. Either he was genuine in his anger over Sanchez, or Janice Crawford wasn't supposed to walk out of that apartment building, and he didn't know what to do with her now.

Gianni was on the phone on the desk opposite Sinclair. He gave Laura a cursory nod when she returned to the vacant desk but continued his conversation. Sinclair shifted sideways and leaned back against the wall. "How's your head?"

"Concussion. Nothing serious." She pulled out the PDA. Hornbeck had called personally, and Saffin was worried his next step would be an unannounced visit. She didn't want to send any response in front of Sinclair, so she slipped the PDA back in her pocket.

He stretched his long legs toward her and crossed them at the ankles. "I was scared shitless when I saw you and Sanchez. I thought you were both dead."

His vocal inflections indicated honesty. She did a quick check on him, but his strong body essence didn't reveal subterfuge. She decided to go with a bit of vulnerability and truth. "You know, I wasn't scared the entire time until I saw Sanchez. Not when we were getting shot at, not when I had to deal with the Inverni or when the crates came down on me. But seeing all that blood and Sanchez sitting there with his hands around his neck made everything real in a way I'd never thought about. I've never had anyone die on me before."

Janice was supposed to be young, with little experience. The part about the fear was true. Being in the line of fire was always scary. Even the most battle-hardened felt fear, although they didn't like to admit it. Laura had seen plenty of friends and colleagues die in the line of duty. It never got easier, and it was always horrifying. She made a mental note that Gabrio Sanchez was the first cop Janice Crawford saw die. It was part of her history now.

"It wasn't my first." The tone in Sinclair's voice indicated a point of information, not an invitation for more conversation about it. And it wouldn't be the last death, she completed in her head. They both knew it. If you made a career on a SWAT team in D.C., the odds were you would become a statistic. Sinclair jutted his chin toward some files on her desk. "I thought you might want to look at those."

"Thanks." She flipped open the folder. Team reports from the raid. She glanced at Sinclair. She wondered if he was being nice or if he was the squad's designated good cop to soften her up. Foyle's report was on top. She read it as Gianni rambled on the phone—to a woman by the annoying cutesy tone in his voice.

To quote Foyle, his report had nothing she didn't already know or surmise. After she and Sanchez had charged the rear hallway, Foyle remained behind. He sent Sinclair and Gianni ahead as backup for Laura and Sanchez. As Foyle waited for his own backup, he became pinned in the cross fire. When his backup arrived, he entered the rear hall alone and met Gianni and Sinclair returning from the computer lab. They searched the workroom, looking for Laura and Sanchez when they couldn't raise them on radio. Sinclair reached them first. He checked Laura's vitals.

She closed her eyes. She remembered Sinclair standing over her in the sweatshop. He looked concerned and professional in the memory, no panic at the sight of two people possibly dead. His face was just a brief flash with no emotional resonance attached to it so she couldn't determine if he had been concerned or putting on an act for whoever else was in the room. Her memory clouded.

The next few reports were from other teams. She gave them a cursory review, trying not to rush. She felt Sinclair's eyes on her and didn't want him to think she had any particular concern about their team. She found his report and Gianni's on the bottom, which confirmed her suspicion that he was waiting to see if she would shuffle through the stack to reach them before the others.

Sinclair reported that he and Gianni had overshot the room where she and Sanchez were. They followed the mission plan by heading to the lab, not realizing she and San-chez had had to break from the plan to follow the Inverni. They joined forces with a side-entry team to take out the lab. An unknown group of shooters came up behind them. Sinclair and Gianni became separated. Sinclair left the lab and pressed deeper into the building after the shooters. When he heard Laura's mayday, he returned to the back hall and entered the workroom with Gianni and Foyle. He spotted Laura and Sanchez and called in the medics.

Gianni's report was short and to the point. His time line matched Sinclair's up to the lab, where they became sepa-rated. He was assisting the other team in securing what was left of the lab when he heard the mayday. He met Foyle and Sinclair at the door, and they entered the workroom. He maintained position at the entry while Foyle and Sinclair secured the room.

She gathered the reports and tapped them on the desk to neaten the pile. She caught Sinclair's eye and nodded. "Thanks."

He shrugged. "You already said that."

"No, I mean for finding me."

He gave her a curious look, as if surprised she would be grateful that he'd done his job. She was, in a way. Just be-cause it was his job, didn't mean he had to do it right—or well. "Sure. You're welcome," he said.

"I'm sorry about Sanchez," she said.

Sinclair frowned and pulled his chair to his desk. "Yeah."

She kept her face neutral. Anger and annoyance hovered around Sinclair, but no substantive grief. When a family member or friend died, a sense of grief became a distinct part of someone's essence for a time. Anger was often part of it as well, but it was unusual to feel no grief at all. Odd reaction to the death of a teammate.

She gestured at the reports. "Can I take these for the night?"

His eyes shifted to the closed door to Foyle's office. "It's probably a good idea to have them sitting on my desk at the end of the day."

Laura affected a confused look, as if she didn't pick up his subtle warning. She handed him the file. She didn't need to take it home. Her natural talent and druidic training ensured that everything she read had logged itself into her photographic memory. Sinclair would be surprised to hear her recite the reports verbatim. Or maybe not. They used to have a druid on their team. Sinclair might be more aware of her talents than his experience would indicate.

Gianni broke the awkward silence by slamming down the phone. Laura startled for effect. By the lack of reaction from Sinclair, she suspected that Gianni was a chronic phone slammer. He didn't look happy. "Let's go for a beer."

"I'm in," Sinclair said.

They both stared at her, almost challenging her to refuse. She hesitated for a moment, debating whether to beg off. Her headache had lessened but not gone away. She still had Guildmaster Rhys's speech to review. But she didn't want to miss the opportunity to make more of a connection with them. Not with Foyle acting so strangely. Something was definitely going on in the squad, and she wasn't going to figure it out by playing the unsocial outsider.

"Sounds good. Where's the locker room?"

A strange tension vibrated off Sinclair while an equally strange sense of satisfaction came off Gianni. She hoped neither emotion indicated one of them was going to take a shot at her.

CHAPTER 7

THE VAULT WAS a club everyone knew by reputation but few under a certain income bracket ever experienced. The clientele varied in character throughout the day, but the atmosphere didn't. Money and power ruled. The upstairs lounge functioned as the power lunch site where lawyers and lobbyists dined with elected officials and their staffs, maintaining the facade of friendship against a backdrop of exchanged favors. By midafternoon, the room evolved into an elite social club that included women and fey, meaning it had the trappings of an old men's club with the vibe of the new century. The bar saw traffic for the after-work decompression and late in the evening for post-charity-event socializing or breaks from late-night strategy sessions. Laura had been there a few times as Laura Blackstone as well as Mariel Tate, her high-level InterSec persona. She was surprised that two midlevel police officers were interested in the place and more surprised they gained entrance without their badges.

Sinclair and Gianni met her after she parked her SUV in a lucky spot on the street. The doorman held the door as they entered—Laura first, which she wasn't sure was courtesy or sexist. As the closing door cut off afternoon daylight from the dimmer foyer, the doorman said, "See you later, Sal."

So Gianni, at least, was known at the Vault. If she had to guess which of her companions was a regular, she would have said Sinclair before Gianni. Sinclair had the look of a Vault bar patron, early twenties to late thirties, dress pants and shirt. She admitted that he looked handsome, equally comfortable in the sports coat he was wearing as he was in the black SWAT-team gear. Without asking or being told, Gianni leaned in to the coat checkroom and retrieved a sports coat that hung with several identical ones under a discreet sign indicating that they were required dress for men. Laura trailed behind them to the bar.

The bartender finished an order, then handed up draft beers to Sinclair and Gianni. He smiled at Laura inquiringly. "Same for me," she said.

No one spoke as they assessed the room. Laura recognized several people, some from meetings as Laura Blackstone or Mariel Tate, some from the evening news, but mostly the room was full of the unknown people who made the wheels of government turn. Years ago, when she found herself in D.C. advocating for the fey more and more, she'd bought a book to learn how the American democratic system worked. A week after her first job at the Guildhouse, she threw the book away.

Washington worked like so many other governments—relationships and favors drove policies more than rules and regulations ever could. The letter of the law was followed, but the intent or the spirit of it wasn't always. Words on a page could mean anything if someone powerful enough wanted them to. That was one of the reasons humans feared the fey, though they might not articulate it that way. There was a fear, sometimes a real one, that the fey would use their power against anyone who threatened theirs. High Queen Maeve wasn't known as the Bitch of Tara for nothing.

The bartender slid a beer next to the first two and walked away. No bill. No tab.

Sinclair picked up a glass. "To Gabrio Sanchez."

"To Sanchez," Laura said, and tapped his glass with her own. Gianni frowned as he tapped glasses but didn't verbalize the toast. He turned a shoulder to them and faced the busy room. Laura sipped her beer, scanning the crowd with a practiced innocent air.

"Have you ever been here before?" Sinclair asked.

She shook her head, amused that it sounded like a lame conversation starter for a pickup. "I'm not much of a bar person."

Gianni walked off without a word. He leaned in halfway down the bar and started talking to two young women. Laura didn't think much of it. While they were out of his price range, they were close enough in age to keep it not-creepy. She scanned the bar again until her gaze settled on Sinclair. He smiled.

"What the hell are we doing here?" she said.

He chuckled and finished off his beer. "Gianni does a detail here every once in a while, so he likes to think he belongs."

"And you?"

The bartender landed another beer for both of them. "I work details, too, sometimes. Mostly I come to watch Gianni make an ass of himself," Sinclair said.

Laura cocked an eyebrow. "Nice. So why am I here?"

"That's what I'm wondering. Why'd you come?"

She shrugged. "I don't know. Maybe I wanted to get to know Sanchez's friends."

Sinclair stared into his beer. "You having survivor's guilt?"

She paused, considering whether Sinclair would like that or not. "No. It was screwed up, but it wasn't my fault."

Sinclair nodded once sharply. "Good. Sanchez wasn't worth the guilt."

Sinclair knew she was a druid. He had to know she sensed things off people, even if he didn't know that she could sense emotion more acutely than other druids. He had to know he was not putting out mourning signals. "Okay, I'll bite. Why didn't you like Sanchez?"

Sinclair leaned into the corner to face her fully. "Maybe

Sanchez disappeared a lot with no explanation. Maybe he asked a lot of questions, then maybe he clammed up if someone asked him anything. Maybe he liked coming down here as much as Gianni does." He took a long pull on his beer. "Or Foyle, for that matter."

"Something about this place I should know?" she asked.

He kept his smile teasing. Laura felt herself blush at his direct gaze. She never thought of the Janice glamour as particularly attractive, more like a simple, plain-looking police officer. She definitely didn't expect someone with Sinclair's looks to be interested in Janice, but that was what that teasing smile sure as hell felt like. She told herself it was the beer. She hadn't eaten all day and was already feeling the soft tickle of alcohol coursing through her. She was tired and seeing things to make herself feel better.

"I'm not talking. I'm just saying. Know what I mean?" he said.

Laura wasn't sure she did. She didn't want to seem eager, so she put a little irritation in her voice. "Maybe you're being real nice to someone you just met. Maybe I could take that two ways. And maybe, considering the freaking bruise on the side of my head, I should be cautious about what I hear. Know what I mean?"

He laughed. She liked his laugh. She wanted to slap herself for thinking it. With everything going on in her life, the last thing she should be doing was clouding her judgment with an attraction to someone who might have shot her. "Yeah, I do."

Laura stopped looking at him. While they didn't speak, the silence didn't stretch to uncomfortable. Assessing, Laura thought. They were assessing their next moves. Offering the raid reports and now hinting at dirty cops was a little too much too soon for her taste. She wasn't sure if she was supposed to bite on something or if she was being warned off. As far as Sinclair knew, she was a low-level staffer from InterSec, farmed out for the cleanup chores and no-brainer jobs. In other words, no one powerful, so no one likely to bring in any noise from InterSec. Considering where they were, if Sinclair was a regular at the Vault, he had plenty of opportunity to connect with someone who might be interested in stirring the pot in a SWAT-team squad room.

Someone on the team had taken a shot at her, and it didn't take a rocket scientist to assume that the same person had killed Sanchez. Laura had to consider the possibility that the bread crumbs Sinclair was laying out could be a trap to see what she knew or remembered.

He finished his second drink. "I'll be right back. I'm going to give Gianni a heads-up that the woman whose ear he just licked is a congressman's daughter."

"So now you care?" Laura shot at him.

He gave her a cocky grin over his shoulder. "He's my ride unless you take me home."

She rolled her eyes. The woman in question did not look pleased, and Gianni wasn't getting the message. Sinclair slipped between them and ordered another beer. He spoke to Gianni, then turned to the woman and introduced himself.

The bartender slid another drink in front of Laura. "On the house," he said, and walked away before she could respond. She picked up the fluted glass and sniffed. Brandy, an Armagnac by the shape of the glass. Sinclair caught her eye. She raised the glass and toasted him. He smiled uncertainly as his gaze shifted to her glass. Gianni said something that distracted him, and he looked away. The amber fluid spread across her tongue and released shades of vanilla and apricot and something earthy she couldn't identify. The crowded bar made it difficult to parse the scents, but it was delicious. Another pleasant surprise from Sinclair.

Intent on watching Sinclair and Gianni, Laura didn't pay any attention when someone stood behind her. The barroom was crowded, and the bar itself was, too, so the sudden presence next to her did not seem amiss. Until the person behind spoke in her ear. "Good teammates watch each other's backs."

She looked into the face of a tall elf. She recognized him immediately from media reports. Tylo Blume smiled pleasantly down at her, his pointed ears showing through long dark hair tied loosely at the middle of his back. Apprehension rippled through her. Blume was a high-profile mover and shaker on Capitol Hill. He had friends in all the right places and was worth millions. The same Tylo Blume that Senator Hornbeck wanted Laura Blackstone to meet and secure a speaking role for at the Archives' exhibit opening. And suddenly here he was, talking to Janice Crawford. Washington could be a small town, but she hated coincidences and always suspected them.

"Teammates?" she asked.

Blume made no overt indication to the bartender, but another glass of Armagnac appeared at his elbow. He must have done a sending. Laura looked down at her own glass. Not Sinclair then. She felt foolish, accepting a drink without knowing who it was from, as if she were a kid from the country on her first city visit.

Blume glanced over at Gianni and Sinclair. "As are you, Ms. Crawford." He held out a hand. "Tylo Blume."

She shook. "And you know me because . . . ?"

He sipped his drink and peered down at her. She debated whether he was sneering or amused. "I heard about what happened to you and wanted to meet you."

Laura played it cautiously pleasant. "Really? Why?"

He nodded up the bar. "Your friends, Gianni and Sinclair, do some work for me occasionally. I could use a druid with backbone."

Laura decided Janice would be clueless about Blume. "I'm sorry, but who are you?"

He continued staring at her with his thin smile. His essence felt amused. Laura had the sense that he was buying the dumb act. "Well, I own this place, for one thing. The building, in fact."

"Nice place. And for another thing?"

"Let's say I have several business interests in town," he said.

She feigned loss of interest, looking around the room. "Oh. I don't really follow politics."

She caught Sinclair's watchful eye. He looked away a fraction of a second later, as if he didn't want her to know he was watching. Blume stayed next to her.

"Are you interested?" he asked

"In a job? Depends. What do you have in mind?" she asked.

Blume took a turn scanning the room. "Look around. Even if you don't follow politics, you probably recognize a few faces in here. We keep the press and the tourists out. Off-duty law enforcement helps our clients and keeps the place safe."

Laura twisted her lips. "I don't know. It sounds like you want a bouncer. I became a police officer to get out of that gig."

"There are interesting security issues as well," said Blume.

"I'll have to think about it," she said.

"My offices are upstairs. Shall we discuss it in more appropriate surroundings?" he asked.

She was tempted. She had followed Gianni and Sinclair to learn what she could about them. Blume was unexpected, and unexpectedly respectable, but clearly one of her "teammates" had told him about her. Under normal circumstances, she would have taken advantage of such a turn of events. But now the timing and situation felt wrong. Two and a half drinks had taken the edge off her alertness, and drinking with a concussion hadn't been the smartest move in the first place. She didn't need to follow up tonight.

"Maybe another time," she said.

"You could use the money," he said.

In one sense, it was true—part of the Janice biography. But Blume spoke with a tone of conviction that revealed he knew it for a fact. She faced him with a touch of indignation in her face. "Excuse me?"

He pursed his lips, his amusement turning smug. "You live in a small apartment and have no family to help you financially. InterSec throws you a short job once in a while, and the D.C. human force has no interest in hiring you.

You're three months late on your student loan, and your cable was turned off last month." He placed a business card on the bar. "Do think about it."

He melted into the crowd without another word. She picked up the card, a plain cream with two evergreen stripes down the side and across the top. The only text gave Blume's name, email address, and a phone number, no title or business.

"I see he made his pitch," Sinclair said.

She glanced at his sudden appearance. He didn't startle her, but she was surprised she hadn't detected his body signature until he was right next to her. Her limited sensing range became more constricted in crowded rooms; but once she knew someone, she was usually more sensitive to the body signature. She frowned. "Thanks for the heads-up."

"It wasn't my idea. Maybe I wanted to see how you reacted," he said.

"Did I pass your test?"

"Did you take the job?"

"No."

He toasted the air. "A-plus."

"I don't like being played, Sinclair. I'll see you tomorrow." She decided to establish her own role as the druid with a backbone. She pushed through the crowd. She'd have plenty of time to make nice in the squad room.

"Wait a sec," Sinclair called to her, when she reached the foyer. He followed her. She continued forward but waited for him on the sidewalk.

"What?" she asked, when he stepped out.

"Look, don't take this wrong. I didn't mean to make you mad. They played me when I was the new guy. You're just newerer."

She glared at him, then laughed. "I hope you're drunk and don't think that's a word."

He had the good grace to hang his head in embarrassment. Laura wasn't buying it yet. "You okay to drive?" he asked.

She gave him a cocky look. "I'm a police officer with a badge. I'm always okay to drive."

She tucked her chin down as she walked away so that he could not see her smiling. His concern about her driving was genuine. She surprised herself by feeling flattered but didn't want Sinclair to see her looking pleased. He might get the wrong impression. Or the right one. Despite her suspicions, she liked him. He had a refreshing honesty in a city seldom known for truth. He wasn't telling her everything—either about himself or what he knew about the raid—but at least he wasn't lying. Yet. She allowed herself to enjoy the attraction. It had been a long time since she noticed a man. Surrounded as she was by beautiful fey people in the Guildhouse, physical attractiveness had almost become a given in what passed for her social life. Finding someone attractive wasn't the problem. Finding someone attractive in the right way was.

She decided to stay the night at the Guildhouse. It was closer than her apartment, and she wanted to get an early start in the morning. She parked her SUV in its usual spot, shifted out of the Janice glamour in the elevator lobby, and rode the elevator to her Blackstone office.

Without pausing, she went to the closet behind her desk and pushed aside the coat and extra outfit she stored there. To the casual observer, the closet was two feet deep. However, the back wall didn't exist in the conventional sense. A masking spell created the illusion of a wall, tactilely and visually. The spell was keyed to her body signature, and it tingled over her skin like cobwebs. It allowed her to pass through to an office on the opposite side of the floor. InterSec had requisitioned the space for her. The people who worked in the nearby department thought the hall door on their side accessed an electrical closet.

A double clothing rack along one side held a variety of outfits. Beneath, dozens of shoes sat toes to the wall, everything from work boots to ballet slippers. An unmade bed took up most of the next wall. Two worktables, a bureau, and a desk filled the rest of the space. The room was cluttered and messy, the stale, filtered air tinged with the faint burnt odor of the herbs that she used for healing and meditation.

Laura slept in the room more often than she liked to admit. As the years went on, she spent more time in it, even thought of it as a home. There was no pretense about the room, no artifice. It represented a world of hidden agendas, but the room itself contained none. It was the one place where she didn't have to be anyone. The problem was, she wasn't quite sure what that meant anymore. Her life had become the room, closed off, contained, and hidden.

She stripped off her clothing. In the cramped bathroom, she examined herself in the mirror as she waited for the hot water to come up. The bruise from the gunshot hit was already fading, a testament to her fey constitution. Despite whatever Cress had done to boost her essence, she looked drawn and pale. She didn't spend much time in the tiny, claustrophobic shower, staying just long enough to get the odor of the bar off her.

In the main room, her gaze fell on a vodka bottle next to the hot plate. Even as her hand reached for the bottle, she changed her mind, picked up the teapot, and filled it from the bathroom tap. A small burn ignited in her chest. After decades on the job watching colleagues disintegrate in an alcoholic rage, she was not going to slide into the trap now. It bothered her that she had reminded herself about it twice in two days. Instead, she made chamomile tea and added healing herbs.

Sitting on the edge of the bed, she wove a chant into the aroma from the tea. It flickered with healing essence as she sipped. Warmth spread in her chest and stomach, and she used her body essence to nudge the spell to her sore shoulder and head. The ache in both places lessened, as though under a mild anesthetic.

Turning off the lights, she stared into the darkness. She had spent too many moments gazing too long at Sinclair. She needed to pull herself together, remember her job, and not get distracted. Not by drinking and not by flirting with Jonathan Sinclair.

She sighed and rolled on her side. The only explanation she had for her behavior was exhaustion. Why else would she be almost actively slipping up? She needed a break, that much she was sure of. As she drifted into sleep, the image of Sinclair's amber eyes floated through her mind. He was handsome. He was intriguing. He was interested. She reminded herself that none of those things were worth getting killed over.

8
CHAPTER

LAURA PLACED HER hand on a granite panel beside the locked door to the InterSec unit. Her body signature—Janice Crawford's body signature—interacted with the ward spell, tickling static across her palm. The spell recognized the glamour's persona and the lock released. Over the years, she had taken pains to avoid connecting Laura Blackstone with InterSec. Whenever she worked on anything other than public relations at the Guildhouse, she wore the appropriate glamour. That way Laura Blackstone didn't have to answer any questions about her presence in an area that had nothing to do with her day job.

Inside the secure area, Cress appeared in the hallway and smiled when she saw Laura. "Feeling better?" she asked.

Laura nodded. "Yeah. Sleeping did me a world of good."

Little feathers of essence flickered over her body essence like small tongues as Cress examined her discreetly. Laura dealt with several different species of fey healers, but the way Cress touched her essence felt overly intimate and intrusive. Always behind it was the hunger of a *leanansidhe*, the palpable desire to drain essence, which Cress kept in check only by her own willpower. "The bruising from the concussion is gone. Are you remembering anything from the raid?"

Laura glanced at her palm, recalling the blood and Sanchez's hand. "I think I had a flash of something, but it's too vague to mean anything."

Cress withdrew a notepad from her white coat and made a brief note. "It will come. Keep thinking about the people involved. Sometimes that rebuilds connections."

"Rebuilds? Is something broken?"

Cress smiled. "You had a concussion, Laura. Brain cells died. Don't worry about it."

Laura poked her in the arm. "Oh, thanks. 'Brain cells died.' That doesn't make me worry."

Cress's smile turned crooked. "Sorry. I'll keep monitoring. Just get as much rest as you can."

Laura sighed. "Yeah, right, Cress. Look at my calendar. Better yet, look at this face. I'm living two lives at the moment. Is Terryn in?"

Cress nodded. "In his office. He's in a bit of a mood."

Laura adjusted her jacket. "I'll try not to provoke him."

Cress patted her on the shoulder as she walked away. "Oh, please do. Dinner tonight will go more smoothly if he lets off some steam before he gets home."

Laura shook her head as she continued down the hall. For all her conflicted feelings about Cress's nature, she was still a person, still more than her nature. At the end of the day—literally in this case—even the *leanansidhe* sometimes had to deal with a cranky boyfriend like anybody else.

True to Cress's word, Terryn was in a foul mood when Laura entered his office. He didn't look up right away but frowned at something he was reading. "We need more info on what was going on at that apartment building."

"Have you seen the case files yet?" she asked.

He gave her a small smile. "About an hour after the raid. All standard op. Several tips on drug manufacturing leading to surveillance to planning the raid and its timing. Nothing to indicate it was other than a straightforward raid."

"There was a computer lab that looked heavily defended," said Laura.

Terryn sifted a folder out of his pile. "I thought that was interesting, too. It was destroyed. Crime Scene hasn't released anything yet, and I'm hearing rumblings that the FBI might take over." Terryn pushed a piece of paper across his desk. "More bad news."

She picked up the sheet, a memo on FBI letterhead, stamped SECRET and hand-delivered. She skimmed it and slipped surprise on her face. "Sanchez was working for the Bureau?"

Terryn nodded. "I confirmed the report through our back channel at the FBI. He was CTD."

A spot of annoyance in her chest quickly blossomed into anger. "Counterterrorism? What the hell did I step in, Terryn, and why didn't we know about it?"

He held up his hands. "I was as much in the dark as you were, Laura."

She threw the memo on his desk. "*Dark?* I got *shot at*, Terryn, by our own side. You can't get more *dark* than that."

He frowned. "Laura . . . I know. I don't blame you for being upset, but you're getting angry at the wrong person. You volunteered for that mission, remember?"

She closed her eyes and massaged her temples. "I'm sorry. You're right, Terryn. I have a headache, and I'm ticked off. It's been a long two days."

She wasn't going to wait for an invitation or assignment to figure out what was going on with Sanchez and the FBI, not when her own life was in the balance. "Who was Sanchez's field director?"

"Lawrence Scales."

She knew the name. Good reputation from all she had heard. "Set up an appointment. I'm going."

Terryn didn't try to hide his amusement. "There's the Laura I know. Would you like me to drive you to the meeting, or do I have your permission to run this unit while you go?"

She bit her lips in false embarrassment. "I'm sorry. What I meant was, may I have this assignment, sir?"

He inclined his head. "You may. It makes sense for you

to go as Mariel Tate anyway. I already set up the appointment and sent a dossier to the Tate office."

"Thanks. She'll get right on it," said Laura. Mariel was
the most formidable persona Laura used. She was smart,
powerful, and had the might of InterSec to back her up publicly. Mariel's phone calls were always taken if someone
was in, and the first returned if someone was out.

Terryn moved papers on his desk. "I've done some preliminary research on the SWAT team. Gianni, Sinclair, and
Sanchez have done paid detail and other side work at a dinner club called the Vault."

Laura nodded. "I know. I was there last night. Tylo Blume,
of all people, owns the place. He offered me a job."

"He's an arms merchant," said Terryn.

Laura's eyebrow flicked up. "That I didn't know. His
firm is running some of the security for the Archives ceremony I'm working on for Guild public relations."

Terryn dropped a corner of his mouth slightly. "Laura
Blackstone and Janice Crawford have both met him?"

Laura shrugged. "It's a coincidence. I've been avoiding
meeting with him about the Archives ceremony as Laura
Blackstone because that ups the pressure to say yes to what
he wants. Senator Hornbeck's the actual connection. Foyle
mentioned to him that he wanted a backup for Corman
Deegan, his SWAT-team druid who's out of commission. If
you remember, Terryn, you were the one that wanted more
contacts with local enforcement. I created Janice the first
time Deegan called in sick."

Terryn leaned back in his chair. "I remember. I also remember saying I thought the situation might produce a persona conflict."

She had no choice but to agree. "Fine, you were right. I
didn't think the two personas would ever have a reason to
cross. Once the Archives ceremony is over, the problem
should go away. Did Corman Deegan work there, too?"

Terryn shook his head. "The SWAT-team druid? I don't
see any indications that he did."

"Where is he now?"

"Still in the hospital with head-blindness," Terryn said.

"Sanchez knew something, Terryn. Now somebody thinks I do and is willing to kill me because of it."

"Maybe you do."

She thought of her memory flashes, Sanchez pressing his finger into her bloody hand. She pushed at the moment, tried to make the scene step beyond what she remembered, but it drifted into nothing. "I think Sanchez did tell me something. He couldn't talk. I remember him doing something to my hand. He might have been trying to communicate something."

"Sign language?"

Laura looked at her palm. Something about the way the lines of her skin crisscrossed made her uneasy. She had never subscribed to palmistry, at least not the way the modern world did. She knew some fey could read health issues in the skin, but that had more to do with how essence points radiated than simple lines. Something about the way her life, heart, and head lines were arranged. "It was a shape, I think. He wrote something."

"A name?"

She didn't respond, but continued staring. The memory flickered on the edges of her awareness. Frustration grew within her, frustration that a druid, of all people, was having a hard time remembering. She shook her head. "It's gone again."

Terryn had the good grace not to look disappointed, but she felt it. "It'll come. In the meantime, let's do the footwork to figure out why the FBI was spying on the SWAT team."

Laura gathered her things. "Will do. I want to talk to Corman Deegan first, see if he knows anything. I'll catch up with you after that."

On the way to the elevator, she passed Cress in the hall. "I made him smile. You owe me lunch."

"A small price to pay, I am sure," she replied.

9
CHAPTER

"WHERE THE HECK have you been?" Saffin said.

Laura was tempted to tell her she had been impersonating a police officer and drinking with an arms merchant, but thought better of it. Instead, she rolled her eyes in shared exasperation as she walked through the public-relations reception area. "Sorry. I got pulled into a meeting yesterday, then had to do some damage control on something last night."

Saffin handed her a stack of mail. "Hornbeck called again," she said.

Laura shook her head as she sorted the mail. "He won't let up, will he?"

Saffin made a sour face. "It gets worse. His office noticed that the two of you will be at separate Senate hearings on the same floor tomorrow. He wants you to meet him as soon as he finishes."

Laura bit back a curse. She was participating in a fact-finding session at one of the Senate buildings about fey homeless shelters. "I forgot about the hearing."

Saffin sighed and frowned in mock-frustration. "Did you not read the three email alerts I sent you? I can't run your life if you don't pay attention."

Laura chuckled, but a sliver of guilt swept over her. She had neglected to check her email. Sloppy. Despite her joking, Saffin's face had a shadow of gauntness about it that suggested stress. That was a minor hint that a boggart situation could evolve. Over the years, Saffin had never become more than highly agitated with Laura. Laura took that as a point of pride for both of them. It meant they knew how to work together.

Brownies didn't like going boggie. The mental strain was bad enough, but the change was physical, too. Their bodies literally transformed, becoming elongated and taut, while their physical strength increased dramatically. Their minds slipped, too, normal rationality becoming suppressed as they became obsessed with completing the task that sparked the change. It happened like an adrenaline rush— fast, intense, and utterly exhausting when it was over. "I'm really sorry, Saf. I've been distracted. I think it's time we pull Rhys into this to get Hornbeck to go away."

Saffin nodded her acceptance of the apology, but the sad look on her face pained Laura. "Sorry to disappoint you, but Hornbeck already called the Guildmaster, and they referred him to you."

Laura slumped against the door in frustration. "Okay, dammit, I'll talk to him. But if Rhys doesn't want to deal with it, then I can't be responsible for what I say."

Saffin followed her into her office. "Speaking of which, Rhys's office has been calling all morning. They want your edits to his speech."

As Laura walked around her desk, she found a small Talbots bag on the chair, Saffin's favorite spot to leave things she absolutely wanted Laura to see. Slipping her hand into the bag, she pulled out a large piece of silk folded in a neat square. She let it slide against itself to reveal a large paisley scarf in shades of red. "Oh, Saf! This is gorgeous."

Some of the stress lines in Saffin's face relaxed. "It's the wrong red for me, but I thought it would look great with your hair. It was an insane deal."

Laura gathered the fabric and slipped it loosely around her neck. "I love it. How much do I owe you?"

Saffin waved her hand. "Nothing. It's a gift."

Laura learned long ago not to argue when Saffin called something a gift. Part of her nature was in the giving of things, whether help or tangible items, and Saffin sometimes perceived even a courteous demurral as a failure on her part. "Thank you, Saffin. I'll get on the speech right now."

Saffin brightened considerably, the tautness nearly gone. "Okay. I'll be right outside."

Laura took her seat and adjusted the scarf. She really did like it.

She opened her email and retrieved the Guildmaster's document. Orrin ap Rhys wrote most of his own speeches. He was good at it. In recent years, he had taken a liking to Laura's editing suggestions, probably because they shared similar approaches to problems. She hardly ever needed to contradict him or attempt to change his position. Usually, all she did was update his language for a modern audience and let him know about current affairs that would enhance his arguments.

His Archives speech demonstrated their mutual concerns. Laura didn't add much for most of the speech. Rhys had hit all the key points in the relationship between modern humans and the Celtic fey. In fact, he had lived through all of the last century's interactions and been a significant player himself, even participating in the negotiation of the Treaty of London.

Near the end of the speech, though, Laura massaged the language with an eye to current politics. She brought in the achievements of a recent summit between Maeve and the Elvenking. It wasn't a resounding success, but enough progress had been made to ensure that the process would probably continue. Except, not everyone was pleased with the idea that the Celts and the Teuts might settle their differences. Some human factions feared that an allied fey was a dangerous fey. Therein lay the difficulty for her—events had different meanings to different groups. Laura tried to keep tabs on all of them and make sure that Rhys soothed the right egos and slapped back at the politically inconsequential and the dangerous. Nuance was key.

As a commander of fairy-warrior forces, Rhys liked to talk too much about conflicts. Laura thought it undermined the message of success and unity of the recent negotiations and the benefits that they would provide the human population. She cut the troublesome material in half, wrote "too negative" in the margin, and slanted the language into a stronger message of triumph, despite the inevitable obstacles naysayers would throw in the way of progress. She made one more pass through the speech and emailed it off to Rhys.

She glanced at her watch and called out the door to Saffin. "I sent the speech, if anyone should ask, Saf. I need you to make a delivery for me."

From within a locked drawer in her desk, she retrieved a sealed envelope. As Saffin entered, Laura wrote "Candace Burke" on the envelope and an address. Burke didn't exist. She was a means to manipulate Saffin away from her desk by sending her on an errand outside the building. She handed the envelope to Saffin. "I probably won't be here when you get back, but call my cell if you need me."

Saffin read the address to herself. "Okay. Don't forget the hearing tomorrow. Wear the yellow suit with the short skirt. Your new scarf will go perfectly, and Hornbeck will be distracted by your legs."

Laura shook her head. "I think you know my entire wardrobe better than I do."

Saffin shrugged. "You surprise me sometimes."

Laura waited a few minutes, then checked the outer hall. Saffin was gone. She gathered her handbag, her briefcase and PDA, and stepped through the closet to her private room.

Dropping her things on the bed, she slipped into the chair at one of the worktables. Two tiers of plastic bins sat on the table, a collection of stones, gems, and wood—the accumulation of years of practice. She removed the chained emerald with the Janice glamour in it and hung it on a wooden stand. The monetary value of the three-carat emerald never crossed her mind. It was worth more than dollars and cents to her.

Any stone could be made to hold a glamour, but a perfect stone—a perfect stone was rare and priceless to someone who manipulated essence. Perfect stones held essence imprints that didn't degrade quickly, and the amount of essence required to power them went down as the perfection of the crystalline structure went up. Laura had never come across a more perfect one.

She sorted through a bin of smaller emeralds. The Janice glamour was rather simple, playing off Laura's existing features and changing her hair color. It didn't require a perfect stone. Laura had used the stone because it was convenient—she wore it all the time—and she hadn't expected Janice to be around for more than the one day of the raid. However, the perfect stone was more suited to the Mariel Tate glamour, so she needed to switch Janice onto a lesser stone.

She selected a serviceable one-carat emerald, threaded it onto a gold chain, and hung it from another wooden stand. Cupping the smaller stone in her hand with a thin wand of oak, she took care not to touch the stone with the wood. Brushing the tip of the wand against the perfect stone, she pulled at the glamour with a muttered cantrip. The essence-template that formed the Janice glamour tingled under her hand as it swirled through the wood. It sought the crystalline structure of the smaller stone and imprinted itself there.

Laura draped the one-carat stone around her neck, cool static chasing over her skin as the glamour settled. She examined herself in the mirror above the table. Janice Crawford stared back at her. Satisfied that the transfer hadn't degraded the glamour, she removed the chain and put the stone aside.

Lifting the perfect stone from the stand, she dropped it in a box carved from granite and covered it with a glass lid. Sparks of essence escaped her fingertips and into the box, dancing with a blue light around the emerald. When the essence faded, she removed the stone and tested it with her sensing ability. No essence registered, the equivalent of sterile. The only glamour on the stone was its own inherent beauty.

She slipped it back around her neck and visualized Mariel Tate. Mariel was a more complicated glamour than Janice. Laura had modeled her on several classic beauties who looked nothing like her. She rarely enhanced her own looks with a glamour, but she had gone all out with Mariel. Physical attractiveness could be a useful distraction.

A mental image was the first step in creating a glamour, providing the basic blueprint. She bound the mental image of Mariel Tate with a touch of essence and pushed it into the stone. The mirror above the table reflected the shift, her true face blurring into a rudimentary version of Mariel's features.

From experience, Laura focused first on the eyes. If the eyes weren't right, nothing else would matter. She shifted the color of her irises from their normal green until they shone golden. The trick with Mariel's eyes was light and depth. For ease of transition, she kept Mariel a druid, but for added effect, she had styled her as an Old One, an ancient fey who had a deep, fathomless aspect to her eyes that spoke of years of experience and survival. To look into the eyes of an Old One was to see history and power, a cool, sometimes cold, detachment of someone who had lived through decades of experience and would continue to do so. An Old One projected the power of triumphant survival. Humans felt insignificant under such a gaze. The physical difference that produced the effect was subtle but intense.

Satisfied with the basic template, she worked the rest of the glamour with little effort. Re-creating a glamour took less time than producing a new one, the uncanny recall that all druids had enabling Laura to call forth the memory of the template. Mariel's ebony hair flowed to her waist—another trick, long hair on women having a history of conveying mystery beneath femininity. For convenience, she added an outfit, a dark gray, form-fitting power suit with a long skirt. Wearing physical clothing was easier since she only needed to maintain a body image, but she wouldn't have time just then to change into Mariel's clothes.

As a final touch, she softly sang an old Irish song as she worked, a cadence of grief and remembrance that touched the soul. Mariel's voice had a mild lilt, which women found endearing and men found alluring, and the song spelled the accent into her voice.

Rising from the worktable, she examined the results in a full-length mirror, a critical eye roaming over the line of the skirt, the shape of her shoes, and the drape of her hair. As Laura, as her physical self, she knew she was attractive. But Mariel went beyond that. She represented a woman who most people aspired to be or be with, and possessed a confidence in herself that everyone wished they had. If a glamour was a mask—a visual lie—Mariel was Laura's lie to her inner self. She was Mariel, but wasn't. Mariel's allure and power were aspects she only pretended to have.

She slipped the Janice glamour stone into a small pouch that was keyed to her body signature. For security reasons, only she could open it. She tucked the pouch into one of the vest pockets of her business suit, closed the plastic bins, and returned them to their orderly cubbyholes.

Instead of passing back through the closet—and risking an encounter with a returning Saffin—Laura paused at the workroom door, which led into the next department. Sensing no one in the hallway on the other side, she opened the door. From the hallway, the view into the room was masked to look like an electrical closet. If a maintenance staff member opened the door, he would see junction boxes and the raw piping of the building but would be unable to enter because of a security spell. If anyone asked why there was a security spell, they were told that the room serviced sensitive experiments in the building and entrance needed clearance from Terryn macCullen. Few people asked. It was a Guildhouse, a building that everyone understood was filled with secrets that often were not healthy to investigate.

An added benefit of the location of her workroom was its proximity to a secondary elevator bank near the back of the building. A crowded elevator arrived, and Laura eased into the front. As the doors closed, she noticed Resha Dunne standing two people away. She caught his glance, a brief flicker laced with the gleam of attraction, before his lidded eyes shifted to stare at the numbers at the top of the car. Even with his docile nature, Resha was still a merrow and didn't suppress his obvious appreciation for Mariel. He had no idea who she really was. Without a mirror, even Laura sometimes forgot. She watched as the lit numbers counted down to the lobby. At ground level, she blended in with people in the crowded lobby, alone and anonymous, but still drawing attention.

10
CHAPTER

ELYSIUM GENERAL HOSPITAL blended into its surroundings like any other neighborhood business building. A solid mass of concrete with cantilevered sides, it had been built in the 1950s as part of the urban renewal south of the National Mall. The brutalist architecture suffered from unfavorable critical reviews. After struggling to find tenants for years, a coalition of fey groups purchased it and founded the hospital. If the Celtic fairies and Teutonic elves agreed on anything, it was quality health care, and EGH was the one place where no one argued politics, of the fey kind anyway.

Laura strolled the fourth-floor corridor, the Mariel Tate glamour drawing its intended attention from hospital staff and visitors. Her high heels punctured the hushed working atmosphere with a firm, measured rhythm. Mariel didn't rush and would not be rushed, her movements steady with purpose, the casual sway in her hips conveying a woman comfortable in her own skin more than one attempting to provoke desire in an onlooker. She had other attributes to do that.

She paused at the door to Corman Deegan's room. For a moment, she thought she might have the wrong room. The file in her hands had Deegan's picture in it, a trim man dressed in jeans and a blue oxford shirt. He appeared more youthful than his picture, certainly younger than his fifty-some years. Druids weren't immortal, but they lived decades longer than humans and aged at a much slower rate. Some were rumored to have lived centuries. In the file photo, Deegan looked to be no more than in his early thirties, his blunt-cut hair swept over his ears to the nape of his neck adding to the youthful appearance. The man sitting in the chair by the window looked considerably older.

He tilted his head to follow some movement outside the window. "I'm not sure why InterSec is interested in talking to me," he said.

Laura chided herself for forgetting that other druids had a wider sensing range than she did. She stepped a few feet into the room until she sensed Deegan's body signature. "My name's Mariel Tate."

He turned, revealing a healing cut on his right cheekbone and a fading bruise under his eye. "I know. I'm Corman Deegan."

She gave him a slow half smile. "I know."

They exchanged bemused stares as they took each other's measure. That close, she sensed he had what would be considered an average-strength body signature, not one of the heavy-hitting powerhouses of the fey world but not to be underestimated. Innate body essence was important in manipulating essence, but it wasn't the only thing that determined power. What you did with it counted. Laura knew powerful fey who didn't have the skills to exploit it. She was an example of someone with ability deficits that she more than made up for in other ways.

Deegan gestured for her to take the guest chair while he remained in the other. "You look too perfect. You're wearing a glamour."

The comment didn't surprise Laura. There were ways to see beneath a glamour, but it wasn't an ability. Druids were particularly skilled at creating glamours. They couldn't see through them, though they had a knack for noticing telltale signs when one was being used. Laura thought, for instance, that the Janice glamour was obvious to most druids, but she worked carefully on the Mariel one to avoid notice or comment. She took Deegan's awareness as evidence of his attention to fine detail rather than a flaw in her glamour skills. "I don't like to fuss with my hair and clothes."

"I've never been very good with them myself."

She wondered if he believed her. With her own essence-sensing deficit, she could sympathize with what he meant. Her limited range might be a flaw in her abilities, but her acute ability to sense emotions made up for it. When Deegan spoke about her glamour, she noted that his tone and manner reflected observation rather than definitive knowledge. She sensed no suspicion from him, reinforcing her belief that he accepted her visual appearance as nothing more than a tidied-up version of her actual appearance.

"Druid Deegan, I imagine you know by now about the raid in Anacostia that did not succeed as intended. I've been asked to review the situation since an InterSec agent was almost killed. Could you tell me for the record why you were not on the mission?" she asked.

"I was here enjoying the Salisbury steak and Jell-O." His voice was calm and neutral without a hint of sarcasm. His eyes, though, sparked with irritation.

She didn't react. "What flavor Jell-O?" He frowned at her, but said nothing. "I asked you a question, Druid Deegan."

His frown deepened. "Lemon."

She arched an eyebrow. "How was the steak?"

He gave her a look of grudging approval. "I have been here for two days. The staff can verify that."

"I asked how your steak was, Druid Deegan."

She watched him suck in his lower lip in thought. Deegan was not a novice. She imagined him considering whether it was worth annoying an InterSec agent he didn't work for. "It was fine, thank you," he said.

"Excellent. Now let's not waste time with sarcasm and word play or this will be a very long conversation. Understood?" she replied. Still irritated, he nodded.

Laura rested her hand on the file on her lap. With her

druidic memory recall, she didn't need to take notes. Humans found it intimidating for some reason to be questioned by someone who never lifted a pen, but druids didn't, so Deegan wouldn't mind. In order to gain rank in druidic training, he had had to develop the same skill. "I understand you were brought here unconscious."

His hand trembled as he adjusted his robe. Since he projected neither fear nor anxiety, Laura assumed that the motion was a physical tremor. "I apparently had too much to drink and got into a fight. When I woke up, I was in this room and head-blind."

Laura raised an eyebrow again. On Mariel's face, it was a significant gesture, her finely arched eyebrow lifting smoothly. "'Apparently'?"

"I don't remember the fight. Too much booze."

"You were at the Vault, I believe." She didn't just believe. She knew.

He nodded. "I was there with Gianni and Sinclair." He let his gaze linger on her legs. "I'm surprised I've never seen you there."

"I'm not very social in D.C." Laura moved her hand a fraction against the file folder. "It's not the first time you've had head-blindness."

"No."

"Have you noticed the pattern?" She had. It was obvious to anyone who bothered to look.

He didn't quite freeze, but the hand stopped moving. "What is this, some kind of intervention?"

Not the answer she expected. Laura picked up embarrassment and a touch of anger. "Would you like it to be?"

He set his jaw. "I do not have a drinking problem."

The response clarified his reaction. In the past six months, Deegan had had five instances of head-blindness, all after being in a bar. She hadn't focused on the drinking angle but the fact that he had been at the Vault. "That's not the pattern I'm talking about."

His eyebrows drew together as he frowned. "I don't understand."

"Each time you've had an episode, you missed work the

next day. The file indicates that on each of those days, you had something on your calendar related to the planning of the raid in Anacostia."

Surprise swept over his face. Laura sensed that the emotion was genuine. "Huh. It never occurred to me. What do you make of it?"

She flashed the half smile again. "I was hoping you might tell me, Druid Deegan."

He bowed his head in thought. "Someone didn't want me on the raid."

"And succeeded."

He shook his head. "It was SOP. Nothing out of the ordinary."

"But it wasn't, in the end, was it?"

He closed his eyes, as if blocking out his surroundings to help him concentrate. Laura knew he was using mnemonic techniques to match the days in his memories to their events. "The brownie security. That was the one consistent topic on each of those days, either a review of their files or interviews with informants."

The brownie security, Laura noted, one of whom turned out not to have been a brownie at all. "You didn't think it was odd that the meetings weren't rescheduled if the task of removing the brownies was yours?"

"I read the summary reports. Everything indicated they had low-ability brownies working the door," he said. "No one seemed concerned. It was like I said—SOP."

"Have you read reports of the raid?"

He shook his head. "Not hard copy. Captain Foyle filled me in."

"You picked up on my slight glamour, Druid Deegan. How refined is that skill?" She hoped the phrasing would reinforce her contention that Mariel Tate's glamour was inconsequential.

Deegan shrugged. "I don't know. Most people screw something up—no texture to fabric, perfectly symmetrical faces, things like that. I notice them."

"Do you think you would have sensed an Inverni fairy glamoured as a brownie?"

He ran a tired hand over his head. "Maybe. Wings are tough to hide. The Inverni have a lot more power than brownies. Under the right conditions, I might have figured out it wasn't a brownie, but probably not what the actual species was."

Unlike me, Laura thought. Had she been so careless? Should she have noticed something like that? She pushed the thoughts aside. "Do you remember anything unusual at the Vault the nights you came down with head-blindness?"

He closed his eyes again. "No. Simple drinking after work."

"Who were you with?"

He answered without hesitating. Now that she was jogging specific memories and he was using mnemonics, his recall had refreshed the memories. "Sinclair and Gianni all five times. Sanchez three times."

"Same bartender?" she asked.

Deegan shook his head. "No. And it was random who put the orders in."

"Were your drinks ever unattended?"

He shrugged. "I know what you're asking, but I don't remember. If I'm not focused on something particular, it doesn't go into the hypermemory. You know that."

She did know what he meant. She was using her hypermemory for the interview, recording every nuance of the conversation. "I'm just asking. What did you think of Sanchez?"

He hesitated. She registered doubt and curiosity and was pleased to have stumbled on something that raised her suspicions.

"I think he was working undercover for someone," he said.

"Why?" she asked, cool, neutral, a simple request for clarification from someone like Mariel, who had a reputation for having seen it all.

Deegan twisted his lips for a moment. "Just a hunch. He asked questions that seemed innocuous, but then he had a knack for following up on them so often that I started to notice the pattern. He never took a personal call at work and said little about his private life. Sometimes he would be late or leave early or take long lunches with lame excuses. Foyle got him on that a lot, but Gabe didn't seem to care."

Laura noted the use of the first name. Not unusual, but rare among the cops she knew. If a cop had a long or odd last name, his brothers shortened it or came up with a nickname that played off it. Women were often called by their first names, and they sometimes called men by theirs. With the guys, it happened between close friends. Buddies. "You partnered with Sanchez a lot, right?"

Deegan nodded but looked at his feet when he did. "Yeah. He was a good cop."

"Did you tell anyone your suspicions?"

He shook his head. "No, it was just gut stuff."

She finally felt some grief. Not the intensity of lovers, but there had definitely been a friendship. She remembered thinking during the raid that Sanchez had no trouble working with her sendings. She sensed no guilt from Deegan. Given the obvious friendship between them, he'd project guilt or regret if he knew someone had set Sanchez up. She didn't think Deegan was involved, not with what she was sensing from him.

"Did you ever meet Tylo Blume?"

"Twice. He offered me a job. I declined."

"Why?"

Deegan shrugged. "Why not? I didn't need the work."

"Sanchez took some work."

"Yeah. They all did. Sanchez was pushing for more."

"Did you eat or drink with Blume?" she asked.

Deegan furrowed his brow. She worried for a moment she had been too clumsy. "Not that I recall."

"So you had head-blindness only when you drank with Gianni, Sinclair, or Sanchez."

Anger colored Deegan's body signature. "Are you implying something about my fellow officers?"

She gazed steadily at him without showing any emotion. "Am I?"

"I trust them with my life," he said.

"Janice Crawford will be pleased to hear that," Laura said.

Deegan leaned forward, essence sparking around him in fragments. Laura didn't move. As Deegan loomed over her, she pushed more essence into her glamour, enhancing her eyes. The gaze of an Old One was not easily held. Deegan flinched. He hesitated in the silence, then leaned back in his seat. "They're good men," he said.

Laura cocked her head to the side. "You don't seem particularly concerned about Crawford. It makes me curious about your loyalties."

He sneered at her. "Race-baiting, Tate? That's a human game."

She leaned back and crossed her legs. "I was talking about loyalty to truth over comrades."

He snorted. "I don't know anything more than what I've told you."

Not quite a lie, but not the truth. He had suspicions about something or someone. She had angered him too much, and his body signature was distorted by emotion.

Laura stood, adjusting some pages that threatened to slip out of her folder. "When are you reporting for duty?"

"Not soon. Something important is apparently damaged. I'm still head-blind."

She walked to the door. "That's all the questions I have for now, Druid Deegan. I may contact you again as the investigation proceeds."

He narrowed his eyes. "You mean you'll stop by to confirm answers you already have."

Laura threw a slow smile over her shoulder. "Don't be too sure what I know or don't know."

She moved smoothly out of the room with a soft, rolling gait, knowing damned well that despite his anger at her, Deegan watched her ass. She wasn't insulted. She often turned it into an advantage.

11
CHAPTER

MARIEL TATE'S OFFICE at the Guildhouse was a floor below Terryn's, far enough away to avoid any persona conflicts for Laura yet close enough to help the transition between personas when necessary. Laura found Liam Wilson, the office assistant, working at his desk in the anteroom. "Hey, Mariel. I had a feeling you would be coming in."

She liked him. Not many humans worked in the Guildhouse, and Liam was the only one that worked in InterSec. The fey had their fears and suspicions like everyone else, and having humans work in the heart of their U.S. diplomatic building was not desirable. Liam had shown knowledge of the fey world that impressed both Mariel and Genda Boone, the colleague with whom Mariel had been hiring an assistant. When his background check came back clean, he got the job.

He blushed when she smiled at him. "And why is that?"

He handed her a stack of pink slips of paper. "Phone messages. They always start piling up when everyone but me knows you're about to show up."

She took the messages and grinned. "Remind me to tell

you about the restaurant in the Bahamas. You will love it. Is Genda in?"

Genda traveled as much as Mariel Tate, at least in theory, did. They both presented themselves as high-level consultants at diplomatic meetings. Laura suspected that if Genda performed undercover work for InterSec, it was minor. Industry news often reported Genda's attending the conferences she said she did. As far as Laura was concerned, the lack of corporate espionage—to say nothing of dead bodies—in Genda's wake validated her suspicion that the woman was nothing more than a diplomat.

Liam followed her into her office. "She's at a meeting, but she's in town. I have four other messages for you: a code call verifying your arrival, two from a police officer named Aaron Foyle, and one from someone claiming to be your mother, who I will not assume is the president of France, despite the accent." The code call was a fake from Terryn. Since she didn't recognize the phone number, wasn't French, and didn't know the French president, she assumed the other call was Cress joking around.

She slid into the chair behind the sleek black desk. The Mariel office was her favorite work space. In her other offices, she avoided personal trappings in order to prevent cross-contaminating personas, but Mariel's space was her repository for souvenirs of world travel. The earth-tone colors of the room made a nice counterpoint to the riot of color in paintings, sculptures, and objets d'art. Pushpins of places she'd been or pretended to have been littered a map on a side wall. Red pins stood out even in the white of expanse of the North and South Poles, though she had been to only one of them.

"And here's a sealed pouch." He placed the leather envelope next to the messages and waited for her to touch it. InterSec eyes-only documents had several layers of spells on them. A courier chain spell registered the body signature of each person permitted to carry the pouch. Another spell rang softly if the pouch was moved more than a few feet away from whoever was supposed to carry it. Getting released from the spell happened when someone else with a registered body signature touched it. The idea that the pouches spent time in bathrooms and bedrooms creeped Laura out, and she thought about it every time she touched one.

The next layer of security was a simple quartz crystal embedded in the zipper pull keyed solely to whoever was allowed to open the pouch. Touching the crystal released the lock and simultaneously disengaged another spell on the papers inside. If someone other than a designated person opened the pouch, the pages disintegrated. Laura opened the pouch and removed the dossier Terryn had prepared on Sanchez's FBI connection.

She pulled a notepad across the desk. "This is for your eyes only, Liam. Please call this Aaron Foyle back and tell him I need a conference room on-site in Anacostia." She wrote a list, ripped the page from the pad, and handed it to him. "Tell Foyle I want to see these three people. I will arrive at 8 A.M. and meet with him first. Have a car pick me up at noon with something wonderful to eat that won't spill."

Liam wrinkled his nose. "Are you sure you don't want to do this here?"

She acknowledged his sympathy with a knowing look. "Sure. But these folks have several investigators coming after them. I'd rather invade their space than make the diva demand right now. I have a meeting to go to this afternoon, but I'll call if I need something, okay?"

He looked crestfallen. "You just got here."

She put on an apologetic face. "I'm here for a bit, though. Maybe we can have lunch in a few days?"

"Great," he said. She knew he meant it. Because of their shared love of food, Laura treated him to lunch at the better restaurants in town or "accidentally" left expense-account vouchers for him when she heard about a new place.

She had a hard time deciding whether Liam had a crush on her or not. The vibe coming off him was intense interest, but it wasn't lust. In general, humans were hard for her to read unless their emotional state was high. She got along well with Liam, but she never thought of him as more than a nice guy. Humans didn't interest her often. They tended to take a much shorter view of circumstances than the fey. The fey, of course, took the long view of situations. If they lived well and took care of themselves, some lived centuries. Laura wasn't that old, but she already had a different, more circumspect, perspective on the future than humans, and she was prone to think more about long-term implications. Which was why her attraction to Sinclair surprised and intrigued her.

She flipped through her mail, separating out a few larger envelopes. Out of habit, she reached for her crystal paperweight without looking and instead grabbed nothing but air. She went through the stack of paper in the in-box and elsewhere on the desk, but the crystal wasn't there. She glanced at the credenza beneath the map. If she didn't purposefully activate her heightened memory—and she might not have for an incidental thing like moving a paperweight—she was subject to the same vagaries of memory as any human. Occasionally, she used the crystal piece as a resonator for a spell and might have left it in her hidden room. She made a mental note to check.

Ignoring her messages, she placed the Sanchez file on the center of her desk and turned on her computer. She scanned Mariel's email, amused and marveling at Cress's ingenuity. Laura knew that Cress didn't personally send the emails. Cress worked with an InterSec tech to create a life for Mariel. She read a couple of real messages from Terryn about InterSec administrative issues.

Laura opened the Sanchez dossier. The InterSec agent mole at the FBI had scant information on him—not even his real name—but had confirmed that he was involved in investigating low-level fey terrorists. Lawrence Scales, his field officer, was known as a straight-up guy, with major arrests notched on his belt. The InterSec report indicated that Sanchez had been working more important cases lately, an indication that he had been a rising star.

Laura leaned back in her chair and stared at the map across the room. She would find out what Sanchez had been doing. It was what she did. He had been undercover. Deegan had figured that out, but not everyone had the observational skills of a trained druid. Sanchez had trusted people to protect him. Deegan did, too. Their trust had failed somewhere. She found no suspicious references to Deegan in the file.

The circumstances of Sanchez's death cast a troubling shadow over her. Whom had he trusted? In whom was that trust misplaced? She grappled with that issue every day of her life. Terryn and Cress never gave her any reason to doubt that they would protect her. She assumed Cress and Terryn thought the same thing about her. But she had lied to them on and off over the years. Sometimes it was to protect their position. Sometimes it was to have something to call her own. But what would that do to their trust in her if they found out? How would they handle it? What would happen to her then? The idea that she might be on her own path to the morgue was disquieting. In his lifetime, Terryn had had his share of betrayals. His family had a long history in the Seelie Court. She knew he hadn't gone from being a potential heir to the throne of Faerie to the head of an InterSec section without making enemies or losing allies.

She gazed out the window at the Mall and wondered if the day might come that he questioned her trust. Would any explanation justify some of the secrets she'd kept from him? Sometimes she worried that she played the persona game too much and forgot where the lines were drawn.

12
CHAPTER

LAURA ARRIVED AT the Anacostia station house at a few minutes before eight o'clock. Liam had arranged the interviews for Mariel Tate as requested, and Foyle had requisitioned space for her. The conference room at the station house didn't have the clichéd peeling paint and forty-year-old furniture. It did have the clichéd faux-wood table, pale blue generic office chairs, and dirt-hiding carpet that was twenty years old. Laura suspected the carpet had looked like dirt when it was installed.

She sat alone, checking her PDA and trying to keep Saffin calm. Between Hornbeck, the Guildmaster, and Resha Dunne, the brownie had her hands full running interference for Laura. Once Laura talked to Hornbeck, she hoped things would calm down, and they could get on with the ceremony.

She made clothing for Mariel part of the glamour for the day. Since she was beginning the day as Mariel and switching to Laura in the afternoon, it made life easier to wear a Laura outfit and glamour it with Mariel's preferences for the morning. For the SWAT-team meeting, she appeared to wear one of Mariel's basic business suits in deep charcoal, with a subtle flare at the jacket shoulders and a long, snug skirt. The image projected assurance and reflected the SWAT-team uniform. She wanted the squad to feel that she was in control yet on the same team.

Foyle arrived wearing his dress uniform. She smiled that she wasn't the only one projecting images. "Please have a seat, Captain Foyle. It's a pleasure to finally meet you."

Foyle sat opposite Laura, still and formal. "The pleasure is mine, ma'am."

Laura folded her hands on the table and leaned toward him. "I don't want to take too much of your time. This is preliminary for InterSec. We know you have other agencies you need to speak with. As co-investigators, we will have access to your other interviews and follow up as necessary."

He gave a curt nod. "We appreciate that, ma'am."

"Anything to keep the paperwork down," Laura said. Foyle didn't crack a smile. She opened a folder on the table and sorted through the various reports that had been filed. She wasn't sure if Foyle was one of those who became un-settled during administrative hearings when druids didn't refer to notes. She didn't want him to feel the hearing was pointless or that a decision had already been made. Some-times that was true, Laura admitted, but not always and not this time.

She pushed the paperwork away and leaned back. "What are you worried about, Captain?"

Foyle's forehead creased. "Ma'am?"

Anger simmered below the surface of Foyle's calm face. Laura didn't want him angry. She wanted him comfortable. She gestured at the file. "I can read all this to you, but you know what it says. Off the record, I'm not all that upset by a bunch of dead drug dealers. I want whoever shot Janice Crawford. You want whoever killed your man. Tell me what you think went wrong."

Foyle shifted back in his chair. "Bad intelligence and in-adequate staff."

"That's what I'm seeing, too. Who is responsible for the intelligence?" she asked.

"I am responsible for the integrity of our information," he said.

She nodded. "I know. You should be. But I recognize the fact that we can all be fooled. Where was trust misplaced here?"

Foyle's anger dissipated into slight confusion and, oddly, a sense of hope. "Our primary contact was through an informant who is missing."

She tilted her head, her expression curious. "Do you think you were targeted for disinformation?"

His confusion relaxed into relief, which could mean a number of things. If he wasn't involved in the shooting, he wanted his team exonerated. If he was, well, he might be relieved she was on the wrong track and not going to implicate him. "It's possible. My team is still responsible for its performance."

Whenever he spoke, she nodded. She wanted to encourage the notion that they were in agreement. "I understand your feelings on that. Who found the intelligence sources?"

"Lieutenants Gianni and Sinclair. It's in the files," he said.

"Do you have any issues with their performance?"

"None."

"Have they been involved in poor data sourcing before?"

"No."

She moved some papers. "You were missing your regular team druid . . . Corman Deegan. Was that a factor?"

The curt nod again. "I believe it was. His substitute was not as skilled, from what I understand."

"Janice Crawford. I believe you requested her?"

"I did, ma'am. She'd performed adequately on two or three previous missions. She seemed up to the task."

Laura nodded. "I see. Do you think the outcome would have been different if Deegan had been with you?"

Foyle hesitated. "Maybe. We still don't know what happened when Sanchez was shot. Crawford is claiming amnesia."

"Yes. The concussion. She was shot, too." A flicker of doubt washed out from Foyle. Laura almost broke her cool demeanor. Foyle had doubts about what had happened to Janice. What had happened to *her*. "You said 'claiming amnesia,' Captain. Do you have concerns about her diagnosis?"

His emotions shut down except for suspicion. "Crawford has been less than forthcoming."

Laura picked up a random page from the file and pretended to read. "From what I understand, temporary memory loss is typical of a concussion of this type."

Foyle shifted in his seat. "She was found at the scene covered with Sanchez's blood. She was with him when he died. No one else was reported in the area. To the best of our knowledge, the fey attacker did not use a gun. I asked her whether Sanchez said anything, and she told me she didn't remember. I think it's important to know his last words."

Mariel nodded. "I do, too, Captain. Agent Crawford was wounded. Your man was killed. If something Sanchez might have said could lead to the perpetrator, InterSec wants that to happen, too."

Foyle nodded, his body signature shifted into mild doubt. Mariel didn't blame him. Despite the multiple-agency cooperation, humans worried about the motivations of the fey. "I appreciate that."

Laura pursed her lips and nodded. "Let's get started then. Please send in Lieutenant Gianni."

She followed Foyle to the door and held it closed when he left the room. Pulling out her cell phone, she hit the speed dial for Foyle's office. His voicemail picked up. Janice's voice was a variation on Laura's own, so she didn't need to swap glamours to use it. "Foyle, it's Crawford. My SUV blew a tire on the bridge. I'll be there ASAP. Sorry."

She disconnected and returned to her seat. She took several pages out of the file and laid them across the table without any organization. During the brief times she had been with Gianni as Janice, she knew he didn't think much of women. Coming on strong would probably not work, so she decided her best course was to play into his condescension. Mariel Tate would act disorganized and indecisive. A knock on the door sounded. "Come," she said.

Gianni stood at attention next to the chair Foyle had vacated. Laura gestured to it with an overly earnest smile. "My name is Mariel Tate, Lieutenant. I have a few questions for you regarding your recent mission."

Gianni relaxed into the chair. She felt calm self-assurance from him, colored with impatience and cockiness. "Shoot."

He tried to maintain eye contact with her, but failed. She picked up a page from his mission report. "Lieutenant, I'd like a few more details on your report. You state that you met Captain Foyle and Lieutenant Sinclair at the door to the warehouse workroom. Correct?"

"Yes, ma'am."

"Who arrived first?" she asked.

"I believe they did," he said. His voice had an odd sense, as if he were telling the truth yet lying.

"Together?"

He shrugged. "I don't know. They were there."

She sorted through the papers, pretending she couldn't find something. Foyle reported he had met Sinclair and Gianni at the door, so Foyle had to have arrived last, not Gianni. She lifted a sheet and smiled with relief. "Um . . . so you were alone from the time you left the computer lab until you met them?"

He nodded. Laura didn't like the nod. Gianni projected resistance. While her empathy picked up emotions, hearing someone speak clarified the emotion.

"Okay," she said. She sorted through papers again. "Who called the medics in?"

"Sinclair." Fast. Assured. Truth. Sinclair's report stated the same.

"Oh, right. There it is," she said. She paused and read the report. The longer she read, the more amusement flowed off Gianni. "Okay, um, did you see anyone else near the door before or after you entered the room?"

Gianni shifted in his seat. "Just the medics."

Laura nodded, staring at the report. "And . . . um . . . okay." She switched to another report. "Lieutenant, how did you find the informant who provided information about the warehouse operation?"

He shrugged. "Street contacts. Sanchez put us onto someone."

Lie, Laura thought. "Did you know Sanchez well?"

He shrugged again. "Well enough. We weren't tight."

"How would you rate his skills?"

"We're SWAT," he said. The phrase rang with pride, but the answer was an easy evasion.

With good reason, Laura thought. She leaned back and twisted a ring on her finger, looking uncomfortable. "Lieutenant, I need to ask an awkward question. Did you think Sanchez might have . . . let's call it . . . had a lapse in judgment that led to his death and the wounding of Agent Crawford?"

Gianni stared at her, his eyes going cold. She sensed calculation in the look, a threat of false anger over insulting a colleague. "Sanchez knew what he was doing when he took the job. It only takes one little mistake for everything to go wrong, and he made his."

Laura forced a blush to her cheeks. "Yes, I see. I meant no offense."

"None taken, ma'am," he said. Another lie, she thought.

She gathered up the reports and tapped them on the table. "Okay, then. My focus right now is on the events in the room where Sanchez died. I may need to speak to you again."

Gianni stood. "Not a problem."

"Thank you, Lieutenant. Could you send Agent Crawford in?" she asked.

Gianni hesitated. "Sure thing."

When he was out of the room, Laura hurried to the door. She heard Gianni call out for Crawford, and a muffled reply from someone. She pulled out her cell and saw three calls to Janice from Foyle. She had a good idea what he had to say to her, so she didn't bother listening to the messages. She hit his speed dial. The connection went immediately to voicemail. Foyle was on the phone. Laura's phone beeped at the same time, and his name come up on the call waiting.

Laura created a small bubble of essence and nudged it into the phone. The speaker crackled with static. "Foyle, it's me. Someone freakin' messed with my tires. I'm waiting for a tow. Be there as soon as the truck shows up."

She disconnected and resumed her seat. A moment later, Sinclair walked in. He had a tentative smile on his face that curiously faltered for a moment when he saw Laura. He extended his hand. "I'm Lieutenant Jonathon Sinclair."

Laura returned the shake but did not get up. "Mariel Tate. I was expecting Agent Crawford."

Sinclair took a seat without waiting to be asked. He seemed confused about something, preoccupied. "Lieutenant?"

Sinclair looked up. "I'm sorry, I was trying to recall something. Captain Foyle said Crawford is delayed and suggested I come in first."

Laura pretended to consider the situation with a hint of annoyance. "Very well, Lieutenant." She moved the folders on the table, then leaned back. "Tell me, Lieutenant, how you would have run the drug-raid mission differently."

He looked surprised by the question but immediately focused on the idea. "We needed more people on the main entry and better intel. In retrospect, we relied too much on the druidess."

"That would be Agent Crawford."

"Yes. She was supposed to take out two brownie sentries," he said.

"She did, though, didn't she? One brownie was secured immediately, and the other turned out to not be what he seemed."

"Yes," Sinclair said. She felt a sense of doubt and hesitation.

"What do you think happened in that room, Lieutenant?"

He didn't shrug like Gianni. He took his time to consider the question seriously, willing to offer his opinion. "I can't say. I've read the reports. The preliminary report indicates that both Crawford and Sanchez were fired upon from the entrance to the room."

"The timing and damage in the room suggest that Agent

Crawford was engaged in the back of the room," Laura said.

Sinclair nodded, but doubt lingered around him. Laura felt it whenever he said or heard the name Crawford. He had suspicions about her, vague, something undefined. She tried to think of anything she had done as Janice Crawford that might have prompted the emotion. Of course, being in the room when a teammate died might have had a lot to do with it. Laura glanced away in thought. "Lieutenant, present me with a plausible situation in which Agent Crawford shot Sanchez."

He didn't startle. "He could have fired on her, and she defended herself."

She thought it interesting that the first scenario that came to his mind characterized Sanchez as the aggressor. She took that as a possibility that his doubts about Crawford lay elsewhere. "I don't believe we've found the bullet that hit Crawford yet. Where it fell would be an interesting test of that theory. What if Crawford fired at Sanchez first?"

He shook his head. "She didn't have a weapon that we know of. I didn't see one when I found her. Crawford didn't look like she was in any shape to hide a gun at that point."

Now that was interesting, Laura thought. He was intrigued enough to read the reports to determine if Janice had fired a gun and think about possible scenarios if she had. Of course, analysis was part of any mission debrief, especially for one that had gone wrong, but his quick response indicated he checked that piece of data specifically. "Lieutenant, how would you characterize your relationship with Lieutenant Sanchez?"

"Good."

Laura raised an eyebrow. She was feeling a sense of embarrassment. "That's it? Did you socialize?"

He nodded. "We went for drinks together regularly. He was a stand-up guy, a little close to the vest. He loved baseball. Couldn't stop talking about it."

"I never understood the attraction myself," she said.

He laughed. Good, she thought. She had finally gotten a

spontaneous reaction from him. She even liked his laugh. "Me either, actually. I'm a basketball fan myself."

"I like NASCAR," she said.

His eyebrows shot up. "Wow."

She surprised herself by the admission since it was a persona crossing. Laura liked stock-car racing, not Mariel. It was a minor point, but she had never done that before. She opened the folder again. "Let's talk about the informant. Gianni found him, is that correct?"

"Officially, yes."

She looked at him curiously. "And unofficially?"

Shutting down again, he chose his words carefully. "Sanchez and I went for drinks one night. We drove by this house. Sanchez slowed a bit and checked it out. Not long after that, Gianni came in with the informant."

"I'm not seeing the connection," she said.

"A week or so later, Gianni brought me to the same house to do an initial interview with an informant for the raid."

"Did Sanchez say anything about Gianni's scooping his informant?"

Sinclair shook his head. "No. It was just a drive-by. I asked him what he was looking at, and he changed the subject."

So Sanchez had apparently been one step ahead of Gianni. Sanchez had covered Crawford's back when she needed him, and he hadn't even known her. He must have been a good agent.

"What do you make of it?" she asked.

Sinclair hesitated. "I don't know."

A lie, she thought. "Come on, Sinclair. You're a smart guy. You must have an opinion."

He sighed. "It could be anything. Sanchez might have had the informant in his sights, and Gianni beat him to it."

"You don't believe that. Sanchez and Gianni would have said something to each other. You would have heard about it."

He rubbed his hands on his thighs, nervousness going up a tick in his emotional state. "Okay, I think Sanchez knew something about the raid."

"He was dirty." She threw it at him as if it were fact.

No cop liked to implicate another in breaking the law, but Sinclair didn't startle like she expected him to. "I didn't say that."

"But you're thinking it. You think Sanchez was involved with whatever was going on at the apartment complex, and they took him out."

Sinclair's anger increased, but he did a good job of hiding it to outward appearances. "I'm not going to speculate about a dead cop."

Laura decided to back off. She had her answer anyway. Sinclair thought Sanchez had been on the wrong side. "Okay. Let's move on. What do you think of Agent Crawford?"

His expression became more neutral, and the anger subsided. "I think she's in a tough spot and doesn't deserve it."

That was nice to hear. He meant it, too. "Do you blame her for Sanchez's death?"

He shook his head. "No."

"You seem sure."

"She was doing the captain a favor. She almost got killed, and now she's got vultures circling."

"What do you mean?"

He met her eyes for several impressive seconds. "The bridge."

Laura, or rather Janice, hadn't reported the bridge incident. "What bridge?"

He smirked, but in a congenial way. "The incident on the Anacostia Bridge. Something like that happens, you hear things."

Laura wondered what else he had heard. She returned his smirk. "We all do, Lieutenant Sinclair. Tell me about the Vault."

His lack of surprise was the perfect reaction. "Obviously, you know I've done some side work there."

"Describe it for me?"

"There's not much to tell. It's routine security work. A lot of politicians go there for meetings."

"With whom?"

"Each other. Business types. There are a couple of private rooms in the club and in the offices upstairs. I've run security for meetings."

"Have you ever met Tylo Blume?"

He nodded. "Twice. The night he offered me the first job and one other time, when I worked with Sanchez."

"When was that?"

Sinclair pursed his lips. "About two weeks ago. A private meeting in one of the function rooms."

This was new. "Did you know anyone at the meeting?"

She sensed Sinclair debating what to tell her or what not to tell her. "Blume. Some guys from the State Department. Senator Hornbeck. A congressman—I think his name is Lewis—and a few elves looked familiar. They didn't speak English."

"What was the meeting about?"

"I wasn't in the room."

"Where were you the night before last, Lieutenant?"

He didn't miss the change in subject. "The Vault. With Gianni and Crawford, before you ask."

She nodded. "Did you leave together?"

He shook his head. "Crawford left early. I followed her outside to make sure she was okay to drive. She was fine, so I went back inside. Gianni was gone, so I left."

"Do you think Corman Deegan drinks too much?"

His startled expression at another change in direction amused her. "What?"

She watched him carefully, curious how he would react. "Your teammate. Do you think he drinks too much?"

Sinclair sighed as he thought about it. "I've seen him drink. I don't know if it's a problem. I've never seen it be a problem on the job."

"You went drinking the night before the raid," she said.

"We didn't go 'drinking.' We went for a couple of drinks, then home," he said.

"Deegan seems to have had more than a couple."

Sinclair paused. "He may have. I left after two drinks. He and Gianni stayed talking."

"Do you think the raid would have fallen apart if Deegan had been there?"

He made a noncommittal gesture with his hand. "Too many variables to say. The intel was bad. Deegan's good, but so was Sanchez. When the intel is bad, anything can happen."

She sensed truth from him. He didn't think Janice had screwed up. He knew the problem was the source of the information. "One last question, Lieutenant. When you heard Janice Crawford's mayday, who reached the room first?"

"I don't know. Foyle and Gianni were already there."

That made three officers claiming they were the last to arrive. "Okay. Thank you, Lieutenant. Can you send in Agent Crawford if she is no longer delayed, please?"

Sinclair held his hand out. "It was a pleasure talking with you, Agent Tate."

Laura smiled at the unexpected gesture. "Thank you, Lieutenant."

She checked her PDA while waiting for Foyle to tell her that Janice Crawford was unavailable. Saffin had everything under control back at the office. Rhys's office liked her changes to the speech and sent along the Guildmaster's compliments. Resha Dunne had decided to attend Laura's Senate hearing in the afternoon. Laura groaned at the thought. She knew he would try to hijack the proceedings to bolster his importance. Liam sent a message to Mariel Tate that her car would be waiting when she left the station house.

Foyle leaned into the room. "Agent Tate, I have to apologize, but Agent Crawford has not shown up and is unreachable."

Feigning annoyance, Laura gathered her files. "I will deal with her through InterSec then. When she arrives, tell her to call my office for an appointment."

Foyle accompanied her to the elevator. "Did everything go well?"

She watched the floor numbers counting down toward

her. "They were acceptable initial meetings. I'll review the other investigative reports and get back to you if need be."

The elevator opened, and Laura stepped forward. Foyle touched her arm. She looked down at his hand, mildly surprised. "Agent Tate, I would appreciate it if you got back to me either way. I need answers."

His tone was sincere and matched what Laura was sensing. "I will, Captain. We all want answers."

A black car waited outside as planned. She didn't know the driver, so she chanted a sound barrier around her. Guildhouse drivers were used to the behavior and didn't consider it rude.

"Gianni shot me," said Laura when Terryn answered her call.

"Your memory has returned?" Terryn didn't sound surprised. He absorbed everything with a calm professionalism that sometimes irritated Laura. She wished he would scream in frustration just once in her presence. He and his clan had seen kingdoms rise and fall. A cop shooting another cop apparently didn't faze him.

She noticed a brown shopping bag in the corner of the seat and pulled it toward her. Lunch from Liam. "No. I noticed that the mission reports were vague about when Foyle, Gianni, and Sinclair arrived at the room Sanchez and I were in. All three claim they arrived after the other two. Gianni was the only one who clearly registered as lying."

"If he shot Sanchez, why didn't he shoot you at the same time?"

Laura considered the scenario. "I don't think he had a clear line of sight on me until I joined Sanchez. There was a firefight going on. Sanchez was shooting at the door right up to the end. Gianni would have had to take cover from both Sanchez and the drug dealers."

"Should we pull him in?"

She withdrew a bottle of springwater from the bag. "Not yet. If we pull him in because I sensed he was lying, he'll think I'm bluffing. I don't want to tip my empathic ability."

"He shot you, Laura. Are you comfortable with him getting away with that?"

Even if Terryn couldn't see her, he had to notice the sly challenge in her voice. "Oh, he's not going to get away with anything. I want to know why he shot me. I'm going to tail him personally."

"Another job is the last thing you need. Let's get a junior operative to tail him," he said.

She took a swig of the water. "It's all the same job, Terryn. Just the faces change."

"Keep me updated," he said.

"Will do." She disconnected and removed a boxed lunch from the bag. Starving, she flipped it open. Two small rolled sandwiches of prosciutto with basil and thinly sliced provolone. A small cluster of french fries smelled of truffle oil. She was going to kill Liam for all the salt and starch. But she had asked for "wonderful."

13

THE BLACK CAR dropped Laura off a block from the Russell Senate Office Building. The building contained administrative offices and hearing rooms for the Senate as well as senator's offices and committee rooms. The Senate was known as the world's most exclusive men's club, and a stroll through the corridors confirmed it. Laura had been around long enough to remember when senators were all male and women were their secretaries. High-profile secretaries but still secretaries. More women worked in the building than ever before, but men still held the power. Interns in the building joked that they always knew a women was a senator because she didn't carry files.

Laura had been a sensation in those days. A woman with the power of the Guildhouse behind her demanded—and received—respect. When she was recruited by the forerunner of InterSec, she'd let go of a rising career as a diplomat and was happy to move into public relations for the Guild. She received the exposure to the politics she enjoyed, without the frustrations of all the political backstabbing. She still dealt with those, but it was not her primary job responsibility.

She ducked into an empty restroom. As she washed and

dried her hands, she reabsorbed the essence out of the Mariel glamour. Mariel's face shifted and faded as Laura Blackstone reappeared. She adjusted her outfit, fixed her hair, and made her way to the elevator.

Despite the surprise, Laura didn't react when the elevator opened and she saw Sinclair standing inside. In the full car, Sinclair rose head and shoulders above the others. The crowd of people edged back to make room for her. Of course, she ended up standing next to him. They bumped and smiled courteously. His essence spiked surprise, too, though he had never met her as Laura Blackstone. He projected an undercurrent of pleasure. She stared down at her shoes trying not to think about it. His emotion shifted, an edge of concern coloring his interest. She wondered what he was thinking but avoided making eye contact.

The doors opened, and they bumped again as they moved to exit.

"Excuse me." He stepped back to let her go first.

She smiled. "Thank you."

"My pleasure," he said. It was. Even without the subtle emphasis he placed on the words, his attraction was evident. He paced a few feet behind her as she walked down the corridor. She resisted the urge to look back but became keenly aware of how she held herself.

When his essence receded behind her, she did look. As he entered a hearing room, her pleasure at his attention faded when the door closed. It was the room where Senator Hornbeck's Fey Relations Committee was meeting. Confused but intrigued, she continued farther until she reached the hearing room for her fact-finding session on fey homeless shelters. Guildmaster Rhys considered the program one of his pet projects to enhance relations with the human population.

She stopped short. The hearing room was empty. A small sign on the open door announced the meeting had been canceled.

A young, earnest intern smiled at her. "Are you here for the meeting, ma'am?"

She glanced in the empty room again. "I was."

"It's being rescheduled for Tuesday. Are you Director Blackstone?"

Laura raised an eyebrow. "Yes."

The intern handed her a note. "You were the only person we couldn't reach. I was asked to give this to you."

In a narrow spidery handwriting it read:

It's a shame you won't be able to speak publicly today. It's unfortunate that you didn't get the message. I would be flattered if you attended my committee meeting since you have an opening in your schedule.

It was signed S. Hornbeck.

Laura's PDA vibrated. Despite the desire to, she didn't crumple the paper. I got the message, you old fox, she thought. She pulled out her cell as she checked the PDA. An urgent message from Saffin flashed:

UR MTG CNCLD, CLL ME!!!

"Did you get my message?" Saffin asked when she answered the cell.

"Just now. What happened?" she asked.

"I'm so sorry. I just got it myself. Everyone canceled."

"Everyone?"

"Yes. At the last minute, too. All of them. Maybe they went to a party and didn't invite you," Saffin said.

Laura glanced up the hall at the closed door to Hornbeck's conference. "That's okay. I've been invited to my own party."

Saffin groaned. "It was Hornbeck, wasn't it?"

"Yeah. I was angry a second ago, but now I'm amused. I had to talk to him anyway. Don't worry about it, Saf. It's rescheduled for next Tuesday."

"That's the day I was going to take off. Do you want me to come in if you're going to be there?"

"No. If we're both out, then people will have to figure things out for themselves."

Saffin chuckled. "This is why I like working for you."

"I'll let you know how it goes." She disconnected.

She retraced her path down the corridor to Hornbeck's hearing room. She entered with a pleasant expression fixed on her face. If she had learned one thing after decades of dealings with politicians, it was that the moment she lost her cool, she lost an argument. Besides, she had to admit that Hornbeck's maneuver was nicely played. He'd disrupted her schedule, demonstrated some political muscle to do it, and gotten extra kicks with an innocently worded sarcastic note.

Laura found a seat near the rear of the crowded room. Hornbeck sat front and center. Six other senators sat on his committee, though only four of them were present. Hornbeck's eyes flicked toward Laura when she crossed her legs in the aisle. Saffin was right about the red scarf and, given the shift in the direction of Hornbeck's eyes, the legs. Hornbeck presided over the room, a reassuring senatorial image with his tousled white hair and masculine face. His family came from old Midwestern stock, the moneyed kind, and it showed in his dress and bearing. He was a man accustomed to control and getting his way. He was also on the right side of enough controversial issues to irritate both political parties and win reelection four times.

Her next surprise of the day was Aaron Foyle sitting to the left side of the room in civilian clothing. As a police liaison to the committee, his presence didn't surprise Laura all that much, only that he had had time to change out of his uniform and beat her through traffic. Sinclair, on the other hand, stood near the rear on the same side. When she made eye contact with him, he smiled politely, then looked away as if he hadn't been staring.

Resha Dunne sat in the second row of observers, which both surprised and didn't surprise her. She knew his schedule and would have noticed if he'd planned on attending anything related to Hornbeck. She had expected him at her own hearing and suspected he had wandered down here when that meeting was canceled. The Guildmaster had conveyed to her in private his desire to keep tabs on Dunne and make sure he didn't say the wrong thing in the wrong place.

I'm here, Resha, four rows back. Don't turn around. What have I missed? She sighed when he turned around. Anyone watching knew they were communicating privately, which was poor etiquette at best.

Senator Hornbeck is upset about several recent incidents. Do we have information on a police action in Anacostia? Dunne sent back.

On your desk for two days, Laura thought. *I'll brief you later. I thought this hearing was about financial funding.*

That was earlier. He's using his closing remarks to make points, Resha sent.

Hornbeck droned on. Neither American political party had a corner on anti-fey sentiments. It was almost a necessary political requirement for election in most parts of the country. People feared the fey. They were foreign, answered to a queen, had misunderstood abilities. And some looked downright frightening. Tragedies and aberrant behavior made headlines, fueling the perception of menace. Hornbeck played on those fears and anxieties as much as possible while giving what Laura considered lip service to unity. Laura wondered how much of his antipathy was personal and how much was political. He certainly dropped issues when he managed to garner support for his own agendas.

Hornbeck gaveled the meeting closed. Laura remained in her seat while the other spectators hustled for the door. The journalists and photographers exited first and quickly, trying to give their media outlets an edge in timely reporting. Various political functionaries shifted and gathered, buttonholing targets as they moved toward the doors. Most of the committee members bolted, intent on getting on with other business, but Hornbeck stayed, listening and nodding as someone whispered in his ear.

Resha moved to the front of the room, waiting to speak to Hornbeck. A few straggling photographers snapped shots

of the Guild director leaning against the paneled front of
the speaker's desk. Laura envisioned the shots—the pale,
sharp-featured merrow leaning in toward the respectable
senior senator. Hornbeck would love it.

Hornbeck spoke to Resha, whose wide face looked ominous as it bobbed toward the senator. Laura made a small
prayer that the merrow would learn to be image-conscious
about more than his skin color, or at least wait until photographers were not around before he looked like he was
about to bite off the head of a human politician. Resha
waved her over. She approached the committee dais with
her patented professional smile.

"Laura, it's good to see you," Hornbeck said.

She shook his hand. "The pleasure is mine, Senator."

"The senator was just telling me there seems to be some
mix-up with the Archives ceremony," said Resha.

Laura feigned surprise. "Oh? Is there something I can
do?" *Be careful, Resha. Rhys doesn't want him interfering,*
she sent.

Hornbeck flashed a thin, cold smile. "My request for
Tylo Blume to be on the program seems to have been misplaced."

Laura nodded. "Oh, I see. Security concerns forced us to
curtail the ceremony, Senator. It was decided to limit the
number of speakers."

Hornbeck pursed his lips sagely in the way authority
figures do when they want to appear to be listening, but will
have none of what they're hearing. "Blume's firm has done
an enormous job."

"Yes, the Guild has been very impressed with Triad."

"I think they've earned a place at the podium. The work
they've done coordinating the concerns of everyone is a fine
example of the unity we're trying to promote between the
human and the fey," he said.

Laura smiled to appear agreeable but had no intention of
changing her mind. "I couldn't agree more that projecting
the right image is important. I think the feeling, Senator,
was that it wasn't a political event and that the historical
nature of the relationships would be emphasized."

Hornbeck leaned back in his chair in a staged relaxed pose. "I am a keen student of the history of human-fey relations, Laura," Hornbeck said.

She nodded again. "I know, Senator. The Guild and the Archives have been flattered by the amount of attention the ceremony is receiving from interested parties."

"Is the program so very tight?" Resha said.

Laura forced herself to look regretful instead of murderous. "I'm afraid so, Resha. We tried to accommodate everyone, but you know how these things go."

"Yes, I do," said Hornbeck. "You might reconsider, though. As an elf with connections to the Teutonic court, Blume will only add to the breadth of voices speaking. I am well aware of the delicate tensions between the Celtic and Teutonic fey."

She marveled at the insinuation that his request would ease tension among the fey. Twenty years in the Senate earned arrogance points, she thought. "Yes, always a concern for the Guild. We prefer to handle such things as an internal matter."

Be careful how you speak to him! an alarmed Resha sent.

I know what I'm doing, Resha, she sent. Unlike you, she didn't add.

"We need to reach out to everyone we can to encourage cooperation, Laura. Even more so now, in these times of increased fey-related terrorist activity," he said.

Laura compressed her lips. "Senator, you know every culture has its malcontents. This ceremony is about celebrating an alliance of cultures and its success. The Archives and the Guild want the focus to be on the documents and what they've achieved. Perhaps the Guild would be willing to develop a symposium to address the important issues you continue to raise?" *Back me up here, Resha,* she sent.

Resha startled as if he had dozed off. "I think that's a wonderful idea. We could even bring representatives from the other Guildhouses to broaden the perspective."

She didn't love the idea, but getting the other Guildmasters to participate would drive Resha to distraction, which

Laura wouldn't mind. She infused her face with animated excitement. "I like that. It would be a great opportunity to move beyond the problems and look to the future."

"I agree," said Hornbeck, "And the ceremony will be a perfect moment to announce the idea." He gathered his papers. "Send my office a revised schedule, Laura. I will defer to Orrin Rhys's decision as to when on the program Blume will speak."

Laura clenched her jaw. "I'll have to coordinate this with the committee, Senator. At such short notice . . ."

He cut her off. "At such short notice, I'm sure Blume will have a speech written and prepared. I suggest the planning committee move quickly, too. It was a pleasure speaking with you as always, Laura."

Without waiting for a response, he lifted his briefcase and walked away. Laura retained her composure. "This is a problem, Resha."

"I don't understand your resistance," he said.

"It's not just me, Resha. Rhys doesn't want him there. Hornbeck would like nothing better than to hijack the ceremony for his own agenda. Don't think it's a coincidence that a U.S. senator is supporting a highly connected elven businessman. The U.S. wants to keep the Consortium as happy as the Guild."

"Isn't that what we've been doing, playing them against each other?" he asked.

She glared at him. "Of course, Resha. And a Guild director shouldn't be trying to level the playing field for the other side."

Her tone wounded him more than she intended. Resha remained popular among the solitary fey because of his desire to treat everyone fairly, which was why they voted for him as their director on the Guild board so often. That attribute, though, often made him a lousy politician in Washington. Laura took a deep breath and placed her hand on his arm. "I'm sorry, Resha. I know that sounded cynical, but I'm trying to honor Rhys's wishes. I'll talk to him."

Resha nodded. "Yes, well, I didn't think offering to let Blume speak would be such a problem. I suppose the

Guildmaster will have a real reason to be angry with me now."

Curious, Laura tilted her head. "Rhys is angry with you?"

He sighed. "I'm surprised you haven't heard. I admired the humidor in his office not long ago. Apparently, it went missing, and Orrin thinks I took it."

The idea was so absurd, Laura chuckled. "Did you?"

Equally amused, Resha shook his head. "No. He's embarrassed me terribly. I hope my little faux pas here won't make things uncomfortable for him."

Laura's jaw dropped. The emotional resonance in his voice was clear. "Resha! You did this on purpose."

He grinned, for once the natural predatory appearance of a merrow conveying his intent. "Oh, let's not speak of this anymore. I think Hornbeck has wasted enough of our time. I have a car waiting. Do you need a lift?"

Laura gave his arm a quick squeeze. "I'm all set, thanks. Nicely played, Resha. You've given me a headache, but nicely played."

She shook her head as he sauntered down the aisle. She caught sight of Hornbeck talking to Tylo Blume at the side of the room. As Laura Blackstone, she had not met Blume in person and had no desire to. She casually mingled with the crowd leaving the room to avoid being seen.

Simultaneously, she watched in her peripheral vision as Sinclair angled along the side of the room toward the door. They made eye contact, and a small smile slipped onto his face before he nonchalantly looked away. She smiled when he wasn't looking. The man was flirting with her and, if she wasn't mistaken, he was timing his exit to coincide with hers. It had been a long time since someone whom she didn't find annoying acted like that around her. She slowed her pace to see if he intended to say anything.

She wanted to kick herself when she sensed the elven essence coming up behind her. By letting Sinclair distract her, she had fumbled her escape from the room.

"Ms. Blackstone?" Tylo Blume said to her back.

She turned nonchalantly. "Mr. Blume, it's nice to finally

meet you. I didn't want to interrupt your conversation with the senator."

Blume's eyes glittered like sapphire crystals. "I wanted to introduce myself and tell you how honored I am that the Guild chose Triad for the Archives project."

She shook his hand without enthusiasm. "I can't tell you how pleased everyone is, Mr. Blume."

He nodded modestly. "I understand from the senator that I've been asked to say a few words at the ceremony. I am flattered by the opportunity."

Laura didn't know whom she wanted to strangle more, Hornbeck or Resha Dunne. She keep her tone civil. "Yes, well, the logistics will need to be worked out."

"If there's anything my people can do to help, let me know. And do call me Tylo," he said.

Laura smiled with a pleasure she didn't feel. "It's Laura, then. Regardless, I look forward to seeing you at the ceremony."

"I wouldn't miss it for the world," Blume said, and continued out the door.

Laura watched him leave, trying to figure his intentions. His power didn't intimidate her in the least. She had worked with Terryn and other fey with formidable abilities so long and often that physical power didn't impress her. Blume wanted to speak in public and needed to ingratiate himself with Laura—and the Guild—for the opportunity. Words had a power of their own, and the only thing more powerful than words was deciding who got to speak. The realization struck her that through circumstances, that made her more powerful than Tylo Blume at the moment.

Sinclair left the room with Foyle. Laura paused on the threshold and spotted them in the hallway with Hornbeck. Sinclair nodded as Foyle spoke, but his attention was focused on the door to the hearing room. As they made eye contact again, Sinclair gave the slightest shrug, as if to say he couldn't help the missed chance to speak with her. Laura made sure he saw her smile as she walked toward the elevator. A little innocent flirting couldn't hurt.

She called her brownie driver to pick her up. As much as

the often servile nature of brownies disturbed her sometimes, it had its advantages. The driver would make every
effort to do as she asked without requiring details or explanations.

She waited across the street from the building, trying to
come up with a plan to disappoint Blume. Foyle and Sinclair exited the building. Sinclair gave no indication this
time that he saw her as they walked in the opposite direction. Fine, she thought. While the flirting was fun, she
didn't want any more distractions.

A few minutes later, Tylo Blume left the building and
stood at the curb. As he waited for his own transportation, a
male Inverni fairy walked up to him. They exchanged
words that became increasingly heated. Blume looked angry. They were too far away for her to read their lips. Nonchalantly, Laura snapped a picture with her cell phone.
Incredibly, right in front of the Senate building, Blume
called up a spark of deep green essence. He thrust his hand
out toward the Inverni, who raised his own hands and backed
away. Security guards from the building ran toward them
with guns drawn, but the Inverni shot into the air and flew
out of sight.

The security guards swarmed Blume, and he extin-
guished the essence. As he talked to the guards, he gestured
up the street in one direction, then into the air where the
Inverni had fled. Moments later, a black car arrived. Blume
slipped into the backseat, and the car drove off.

As his car drove away, she zoomed in on the picture on
her cell. A chill went through her. She recognized the Inverni as the one who had escaped during the drug raid. She
rushed into the street, searching the sky. A car horn wailed,
and she jumped back, swearing under her breath. Her car
arrived. Frustrated, she settled in the back and sent the picture to Terryn. Given his other life, he knew most of the
Inverni fairies in the city. Maybe he knew the one who had
tried to kill her.

14
CHAPTER

LAURA PACED IN front of Terryn's desk. She didn't like not understanding what was going on, when events ran a course she couldn't predict. One small decision could change everything, one wrong move cause disaster. The creation of a simple glamour to infiltrate the local SWAT team, so mundane at the time, a routine information-gathering task, had set in motion a strange path of overlapping agendas among unlikely players.

She threw herself in the guest chair for the fourth or fifth time. Terryn's office was Terryn. Photographs lined the walls, landscapes of his ancestral home in Ireland, including a shot of a depressed city. He told her once that the city had grown up over a battlefield that was once a place of beauty and sadness. He wanted to remind himself that the future doesn't always improve on the past. She didn't like the idea.

Terryn's body signature preceded him into the room, and she jumped to her feet. "Dammit, Terryn, I've been calling you for hours. Who the hell is that guy in the photo I sent you?" she asked.

He dropped a messenger bag on one of the side chairs and a stack of files on his desk. "Simon Alfrey. I knew him long ago," he said.

She stood in front of his desk with her arms crossed. "He's the Inverni from the drug raid. What the hell does this mean, Terryn?"

He narrowed his eyes in thought. "I don't know. He's been in Maeve's service since Convergence. The Alfreys submitted to the Seelie Court before any of the other Inverni clans. Simon likes to style himself as Maeve's loyal servant, despite any political differences he has with her."

"By running drugs and trying to kill me?"

Terryn's brow twitched in thought. "I agree it doesn't make sense. Maybe this is part of a Guild mission that InterSec doesn't know about."

Laura jabbed her finger against the desktop. "He tried to kill me, Terryn, and nearly provoked an essence fight with Bloom in front of the Russell Senate Building. That's one helluva mission directive."

Terryn continued unperturbed. "I'm speculating, Laura. I know Maeve manipulates him, and he her. It wouldn't surprise me if the High Queen is using him to stir up trouble somewhere. She's done it before. Simon likes to be involved in things that may backfire on Maeve," he said.

Laura realized she was leaning over Terryn as if he were somehow at fault. She stepped back and sat. "Isn't that the question? What is he involved in? Who's really involved here? What are they doing that they are willing to kill FBI agents and police officers? It can't be drugs. Not at this level," Laura said.

He shook his head. "You're right. It's not drugs. I've penetrated the spell on the USB drive you recovered. The data was degraded, but the apartment complex was a makeshift communications center. You stumbled on some kind of shadow network."

Laura sank into the guest chair. "Okay, this sounds ominous."

He gestured at the files on his desk. "There's data relating to manufacturing operations and financial resources. An odd collection of people are either involved or at least targeted for research. There's information about Blume's operations, several human businessmen and politicians in the

U.S., an unusual assortment of Celtic fey. I don't know what to make of it yet. I also found several itineraries—including this week's schedule for the president and Hornbeck," he said.

She leaned forward. "Both Hornbeck and the president are going to be at the Archives this week. Should we consider canceling the ceremony?"

Terryn divided the files into different stacks. "Rhys and the president don't like impulsive reactions to these things. I don't want to look foolish if it's something else. There are several high-profile itineraries in here. Based on what I'm seeing, it could be anything from money laundering to blackmail. There's also a manifesto of sorts on the drive."

"Manifesto? Like crazy manifesto?" she asked.

He smiled at her. "Is there any other kind?"

Laura looked at the files. "I'd like to see it."

Terryn pulled a thick, bound report out of the top folder and tossed it to the edge of his desk. "I made you a copy. There's a profile of Alfrey in there, too."

Laura started flipping through it. "We have two days to figure out if the Archives ceremony is related. I'm betting it is. You're naming too many people in that file who are going to be at the ceremony. I don't like coincidences."

"I'm putting some of it in channels so we can see what the other agencies think," he said.

She gathered her things and stood at the door. "Blume just got himself invited to the ceremony this afternoon, Terryn. I'm going to see if I can get rid of him. Keep me updated."

With normal business hours almost over, Laura didn't want to return to the public-relations department and get sucked into a last-minute project or crisis. She rode the elevator to the garage instead and jumped in her Mercedes. At first she drove with no direction, even no thought, just listening to music and going through the motions of driving. Eventually, rush hour reared its head, and the pleasure and distraction of driving vanished.

She had no desire to return to one of her persona apartments—even her so-called real one in Alexandria. All of them had a work connotation that would intrude on her in distracting ways. Jumping among three personas was tiring, and she didn't want to feel like she was Mariel or Janice or even Laura, the public-relations staffer.

She parked on the opposite end of town near the Congressional Cemetery. No one she knew would stumble across her in that out of the way corner of the city. The cemetery was not on the major tour routes and had few visitors late in the day. She roamed the graves until she reached the far end away from the road, a shallow depression with tumbled grave markers. Earthmoving machinery was in evidence, and she idly wondered if the landscaping was being repaired or redesigned. She found a low retaining wall to sit on and pulled out the Alfrey profile.

Simon Alfrey was an opportunist, that much was clear. Terryn had collated a laundry list of shady financial dealings, real estate transactions, and political maneuverings that stretched back almost a century. Connections to the Seelie Court were evident, but no firm link existed between him and high-level court officials. As she went deeper into the report, she saw why. The Seelie Court might enjoy using him, but they didn't trust him.

The Alfrey clan had a history of politically opposing Terryn's clan for the rule of the Inverni fairies. The mac-Cullens had even ruled the Seelie Court before their defeat by the Danann fairies. As former enemies, Terryn's family walked a delicate balance between keeping their kindred united while at the same time not overtly threatening the rule of the Seelie Court. The Dananns had numbers on their side, and when Convergence happened, the major clans united around Maeve to protect them in the strange modern world. Except the Inverni. With the instigation of the Alfrey clan, the Invernis made an attempt to win the throne during the confusing early days of Convergence. Terryn's father, Aubry macCullen, led the effort against Maeve and lost his life when the revolt failed. The Inverni submitted to the crown, but not before blood had been shed and alliances were broken. The Alfrey clan had seen the inevitable and blamed the insurgence on the macCullens.

She went back to her car and drove a few blocks to a coffee shop. As twilight fell, she sat at a corner table reading the manifesto. It was definitely crazy. Well-written crazy, but crazy. She'd seen it all before, the rants about failed government and suffering peoples, the need to replace it all with something shiny and new. Except the cynical secret of all manifestos was that they sought a result no different than the state of affairs they claimed to despise. Only, of course, things would be much better if the crazies were in charge.

She finished her coffee and ordered another to go. What made her pause about the manifesto, though, was its breadth. It wasn't about taking down the U.S. or the Seelie Court or the Teutonic Consortium. It was about taking down all of them, sweeping away all three structures and replacing it with another one. The fatal flaw in the plan that the authors missed was the point of most political history and goals, the hope that everyone would compromise and unite and get along. It wasn't going to happen overnight because someone thought it should and wrote it down.

Between the manifesto and Alfrey, Laura had a good idea of what the drug raid was about. Money, of course, and politics, as usual. It wasn't a huge leap to make the connection that Alfrey still opposed the Seelie Court and needed money to do something about it. Under normal circumstances, security agencies would contain the group and write off the ideas. But between Alfrey's history and his connections to the Seelie Court, Laura thought he needed to be taken more seriously.

She drove by the Vault. Restless, she circled the block. She didn't want to go home to an empty apartment and read through the files again. After another two passes down the street, she spotted the InterSec agent watching the club and parked not far behind him. She pulled out Mariel's cell phone and called Terryn.

"Hey. I want to take over the surveillance at the Vault. Can you call off our babysitter?" she said when he answered.

"Go home and get some sleep, Laura," he said.

"I'm bored."

"Laura . . ." he began.

"Can we not do this, Terryn? I can handle this. I just don't want to go home right now."

He didn't answer right away. A moment later, the Inter-Sec agent started up his car and drove off. "Are you okay?" Terryn asked.

"Yeah. Stuff on my mind."

"I know what you mean," he said. She waited, expecting him to elaborate. After a long silence, he said. "Call when you want to be relieved."

"I will. See you tomorrow." She disconnected and settled more comfortably in her seat. After Aubry died, Terryn had delegated his authority to his siblings, come to the U.S., and joined the Guild. That much she knew. But old clan politics from before she was born was something else. Terryn knew Simon Alfrey better than he'd let on.

The dinner crowd trickled into the club. Obvious couples arrived—pairs and groups of four. High-level business people, financiers in particular, exited limousines. Several acknowledged each other without surprise. She watched with a mental hyperawareness, using the mnemonic tricks druids were adept at, attaching names to human and fey guests she recognized, while she made memory imprints of the faces she didn't. At her leisure, she would activate full recall and scan through the InterSec databases for more names to give Terryn.

During a lull, she released the mnemonic spell, and her sensing ability reasserted itself. A body signature registered on the edge of her range, a stationary body signature, as if someone waited nearby. The moment she noticed it, it withdrew. On a busy street with people socializing, a stationary body signature was not unusual. She'd noticed it only by chance. Still, she checked her mirrors.

Patrons leaving the Vault began to outnumber those going in. Laura relaxed again to take a break, and immediately sensed a body signature again. Earlier, it had been behind her, but now it was somewhere off to her left, too far for her to make a positive identification. She boosted more essence into her sensing ability. As soon as her ability touched it, it withdrew again. Someone was watching her.

Considering that she had been sitting for a few hours, an alert security guard might have noticed her. With a short spell, she changed the basics of her facial features, flattening them out and shortening her hair, and got out of the car. She didn't want Janice or Mariel seen near the club tonight. She leaned against the door and pretended to drink from her long-empty coffee cup. No one on the sidewalk paid her any attention.

She searched for Gianni. He operated at the Vault as senior security and might be there. She sipped air again. She knew his personality type. He would consider foot patrol beneath him, but that didn't mean he didn't have someone else looking. The body signature didn't reappear. With a last casual glance around, she got back in her car.

The night lengthened. The limos returned. She saw Blume depart alone in a black Town Car. Two congressmen left so soon after that she guessed that the three had attended a meeting together. More businesspeople, two well-known lobbyists for the banking industry, and a dwarf she remembered from an accounting scandal several years earlier. A large cluster departed at once, many of the same group that had arrived together. A meeting had definitely taken place.

Gianni appeared with his cell phone jammed to his ear. He looked neither right nor left, but cut into an alley beside the club. Moments later, his truck appeared. She followed him as he drove a direct route to Georgetown. Unlike the Vault, the bars and clubs along M Street whirled with late-night activity. Gianni cruised past clubs and cafes, slowing to check out the lines of people waiting to get in. Laura couldn't tell if he was looking for someone specific or scoping the scene.

She slouched in her seat, wondering what the hell she had stumbled into. Gianni and Alfrey had been at the drug raid. Both had connections to Blume, who also had con-

nections to Hornbeck. If Blume were involved, she couldn't
see an angle on his desire to attend the Archives ceremony.
He certainly hadn't been happy to see Alfrey. If something
were to happen, she imagined he'd want to be as far away
as possible.

Gianni turned onto a narrow side street. As she made the
corner, the red brake lights on his truck blazed in the dark.
She drove past. The street was too narrow to pass him, and
she didn't want to risk a face-to-face encounter. She made a
U-turn and drove by again. Gianni's truck remained with its
hazard lights on. Laura pulled to the curb in front of a fire
hydrant. The Guild would pay the ticket if she got one.

She strolled down the sidewalk. Nondescript storefronts
occupied the ground floors, offices for lawyers and insurance agents broken up by the occasional dry cleaner or
convenience store. Not the trendy boutiques and wine bars
M Street was known for. She reached the corner and peered
up a lane that looked like a service road. Gianni stood outside his truck. Across from him, a black car idled behind a
large building. The building hid most of the car except the
front end.

She slipped into the alley. Two cars parked on the curb
blocked her from view. From the new perspective, the black
car looked like a diplomatic vehicle with missing flags. It
could mean any foreign government—or a fey diplomat. As
a precaution, Laura pulled in her body signature tightly to
limit exposure. She didn't want to risk someone fey in the
car sensing her from a distance. The downside was that she
also reduced her own sensing ability.

She moved into the recessed space of a closed garage
bay. Closer, but then Gianni's truck blocked her line of
sight. Gianni had moved to the car to speak with someone
in the backseat. Laura assessed the open space of the lane.
Shadowed service entrances offered some concealment.
She slipped to the first door without a problem. She passed
to the next two, exposing herself for no more than a few
seconds. A long stretch of empty pavement lay between her
and a garage door. She would stand out against a white-
painted wall for several long seconds, but the vantage point

would offer a direct view of the car. She stepped out of the shadows.

A rough sending rumbled in her mind as a large hand clamped over her mouth. *You're safe.*

She slammed on her body shield as her attacker's other arm snaked around her from behind. Too late. He was close enough for her shield to envelop them both. He hugged her as she fought to break his hold. His body signature was a bundle of noise in her senses, human and something else.

Stop. Look at the roofline, he sent.

Against her better judgment, she stopped struggling. Something moved in the blackness above, a dark shadow and a ripple of pale light. Another appeared, then a third launched into the air. They flew over the alley to the roof of the building above and behind her. Shielded fairy sentries, Dananns by their stealth. She hadn't seen, felt, or heard them.

She stopped fighting. *Thank you,* she sent.

He leaned in close to her ear and whispered, "Don't mention it, Ms. Blackstone."

Laura froze at the sound of Sinclair's voice.

15
CHAPTER

GIANNI CONTINUED TALKING while Laura huddled in the doorway with Sinclair. Sinclair removed his hand from her mouth but stayed close enough to touch her back. She puzzled over his body signature. Her sensing ability slid over it, not recognizing the man she knew, but something vague and nondescript. The signature fluttered and changed intensity, like a glamour with no body. The change baffled her. She had never sensed anything other than human from him.

Gianni returned to his truck. The brake lights came on, and the hazard lights went off. Laura pressed back into the shadows, keenly aware of Sinclair's body. Gianni drove off, and the black car followed, its tinted rear window rising. By the time it turned broadside, the window had closed. She didn't see who was inside.

The Danann sentries swooped off the building and followed the car. Laura began to step forward, but Sinclair pulled her back again. *One more,* he sent. Laura breathed shallowly, scanning the roofline. Sinclair held his hand on her waist. She reached down and removed it, not roughly, but firmly. Fifteen minutes passed before the dark shadow of one last fairy detached from the depths of a loading dock and trailed after the others.

Laura pushed out of Sinclair's embrace and strode up the alley. He followed her into the lights and noise of M Street. They regarded each other at the curb. Laura noted that they both wore black jeans and T-shirts, his long-sleeved, hers three-quarter. He wore regulation police boots, to her running shoes. They looked like spies. They were spies. "Who are you?" she asked.

"Jono Sinclair. I'm a police officer," he said.

Jono. She hadn't heard him use the nickname before. She also wasn't sure how to handle him under the circumstances. "Am I under arrest?"

He smiled. A rather warm smile, she thought. "No. You haven't broken any laws that I can think of. Besides, I suspect it would be awkward if I did arrest you, Ms. Blackstone."

She cursed to herself for not using a stronger glamour. The sloppy move bothered her more than getting caught by Sinclair. "That's the second time you've called me that. Why?"

He shrugged. "Because you're Laura Blackstone. We shared an elevator in the Senate building earlier this afternoon."

"You have me confused with someone else."

He shook his head and looked up the street. She followed his gaze to a wine bar. "I know what glamours are, Ms. Blackstone. Let's have a drink."

"I don't think so, Officer Sinclair. I'll be going now."

She stepped around him and moved toward her Mercedes.

"I know who was in the car," he called out to her.

She turned. "Well?"

He gestured toward the bar. "Shall we?"

She hesitated. She could continue the pretense that she wasn't Laura Blackstone, just someone who looked like her. But she wanted to know, and she wanted to know what Sinclair was doing there. Without a word, she walked back past him toward the bar.

Laura eyed the interior. The place smelled of beer and old smoke. Flat-screen TVs littered the corners, and team banners decorated the walls. Not a place she would go for a drink unless it was something that fit one of her personas.

"What will you have?" Sinclair asked, when they entered.

The ceiling was a bit low, the bar a bit worn and the floor a bit sticky. "I think I'll play it safe with something in a bottle. A Corona."

A younger crowd filled the room, women in tight tops and tighter jeans, and guys in oversize shirts and baggy jeans. No, definitely not Laura's usual kind of place. Sinclair returned with drinks.

"Who was in the car?" she asked.

"Why do you want to know?" Sinclair lifted an amber draft to his lips.

"Just curious. I was out for a walk, and it looked funny," she said.

He smiled. "The public-relations director of the Fey Guild just happened to be lurking in an alley where a secretive meeting was taking place between a D.C. police officer and someone who wishes to remain anonymous. I bought the drinks, but I'm not buying that."

"What were *you* doing there?" she asked.

"Me? Now, I was definitely curious. I know the guy in the truck."

"Why were you following him?"

He shook his head. "Your turn, Ms. Blackstone. Why don't we start with admitting who you are."

She stared into his eyes. He wouldn't stop her from leaving. If she left, he would assume he was right anyway. If she admitted it, she would confirm what he already knew. She was caught either way, but one option at least gave her a chance to get more information out of him. "Fine. I'm Laura Blackstone. Now tell me who was in the car."

"I don't know," he said.

She sensed truth and wanted to slap the smile off his face. Instead, she put her bottle on a nearby ledge. "This is pointless then."

Again she walked away from him.

"It's not the first time I've watched him," Sinclair said.

She glared at him. "Are we going to play this game all night?"

He grinned. "Are you planning on spending all night with me?"

She did raise her hand to slap him then, but held back. "What do you want, Sinclair?"

"Answers, just like you. Why does someone I know have secret meetings? And now I'm wondering, why is the Guild interested?"

She regarded him with cool annoyance. "Gianni is connected to a drug raid that involved the fey. The Guild doesn't know what happened and is being shut out of the investigation."

"So you know who he is," he said.

She hadn't revealed anything that wouldn't be easy to find out. "Of course. I also know he works at the Vault."

"He does security there."

She nodded. "For some very high-level people. The Guild is concerned about security risks."

He sipped from his beer again. "They must be very concerned to send a PR director."

She frowned at his snide tone. "I'm not going to explain Guildhouse politics to you."

He shrugged. "Fine, whatever. My concern is my life. A police officer was killed in that raid. I don't think it was an accident," he said.

Laura retrieved her beer. "Why?"

"Someone tried to run me off the road the other night. It was a professional," he said.

That made murder attempts on two people who were present at Sanchez's murder. "Has anything happened to Foyle?" she asked.

He hid it well, but Laura felt his surprise at the question. "He doesn't share information with me. I'm not sharing with him . . . yet."

"Why didn't you let me walk into an ambush in that alley?" she asked.

He smiled again. "Self-preservation, for one thing. If they spotted you, I doubt I could have evaded fairy sentries. And if they killed you, I might never know whether you're really Laura Blackstone or Janice Crawford or Mariel Tate."

Her hand blazed with essence as she thrust her fist under his chin, just short of touching him. She let him feel the heat and power waiting to be released. "We're leaving right now. Don't make me fry your brain."

16
CHAPTER

SINCLAIR DIDN'T MOVE. "I suggest you drop your hand, Ms. Blackstone. You are threatening a police officer."

"This is not a discussion," she said. She chanted a short phrase in ancient Gaelic. A burst of essence froze Sinclair in place as a binding spell draped over him. His eyes went wide when he discovered he couldn't move his lips. She muttered another incantation, and he rose a few inches off the floor. Laura wrapped her arm around his waist and floated him toward the door. The movement did not look natural, but no one paid any attention. Only in a bar, Laura thought, could someone cast a spell and have no one notice or care. Outside, she propelled Sinclair along the sidewalk to her car.

She released the levitation spell and propped him near the open passenger door. "I'm going to release the binding, and you're going to get in the car. If you make any sudden moves, I will take you down before you finish the thought. Blink twice if we're clear."

He blinked twice. She fluttered her fingers in the air and faint wisps of white essence coiled off Sinclair. He swayed in place, caught his balance, and lunged at her. As promised, she hit him in the chest with a handful of white essence. He flew off his feet, hit the car, and dropped to the sidewalk. She didn't blame him for trying to escape, but it complicated things.

Laura glanced around. A young couple watched from outside the bar. The man lifted a cell phone to his ear. Swearing, Laura checked Sinclair to see if he was breathing. Satisfied that he didn't have any major injuries, she hauled him up and pushed him inside the car. She adjusted his position on the seat and recast the binding spell before he came to.

She pulled in to traffic and called Terryn. "I need to meet you at the day-care center."

"I'll be there," he said, and disconnected.

A pit formed in her stomach. She kept a keen eye for anyone tailing her. Sinclair never said he was alone. She pulled to the side of the road and braked in the lane. Traffic flowed, but no one slowed more than necessary or looked in her direction. She merged back into traffic.

How in hell Sinclair had made the connection between her glamours stumped her. No one had ever linked her to one of her personas, never mind two. At a stop light, she glanced over and saw that his eyes were open. With a few words, she peeled the binding spell off his head. He stretched his neck.

"Where are you taking me?" he asked.

"Who are you?" she answered.

"Lieutenant Jonathan Sinclair," he said.

Truth, at least a truth he believed. "Why were you following me?"

"I wasn't. I was following Gianni."

More truth. "How did you know I was Laura Blackstone?"

"I asked someone at the Senate building."

Truth. "Why?"

"Because I thought you were attractive and wanted to ask you out."

The answer startled a laugh out of her. Truth. "I'm guessing this isn't what you expected."

He let a smile play on his lips. "I was having fun until you shot me."

Despite the smile, he wasn't relaxed. Not nervous, but disquieted. Laura didn't find it surprising considering the previous fifteen minutes. "I didn't shoot you. I used a mild essence shock. That's different."

"Tell that to my ribs," he said.

"They're bruised. If you cooperate, we'll fix that," she said.

"Cooperate how?"

A list of responses sprang to mind. She didn't want to make any promises. Terryn might have his own ideas. "We'll see."

"Where are you taking me?" he asked again.

"You have to sleep now." She raised her hand and spoke an ancient Welsh phrase. Sinclair's eyelids drooped shut.

The Guild owned hundreds of properties, some official, some not. Laura drove out of the District and into a Maryland suburb. The neighborhood consisted of street after street of similar houses, the homes of the bureaucrats who some people contended truly ran the government. Laura pulled in to the driveway of a house that looked like a dozen others on the street except for the landscaping. She tossed a ball of yellow essence at the garage door. It closed behind the car after she pulled in.

Terryn stood at an inside door that led to the main section of the house. She got out of the car and gestured to Sinclair. "Would you do the honors?"

He raised an eyebrow when he saw the passenger. "What happened?"

She told him as he lifted Sinclair from the car. Terryn led her into the house and down into the basement. Not the typical finished basement of a colonial house. A warren of rooms had been constructed, incongruous holding cells with iron and glass walls. Terryn shifted Sinclair across one shoulder, passed through a small anteroom with a viewing window to a larger iron-lined room that contained a table and four chairs. He placed Sinclair upright in one of the chairs.

Terryn's hands rested on his hips. "Assault and battery on a police officer and kidnapping. You crossed state lines, too. I think that makes it worse if I remember correctly. Anything else I should be worried about?"

She tried an ingratiating smile. "No, my car's fine."

Laura released the binding and sleep spells. Sinclair slumped forward but caught himself before his face hit the table. He shook his head as if he were trying to clear it. "Where am I?"

Laura pulled her chair closer. "It doesn't matter. I'm going to ask you again, who are you other than Jonathon Sinclair?"

He stretched with care, wincing at the pain from his ribs. "That's who am I."

Laura leaned forward. "Jonathon Sinclair is a human. You detected four fairy sentries I didn't sense at all. That's fey ability. Who are you?"

He held his arm across his torso, glaring at them. "I am a police officer with the Washington, D.C., police."

Terryn unfolded his wings up and out, the dark indigo points curving toward each other. "Let me explain what is at stake, Mr. Sinclair. At this moment, you are a security threat. I can make the case that you are technically no longer on U.S. soil. It will take some time to sort that out. You can either start answering questions or leave your loved ones wondering what happened to you."

Sinclair gave him a cocky grin that hid the anger and anxiety Laura sensed. "I want a lawyer."

Terryn inclined his head. "If one should find his way in here, I will recommend him to you."

Sinclair's confidence slipped.

"Who are you, Jono?" Laura asked, her voice pitched low.

"I told you."

She laid her hands flat on the table. "I know what you said. I think you're someone else, too."

"I'm not the one pretending to be someone I'm not," he said.

"That's what I mean. What do you think you know about Janice Crawford or Mariel Tate?" she asked.

"All three of you are the same woman. I was pretty sure before. Now I'm positive," he said.

"Why is that?" asked Terryn.

He flicked an annoyed glance at Terryn. "Locking me in a basement has something to do with it."

Laura changed the direction of the conversation. "I didn't sense you come up behind me in the alley. How is a human able to do that?"

"Your essence field is weak. When you pulled your body essence in to hide your signature, I slipped into the blank spot left behind."

Only someone fey can do that, Laura. He's not human. Terryn sent.

We're missing something, she replied. The only species the fey couldn't glamour well was human. A glamour can make someone look human, but it was, for all practical purposes, impossible to hide the fey essence underneath. Sinclair didn't read fey to her at all. In fact, he still felt vaguely null.

"How do you know how to do that?" Laura asked Sinclair.

"I would be risking my life if I answered that," he said.

A cold white light flickered in Laura's eyes. "You're already at risk, Jono. We can't let you go if we don't believe we can trust you. You have to tell us how a human can read essence as if he is fey."

Sinclair considered for a moment, then reached for his collar. Terryn shot his hands out, sparking them with blue-lit essence. "Stop."

Sinclair froze. He wasn't afraid, but he recognized power when he saw it. "I have a sort of glamour on. It makes me read human to the fey."

Terryn reached across and fished a neck chain from beneath Sinclair's T-shirt. A small flat medallion of a sun with three Teutonic runes inscribed on it hung from a simple gold chain. Laura sensed a deadening field radiating around it, devoid of any essence at all. "Take it off," she said.

Sinclair pulled the chain over his head and dropped it on the table. His body essence flared brighter, human, but stronger than any Laura had encountered. She played her sensing ability over it, then thrilled as she probed deeper. His human signature had the distinct edge of fey about it. Stunned, she rocked back in her chair. "Danu's blood, Terryn, he's a human-fey hybrid."

"You make it sound like I'm some kind of experiment," Sinclair said.

"Are you?" Terryn asked.

"My grandfather was fey," he said.

Laura and Terryn exchanged glances. The fey and humans did not crossbreed well. Their children usually didn't make it to term, and when then did, they suffered from mental and physical disabilities. Few survived with no discernible effects. It happened, but it was rare. "Who was he?" Laura asked.

"That's all you're getting," he said.

"What species was he?" asked Terryn. Sinclair wouldn't answer.

Laura closed her eyes and focused. Sinclair's signature was unlike any she had known, more human than not. Technically, she would call him a solitary fey, something unique, yet fey. She probed deeper. A faint image burned within him, like a ghost pattern within his human body signature. She pushed harder, mentally discarding the human essence to expose what lay beneath.

Her eyes flew open. "Jotunn!"

Terryn looked dubious. "Are you sure? The giants hardly breed among themselves, Laura."

Laura nodded. "Positive. I can even tell you more precisely—he's logi-jotunn. I've met one before."

Terryn peered at Sinclair. "A fire giant? Does he have any ability?"

Laura assessed the strange body signature. "The essence doesn't look active."

"Stop talking about me like I'm a specimen on a slide. I'm sitting right here," Sinclair snapped.

I think he would have done something by now if he could, she finished in a sending.

"You can do sendings," said Laura.

He nodded. "Not well. They exhaust me."

Terryn subtly raised his body essence. "If you have such limited abilities, explain how you sensed Laura's essence. I don't know anyone who can see through a glamour without special means."

Sinclair shrugged. "Neither did my grandfather. I don't sense essence. I sense its shape. Everyone's shape is unique. Glamours don't change that. I can't tell your species, but I sense the difference in the shapes of your body signatures. When I met Mariel Tate, I was surprised that the shape of her body signature matched Janice Crawford's. I was trying to figure out which one was wearing a glamour. Then I met Laura Blackstone."

"That's why you said hello to me at the Senate building," Laura said.

He shook his head. "That was coincidence. I have to actively use my ability. When I'm around a lot of people, it's exhausting. I told you the truth about why I wanted to know your name. I didn't match your essence until tonight."

Realization dawned on Laura. "You're the one I've been sensing!"

"Could you clarify that?" Terryn asked.

Laura shook her head. "I thought someone was following me. At the drug den and at the Vault. Someone came to the edge of my sensing range and backed off. Someone with an ability to sense the shape of my body signature, isn't that right, Jono?"

He nodded. "I had to know if I could trust Janice, so I imprinted on her. I was watching Gianni tonight, too, when I saw you park. I thought you were scoping out Blume's meeting, but when you followed Gianni, I followed you."

"Where did you get the medallion?" Terryn asked.

Sinclair picked up the chain and rubbed the medallion.

"My grandfather made it. He didn't like the human tendency to kill what it doesn't understand. He thought I would have an easier time in life if people thought I was fully human. He was afraid if anyone knew about me, I would be studied like an insect. Much like this moment, I imagine."

"We're not examining you, Jono. We're talking," said Laura.

"Interrogating," he said.

"Fine. Call it that. But you have to understand the position this puts us in—puts me in. Lives would be at risk if people knew what I do."

"My life feels at risk right now," he said.

We can't let him go, Terryn sent.

There has to be another way, she sent back.

"Who are you working for?" Terryn asked.

Sinclair shook his head. "I'm done. I told you about the medallion because you would have found it anyway. We're even. You keep your mouths shut. I'll do the same."

"Why should we trust you?" Terryn asked.

He shrugged. "Why should I trust you?"

They stared at each other across the table. A pit formed in Laura's stomach. This is what she had always feared would happen to her someday, glamours removed, trapped in a room, and interrogated. When that day came, she would pay the price for years of lies and betrayal.

"We have more to lose than you do," said Terryn.

Sinclair snorted. "Sure. My life's not worth much, right?"

Laura glared. "That's not what he meant. If we expose you, you can disappear and start over. If you expose me, I might manage to stay alive, but there will be political ramifications. You'll probably become a target, too. There will be angry people who will blame you and be a lot more relentless in looking for you than anyone you'll have to deal with if we expose you."

"Now that's a subtle threat," he said.

Laura shrugged. "Those are the facts, Sinclair. I'm not

happy you're in this position either. I wish I had never met you. But I have to tell you, if you expose me, I will not stand in the way of anyone who wants to kill you. I might even help."

He smiled. "Does this mean you'll say no if I ask you to dinner?"

Terryn raised an eyebrow. *Cheeky.*

"Your lack of seriousness isn't helping you," Laura said.

Sinclair leaned back in his chair. "I don't for one minute believe you will let me walk out of here alive. Excuse me if I don't beg for my life. It's not my style."

"You said someone tried to run you off the road, Sinclair. I've had two attacks on my life the last three days. What makes you think you'll have a better chance outside than in here?" she asked.

He smiled. "I don't."

She stared at him. "Did you try to kill me?"

"No," he said. No hesitation. Firm voice. No fluctuation in his essence. Truth. She sensed truth.

"Who do you think did?"

"Gianni."

"That's one possibility," she said. "So we both suspect the same person. I think we can help each other."

"What do you propose?" he asked.

Laura refused to look at Terryn. "How would you like a new job?"

"What kind of job?" Sinclair asked.

I think we should discuss this, Terryn sent.

Later, Laura replied.

As Sinclair shifted his gaze between them, she wondered if he had another aberrant ability and could eavesdrop on sendings, something no fey could do. She formed as lascivious an image in her mind as she could, but he didn't react. However good Sinclair was at keeping his composure, she doubted he would have had no reaction at all.

"What you do now: investigations. InterSec could use a human staffer," she said.

"Under what legal authority?" he asked.

"InterSec's. We're governed by treaty and agreement with the U.S. government," Terryn said.

"What if I don't want to do what you want me to do?"

Laura shrugged. "Quit."

"What if I quit right now?"

Laura frowned. "Cute."

"What's the catch?" he asked.

"Trust, Jono. We need to trust each other, and we need to get out of this mess," Laura said.

"What's in it for me?" he asked.

"Protection. You'll need it. The pay's pretty good, too," she said.

Am I going to have any say in this? Terryn sent.

Laura ignored him.

"I don't know. I've got a pretty good career going," Sinclair said.

"Which will likely be cut short by your death in the next few days," said Terryn.

Thanks for joining the party, Laura sent him.

Terryn's comment took the cockiness out of Sinclair. He leaned on his forearms and stared at his hands. "I won't kill anyone."

"No more than you're asked to now," Laura said.

"What's in it for you?" he asked.

"Protection as well. We watch your back; you watch ours. I think we can trust each other," Laura said.

"What if we can't?"

She shrugged again. "It's simple. One of us dies."

He chuckled. "Yeah, simple."

Terryn leaned forward. "Let's make this provisional. We make it through the current situation, then decide whether you stay or not."

Sinclair slowly shook his head while he considered. "But I don't get a choice until then, right?"

Terryn didn't crack a smile. "Who said the choice would be yours then either?"

Sinclair's eyes shifted back and forth, not looking at them or anything else. Laura watched him closely. She remembered how calm he was when she first met him. The stress flowing off him now was understandable, but beneath it was a strong focus. He weighed his options and tilted back in his chair. "When do I start?"

Laura released the breath she hadn't realized she was holding. "Now."

17
CHAPTER

"I DON'T LIKE this," said Terryn.

Sinclair remained locked in the basement. When Cress arrived, she went down to tend his bruised ribs. Laura leaned against the counter in the kitchen. "We don't have a choice, Terryn. I'm exposed."

"We don't know if we can trust him."

She crossed her arms loosely and stared at her feet. "He could have let me get killed tonight."

"Or he could be lying to gain our confidence," Terryn said.

She arched an annoyed brow at him. "Ahem. Are you questioning my ability to sense truth?"

She thought she detected embarrassment. Actual embarrassment from Terryn macCullen. "I didn't mean that. I'm worried."

"I've been sensing only the truth from him," she said.

Terryn nodded. "I don't dispute that. But he was also able to hide his fey nature from you. We don't know if he can hide lies from you."

She shook her head. "We've never disclosed my truth-sensing ability, Terryn. Every arrest or report we've ever made, we've used independent verification. No one knows about it. Sinclair wouldn't know to hide from it."

"You can't be sure of that," he said.

She stared at him. "Terryn, if I can't be sure of that, then we have a bigger problem. Our agreement was that you and Cress would never tell anyone about my truth-sensing, not even Maeve herself, unless I agreed. Is there something you need to tell me?"

Again, embarrassment rolled off him. "No, we've never told. I'll trust you on this."

She ran water into a glass and watched him as she sipped. "This isn't like you, Terryn. You're never this unsettled. What's wrong?"

He closed down his emotions. It was a natural reaction, Laura supposed. He knew she could read him. She wondered what it must be like for him to have two people he couldn't lie to. She could sense lies in his tone, and Cress could feel them in the core of his essence. Laura could not fathom what it was like to have not one, but two people know him that intimately. It had been years since she allowed someone that privilege.

He closed the door to the basement, a move that surprised Laura. Terryn hid nothing from Cress as far as she knew. "Like I said, I don't like this. You've had persona conflicts before, but never this many connecting to the same case and never with Laura Blackstone involved. I'm worried things could slide out of control."

She swallowed water. The true reason her personas were tangled was her poor decision to create Janice. Janice Crawford wouldn't have happened if Laura Blackstone hadn't been involved with Foyle through Hornbeck's office. "Are you sure that's it?"

"What do you mean?"

She rubbed at the tense muscles in her neck. "I read the Alfrey file. He's dredging up a lot of bad memories, isn't he?"

Terryn glanced at the basement door again. "I know I can't lie to you, Laura, so, yes. The Alfrey clan has always been a problem for my family. I don't think this investigation is about me, but I'm concerned about where it can lead."

Laura frowned. "Are you afraid it might lead to Ireland?"

He shrugged, a long, languid gesture for him that sent his wings rippling. "'Afraid' isn't the word. My sister has things well in hand leading the macCullens. It's the larger issue. I walked away from Danann and Inverni politics because it never ends, but I'm wondering if Simon Alfrey's appearance is a sign that I made a mistake."

"How would your being in Ireland have made a difference?" she asked.

He frowned. "I don't know. But I do know that I would have a clearer sense of the nuances of what is happening with Alfrey." His eyes slid to the basement door again. "And I don't know if I can go back."

She realized his conflict was about Cress. The clan would have a hard time accepting a non-Inverni as a mate for their leader. That Cress was a *leanansidhe* made matters worse. No one trusted them. With the failures of the past haunting the Inverni, they would find Cress's influence disturbing. Hell, she thought, I find it disturbing sometimes. Their intimacy had a palpable texture to it. Everyone could feel it when they were together. That intensity for anything other than the good of the clan would be looked on as suspect. "The Wheel of the World, Terryn," she said instead.

Terryn said nothing. The Wheel of the World, the fate of them all, a question of faith to which both she and Terryn subscribed. Things happened because they needed to happen for whatever reason fate dictated. They all rode the Wheel as It turned. Sometimes It ran its course as it would and sometimes people affected its course. At least that was what Laura believed. Otherwise, she was a pawn in the hands of some vast unknown Power. As far as she was concerned, if such a Power existed, she doubted it would care much about her as an individual.

"Sometimes I forget that," he said.

"We all do."

He changed the subject. "Sinclair stays off the books until he proves himself."

"That's fine with me," Laura said.

Terryn allowed himself a tired smile, which was telling. Powerful fey didn't tire easily. "Good. Because he's your responsibility until then. He doesn't go anywhere without you except when he's at work."

Laura nearly dropped her glass. "You're joking."

He shook his head. "No joke. I don't trust him. I trust your judgment, but that doesn't mean I won't set precautions. You should decide where you're going to live. The two of you can't stay here. It will raise questions."

She put the glass down. "You want me to *live* with him?"

"Is there a problem? You've done things like this before. If he's willing, maybe he'll let Janice Crawford move in to his place. The Crawford apartment is rather small, and the cable's been disconnected."

She retrieved the glass and turned away to refill it at the sink. "Fine. Bring him to the Guildhouse. I have to get some things from my apartment, and I'll pick him up afterward."

"Okay. Cress should be done by now. Do you want me to help debrief him?" Terryn said to her back.

She shook her head as she stared out the window. Someone had set up a swing set in the backyard. "It'll help build trust if I do it alone."

"True. Let me know if there's anything I can do," he said.

She kept staring out the window. She didn't know whether to laugh or scream.

18
CHAPTER

DROPPING HER DUFFEL bag on the threshold, Laura stood in the doorway of Sinclair's apartment. The small, spare living room was furnished with two armchairs and a couch. A pile of books and magazines teetered next to a used coffee cup on the coffee table. Throw pillows pressed to one side of the couch with a blanket hanging half on the floor. A flat-screen TV was mounted above the fireplace.

"Sorry the place is such a mess," Sinclair said.

"It's fine." All in all, Laura thought, a helluva lot cleaner than her room at the Guildhouse.

Sinclair picked up the blanket and folded it. "Make yourself at home."

She closed the apartment door. While Sinclair tidied the magazines, she scanned the room for essence. Moving along the bookcases to either side of the fireplace, she noted a few classic novels, plenty of mysteries and thrillers, and a substantial amount of nonfiction. Sinclair read biographies of politicians and histories. Or at least owned them, Laura thought. She mentally slapped herself for the unspoken dig at him. She couldn't deny he read. There were too many books and too many categories for it to be one of those contrived libraries. She had been hoping he wouldn't be interesting.

A stone cup sat next to a history of the Seelie Court in the twentieth century. It threw off the subtle essence of a listening ward. As Sinclair passed it on the way to the kitchen, the cup's essence faded and reappeared when he was gone.

The dining area was large enough for a table and four chairs. Sinclair scooped an empty glass and a plate with crumbs off the table and carried them through an archway. A framed photograph hung on the wall. Other than that, the space held nothing that could be a ward.

To the left of the dining room, the archway led to a galley kitchen. She watched Sinclair place the cup, plate, and glass in the sink and run water. "Would you like a drink?" he asked.

"Sure. I'll take any kind of beer," she said. She opened the cabinets and scanned inside. No listening wards. Sinclair moved to the end of the counter and took two beers out of the refrigerator. She caught a subtle current of essence when he moved away. A ceramic canister outside the range of his medallion had been charged as another listening ward. She pointed it out to him and held her finger to her lips.

In the living room, he popped open both bottles and handed her one. He held his out, and they tapped bottles. Laura took a sip and set the bottle on a magazine. She opened her duffel bag. *Ask me what this is,* she sent.

"What's that?" Sinclair asked.

She held up a small granite obelisk. "This? I like to mediate in a cleansed space before I go to sleep. Do you mind if I set it up?"

"No, go ahead. Can I watch?" he said. He put a mildly lewd tone to the question.

She glowered at him. "Sure, if that's your thing."

She placed the obelisk next to the stone cup on the bookshelf. She caressed it, strands of blue essence dripping from the tips of her fingers into the stone. Retrieving her beer, she sat in an armchair. "That cup's a listening ward. The obelisk is basically a jamming device. We can talk freely in here. There's another listening ward in the kitchen and probably one in your bedroom."

He slouched across the couch and frowned. "Why the hell would someone do that?"

Laura shrugged. "I believe someone thinks Sanchez said something to me before he died. If I had to guess, they think I told you something when you found me in the warehouse."

He looked dubious. "They bug my apartment and try to run me off the road on the off chance you might have said something to me?"

She took a swig of beer. "I've seen people killed for less reason, Jono. Depends on the stakes involved."

A flash of satisfaction passed over him when she called him by his nickname. She stretched her legs out, watching his eyes shift to them and back to her face. Flirting with someone to manipulate them was so much easier when she actually enjoyed the flirting. She sipped her beer again. "Do you know much about how your medallion works?"

He shook his head. "No. My grandfather made it and told me to wear it. That's good enough for me."

She pulled off her barrette and shook her hair loose. "Want to hear something funny? The listening wards are pointless. The medallion neutralizes them when you're near them."

He grinned. "Thanks, Gramps."

"Have you had any houseguests since the raid?" she asked.

He raised his eyebrows. "Are we at the point where we talk about past relationships?"

Laura rolled her eyes. "No, we're at the point where I try and figure out if they've realized you have that dampening medallion. If you've been home alone, there's been no reason to talk, so no reason to hear. With me here, they'll notice if they can't hear conversation."

"Like now," he said.

She nodded. "Like now. Only I just gave them the reason. They know a cleansing ward is meant to suppress other essence. Lots of fey like cleansed meditation spaces, so they shouldn't find it suspicious they can't hear. As long as they think the other wards are fine, they might not worry about the living room."

"No one's been here," he said.

"We'll have to be careful what we say when you're not near the listening wards. They'll pick up anything up to ten feet away, but not something near that obelisk and not if your medallion is near."

"Got it."

"Any word on what's going down at the apartment complex?" she asked.

Laura caught herself noticing the way his widow's peak curled off center, a satisfying quirk that broke the sharp planes of his face. He shifted to a more comfortable position on the couch. "The FBI shut us out. They're claiming we stumbled into a European drug cartel they've been investigating, so they're going with that."

Laura nodded. "That's become their standard excuse the last year or two."

He grunted as he downed half his beer. "All drugs are connected to a cartel somewhere."

"Is Foyle taking heat for the bad intel?"

She watched him hesitate, as if he were about to say something and changed his mind. "He's been in his office with the door closed. I think he's been sidelined. Are you going to be Crawford all night?"

She smirked playfully at him. "Who do you think is more attractive, Janice, Mariel, or Laura?"

He smirked back. "That sounds a lot like that who-do-you-love-more game parents tease kids with. How about you pick whoever you're most comfortable with?"

Her impulse was to say Laura. That was who she was, physically. That was the face she put to the world, her real face without any artifice. Laura was her default, but in that moment, she didn't think that meant the same thing as comfortable. Laura wasn't a person anymore. These days, she was only someone when she was Laura Blackstone, director of public relations. By definition, she was a persona about presentation and image, not a fleshed-out human being with an existence outside her office.

She shoved the reflection aside and released the Janice glamour. Her hair lightened and face narrowed. Her body lengthened a bit and thinned, but the clothes remained the same black jeans and T-shirt. Sinclair showed little reaction at the transition except a slight lift to his eyebrows. His eyes shifted, as if he marked off something on a mental checklist. "I'll get us more beer."

She liked the way he walked, the way his jeans hugged his hips but hung loosely enough on the legs that she surmised he didn't think much about it. Of course, like all elite cops, he had a gym body, the V-shape of his torso flaring to fill the T-shirt. His giant heritage showed in that, now that she knew to look for it, the height, the thick muscle, even the wheat blond hair.

Stop, she thought. Everything was complicated enough. She was lonely and tired and frustrated. He was handsome and smart and different. The wrong combination for her at the moment. He startled her by dangling a beer bottle in her face. Between her weak sensing field and the medallion dampening his fey nature, she didn't know he had returned. Even that lack of warning intrigued her. She literally couldn't see him coming.

"What's so funny?" he asked.

"What?"

"You're smiling. You've been aggravated all night, and now you're smiling," he said.

Tired, she shook her head. "Long day."

"Liar," he said, around the opening to his bottle of beer.

She lifted her head, a little too quickly, wondering if the jotunn had truth-sensing abilities after all. They were an enigma among the main branches of fey species, not so few to be considered solitaries, not so many that they posed a threat to anyone as a group. She knew few truth sensers other than herself. Jotunn were among the least studied species, which probably was another reason to be careful around Sinclair. And hybrids like him were even rarer and less studied. "I was just thinking you met Janice Crawford only a couple of days ago, and now anyone watching will have seen me show up here with an overnight bag. Makes you look like you take advantage of women who might be a little emotional about getting shot at."

"Nah. Makes Janice look a little easy," he said.

Laura surprised herself by snatching up a bottle cap from the coffee table and playfully flinging it at him. He pretended it came at him harder than it did, then tossed it back at her. She snatched it out of the air and took another deep draft of beer. "So what were you doing at Hornbeck's hearing yesterday?"

The smile on his face went out like a light. Mood killer, she thought. "Foyle asked me to drive him. The overtime's good. It's interesting sometimes."

She chuckled. "You must be the only person who thinks driving in D.C. is interesting."

He smiled. "I meant it's interesting to see what Foyle does when he's not running the unit. I like politics."

"Tylo Blume was at the hearing yesterday. Did Foyle talk to him?"

He nodded. "He owns Triad, one of the security contractors that Hornbeck recommended for a ceremony at the National Archives. Are we back to the interrogation already?"

She rolled her eyes and lied, "No. Lighten up, Jono. A subject we have in common happens to be related to an investigation. We're not friends yet. This is called getting-to-know-you conversation."

"You want to be friends?"

She shrugged a little. "Let's say I don't want us to be adversaries. I'm putting my ass on the line for you, and it would be nice to know if my gut is right."

"Me, too. Tell me why you're spying on the SWAT team."

She rested the beer on her hip. "Fair enough. To be honest, I wasn't this time. A year or so ago, Foyle needed a druid to fill in for Deegan when he was on sick leave. InterSec thought it might be beneficial to have someone on the inside there, so I created Janice. It didn't go anywhere, but I got stuck doing Foyle a favor as a result. That was how I ended up on the drug raid."

"You want me to take over that job," he said.

Laura played with the label on her beer. "More or less. I'm stretched too thin to keep it up for much longer. There might be other things."

"Like what?"

"Like, let's cross that bridge when we come to it. You're on probation until Terryn is satisfied you aren't a double agent," she said.

"Like you," he said.

She sighed. "For the right side. I'm not going to apologize for what I do, Jono. It's fair game in this town. I've accomplished a lot of good, positive things over the years."

He laughed. "Yeah, I forget how the good guys kidnap people and threaten to make them disappear."

She tore the edge of the label. "Is this how it's going to be? Because I don't need it."

He chuckled again and stood. "Yeah, this is how it's going to be. I'm not the only one on probation. You'll have to figure out when I'm joking and when I'm not. Come on. Let's find the bedroom ward so I can get some sleep. We have to work tomorrow."

She followed him through the door at the back of the dining room. A short hall had a clean, well-lit bathroom to the left next to the kitchen. To the right, a space too large to be a closet and too small to be a room served as a study area. Laura found another ward—stone pencil sharpener—and held it up for Sinclair so he knew where it was. The bedroom at the back of the apartment had a clean, masculine feel—midcentury modern nightstands and bed, minimalist bureaus, and crisp white sheets.

"So this is my bedroom," he said.

"It's nice. Are the nightstands original?" she asked.

He shrugged. "I'm not sure. They're secondhand, though. Found them in a shop."

He sat on the edge of the bed and pulled off his boots while Laura made a circuit of the room. She found the listening ward. The base of the lamp on the alarm-clock side of the bed had been charged. She pointed it out to Sinclair.

"Why so shy, Crawford? We've been wanting this for days," he said.

Startled, she pointed again at the lamp. He wasn't close enough for the medallion to block the sound of his voice. Sinclair chuckled loud enough for the ward to pick it up. "Mmmm. Lift your shirt a little higher."

She crossed her arms firmly across her chest. *What the hell do you think you're doing?* she sent at him.

He grinned and slipped off his jeans. She met his challenge and refused to look away as he stretched in his T-shirt and navy boxer briefs. At least he didn't push it with an arousal, she thought. "Very nice," he said, his voice soft with seduction, "now slide the jeans down slow."

Knock it off!

"I love thongs," he said.

She grabbed a pillow and threw it at him. He caught it with one hand and moaned. "I knew I'd love the way your skin smells. Talk, Janice, I like to hear you talk. Tell me how good this feels."

"You like to play games, don't you?" she said, as annoyingly sweet as she could while maintaining the threat in her eyes.

He groaned again. "Oh, yes. Let's play more."

Stretching out on his side and closer to the lamp, he propped up his head on his hand and grinned up at her. Behind him, the essence ward faded as the field from his medallion touched it.

Laura put her hands on her hips. "You are dead meat, Sinclair."

He patted the sheets next to him. "Time for bed."

She sat down hard with her back to him, then lay fully clothed on her side. "You can sleep on the couch," she said.

"Uh-uh," he said. "If someone's listening in when I bring a woman home, you can be damned sure she's sleeping in my bed with me."

She half rolled toward him. "Sleeping is all she'll be doing."

"Got it," he said, still grinning. He slipped under the sheets and turned out the light. "There's a blanket at the end of the bed if you want it."

She found the blanket, arranged it over her jeans, and lay back down. "Thanks."

"You're welcome. Do you need another pillow?"

"I'm fine."

Sinclair shifted on his side, not crossing the space between them. She closed her eyes and listened to him breathe.

"Would you like a glass of water?" he asked her back.

"I'm okay, Sinclair. Good night."

"How about a story then?"

"Good night, Sinclair," she said loudly. He snickered behind her.

She smiled in the darkness, watching leaf shadows cast by a streetlight dance in dark gray against pale walls. The last time she'd slept in the same bed with someone was . . . a long time ago, she realized. Although technically, she was working. And wearing her clothes. And on top of the sheets while Sinclair was under them. But she was sleeping in the same bed with someone. Technically.

Sinclair breathed lightly behind her. She knew he was awake, probably staring at the back of her head like she was staring at the wall. He had started out the night as a cop following up a hunch on his own and ended up sharing his bed with a druid who had threatened to kill him. She tried to imagine being in his situation, and if their positions were reversed, would she have a sense of humor. She admired that he could. She liked it.

She adjusted the pillow. That was as far as she was going to take that line of thought. It was fun—fantasy always was—but Sinclair was the wrong person at the wrong time. And maybe a little too cocky. He definitely was too cocky. She pictured him swilling beer every night at his dining-room table, completely oblivious to food stains on his T-shirt. Yeah, she thought. That was what he was probably really like. Behind the handsome face, the attractive body. An arrogant cop who would take any opportunity to trip her. She didn't need the hassle. She had gotten along fine without it for years. His breathing became rhythmic, a slow deep inhale, a soft exhale. It soothed her into drowsiness, then sleep.

She dreamed of a city empty of people, the sky a stark white above, something acrid in the air. She ran, darting around corner after corner, looking for something while something looked for her. A sound gained on her, like the panting of a large animal, its breath broken by the lunging of a heavy body. Light flashed across her vision, bright white and blinding. Whatever followed was coming closer. Panic took over as she ran between parked cars and dodged down broken sidewalks.

Her hair became damp with sweat. The stark white sky turned orange and red, thick black smoke smearing against the horizon. Something was wrong, and she didn't understand if she were trying to fix it or escape it. The thing behind came closer and closer. She tripped. Of course. She always tripped in moments like this in her dreams, an abrupt twist of an ankle caused by some minor heave in the sidewalk, a slow-motion fall as she curled into a ball to land with the least damage. She rolled onto her back and it was night. Something huge and dark loomed over her while flames roared behind it. It descended.

Laura gasped, and her eyes flew open. Sinclair had his hand on her arm, rocking her gently. She let him continue to hold her while her racing heart slowed. She took deep breaths to calm down.

He must have sensed she was awake because he stopped rocking. "You okay?"

"Nightmare. Sorry I woke you."

His arm slid down, his hand lingering on her biceps. He gave it a soft squeeze and let go. "Yeah, I get them, too."

He rolled away. She stared at the leaf shadows, Sinclair's scent tickling at her nose. "Thanks, Jono."

"You're welcome," he said in the dark.

She dropped into sleep again.

19
CHAPTER

LAURA HAD BEEN around Washington long enough to remember when she could walk in the front door of the FBI building without an appointment. Security had tightened over the last decade, and the building was closed to the public. The Bureau no longer offered tours, and nonstaff visitors were invitation-only. Her driver looped around the block, waiting for a space to open in the drop-off zone.

She retrieved the dossier on Sanchez from her briefcase. Terryn had collected scant information. Whatever Sanchez was involved in, even the InterSec back channels couldn't pick up on it. That meant his mission was compartmentalized, records would be limited, and few inside the Bureau would have direct knowledge. That also meant it was a sensitive mission that the FBI wanted to move on carefully.

Her mind wandered to Sinclair and the morning. She awoke before he did and jumped in the shower. When she came out of the bathroom, he had coffee ready. They spoke little, bumping into each other in doorways as they passed between the rooms in the small apartment. An awkwardness marked their movements, as if they had done more than sleep. Neither mentioned Laura's nightmare or the moment after it that was oddly more intimate than sex. As Sinclair went out the door, she warned him to stick to main streets and not take shortcuts. InterSec would be watching in case someone decided to stage another accident for him. He leaned down to kiss her but darted back with a smirk before making contact. She glared at him all the way to the car, and he returned her look with a mock-innocent expression.

Sinclair's manner intrigued and confused her. He made his blatant come-ons with an obvious awareness that she wouldn't react to them, at least not react positively. He made no secret that his attraction to her was genuine, yet he continued the antics. Maybe he thinks he'll wear me down, she thought. Maybe after we figure out what was going on at the drug lab, and we manage to live through it, I might let him buy me dinner, but not now. She laughed. Given that she was considering seeing him under these circumstances, maybe he knew exactly what he was doing.

The black car pulled to the curb. Laura thanked the driver and stepped out. She ran a quick check of the Mariel glamour, making sure her outfit clung snugly in all the right places. Walking the half block to the building entrance, she displayed her ID badge on its lanyard. From experience, she knew that the military police who patrolled the outside perimeter were not shy.

Despite the lack of public access, the lobby bustled with people. The Bureau was a huge, sprawling entity with thousands of employees, even more investigations and research projects, as well as being actively involved in programs with other government groups. Except InterSec. They gave some token support, but integration with a security group that included foreign nationals did not sit well with them.

She queued through the first layer of metal detectors, pretending not to notice the sideways glances from men. A wall of bulletproof glass blocked the main hallway, and she waited with others to be photographed and demonstrate that she was approved for entrance. Once through, a guard escorted her to the elevators. While the Bureau didn't love InterSec, they honored her security status and left her alone at that point. Nonsecurity staff were escorted for their entire visit.

Lawrence Scales waited outside his office. He didn't outrank Mariel Tate, but she had cultivated a formidable reputation for courtesy and expected it to be returned. Not a few people tested her patience and found themselves waiting a long time to speak with her, if they managed to get an appointment at all. It was all part of the D.C. game.

Laura held out her hand, automatically imprinting his body signature into her memory. It was an old habit that served her well. "Section Chief Scales, I'm Mariel Tate."

"Pleased to meet you, ma'am. You're early." He ushered her into his office with cool professionalism. The stark, utilitarian room had few personal touches that did not relate to work with the exception of a small framed photograph of a woman and two children that graced his desk. The kids looked like him. Laura did not wait to be offered the guest chair but made herself comfortable.

She slipped her briefcase to the floor. "I thought I'd be longer getting through security, so I padded my schedule."

Scales took his own seat behind the desk. "I'm not sure why your office requested this meeting."

Mariel folded her hands in her lap. She knew he was lying by the tone of his voice. Anxiety fluttered from him when she turned her deep gaze on him. "A D.C. SWAT-team officer named Gabrio Sanchez was killed five days ago. An InterSec agent with him was almost killed, and another attempt has been made on her life since then as well as an attempt on another police officer. It is our understanding that Sanchez was working an undercover operation for the FBI."

He gave her a false, professional smile. "That's where my confusion comes in. No one by that name works here."

Not by the name of Sanchez anyway, Laura thought. That a lie could be the truth amused her. She knew Terryn had made the same claims about her personas on more than one occasion. "We have an agent who is being targeted, Chief Scales. If InterSec opens its own investigation, we will eventually stumble into each other. I would prefer that our agent not die in the meantime."

Scales nodded, his manner sympathetic, yet resistant. "I

understand your concerns. I would feel the same way. As of now, I can only say your information is mistaken and that I can have someone look into clarifying the situation for you."

Laura let her body essence seep out, not enough for a physical manifestation, but enough for Scales to feel a change in the air. A mild static would tickle along his arms and legs, maybe the back of his scalp. It was an old druid trick to tease out anxiety, and one that worked particularly well with humans. "Chief Scales, I cannot stress enough the interest in this case. If there is anything you can tell me off the record to assist in protecting our agent, I would appreciate it."

His gaze slipped away as he tidied things on his desk, moving a stapler, then some pencils. "If I were to conjecture, maybe this Sanchez—if he were an agent—might have exposed something unexpected. I imagine it would be fairly high-level. Perhaps he even had names."

Laura nodded. "Assuming he was an agent, do you think he would have reported those names?"

Scales nodded. "As part of his duties, of course. He might have already provided one, and the night he died, he might have thought he would provide more."

"I see." She did. Scales headed Counterterrorism. Even a low-level case for him was off the charts for other agencies. If someone took out Sanchez to keep him silent, Janice Crawford would not be left alone if that same someone thought she knew something. Scales effectively told her that Janice Crawford was in grave danger. She shifted in the chair, boosting the essence in the room. "I imagine the FBI would be keen to keep any information confidential until they sort things out themselves."

"It's quite possible," said Scales. Probable, thought Laura. The message from him was clear. He couldn't and wouldn't say anything that might jeopardize their investigation. Which meant the Bureau was going to stonewall at the drug-den site. They weren't going to share because Janice Crawford was not important enough and not their immediate problem.

Laura stood, keeping her face cordial. "Thank you for your time, Chief Scales. Unfortunately, I may have to pursue this through higher channels."

He rose and shook her hand. "Understandable, Agent Tate. Please keep in touch."

He walked with her to the door. "Have you ever been to the Vault?" His voice changed, shifting to a more relaxed tone to indicate they had moved to more social conversation.

"The club?" she asked.

He nodded. "Yes. I recommend it. A surprising number of politicians enjoy the place. You might say the names that go through the door are very interesting."

She smiled to indicate she understood what he meant. He wasn't going to tell her what he knew, but he was giving her a lead. "Perhaps we will run into each other there."

Amusement danced in his eyes. "It's a small town, Agent. You never know who you will run into."

She kept her pace steady as she walked down the hallway. The stonewalling didn't bother her. It had happened before and would happen again. She already suspected something was going on with the Vault, but Scales's hint of a political connection gave the situation a different spin.

Her sensing ability flickered as a shimmer of essence passed over her. She hesitated at the elevator. Someone was casting a spell, a damned large one, big enough to cause a wave front. Her skin prickled.

Back up the hall, a young man left Scales's office and made his way to the floor exit at the far end. On his heels, Scales appeared at his office door with a box in his hands and a confused look on his face as he watched the retreating figure. As he turned back, he noticed her, nodded, and retreated into his office.

Something wasn't right. The FBI didn't have any fey on their teams. They didn't *like* the fey on their teams. The president and Congress had determined it was a national-security issue to have nonhumans in the Bureau. Either she'd sensed something she wasn't supposed to, or something was wrong. She decided not to let it go and walked back toward Scales's office.

The essence intensified, and her body shield slammed on. Another wave front swept over her, strong enough to produce a hazy white light against her shield. She stumbled within it, surprised by its force.

The hallway exploded. A roaring sound filled her ears as plaster and wood and concrete showered down and hot black smoke billowed around her. She heard a high-pitched hiss as the sprinkler system sprang to life, cold water mixing in with the smoke and dust.

Coughing, she steadied herself against the wall. Smoke and water filled the air. Debris crowded her legs to the knees, but her body shield prevented them from being crushed. She grabbed a doorjamb and pulled out one leg at a time. The smoke thickened. She doubled over, coughing to clear her lungs. With a short-focused spell, she altered her body shield around her mouth—a simple cantrip to filter essence away from her, but it helped keep some smoke out of her lungs, too.

The smoke had an acrid, burning odor. She heard a deep hissing crackle. Fire. The building was on fire. Behind her, the elevator doors were bent inward, obviously jamming the car. More debris blocked the office doors around her. In the opposite direction, bursts of cooler air tangled with the heat.

"Scales?" she yelled. No answer. She called up his body signature in her inner vision and threw out a sending. *Scales, it's Tate. Shout if you can hear me.* No answer. Laura kicked off her heels. Using the body shield to protect her feet as best she could, she moved in a crouch down the hall, avoiding the thicker smoke along the ceiling.

The smoke brightened with an ominous orange glow. The temperature increased, and the roar and crackle of fire filled the air. Wind buffeted the smoke, and flashes of daylight pierced the darkness. Even through the body shield, the heat pressed against her like a physical thing.

Scales? she sent again. Her limited range prevented her

from directly sensing his body signature. He couldn't return the sending, but she hoped he would at least call out. She hoped. Depending on where he was when the spell bomb blew, he could be either dead or unconscious.

She neared where she thought his office was. Her body shield rippled as it interacted with a sharp stroke of essence. Laura reached into the smoke and encountered something metallic. And hot. She jerked her hand back, feeling the fingertips blistering.

Calling up a ball of essence, she pushed the smoke away for a moment. It receded, and a piece of metal embedded in the wall became visible. The smoke coiled forward and hid it from view again. She closed her eyes against the stinging air and used her sensing ability to see. The metal radiated essence in her mind, a dark shape burning with a cool green light on the edges.

Fire engulfed the remains of Scales's office. Flames shot outside the building through a gaping hole where his windows used to be. She sensed no living essence. Moving closer, the heat seared against her skin even through the body shield.

"Scales?" she shouted. As she stumbled in the rubble, she spotted two legs protruding from a pile of plaster and wood. Not far off, an arm jutted up. Not far, but too far away from the legs. She sensed nothing. Scales was dead. Superheated air started overwhelming her body shield. She backed out of the room, avoiding the slick fluid gushing from the ceiling and saturating everything.

Scattered metal vibrated around her with green essence. Metal conducted essence but didn't have any appreciable essence of its own. She picked up a piece and touched a tentative finger to a small chunk the size of her palm. It was cool enough to hold and had essence radiating from it.

A wave of dizziness hit her. The fire was eating the oxygen out of the air. She closed her eyes again to concentrate, sensed the vague shape of an opening, and climbed her way toward it. Wind pressed against her back, funneling the smoke ahead of her. She reached a point where the floor became clear of debris. She ran. A fire exit came into sight.

She hit the emergency release bar and staggered into a crowded stairwell. Hands grabbed her as she fell. The door was kicked shut.

"Keep moving!" someone shouted. Several more hands steadied her on her feet as a crush of people pushed down the stairs. Wracked with coughing, she forced herself to move with them. As they descended, the hazy air lightened and became cooler. Bright white light shone below. Laura turned at a landing, and a door to the outside stood open. In a wave of bodies, she stumbled out onto a sidewalk in blinding sunlight.

She wandered into the street. Smoke and fire shot through a hole in the side of the building. Fire trucks and emergency vehicles choked the street. She moved to the opposite sidewalk and scanned the crowd around her. People moved all around her, civilians running from the building or emergency personnel running in.

A cell phone rang. She looked down at her side, too stunned to laugh. Without thinking about it, she had walked through the chaos without losing her handbag. She opened it, dropped the chunk of metal inside, and retrieved the phone.

"I'm fine," she said as she connected.

"Thanks be," said Cress. "Get back here as quickly as you can. The city's under attack."

20
CHAPTER

SHE NEARLY COLLIDED with Cress as she came through the door to InterSec. "What the hell is happening?" Laura asked.

They hurried down the corridor. "Three bombs have gone off in the city," said Cress. "Targets hit are the FBI building and the Guildhouse. A car bomb heading for the White House blew up at the gatehouse."

At the end of the corridor, they swept into the InterSec situation room. Terryn sat on the long side of a table facing several monitors. Newsfeeds from across the city lit the wall. One monitor showed smoke billowing out of the FBI building. The outside wall of the building was scorched, and several windows were broken, but otherwise the damage looked minimal. The fire trucks on the scene seemed to have everything under control.

"Are you okay?" Terryn said.

Laura nodded. "Scales is dead. I was leaving his office when a bomb went off."

"The gods were with you," Cress said softly.

Guildhouse security feeds filled a second series of monitors. A car burned next to a shimmering white wall of essence in the alley behind the building. News channels showed distance shots of the entire building. Behind its large, activated essence barrier, the Guildhouse was undamaged.

Laura placed her handbag on the table and opened it. She pulled out the chunk of metal. "We need to get this analyzed. It's a piece of metal from the bomb, with some kind of spell on it."

Cress stepped back and activated her body shield.

"Sorry, I wasn't thinking," said Laura.

"It's fine," she said. Absorbing essence enabled *leanansidhe* to survive, but it also exposed them to potential attacks through manipulated essence. With her body shield protecting her, Cress held up the metal fragment. She half closed her eyes as she sniffed at it, her lips and nostrils trembling. "It feels like a shield. I do not sense an active spell but the shadow of some kind of trigger spell."

Terryn took the metal from her. As his own precaution, he protected his hands with a warding barrier of hard blue light. "The material is hardened with essence. The spell increased its density. We used to do this with projectiles."

Rocks, Laura thought. Terryn was talking about rocks flung from catapults or something similar. She worked with a man who made connections between a modern bomb and an ancient weapon. His nonchalant references to his age and history disconcerted her at times. He handed the metal piece back to Cress. "Dispatch agents to the crash sites in case there are delayed or untriggered spells in the debris."

Cress held the metal chunk with a cupped hand as she left the room. "I'll take this to Forensics for a deep probe."

Laura stared at the monitors. The bottom row ran incoming updates from local, national, and international news. A screen banner caught her eye. Several street-level news crews were picking up house fires in a residential section of Anacostia. The scene looked more chaotic with civilians present. She pointed. "What's that?"

Terryn pulled the channel onto a larger monitor. "House fire."

Laura stared at the screen. A simple three-story was entirely consumed in flames. Secondary fires were burning on the houses next door. "That's a big house fire. When did it start?"

Terryn checked the computer screen that lit up the table-top, then raised an eyebrow. "Within minutes of the bombs. Wait a moment . . ." He tapped the keyboard of his laptop and monitors shifted to an internal computer directory. He opened a document. "I thought so. This is from the SWAT-team files we were able to get before the information flow stopped. Check out the address of one of the informants for the raid."

Laura read quickly through the form on the screen. "The house in the middle happens to be the home of Gianni's informant. Scales happened to be the director in charge of an undercover operation investigating the SWAT team. Both targets were softer than the other two. It's almost pointless to go after the White House or the Guildhouse with small bombs. They were a smoke screen to draw attention away from these two."

Laura slid into a chair. She let Terryn's theory sink in. A chill ran over her. "Mariel Tate was a target, too."

"How so?" Terryn asked. Laura was always impressed that nothing surprised or struck him as bizarre.

"I was early. The meeting was short. I left Scales's office about when the meeting was originally scheduled. I saw the bomb delivered," she said.

"That could be a very lucky coincidence," he said.

Laura shook her head. "I think I triggered it, Terryn. I sensed a strange essence field in the hall. When I went toward Scales to tell him, the bomb blew."

"No one knew you were there," he said.

"Scales did. Someone knew his schedule."

"Did you get anything from him?"

She shook her head. "Scales implied there is a political angle to what was going on at the raid. That's never a good sign for internal security."

"Did you get any names?"

"He went secret on me, so I couldn't get details. He made sure to mention that I should visit the Vault."

Terryn arched an eyebrow. "We've updated Tylo Blume's

dossier since your visit. I'll look a little deeper into his political connections."

Laura's gaze wandered back to the monitors. "Is Foyle's team at the Anacostia crash site?"

Terryn checked something on his laptop. "They went in with the first responders. They needed a spell senser, and Foyle asked for you. I told him I'd put Janice Crawford on sick leave."

Laura gathered up her handbag. "I'm going out there. If Sinclair ends up alone with Gianni, that might not be a good thing."

Terryn pursed his lips. "Are personal feelings clouding your judgment?"

Laura paused at the door. "What is that supposed to mean?"

Terryn gazed at her. "I don't see a rational basis to trust him. Maybe we need to retire Janice Crawford."

She didn't say anything for a moment. It would be a relief to retire Janice. Working one glamour persona was tough enough to balance against her Guild responsibilities—to say nothing of making time for assignments from InterSec. But Janice was her in with the SWAT squad. Mariel Tate would only hear what they wanted her to hear, but in the downtime in the bull pen, Janice was likely to hear a different story. "Not yet, Terryn. We need her. As long as I'm with Sinclair, he's not acting on his own. If he's exposed me, now would be the time to find out."

Terryn returned his attention to the monitors. "I never like to put you in jeopardy, but I have to agree. Be careful."

"Call Saffin for me and get her away from her desk," she said. Retracing her steps down the hall, she pulled her essence out of the perfect stone and the Mariel persona slipped off in a sweep of cool static. Beneath the glamour she wore jeans and a T-shirt. With soot in her hair and on her face, she looked a bit mad in her bare feet. The idea amused her. She felt a bit mad.

By the time she reached the public-relations department, Saffin was gone from her desk. Laura hurried into her office and through the closet to her private room. Without pause, she pulled on her regulation SWAT-team boots, the flak jacket and helmet over her jeans and T-shirt. She didn't want to waste time dressing. Activating the Janice glamour completed the rest of the uniform. When she hit the parking garage, she jumped in the SUV and tore up the exit ramp, with a metal band blasting from the stereo.

21
CHAPTER

WITH THICK CLOUDS of smoke billowing in the air, Laura didn't need directions to the house fire in Anacostia. She parked her second SUV of the week in the middle of a road blocked by police cars and fire vehicles. She jogged up the street, weaving in and out of emergency support trucks until she reached the site.

Houses on three adjacent properties were on fire, the center one completely engulfed by flames, its upper floor and roof missing. They had blown off, not collapsed, evidence of more than a simple house fire. At either end of the block, local police kept neighbors and bystanders back. In contrast to what she had seen outside the FBI building, no one was panicked, security wasn't running roughshod over anyone, and the professional responders were treating the fire as they normally would.

She spotted the SWAT-team van on the far end of the street, then Foyle as he came around a police car. He had a wary look about him, professional anger. "Are you sure you should be out of bed, Crawford?"

"I'm fine, sir. I heard you needed a spell senser, and I volunteered."

Foyle didn't answer. Laura hid her curiosity behind Janice's look of discomfort. She nodded up the street to the fire watchers. "These people don't look too upset."

Foyle surveyed them with indifference. "No one's going to cry for the guy who lives here. They're probably better off without him."

The two of them were alone except for a communications tech in the open van. "He was trouble?" she asked.

Foyle gave one curt nod. "A dealer. We knew him."

And didn't do anything about the drug dealing because he was supplying you with information, she thought. False information. No one was going to be crying about him at the station house either. "Was he inside when the bomb went off?"

Foyle narrowed his eyes at her. "What bomb?"

Janice shrugged. "I just assumed with the roof missing and what's going on in the city . . ."

He shook his head. "There was an explosion, but I wouldn't call it a bomb. Probably a meth lab or something. Neighbors said they saw him go in before the house went up. We won't know for a while."

Laura watched the roaring flames and thick smoke. She didn't need her sensing ability to find survivors. Nothing short of a miracle could enable a person to live through the intensity of the flames. Neighbors were a better source of information anyway. In the immediate aftermath of any drama, people were too excited to keep quiet. If they saw the informant go in the house, he was in the house. And dead. Besides, whoever managed to pinpoint an attack on an office in a federal building would not be sloppy enough to miss the dealer.

Laura prodded Foyle. "InterSec said you needed a spell senser."

"Yeah. Are you sensing anything?" he asked.

Anger, she thought. Something was irritating him, but she didn't think it was her. "Nothing from here. I'd have to get closer, but it doesn't look like a good idea yet."

"Sinclair is securing the rear of the building. Check in with him," said Foyle. He climbed into the van. Laura stared at his back for a moment. If Sinclair had told him who she was, it might explain Foyle's abruptness. But he had been that way with her from the beginning of the mission, before Sinclair figured out her glamours. Whatever he was thinking, it wasn't making him happy.

She threaded her way through more cars and into the yard of the first house next to the fire. Halfway down the driveway, the backyard came into view, open to the next block. She cut through it to find more police and another fire truck in case fire blew in that direction.

Sinclair walked behind her on the edge of her sensing range. She kept moving, making a show of searching for him. He paced her, tracking the edges of her body signature. Whether he did it out of habit or was demonstrating that he could do it, she couldn't tell. He moved closer. She ignored him, letting his field overlap hers, testing whether his ability merely reacted to others around him or if he had to get some reaction.

"Who were you today?" he asked.

She glanced over her shoulder. "Excuse me?"

He smirked. "Shift's almost over, and you didn't report in."

She rolled her eyes, but smiled. "Yeah, well, Foyle's not the only one on my ass. InterSec has been picking apart my report all day."

"Am I supposed to play this game, too?" he asked.

She frowned. "What game?"

"The Janice Crawford, SWAT-team officer, game." She tapped at her headset. He exhaled sharply through his nose. "Do you think I'm stupid? Of course, I wouldn't talk with my channel open."

She stared at the burning house. "I'm careful, Sinclair."

He grinned. "I am, too. And you can call me Jono."

"Thanks. You can call me Officer Crawford."

He chuckled and jerked his head at the nearest burning house. "We need to shift positions. You're with me."

Despite having his weapon ready, he walked with a casual gait to a fence between the burning houses. They crouched and checked their sight lines.

"This looks like a bomb, like the ones downtown," she said.

He glanced at her sideways. "Is that what InterSec thinks?"

She focused on a house across the street where someone watched the fire from an upper floor. "CNN, actually. They noticed the flames."

"Well, that works in their favor," he said.

"Whose favor?"

"Whoever intended to blow the house. You know who lived there, don't you?" Sinclair asked.

She nodded. "That's why I came down. Foyle wants me to go in and check for spell bombs."

Sinclair peered over the hood of the car. "And you'll find one."

She gave him a sharp look. "How the hell do you know that?"

Sinclair ignored her, still scanning the area. "Foyle already had a spell senser come in. He made up an excuse to keep everyone away from the back of the buildings. I was in the tech bus. I guess they didn't know one of the video feeds was already set up. An Inverni fairy went in. I went outside and stood close enough to the house when he came out. He hid his face, but I've seen the shape before at the Vault. Alfie, I think is his name. Nasty personality."

Laura kept her eyes on the fire and not Sinclair. Alfrey, not Alfie, she thought. As far as she knew, InterSec and Foyle were the only people who knew about the Inverni. No one else knew he had been identified. She decided to keep it that way, and stayed silent about "Alfie's" real name.

"I'm willing to bet if there's a bomb in there, Alfie planted it. If they want you to go in there, someone wants you dead . . . Officer Crawford," he said.

She smiled grimly. "Guess who's my backup going in . . . Jono?"

He met Laura's eyes with a flat stare. "I don't think I want to work with you anymore."

She shrugged. "And this is just the day job. Wait until we throw you some freelance work."

He shifted on his haunches. "Looks like they've knocked the fire back."

She shielded her eyes against the sun. The two side houses were no longer burning. Gray smoke billowed from the middle one, but no flames were visible. Without another word, Laura ran across the backyard to the burning house. The smoke lightened, steam mixing in with it as the fire trucks continued to shower water. Faint wisps of smoke came out the back windows. She dodged inside a door that led to a kitchen, out of sight from the rest of the SWAT-team members and other police. Sinclair took up position at the entrance.

"I'm on the first floor. All clear," she radioed for everyone to hear.

There's an essence anomaly up ahead. It's our trap, she sent to Sinclair.

"Check. Following into position," Sinclair radioed. He joined her in the kitchen and signaled Laura to cut her radio. "What's the plan?"

"It's probably set to explode when it feels a body signature near it. I'm going to set a spell that should trigger the trap. I'll put a delay on it. Then you're going to save me from a medical emergency. Are you good with that?"

He nodded. "Where do you want me?"

"Right here. Don't move. The timing's going to be important," she said.

"Got it," he said.

She clicked her headset on. "Come again, Sinclair. I lost you."

He turned on his headset. "Sinclair, here. I think there's some interference. Reading you now."

She moved deeper into the house. "I'm in a hall. I see a staircase. Still clear."

The trap is in the middle of the staircase. It definitely has an essence trigger. When my field touches it, it's going to go off, she sent.

"Coming in behind you," Sinclair said.

"Negative. Hold position until I clear the stairs," she radioed back.

Laura turned off her headset again. She cupped her hands and drew on her own body essence. Faint amber light welled up from her skin. It coalesced into a bright ball of orange light that hovered in the air. She tethered it to the essence of one hand and used the other hand to inscribe Celtic runes in the air. They glowed white as they danced around the amber ball and melted into it.

I'll be right back, she sent to Sinclair.

She moved down the short hallway into more smoke and heat. At the staircase, she released the tether on the spell. The ball of light hung suspended at the bottom of the staircase. As she backed away, the activation delay initiated.

Dropping her body shield, she took a tentative breath. Acrid air burned the back of her throat. She said a short prayer, surprising herself. She still believed in honoring the Moon and the Lady, but had lapsed from real prayer long ago. She inhaled deeply and doubled over coughing. Tears sprang into her eyes, and her nose ran freely. She slapped on her headset and coughed loudly over the link. "Crawford 88. Repeat, 88." She didn't have to pretend that speaking was difficult as she transmitted the distress code.

"Crawford? Where are you?" Sinclair radioed.

She staggered to the kitchen. Sinclair stood silhouetted against the bright light of the open back door. She paused, as a memory bubbled up. A figure in SWAT-team gear surrounded by swirling smoke at the doorway in the warehouse. She tried to focus on his body, resolve the silhouette into someone she knew. The shadowed figure in her mind raised his gun, and the memory faded.

Sinclair rushed through the thinner smoke of the kitchen. She let him drape her arm around his shoulder. The air trembled and shuddered as Laura's spell released up the hall, a short burst of her body essence expanding in a sphere. It touched the spell trap, and white light flashed as Sinclair yelled for a medic. He half carried, half supported Laura through the door as the staircase exploded. The force of the blast lifted them into the air, and they sprawled into the yard with debris raining down on them.

Laura landed roughly on her side, but her body shield

absorbed the impact. She curled to her knees as coughing wracked her body again. The one inhalation had been enough for appearance sake. Oily soot smeared across her upper lip as she wiped at her running nose. Sinclair lay facedown about ten feet away.

You okay, Jono? she sent.

He stirred as her words touched his mind, raising himself to his knees. They faced each other in the same position, their faces covered with soot and scratches.

Okay, he sent back.

Emergency personnel rushed into the yard. Someone slapped an oxygen mask over Laura's face. Two EMTs lifted her, one on either side, and carried her to the front of the house. In seconds, she was in an emergency van.

Foyle appeared. "Are you okay, Crawford?"

She nodded, letting the mask speak for itself. She watched Sinclair being led to another van behind Foyle. She pulled the mask down. "Too much smoke. I burned out my sensing ability."

"Why the hell didn't you use your mask?" Foyle said.

He confused her again. His concern was genuine. "I thought my body shield was good enough. I'm sorry."

"Can you go back in?" Foyle asked.

She made a show of taking another hit of oxygen. "I'm sorry. You'll have to get someone else."

Over Foyle's shoulder, Sinclair caught her eye. He nodded, impressed. Foyle was buying it. He believed she was overcome with smoke inhalation. She allowed herself a small inward smile. If there was one thing she was good at, it was appearances.

22
CHAPTER

CRESS PEERED INTO Laura's mouth. The *leanan-sidhe*'s dark orbs shifted back and forth, her unique vision affording her more than simple sight. She didn't need a flashlight.

Glass cases lined a wall of her office, jars and canisters filling every available space. Protection wards hummed at various levels of intensity, warding against herbs and spells interacting or activating. As a fey healer, she combined traditional medicine with the esoteric needs of the fey. She dropped her hand from Laura's chin and rested it on her shoulder. "There's some mild inflammation, but no essence implications. You're fine."

"That was risky," said Terryn.

Laura let Cress lift her hair to examine the faint remains of the concussion bruise. The physical aspect of the injury had healed so quickly that Laura had not thought about it for a day or two. "I was careful," she said.

Terryn leaned against the open door. "You're pushing yourself too hard. You forget you're not immortal sometimes."

Laura dangled her feet off the short examining table.

There was no denying she was tired, and Terryn wouldn't believe her if she said she wasn't. You don't get almost blown up by a bomb, escape from one burning building then run into another one without getting winded. He was right. As a druid, she had a stronger constitution than humans, but it didn't come close to the strength of other fey. She didn't bother hiding the exhaustion in her voice. "I didn't ask for this, Terryn."

"I want to sideline Janice. You don't have to do two glamours," he said.

She hopped off the table. "You mean three. Just because I don't change my appearance as Laura Blackstone doesn't mean it isn't a job. I still have the Archives ceremony to work on. At least no one's trying to kill me there."

Terryn shook his head. "That doesn't help your case, you know. Let Sinclair prove himself. Put him to work with Foyle instead of Janice."

She rubbed her eyes. The tender skin felt raw and dry. "Okay."

He didn't try to hide the surprise on his face. "Okay? That was easy."

She gave him a lopsided smile. "Because you're right. I'm stretching myself thin. If I lose my edge, I start missing things. We put Crawford on sick leave and Sinclair on Foyle. That will free up time for me to work on Blume."

Cress paused at her work space. "You need to rest, Laura. The physical aspect of the concussion is healed, but your body essence is working at near capacity to heal the rest."

"I'll deal with Blume in the evening. I can swing that. I don't sleep much anyway," she replied.

Cress stared with those inscrutable black pools she called eyes. She glanced at Terryn, and Laura felt the light flutter of a sending pass between them. They were worried about her. It was comforting—she was worried about herself—but she had continued working with worse injuries before.

"Have you remembered anything more?" Cress asked.

"Nothing helpful. You were right, though. It's coming back," Laura said.

Cress nodded. She picked up two sealed jars from the counter. She held up one with a thick solution in it, vibrant green. "Drink this when you get home. It'll fortify your body essence and soothe the throat burn." She handed Laura a smaller, opaque jar. "You have burn patches that aren't much worse than a sunburn, but they're still draining essence from you. Draw a bath when you get home and dissolve this in it. Your skin will heal faster."

Laura held both jars, thinking she'd rather eat the paste than drink the vibrant green sludge. "You're ordering me to take a bath?"

Cress smiled. "Exactly. You'll smell better, too."

Laura slipped the jars into her bag. "I have had a couple of stinky days."

"Can we talk about Blume before you leave?" asked Terryn.

Cress pushed Laura toward the door. "No, she can't. She needs to go home and take a bath and go to bed. Now."

Laura made a show of resisting, but it was obvious she wanted to leave. She stopped by her InterSec office to pick up the rest of her things and took the elevator down to the garage as Laura Blackstone, working-late public-relations director. If Cress was so concerned about her comfort and health, the least Laura could do was drive her Mercedes home.

Realization hit her when she started the car. She couldn't go home. She rested her head against the steering wheel listening to music, trying to drown out thoughts of anything else. At the end of the third song, she turned off the car and went back to the elevator lobby. In the blind spot of the security camera, she resumed the Crawford glamour.

She jumped in the SUV. Cress might have thought it best that Laura go home, but Janice still existed and now had the seeds of a private life. Under the circumstances, Janice couldn't disappear for no established reason. Someone would notice. Whoever wanted her dead would notice and find it curious. Inspiring curiosity was something Laura avoided when it came to her glamours. It was how she had gotten into her newest persona tangle. She pulled out of the garage and drove to Sinclair's apartment.

23
CHAPTER

SINCLAIR OPENED THE door the moment she knocked, his relief obvious. "I've been waiting to hear from you. Everything okay?"

Her first reaction was irritation. She barely answered to Terryn, never mind Sinclair. But she quickly bit back a barbed comment. His concern was genuine. She wasn't used to that from someone she barely knew. Terryn and Cress often expressed concern for her welfare, but it always felt professional, never intimate. Emotional expression was something she avoided. She dropped her duffel on the floor by the door. "Sorry. I had an errand. You should give me a spare key."

He stepped back, as if embarrassed by his concern, and she regretted not being as responsive. He glanced pointedly at the listening ward on the bookshelf. "Isn't that rushing things a bit?"

She closed her eyes and examined the essence on the obelisk to confirm that the dampening field remained active. "It's okay, Jono. The obelisk is jamming. We can talk freely."

He looked innocent. "Oh. I was."

She fished in her bag for the two jars from Cress. "You

never let up, do you? Even if I was interested, I don't date colleagues."

"You went out with me for drinks twice already," he said.

Laura put the jars on the coffee table and dropped into the armchair. "That was work."

He grunted. "Really? I didn't notice you breaking a sweat."

She chuckled. "Speaking of drinks, do you have any vodka? I need to drink this thing from Cress, and I have a feeling I'm going to need a chaser."

"Sure. Are you hungry? I can throw something in the microwave," he asked.

She unscrewed the lid to the jar with the vibrant green liquid. "Not yet, thanks. I'm tired and need to take a bath."

Sinclair wandered into the kitchen. Jeans and tight T-shirts must be his civilian uniform. Not that I'm complaining, she thought.

As she leaned forward to examine the open jar, she heard the bathwater go on. She sniffed the liquid and decided it might be palatable. Cress made an effort to make her potions inoffensive. Laura sipped it. Not bad, a bit grassy with some mint and menthol. Taking a deep breath, she downed it. It went down thick and slow, but it went down. She smacked her lips at the pasty aftertaste.

Sinclair returned with a beer for himself, handed her a mixed drink. He slid a key across the coffee table. Laura pocketed it without a word and nodded at her glass. "I put some lemonade in it," he said.

She leaned back in the chair. "Thanks. How are you? Do you need Cress to do anything?"

He sat sideways, dangling his legs over the arm of the other armchair. "I've taken harder falls. I think I'll pass on any more healing."

She sipped her drink. The alcohol spread across her tongue, washing away whatever was making the sticky sensation in her mouth. "Why? Cress is an excellent healer."

He exaggerated a shiver. "I appreciate that she took care of my ribs, but when she did it, I felt this sort of desire from her. Like a hunger. No offense if she's a friend, but I thought it was creepy."

"She's a *leanansidhe*."

His eyebrows shot up. "Really? I thought they were dangerous."

Laura didn't want to admit her own occasional discomfort with Cress. "They are. Not Cress, though. She has her . . . needs under control."

He took a swig of beer. "Hmm. Yeah, that sounds convincing." He nudged the unopened jar on the table. "What's this?"

"For the bath. Some kind of healing agent."

He picked it up. "I'll drop it in. Finish your drink."

He was out of the chair before she could protest. It was a nice gesture, she decided, and she was too tired to make an issue of it. She retrieved her duffel and pulled out her overnight tote bag, a pair of sweatpants, and a T-shirt. One night of sleeping in her clothes was enough. She bumped into Sinclair at the door to the bathroom.

"All yours," he said, and moved away quickly.

Bubbles filled the tub. Thick towels sat on a wicker hamper, and three lit candles gave a warm glow to the room. She smiled toward the living room. Only Sinclair's bare feet were visible, propped over the end of the couch.

She closed the bathroom door and stripped out of her clothes. They fell to the floor in a rank heap. As she slipped into the hot water, she groaned with pleasure. Cress was right. It had been a long, smelly day.

Sinclair knocked on the door. "Are you under the bubbles?"

She leaned her head back. "Yes. Thank you. Could you call me in thirty minutes in case I fall asleep?"

Sinclair opened the door.

Surprised, Laura ducked deeper into the water. "What do you think you're doing?"

He had his beer in one hand and her drink in the other. He set hers on the edge of the tub. Closing the lid on the toilet, he sat and propped his feet on the hamper. "You forgot your drink. I freshened it for you."

Surrounded by bubbles, hot water, glowing candles, and a strong drink, she decided to be polite instead of annoyed. "You didn't have to do that."

He gulped some beer. "I wanted to. You saved my life today. I made you a bubble bath. Seems fair."

She chuckled and lifted her drink. "You did warn me about the spell bomb."

"Is it me, or was that a crazy stunt you pulled at the fire?"

She tilted her head forward and sipped, being careful not to dislodge any bubbles. "A little. Terryn wasn't too happy about it. Sometimes you have to take risks to keep your cover."

"You didn't say anything to me at the drug raid, you know," he said. Truth resonated in his words.

"That's too bad for both of us. I can't remember if Sanchez said anything, and someone tried to run you off the road for nothing."

He smiled around the lip of the bottle. "Well, I did get to meet you."

She let her head drop back against the tub again. "You seem fixated on me. You know that, don't you?"

He shrugged. "I like your vibe. I don't feel that often."

"I have a vibe?"

"Your essence," he said. "Sometimes essence shapes feel right to me. When I meet someone I also think is good-looking, it's a combination that's hard to resist."

She gave him a sly smile. "What if I were a guy?"

"Then I'd ask you to go bowling," he said without missing a beat.

She laughed. "You do *not* bowl."

He chuckled. "And you're not a guy."

She arched an eyebrow. "You're sure about that?"

He drained his beer. "If you were a guy, you wouldn't have been tugging at your tight flak jacket in the van the night of the mission. Even with a glamour."

She flicked soap bubbles at him. "I knew you were staring!"

He flinched and grinned. "So sue me."

She settled back again. "What's with all the candles?"

His forehead creased. "What? Don't you like them?"

She shifted in the water, then darted her eyes to the bubbles to make sure she was covered. "It's not a guy thing, in my experience."

His eyebrows went up. "You have a lot of experience with fire giants?"

Laura debated whether to be afraid he was about to announce an ability she wasn't prepared for. "You have a fire ability?"

He took another swallow of beer. "I wish. They're for meditation and prayer."

"Prayer! You're devout?"

He slowly shook his head. "I am not about to debate jotunn theology with a Celtic druidess."

She allowed herself a snicker. "Oh, right. Fire and water."

Silence filled the room. Sinclair sat with an amused expression as he toyed with his beer bottle. She closed her eyes. "Thanks for the drink. I'll be out in a bit."

Sinclair didn't move right away, and she wondered if he were going to push the situation. Instead, she heard the hamper creak as he removed his feet, then the bathroom door close softly.

The water and Cress's concoction soothed her tired muscles. She wondered how many more layers there were to Sinclair. She liked his look and his manner. Even his constant flirting had its appeal. He seemed almost too good to be real. Which is why you shouldn't trust him, she thought. If she were working for Blume or Alfrey or whoever, she would do the same thing—seduce, subvert, and deceive. No, despite her attraction, Jonathan Sinclair had to remain at arms length until she knew his full story.

When she stepped out of the bathroom in her sweats and T-shirt, Sinclair was working at his laptop in the study area. He glanced at her in a distracted way, then returned to his screen. She carried her filthy clothes into the living room and stuffed them in the duffel bag. In an inside pocket of the duffel, she tucked the spell-secured case that contained her perfect stone with the Mariel glamour. She wore the stone for the Janice glamour in case she needed to activate it on a moment's notice.

Clean and relaxed, she finally felt hungry. She went into the kitchen and opened the refrigerator. Despite cluttered shelves, she didn't see anything to eat as an actual meal. She checked the freezer and found two frozen dinners. "Are you hungry?" she called out.

"Yeah, I'll be there in a sec," he replied.

She slid the dinners from their boxes and popped them in the microwave. Sinclair joined her and leaned against the counter near the listening ward. Its essence faded away.

Laura leaned against the opposite counter. "We're shifting our investigation. Janice Crawford is going on extended sick leave, and you're taking over."

He crossed his arms. Her eyes went to the prominent veining on his biceps. "What does that mean?" he asked.

"We want to know who Foyle talks to, where he goes, and anything that strikes you as out of the ordinary," she said.

"You're telling me my commanding officer is under suspicion," he said.

She nodded. "Foyle's been instrumental in blocking information to InterSec, and you said he pulled back teams at the fire so that the Inverni could get in. That makes him fair game."

Sinclair rubbed at his crew cut. "I can see that. It puts me in an uncomfortable position."

Laura snorted. "Welcome to my life."

"Except, I have nothing to prove you're the good guys or that I'm legitimately working for you. I'm not stupid. You could be setting me up."

Laura watched the frozen dinners revolve in the microwave. He had a point. "What can I do to make you trust me, Jono?"

He laughed. "Call off your watchdogs. You can stay, but the tail on me has to go."

She shook her head. "They're protecting you."

"Maybe. They're also watching. If I'm going to be part

of whatever this thing is that I've gotten tangled in, I'm going to have to survive on my own. You want trust, and so do I. Trust me to take care of myself without the spies."

"I'll talk to Terryn," she said.

"Good. When you do, tell him Foyle talks to Alfie a lot."

"His name's Alfrey," she said.

She hadn't corrected him earlier. By the way Sinclair paused, she wondered if he caught it. If he did, he decided not to mention it. "He's talked to Foyle a number of times about Triad."

"He's with Blume's company?"

Sinclair shook his head. "Used to be a long time ago. They had some kind of falling-out, but Hornbeck's been trying to get them back together. Alfrey's consulting or something."

"Just because Hornbeck or Foyle are involved doesn't mean he's a good guy."

Sinclair frowned knowingly at her. "Oh, I definitely will keep that in mind."

Laura reddened at the accusation. The microwave bell went off. She hit the door release. "Dinner's ready."

24
CHAPTER

A BENEFIT LAURA enjoyed with staying at Sinclair's apartment was one less glamour transition at the Guildhouse. Instead of arriving at work as Laura Blackstone and contriving excuses to Saffin for absences, she arrived as Janice Crawford and took care of business. Leaving her SWAT-team gear in the duffel, she glamoured a simple, ill-fitting suit that reflected Janice's inattention to clothing. Within ten minutes of pulling in to the Guildhouse garage, she knocked on the door to Mariel Tate's office suite.

Liam acknowledged her as she came in the door. "Can I help you?"

"I'm Janice Crawford. I have a ten o'clock with Mariel Tate," she said.

Liam made a show of looking at his watch. "You're early. She's out of the office at the moment, but she'll return shortly. Take a seat—there's coffee if you want it."

Laura took one of the leather armchairs. Since Mariel and Genda operated as outside consultants, neither tended to have large meetings. The reception area had room enough for only two or three people to sit.

Laura sorted through magazines on the low coffee table. Liam engaged in a number of sports, including skiing and rock climbing, and brought in old copies from his subscriptions. She noticed he didn't always rip off his mailing address labels. Mariel wouldn't like that. It made the Guild look cheap and was bad form for someone in InterSec to be so casual about personal information.

She pushed aside both the sports and business mags and found the general interest ones. Fortunately, the current editions were there, so she was able to catch up on pop culture. She planned to kill half an hour before giving up on Mariel. It was a game she had to play rarely, one glamour supposedly meeting another. Janice Crawford didn't have much shelf life left as a persona, but given the level of investigation with the drug raid, she wanted the file to reflect a clean investigation with no questions.

She made herself a cup of coffee and settled in to read book and movie reviews. Laura read, sometimes voraciously, but did not have much time or energy to go to movies. Occasionally, she would rent one, but most films bored her. Television fared even worse on her entertainment schedule. It wasn't the programs so much as the rampant, aggressive advertising. Having lived through several wars, she had a strong sense of the meanings of want and need. Consumer culture made her uncomfortable.

Liam answered the telephone and handled general office tasks. He had little to do for Mariel, so most calls were for Genda. Laura made a mental note for Mariel to have lunch with Genda while she was in town. Despite glaring conversational voids when they touched on their respective jobs, they found things to talk about to while away an hour or so. With not much of a social life, Laura enjoyed the company.

Genda arrived in a flutter of white hair and undulating wings. She was a Danann fairy, not a royal family member but still part of the ruling clan of the Seelie Court. She wasn't considered powerful in the essence department, but even a low-powered Danann was formidable. She gave Laura a cursory look as she passed, then leaned in to ask Liam if he had seen Mariel.

Liam glanced at Laura. "No. She's running late for an appointment."

"Tell her to stop in if she has a chance." Genda disappeared into her office without another look at Laura.

Laura checked her watch more frequently. At first she did it to mimic impatience, but after a while, she did it because she was bored and wanted to leave. The phone rang, and Liam answered it. Out of habit, Laura focused attention on his words when he dropped his voice. When people dropped their voices, it was generally something they didn't want others to hear. "I don't know," he said, then, "I haven't seen her in three days . . . She doesn't always tell me her schedule . . . I put it back . . . No, I'm not. I'm uncomfortable about what happened . . . If it was a coincidence, then fine . . . I'll see what I can find out. I have to go."

He hung up and didn't move. Curious, Laura glanced over. She didn't think he had a girlfriend, but his tone sounded evasive and defensive. When their eyes met, he acted self-conscious, as if he had forgotten she was there. He turned to his computer.

"Excuse me, but has Ms. Tate called or anything?" she asked.

Liam continued typing without looking up again. "No. She's usually on time. She'll be here."

Laura looked pointedly at her watch. "I have a doctor's appointment that I don't want to miss. At this point, I don't think I'll have time, so can I reschedule this?"

He did turn then. "Is it over at InterSec? I can have Mariel rearrange that for you."

Liam's intuition made sense. He facilitated the job with Foyle, so he knew she was InterSec. "Um . . . that's kind of personal, but thanks. I'll call Ms. Tate to reschedule."

She left the anteroom and rode the rear elevator to the seventh floor. Entering her room through the back hallway, she shed the Janice glamour, including the outfit. Catching sight of her jeans, she rejected the idea of another plain outfit for the day. Saffin would be sure to mention it, and even more sure to be disappointed in Laura. If Laura allowed herself any indulgence, it was an expensive wardrobe for her public-relations work. She changed into a designer label, a lightweight caramel-colored pantsuit with a black-and-white horizontal-striped blouse.

As she fixed her hair, she put her phone on speaker and called Saffin. "Hi, Saf. It's me. Can you do me a favor and see if I left a folder at Rhys's office? I was down there this morning, and now I can't find it."

"Sure. Are you coming in?" Saffin asked.

"Yeah. I'm down grabbing a coffee and will be right up."

"Got it." Saffin hung up.

Laura repacked her overnight bag for later and dropped it in the closet on her way through to her office. She called the reception desk on the Guildmaster's floor. "Hi, it's Laura Blackstone. Saffin's on the way up. When she gets there, can you tell her I found the file I was looking for?"

The receptionist acknowledged and hung up. Laura hated manipulating Saffin. Between her natural tendency to please and her brownie predilection to accomplish tasks at all costs, Saffin's compliance bordered on submission. After working together so many years, Laura knew the woman had bonded with her, and the connection was strong. It was a level of trust that Laura did not take lightly.

Saffin breezed into the office. "Hi. Did Rhys rewrite his speech again?"

Laura rolled her eyes. "He wants to impress our special guest."

Saffin nodded. "Speaking of which, Secret Service sent over another revision on the outside security. They're closing down Constitution Avenue during the speeches."

In the original plan, the secretary of state was to represent the U.S. at the Archives ceremony. She would still speak, but High Queen Maeve had a major fan in the current president. He had sent word to be put on the program as a surprise guest. Of course, the presence of the media and his desire to expand mutual security initiatives with the Seelie Court had plenty to do with it.

"And speaking of the speeches, have you heard the news?" said Laura. "Hornbeck got what he wanted. Tylo Blume's in. The chief archivist is going on first, so let's stick Blume right after him. He gets five minutes. With any luck, everyone will have forgotten he was there by the time the president arrives."

Saffin grinned. "I love when you do stuff like that."

Laura scrunched her nose. "I hate all the gamesmanship, but it's part of the, um, game in this town."

"I'm going to go to the Archives this afternoon for an event run-through. Anything you want me to focus on?" Saffin asked.

Laura shook her head. "Use your judgment. You probably know more than I do at this point."

"Can I have a company car?" Saffin asked.

Amused, Laura shook her head. "No. It's five blocks."

Saffin giggled as she left. With a touch of envy, Laura watched her leave. Despite all the evident frustrations of dealing with Laura's odd schedule, Saffin loved her job—the big personalities, the complicated schedules, the politics and drama, even the mysteries of her boss's unexplained absences. Laura wouldn't trade her as an assistant for anything.

She finished up her email and checked her watch. Time to put in one last glamoured visit at the Guildhouse before focusing on other matters. She closed down her computer and retrieved her overnight bag. Down in the parking garage, she stepped into the security-camera blind spot and activated the Janice glamour, walked to the SUV, and left the bag in the back. Returning to the elevator, she hit the blind spot, swapped Janice for Mariel, and went back up to InterSec.

Liam jumped up when she entered the anteroom. "You just missed Janice Crawford."

Laura frowned as she checked the time and continued into her office. She kept up the annoyed attitude to reduce Liam's hang-around time. "I was in a meeting I couldn't get out of. When did she leave?"

"About twenty minutes ago," he said from the doorway.

She pulled her chair up to the desk and started her computer. "Call her and get her back in here. If you get her voicemail, give her my work cell and tell her she's to call immediately."

"Got it," he said.

Janice Crawford's cell phone vibrated. Laura checked the number to confirm it was Liam. With that out of the way, she removed the crystal-sphere paperweight from a pile of mail and sorted through correspondence.

When the political nuances of her career as Laura Blackstone exhausted her, the intellectual challenge of Mariel Tate's position came as a welcome relief. Mariel played corporate politics like anyone else, but the nature of her diplomatic missions were more research-oriented and in-house consultancy. She advised, and other people took the matter from there. It was nice not to have final responsibility.

She separated out a number of white papers to read at home and collected the correspondence that needed responses. The rest of the mail she organized, returned to her in-box, and placed the paperweight on top of it.

She leaned back in her chair, scrolling through email. In the middle of everything, Terryn was passing Mariel Tate an invitation to a summit meeting of defense executives next month. He had a remarkable ability to compartmentalize projects. He mentioned hard-copy correspondence he had sent, and she pulled the in-box toward her.

As she reached for the paperweight, she paused, her hand hovering an inch away from the clear crystal. She dropped her hand beside the in-box and stared. Essence accumulated with repeated contact and dissipated with the lack of it. Since her sensing ability worked at all times— was effectively always "on"—she sensed the faint trace of Mariel's body signature on the paperweight. Too faint, though. Crystals worked as essence capacitors, and she used the Mariel persona frequently enough for there to be significant buildup on the paperweight. There wasn't. She boosted more essence into her sensing ability to fine focus and found only enough essence from moving the crystal moments before. It should have had more. Much more.

Her eyes shot to the door to her office. Liam's comment on the phone earlier became clear. "I put it back," she remembered him saying. Last time she was in the office, she hadn't forgotten taking the paperweight to her room. She hadn't taken it at all.

She picked up the phone. "This is Mariel Tate, Suite 835. I need a security agent."

"Is there a problem?" the dispatch asked.

"No. But there will be in a moment." She hung up.

"Liam, I need you," she called. She watched him come around his desk. "Close the door and have a seat."

He smiled at her seriousness and complied. "What's up?"

She picked up the paperweight and placed it on the edge of the desk in front of him. "Explain."

He paled. "What?"

"Are you going to tell me you didn't take this from my office recently?" she asked.

He shifted in his seat and licked his lips. "Uh, no. I use it when you're not here. I should have asked. I'm sorry."

His words registered heavily as untrue. "That would be plausible if your essence was on it and mine wasn't completely stripped. Neither is the case. You have no fey abilities to do that. Who did you give it to?"

A knock sounded on the door. "Come in," Laura said.

A Danann security agent entered, his wings flared open and glowing white with charged essence. The Guild's elite force wore black uniforms designed to intimidate and a chrome helmet that completely covered the head and hid identity. They were highly trained, faithful, and utterly discreet. If possible, Liam turned even more pale.

"Let me repeat my question. Who did you give my paperweight to?" asked Laura.

"Mariel, I don't understand what's going on," he said.

Laura tapped her inner essence until her eyes glittered with shots of white and gold. She slapped her hand on the desktop. The wood cracked. "Answer me!"

Liam flinched. "He said his name was Sean Frye. He's an Inverni that works for the Guildmaster's office. I checked."

"What did he want?" she asked.

Liam shifted his eyes between Laura and the security

guard. "He said you had been implicated in acts against the Guild, and they needed a sample of your essence. I checked with the Guildmaster's office, and they confirmed who he was."

"He lied, Liam. Sean Frye is a false name the Guildmaster's office uses for undercover agents. You didn't go through proper channels," she said.

Sweat broke out on Liam's upper lip. "He came to my apartment, Mariel. He scared the hell out of me."

"What else did you give him?"

"Your schedule. He said they needed to set up surveillance to see who you were passing information to."

Laura went cold with realization. "What schedule did you give him, Liam?"

"Your appointments in Anacostia and the one at the FBI," he said.

She wanted to lash out in rage. "What else?"

Liam shifted agitatedly. "Nothing. He called this morning. He wanted your updated schedule. I didn't give it to him."

"How do you contact him?"

"He gave me a phone number," Liam said.

Laura slid paper and a pen across the desk. "Write it down and give me your cell phone." He did as she asked. When he placed the cell on her desk, Laura let the essence retreat from her eyes. "You should have gone through channels, Liam. You should have called Terryn macCullen."

Liam was on the verge of tears. "I was going to. After that bomb went off at the FBI, I didn't know what to do. I was afraid the Inverni had tried to kill you, and I was afraid you might have set it off to kill that agent. I was going to call Mr. macCullen today."

The fear and truth in his voice pained Laura. She slumped back in her chair. "You thought I set off a bomb that killed an FBI agent?"

Still afraid, he became defensive. "I don't know what the hell you do, Mariel. You disappear for days and weeks at a time. I never know where or why. You could be an assassin for all I know. I thought that guy checked out, but I screwed up."

She felt sick to her stomach. And angry. "Do you know what happened at the FBI building, Liam? Let me tell you . . ."

"I heard about the bomb," he said.

Laura stood and trembled. She dropped her voice low and deadly. "Do not interrupt me. I'll tell you want happened at the FBI, Liam. I was early for my appointment with Lawrence Scales, a husband and father of two young children. We talked and I left, Liam. You know what happened then? A package with essence radiating off it was delivered. I went to warn Scales, and the bomb blew. My essence triggered it, Liam. The bomber used my essence from this paperweight to set a trigger."

She slammed the crystal sphere on the desk. "A man is dead because you didn't make the right fucking phone call."

Laura nodded to the agent. "Detain him until you hear from me."

The agent stepped forward, giving Liam the opportunity to stand on his own. Tears streaming down his face, Liam didn't hesitate to join him. "I'm sorry, Mariel. If there's anything I can do to make up for it, I will."

He meant it. She didn't care. Showing no emotion, she turned to her computer. "Get out."

The door closed behind them. They were gone. Laura's fingers trembled as she reached for the keyboard. She had trusted Liam. She thought he liked her. She thought the Mariel persona was above suspicion for everyone, especially her own assistant. To think that someone so near found her so unknowable nauseated her. Had she become so lost in her personas that nothing of her true self showed? Had she become so shut off from her own self-awareness, she didn't even recognize herself anymore?

She brushed a tear off her cheek and thought of Sinclair. What was he seeing? Did he really want to get involved with someone like her? Why would he? Why would anyone? She shoved her fears aside and took a deep breath. She was Laura Blackstone. That much she knew. That she could hold on to. Laura Blackstone knew how to get a job done. She would worry about who she was later.

If there was a later.

25
CHAPTER

FROM THE CHRONIC state of disarray in Laura's Inter-Sec office, it was obvious no assistant cleaned up after her. The desktop and two credenzas held stacks of reports she never got around to filing. Someone scanned major reports into the computer system anyway, giving her even less incentive to tidy up. Even the guest chair that Sinclair occupied had papers on it. He didn't bother to remove them before he sat.

Laura rubbed her finger along the edge of Blume's business card as she waited for the number to connect. The simplicity of the card struck her again, the lack of need or desire to impress.

"Officer Crawford," Blume answered.

Laura pursed her lips. She hadn't given him Janice's cell number. "Yeah, it's me. I need some work."

"I believe you are on sick leave," he said.

"It's a respiratory thing. I was wondering if you could use me for something that doesn't involve running." A trickle of essence came out of the phone. Blume didn't hide his attempt to sense her location. She pushed back before his spell had time to take an imprint of her surroundings. She didn't really care if it did, since the Guildhouse wouldn't have surprised him, but she didn't want to look sloppy when she was applying for a security job.

"Why the change of heart?" he asked.

She rolled her shoulders in a disinterested shrug. As Laura or Mariel, she didn't use much body language on the phone. It felt right for Janice, though. "I don't see any overtime in my future, and I need cash."

"I can offer you door security," Blume said.

Exactly what Janice had told him she didn't want to do. If anything, Blume was a game player. "That's fine. I'm free tonight and next Tuesday."

Amusement colored Blume's voice. "Oh? I may not need you then."

Laura threw her hands up. "Whatever. You offered. I'll look somewhere else if you don't have anything."

"No, it's fine. Let's start you tonight and see how things work out. Nine o'clock." He disconnected.

Laura glanced at Sinclair. "He bit. I'm on the door tonight."

Sinclair stretched out his legs and knocked over a stack of journals. They both ignored it. "I'm working security for a meeting at seven. What's the plan?"

She walked around the desk. "Ingratiate. We get the lay of the land. I want to know if Blume is more connected to Alfrey. I'm getting coffee. Want any?"

Sinclair grabbed her arm as she passed. "What's up? You've been quiet since I got here."

She arched an eyebrow at his hand. "Let's call it a bad day at the office."

He smirked. "Which office?"

She shrugged out of his grasp. "Really, Jono. Not a joke."

His amusement faded. "Sorry. Cream and light on the sugar, please."

She returned and set a cup on the front of the desk as she circled to her chair. Sinclair picked up the cup and sipped. "Mmm. Better than the station."

Laura held a mug with both hands. "Cress brings in her own beans."

Sinclair propped his feet up on the corner of her desk. "You want to talk about it?"

She shook her head as she swallowed. "It won't change anything."

"Might change your mood," he said.

"I don't know if I want to change my mood."

He nodded slowly and sipped his coffee. "I like a good wallow myself sometimes. I usually drink beer, though."

Laura snorted. "How many cops have I heard that from?"

He narrowed his eyes. "Are you looking to pick a fight? 'Cause we can do that if you want. I like a good tussle, too, ya know."

She stared into her mug. She did want to fight. Something. She wanted to exhaust the anger out of herself, hit something to make things right again. She wanted to go back in time and ask Liam where her paperweight was when she first noticed it missing. She wanted Lawrence Scales to be alive. "A man died because of me," she said.

Sinclair nodded. "Was he on the job?"

"Sort of."

"Then it wasn't because of you. It was because of the job. It's what we sign up for. All of us," he said.

She put her mug down and crossed her arms. "Bullshit."

He shook his head. "No bullshit, and you know it, babe. I don't carry a gun because I think no one else does. You don't do your mojo because you think no one else will. When we get into this, we know the bad guys shoot back. It's why we do it and why it sucks. Unless you pointed a gun or your finger at his head and pulled the trigger for no good reason, I'm not going to listen to any blame laying."

She ran a hand through her hair and stared at the ceiling. "I know. It doesn't make it any easier. Don't call me babe, by the way. I'm not your babe."

He affected surprise. "What? You don't like nicknames?"

"Not the sexist kind."

He shrugged. "Oh, it wasn't sexist. Babe is short for

baby, as in too immature to deal with grown-up stuff. I was being condescending."

She gave her eyes a derisive roll. "Do you really think you can bait me that easily?"

He grinned. "Yep."

She shook her head. "Really, Jono, knock it off. You want to get to know me, not taking me seriously isn't the way to go."

He held up his hands. "Okay. I'm sorry. Really. I'm just trying to figure out why a woman who threatened to kill me is suddenly having such a hard time because someone died."

She met his eyes. "Maybe I'm not who you think I am."

He shook his head. "I may not know who you are, but I know what you are. You're human."

She chuckled derisively. "No. No, I'm not, Jono. I'm fey. I leave destruction in my wake. Isn't that what the humans say?"

He walked around the desk and crouched in front of her. She thought for a moment he was going to touch her. Instead, he clasped his hands and smiled up at her. "Skip the labels, babe. You're human because of what you feel right now. Being human has nothing to do with race or essence ability."

She stared down at him. He meant what he said. "You called me babe, again."

He poked her in the knee. "I guess I did. Now, I'm going to leave and get ready for work. You are going to finish your coffee, take a hot shower, and remember you're one of the good guys. Got it?"

His sincerity touched her. "Got it."

He leaned on her knee as he stood. "I'll see you later then."

She stared at the empty doorway long after he left. Intellectually, she knew he was right. Emotionally was harder. She spent so much time hiding her emotions from other people, it had become ingrained. Liam, whom she thought a friend, had proved it to her. Mariel was her most complete persona, and yet Liam had no idea whether to trust her.

She'd thought he did. She thought she had created a personality for Mariel that no one would doubt. But somehow, she missed the wall she put up for the persona. She realized that wall was part of all her personas and had become a part of herself. It had become so natural, she didn't even see she had walled off herself. That had to change. She couldn't do it anymore.

She sighed and dropped her head back to stare at the ceiling. A vacation was in order, maybe even a leave of absence to sort through her feelings. The world wouldn't end without her. And if it did, a tropical beach wouldn't be the worst place to be.

26
CHAPTER

IN THE VAULT'S lobby, Laura felt like an out-of-her-league naif waiting for a no-show date. The Janice persona's plain-Jane business suit puckered at the waist and shoulders and screamed off-the-rack discount store. The appearance was intentional, of course. Laura had designed Janice to appear less than sophisticated and out of her depth. The Vault was the perfect place to emphasize it. Well-heeled customers filed past her without a second look.

Businesspeople filtered in as the younger crowd moved elsewhere for the night. The bar area became quieter, though no less full as midlevel bureaucrats settled in to have a quiet drink with industry allies.

Blume was late. She didn't expect anything more from him. People of a certain power level worked their own schedule, skimming through their appointments with an unspoken hierarchy of importance. Everyone was on time for the president of the United States or a senator or certain CEOs. A police officer looking for side work was kept waiting.

She watched the faces of the clientele and considered their emotional states. They hid their true feelings as much as she did, only instead of glamours, theirs were practiced facial expressions. The avid, interested look of a lobbyist hid contempt for the politician in front of her; the bright, friendly smile of an assistant director hid anxiety about his job status; the obvious upset of a congressman hid the cold calculation of strategic maneuvering. All masks of one kind or another, attempts to hide or betray the truth to further goals.

Gianni arrived. Where Laura's clothes hung loosely in all the wrong places, Gianni's black suit stretched across his broad shoulders in as many wrong places. Buttons barely held the jacket closed. "Good, you're on time. Blume likes punctual," he said.

"In other people, I guess," she said.

Gianni lowered his eyes at her. "I'd watch my mouth if you want the job. Let's go."

He walked into the bar. "Where are we going?"

He didn't answer. She followed him to a corridor in back that led to a wood-paneled elevator door. Gianni inserted a key into the elevator's floor panel inside the elevator. They rode in silence up one floor. An undercurrent of amusement colored Gianni's body essence, but his face remained impassive. Laura ignored the intent to unsettle her.

The doors opened onto a quiet office corridor lined with closed doors. Laura took note of the security camera tucked into the corner of the ceiling and another at the far end. She followed Gianni down the hall to where two men in black suits guarded a closed door. Gianni nodded at them and entered the room.

The first thing that Laura noticed about Tylo Blume's office was the odor. A musty burnt tang permeated the room, the aftereffect of burning incense. Laura detected the essence of juniper, cedar, and elm. Elves used incense in spells for protection from negative forces during chanting as well as for inspiration during meditation. Blume sat behind an antique desk, a mahogany Victorian. An Art Deco lamp illuminated a dull, worn leather surface that was clear of clutter. The elf read a document, its paper a brilliant white under the lamp. "Officer Crawford, I'm pleased you agreed to come."

"Why?" she asked.

"Why I'm pleased or why you came?"

Laura frowned. "Both."

"You came because you need money. I'm pleased because I need help. Your employment will solve both our problems," he said.

She sensed truth in his words but didn't see the point. "Why do you need my help?"

He peered at her from the dimness beyond the desk lamp. "I need a druid on staff."

"And Corman Deegan shot you down."

Blume nodded. "Yes. We did not have mutual needs."

"Why me?"

Blume glanced at Gianni before answering. A flutter in the air meant he'd projected a sending to him. "I have heard about this mission you were on. I am impressed with your ability to think on your feet. From what I understand, you are no match for an Inverni fairy, yet you managed to survive his attack."

"So if I'm no match, what do you need me for? Hire someone with power."

He smiled. "That I can do. What I can't do is be assured of someone's fortitude, of the commitment to a task. I need someone who will put herself on the line and follow through despite personal jeopardy. You've proved you can do that."

She nodded. "For the right reason. Money isn't always the right reason."

His lips quirked in amusement. "True. The reason has to come first, not the money. I can provide you with an opportunity to help me ensure a better future for the world."

"Sounds like political bullshit," she said.

He chuckled. "If this is an example of your interview skills, I am not surprised at your lack of work."

"I asked for a job, Blume, not a lecture. Give me a reason not to walk out of here."

He nodded. "I have many businesses and many friends. We hope to bring our abilities together to end the strife between human and fey, even between the Celtic and the Teutonic fey. Some of our ideas will be perceived as radical. We need protection from people who might seek aggressive means to stop us."

She forced herself to smirk. "You think you can accomplish what High Queen Maeve and the Elvenking have been trying to do for a hundred years?"

He stared directly into her eyes. "Yes. Do you think that's enough motivation to keep what you see and hear to yourself?"

She suppressed a shiver. He believed he could do it. "Sure. More power to you."

He nodded. "You have a job."

"I have one condition," she said.

"Name it."

"I'm not a merc. I won't kill someone on orders."

"I wouldn't ask that," he said.

She had a moment of confusion. He wasn't lying. Gianni was right by the door, and he had tried to kill her and probably Sanchez on someone's orders. Either Blume hadn't ordered it, or he was saying he wouldn't use her in that way. Yet.

"I'm in," she said.

27
CHAPTER

"IN," LAURA DISCOVERED, meant boredom. Gianni did put her on the door, checking IDs. She knew it was a test, to see how she would handle it. The irony, she thought, was that acting as a bouncer brought a welcome relief from the reality of her job. Tiring on the feet, but at least no one tried to shoot her.

When she came on shift, she saw Sinclair in company with several other security guards in the back of the bar. He gave her a subtle wink when their eyes met, but she didn't see him again after that, which meant he was working in one of the private areas of the club.

As the evening wore on, the club reached capacity, and a line formed on the sidewalk. Tedium set in. She wished she could skip the ID checks and confirm ages by using her truth sensing. At least she was allowed to let obvious adults in without checking. In fact, most of the clientele was older, and a good segment of it had the privilege of not waiting in line. She didn't know all the players, but the other bouncer seemed to know everyone. She tried to pump him for information at first, but he didn't have much to say about anything.

The meeting with Blume ran through her head. She had met his type dozens of times—the self-assured power broker with grand plans. His notion of solving the animosity among the fey and humans spoke to his enormous ego. It was no surprise that Blume's desires echoed the manifesto Terryn found on Alfrey's USB drive. Maybe the two had gone their separate ways, but they still were in basic agreement.

Gianni came outside and tapped Laura's door-security companion. "Take five minutes."

The other bouncer went inside. Gianni made no move to check anyone in line. Laura clicked departing patrons off the tally counter in her hand and let more people in. As she leaned over to check a young-looking woman's driver's license, someone cut the line and brushed against her back. The hair on the nape of her neck bristled as she recognized the essence. She returned the woman's license.

When she turned, Gianni was lifting the velvet rope to let Simon Alfrey pass through. She pretended not to take any particular notice. Gianni replaced the rope. When the other bouncer returned, Gianni disappeared inside.

Laura waited a few minutes before turning to her companion. "I'm taking a bathroom break."

Alfrey just arrived. I'm checking it out. Where are you? she sent to Sinclair.

Third-floor meeting room. Sinclair's sending was faint, as if he were calling from far off.

Patrons packed the bar lounge. The music was louder than earlier, not dance-club level, but enough to prompt people to raise their voices. In the close quarters, species essences mingled in a confusing concentration. Someone with a more fine-tuned ability might be able to pick Alfrey's signature out of the crowd and follow it, but Laura had to rely on her eyes.

She didn't see him. She slipped into the back corridor and called the elevator. When the doors closed, she shot a burst of essence into the override lock and pressed the button for the next floor. With a momentary hesitation, the locking mechanism malfunctioned, and the elevator rose. Alfrey's body signature hovered in the air around her.

When the doors opened, she held them with her foot while moving her hands in the air. Essence trailed from her fingertips in faint amber light that formed ogham runes—a long line with hash marks. The line coiled and stretched, then faded. She saw it still, invisible to the naked eye, but not her essence sensing. With a gentle nudge of thought, the spell floated out of the elevator and down the hall. Seconds later, it passed across the open elevator in the opposite direction. A few seconds more and it returned to her, spent and unactivated. It had found no living essence. The hall sentries were gone.

Alfrey's body signature trailed left toward Blume's office. As the runes dissipated in front of her, she decided against her initial plan to disable the cameras. Doing so would raise an alert and decrease her already limited time. Instead, she activated her body shield and tuned it to reflect her surroundings. Her body faded from view, not disappearing, but taking on the colors and patterns of the environment around her. The spell worked much like a glamour, but rather than a fixed template in stone, it fluctuated like a reflective veil.

She moved into the hall, her silhouette a rippled distortion against the wall, and followed Alfrey's essence path to Blume's office. Residual essence pooled in the air outside the door, layered over her own from her earlier visit as well as Gianni's and Blume's. Alfrey's essence continued farther up the hall, a single sinuous line that meant he hadn't returned. Yet. Either he'd left by another exit, or he was on the floor still.

She froze as an angry voice penetrated the quiet.

"Of course she knows something. Why do you think she's here?" Blume was in his office. A lower, indecipherable response revealed someone in the room with him.

"Then find out," said Blume. "I want to know what connections she's making and who she's talking to."

More murmuring, then: "With Sinclair? So what. Of

course, there's more. You people are so damned short-sighted."

She leaned closer, trying to hear the other voice, but the soft reverberation told her only that the speaker was male.

"Then do it. I want it taken care of," said Blume.

The elevator signal chimed behind her, followed by the scraping sound of the doors closing. At close range, her spelled veil would not fool anyone. She hurried from Blume's office in the opposite direction. As she reached the far end of the hall, the elevator chimed again. She ducked around a corner when she heard footsteps coming nearer.

She reached a brightly lit elevator lobby and hit the call button. When an elevator arrived, she rushed in and slammed the DOOR CLOSE button. The door slid slowly together as the sharp sound of footsteps rang in the lobby. A shadow appeared on the floor. The doors closed. She leaned against the wall and laughed as the elevator descended.

The elevator opened onto the main lobby for Blume's building. Laura moved quietly within the area behind security. The two guards on duty didn't even look to see if anyone exited the elevator behind them. She rounded a corner and faced a set of doors. A burst of voices and music greeted her when she opened the door to yet another corridor, the one that led to the rear of the Vault. She shed her masking veil and walked toward the bar.

As she reached the private elevator, it opened, and Gianni stepped out. He frowned when he saw her. "What are you doing away from your post?"

Laura threw an annoyed look at the nearby restrooms. "I needed to take a break."

Gianni glanced at the restrooms and back at her. He gave her an insincere smile. "Your shift's over anyway. Let's have a drink."

Instead of taking her to the bar, he unlocked a nearby door, and they entered a small, cluttered office, no closets, a sealed window. In the small space, she sensed no one else—no Inverni fairy masking himself from view. To be on the safe side, she activated her body shield. The room had no exits. Laura hesitated on the threshold. Being alone with the man who'd tried to shoot her wasn't high on her list.

Gianni eased himself into the desk chair. "Don't just stand there, sit. You did okay tonight."

She gave him a tight smile and eased into the guest chair. "Thanks."

A knock sounded, and a bar server in her early thirties came in with two drinks on a tray. She smiled. "Hey, Sal. Starting earlier tonight?"

Gianni laughed too much. "I never stop. When you getting off?"

Still smiling, she shook her head. "When my husband comes to pick me up. You need anything else?"

He grinned. "Sure. Tell your husband I'll drive you home if you want."

She laughed at that and tapped Laura on the shoulder as she left. "You watch that one, hon. He's not as nice as he seems."

"I'll keep that in mind," Laura said, unable to keep the dry tone out of her voice.

Gianni held one of the glasses in the air, waiting for Laura to pick up hers. He tapped her glass. "Blume sends his compliments and thanks. Me, too."

She nodded and sniffed the drink. Mead. A nice one if she wasn't mistaken.

"We got off to a bad start," he said.

"Really? I hadn't noticed."

Gianni leaned back with his glass. "Yeah. The whole Sanchez thing had me bad. I couldn't help thinking if it was me instead of you, he'd be alive."

His vocalization dripped with falsehoods. "It wasn't my fault, Gianni."

He nodded vigorously. "I know, I know. Like I said, the Sanchez thing screwed with me. We were tight."

"Why the change of heart?" she said, echoing Blume's words to her.

He shrugged. "I thought I'd clear the air since you're going to be working here."

"Then I get a steady gig?"

Gianni nodded. "Until Blume says otherwise." He rocked his head from side to side. "Yeah, Sanchez was a good guy. You know?"

She shook her head. "He wasn't with you guys last time I worked with the SWAT team."

His look of realization was on the overboard side. "Oh, right. Good guy, though. So you didn't get to talk to him much?"

She sipped the mead. "No more than you and me."

He gave a long, considering look. "Anyway. I have something else to take care of, so you're good for tonight."

"Already?" she asked.

He stood. "Policy. New employees are monitored until background checks are complete. I have something else to do now and can't watch you."

She furrowed her brow. "You run a background check on an InterSec staffer who works for the SWAT team?"

Gianni held out his glass. "This isn't Little League in here. Bottoms up."

She tapped glasses with him again. They finished the mead. Gianni walked her back to the bar. "See you next Tuesday," he said.

Laura pursed her lips as he walked away. His voice had been modulating in the false spectrum when he said goodbye.

I'm leaving. Watch for Alfrey, she sent to Sinclair.

Everything okay? he asked.

Yes. I'll wait for you outside, she sent.

She made one more visual check of the bar. Gianni was gone. No sign of Alfrey. Not engaging Blume too quickly was acceptable. The key to gaining confidence was not looking eager, but given the overheard conversation, she thought she might have tipped her hand. She considered that Alfrey might have been the one with Blume, though given Gianni's odd behavior, she surmised his was the muffled voice. She had no doubt the overheard conversation was about her. How—and if—it connected to the drug lab was one question. She was more interested in the strange exchange she had witnessed on the street between Blume and Alfrey.

Whomever he was talking to, she was sure of one thing. Blume was afraid of something.

28
CHAPTER

LAURA JUMPED AT the blare of a car horn, surprised she had wandered into the crosswalk not far from the entrance to the Vault. Too much in your head again, she thought, annoyed. She had stamina, but the physical toll on her was affecting her mentally and emotionally as well. She was letting herself get distracted, and in her line of work, that could be fatal. Even Gianni had said as much when she questioned him about Sanchez. Every error, even small ones, had consequences.

She approached the SUV with her keys already out. As she played with the ring to separate the ignition key, it slipped from her hand. A wave of dizziness swept over her when she bent to pick up the ring. Light-headed, she leaned a hand against the SUV. The mead had been strong, but it was only one drink. Taking a deep breath, she steadied herself, annoyed that Terryn was right. She was overextending herself. Running multiple personas was possible, but not without enough sleep.

She slid into the driver's seat and watched the front door of the Vault. Her mind wandered to Sinclair. Again. Either he was playing her well, or he was genuinely interested in her. She was letting Sinclair get to her, and damned if she could come up with a good reason why not. People hit on her—it was part of the Washington scene whether or not anyone admitted it—but Sinclair had something sincere about him that attracted her, despite the fact that he lived a lie, pretending to be a human normal. She could understand that, too. It only served to enhance his appeal. He could have hidden in any number of occupations, unseen, undetected, but he chose law enforcement. That said a lot about him as far as she was concerned.

The night reached its tipping point, and people left the club in larger numbers. Black cars and limos pulled up, and a series of businesspeople departed with their security guards. At closing, a cluster of patrons spilled out, followed by security staff. A flurry of waitstaff left in the final wave. The outside door of the Vault closed for the last time. A lone light remained on as the club closed for the night. Still no sign of Alfrey.

You still there? Laura sent Sinclair.

Yes.

Did you see Alfrey?

No. Gianni's gone, too.

She tapped the steering wheel. Gianni hadn't left in his truck, so he must have left another way. She scanned the floors above street level. A few lights were on, but no one moved in the windows. Either Alfrey had settled in for the night, or he'd left another way. Fairies thought nothing of hopping out windows.

I'm going to the apartment. Send if you need anything.

She pulled in to traffic. A car horn beeped. She looked up at the red traffic light. She hit the brakes in the middle of the intersection. Swearing under her breath, she realized she was on the wrong street. She turned wide at the next corner and wrenched the steering wheel back to compensate. The SUV swayed. Nausea welled up in her stomach.

At the next red traffic light, she closed her eyes against the glare of an oncoming car. Her eyes felt sore and gritty from too little sleep. A car horn sounded, and she realized she had driven over the center line. She jerked the steering wheel and slammed on the brakes. Sweat blossomed on her forehead. She was blocks away from the traffic light where she'd closed her eyes.

A buzz filled her head, a static, crackling hiss. She cast out around her and felt nothing. She was head-blind again. She reached out to the dashboard to call Terryn when something jolted the SUV. The stench of essence-fire on metal surrounded her. She called up her body shield, straining with the effort. She blacked out.

Consciousness returned in a flash of headlights and careening cars. Panicked, Laura swerved. The SUV jumped the curb and scraped a mailbox. She lurched to a stop, and she took a deep breath. Drugged. The sluggish thought drifted up. Something in the mead. It was too fast, too sudden to be anything but a drug. Gianni. He had to know it would be obvious to her that he did it. Which meant he didn't care if she knew.

She gathered a burst of essence for a sending, but it shredded and dissipated. She was head-blind. She had the uneasy sense that she'd known that already. She tried to call Terryn from the dashboard system, but her eyes wouldn't focus. Leaning across the seat, she fumbled in her handbag for her cell phone. The smooth case felt slick in her hand and her fingers slipped off its edges. As she opened it, she lost her grip and dropped it. Leaning forward, another wave of nausea hit. She groped along her sleeve for her InterSec transmitter, then swore aloud. Her fingers felt thick and numb, and she couldn't find it on her skin.

Twisting in the seat, she attempted to climb in back for her duffel bag to get the secondary transmitter she kept in it. She slumped sideways when she released the seat belt, the sudden motion unsettling her. As she crawled between the seats, her stomach undulated violently. For a moment, her head cleared, and her stomach lost its cramped grip. Digging in the duffel, her hand closed on the transmitter.

She awoke twisted between the front seats with her head toward the back. Her body shield was activated. Someone yanked on the passenger-door handle, a male voice shouting. He sounded far, far away. Not friendly. With a limp hand, she shot essence in the direction of the voice. White

light danced and ricocheted through the car. She passed out
again, street noise and warm air rushing over her.

Her eyelids, thick and sluggish, resisted opening. An in-
cessant static buzzed in her head. A shudder ran through
her as feeling returned to her body. She hadn't realized she
was numb. She shifted out of an awkward position and felt
the SUV moving. She struggled to open her eyes. The street-
scape tore by the windows in a blur of lights, smears of red
and yellow against the darkness.

Terryn was at the wheel. His face was grim as he looked
over his shoulder at her. "Can you hear me?" he asked.
Can . . . hear . . . ? he sent.

"Head-blind," she said. She thought she said it. She
wasn't sure her lips moved.

She blacked out again. Something burned in her chest. A
deep warmth, not painful, a glowing ember of soothing
essence. She wasn't moving. The SUV wasn't moving. She
smelled cool, dank air, the bitter odor of exhaust and oil,
and the flinty edge of stone. Hands moved on her chest, and
the warmth spread. Sharp pains spiked through her rib
cage, and she lurched forward with a gasp.

She opened her eyes to find herself splayed on the
backseat, one leg hanging out of the rear passenger door,
her calf cramping against the cold, hard edge of the door-
frame. The other leg twisted under her. She hung sideways
in the seat, with the armrest thrusting her back into an
arch.

Cress crouched over her, her fingers clamped onto
Laura's shoulders, whiteless eyes showing no emotion. She
panted, baring her teeth, faintly blue-tinged teeth glossy with
saliva. *Let me in, Laura. You must let me in,* she sent.

The words echoed in Laura's mind as if from someplace
far away. Her mouth stretched open as she tried to shout.
Daggers of bitter violet essence stabbing at her body essence. Cress was trying to get inside her. Panic rose at the
violation, at the wrongness of the *leanansidhe* essence, and
the hunger behind it.

Let me in. It won't hurt if you let me, Cress sent. Softer,
farther away. Was she leaving? Laura wondered. *Or am I?*

A dagger of light pierced something inside her, and she felt Cress, felt her presence like no one she had ever sensed. She screamed.

Don't fight me. It's Cress, Laura. Cress.

Another voice joined hers. *You're safe, Laura. Let Cress in. You're safe.* Terryn. Cress and Terryn. Friends. They were friends. She knew them. Friends. She let go, stopped fighting the strange essence, fought the panic she was feeling. The daggers lost their edge, became thick feathers, bending and weaving inside her. Something shifted, as if she moved beside herself, a new angle of perspective opening in her mind. Cress's perspective. She rode along with Cress, looking at her own body essence as if it were someone else's.

Something moved inside her, something virulent and green, a spiderlike essence that twisted into her own burning amber light. It coiled and cinched around her essence, the amber light fading to green and fading away. Cress tracked it with her own essence, her feathery strands blossoming into fronds of violet and lavender. They embraced the strange green thing, smothering it, constricting its movements as Cress leached its energy. Power surged through Laura, a hot, burning rush as Cress's essence flared.

Laura shivered violently as the pulsating violet essence drained the green, sucking the light out of it. A yawning ache built in her chest, a hunger and desire to devour. Cress's essence raced through her, siphoning the spider-shape into itself until the last faint flicker of green dimmed and went out. The purple light hovered around her, slithering around her body signature. Hunting. Stalking. Disappointed, it withdrew, like a reluctant wave retreating from shore.

Laura wrenched forward and slammed into Cress. They fell out of the SUV in a tangle of arms and legs, hit pavement, and sprawled away from each other. Laura dragged herself to her hands and knees as dry heaves wracked her. She sat back on her feet and let her head fall back.

Exhilaration raced through her, an adrenaline surge that made her skin prickle. She pushed sweat-damp hair off her face and wiped her mouth with the back of her hand. Herself again, her essence shining within on its own, no strange spiderling dancing on her life spark. No Cress either.

Cress squatted nearby on the ground, arms wrapped around knees as she swayed. She stared, not looking at Laura, not focusing on anything but the patch of concrete at her feet. Laura sensed a deep purple corona smoldering darkly around her. Cress lifted her head, her eyes closing as she opened her mouth. With a strange, soft cry, a small cluster of darkness floated out of her mouth. It danced like a cloud of nothing, then dissolved into motes of black and was gone.

Terryn waited near the front of the SUV, his dark wings open high and wide. Around him, around them all, the air wavered like a curtain of water, the distorted images of cars and columns undulating beyond it. They were behind a protection barrier in the Guildhouse parking garage.

Laura felt the flutter of sending. Cress lifted her head toward Terryn. She nodded with a weak smile and stood. She held out her hand to Laura. "How do you feel?"

Laura pulled herself up. "Fine. Considering."

Anytime Cress looked at her or anything else, Laura thought of it as staring. The weird, whiteless eyes acted like normal eyes, the raised bumps of pupils shifted as Cress focused or cocked her head to examine something. But without that small defining white to either side, she always looked like she was staring. "Do you remember what happened?"

"I started going head-blind and blacking out. Every time I stopped the SUV, I woke up driving the damned thing again."

Cress nodded. "There was an essence infusion of henbane and moonflower in your system. It was short-circuiting your brain. You threw up the physical poison, but the killing spell released."

"How the hell did you find me?" Laura asked.

Cress tilted her head. "You called us on the cell and activated your transmitter."

Laura rubbed the back of her neck. She remembered taking out the cell, then blacking out, then taking the cell out again.

She jumped to her feet. "Sinclair!"

"He's fine," said Terryn. "As soon as we received your distress call, we sent someone to pick him up at the Vault. He made an excuse to leave his post and left before anyone knew he was gone."

Laura slumped down onto the running board of the SUV. "I screwed up."

"You're tired and still recovering from the concussion," Cress said.

"I screwed up, Cress!" Cress took the outburst without reacting. She knew the anger wasn't directed at her.

"What happened?" asked Terryn.

Laura shook her head. "Alfrey was in the building. I had a drink with Gianni. He slipped something into it."

Cress leaned against Terryn. "We need rest. We can talk tomorrow. I will remain on call."

"You don't need to do that, Cress. I just need sleep now," Laura said.

"I think it's better I sleep alone tonight anyway," said Cress. Laura glanced at her, then away. She didn't want to think about what Cress had done to her—what Laura had let her do.

Terryn wrapped his arms around Cress and kissed her forehead, a rare show of public affection. "Go upstairs then. I'll take care of the body."

Cress held him. Laura felt a surge of essence and watched without comment as Terryn allowed Cress to siphon some of his body essence. She wondered what Terryn would have done if he had fallen in love with Cress and wasn't an Inverni. With the powerful reserves of essence innate to his species, he had little to fear from a *leanansidhe* absorbing some off him. It didn't mean she couldn't hurt or kill him, just that he would last a lot longer against her than most fey. Cress pulled away from him and walked through the shimmering barrier that hid them from prying eyes.

Body. Terryn said he would take care of a body. Laura spun toward the SUV. Through the open door, she saw a dark shape in the back. She sensed the essence of an Inverni fairy. It should have been stronger that close to her.

"Dammit," she muttered.

She popped the hatch of the SUV. A shirtless Inverni fairy lay on his back, pale skin bearing ancient blue tribal tattoos across the chest and shoulders, faded with time. In life, Inverni wings flicker with light and color, notably whites and deep blues. In death, they were dim and gray, their diaphanous nature hardening to a fragile membrane that crumbled at the slightest touch. The translucent wings twisted around his arms and legs, a nauseating tangle that would never happen in life. A deep burn mark marred the left half of the fairy's face. It wasn't Alfrey.

On top of messing up, she'd put Terryn in a position of having to kill someone. He went for a head shot. Laura spoke a prayer of departing to herself. She didn't want the Inverni to leave an echo of anger behind for her as he made his afterlife journey to TirNaNog.

"I'm sorry you had to do that, Terryn."

He shrugged. "The Wheel of the World turns as it will, Laura. It chose me to be at the end of his path."

Laura didn't respond as he lifted out the body. She believed in the Wheel of the World, the grand turning of events large and small that determined the course of one's life. She accepted that things happened for a reason and for no reason at the same time. That didn't mean she wasn't responsible for her role in events. It didn't mean she had to like it. It didn't mean she knew what her future held. What it meant, to her, was that actions begot reactions and mistakes had ramifications. A dead body was never a good thing to leave in one's path.

29
CHAPTER

LAURA LET TERRYN unlock the door to the Mariel Tate apartment. She rarely used the place. Mariel had to appear to live somewhere, and the nondescript building where the Guildhouse kept corporate residence suites fit the bill. She turned on the lights as she entered behind him, illuminating the large open studio. If her apartment in Alexandria lacked personality, the Mariel apartment had the bland style of a hotel room.

She dropped her bags on the floor. "Really, Terryn, you had someone do a sweep of all my places yesterday."

He circled the room with a small obelisk of granite that glowed a steady blue. It was keyed to change color if it encountered other essences. "I'll remind you that someone managed to get a bomb through security at the FBI building."

He had a point. She went to the kitchenette in the corner and pulled two bottles of fruit juice out of the refrigerator. She opened one and left the other on the counter. "Whose orders do you think Gianni is following, Alfrey's or Blume's?"

He hovered off the floor to check along the top of the wall of curtained windows. "Alfrey's."

She pursed her lips. "That was a quick answer."

Terryn settled to the floor and placed the obelisk on the coffee table. "It's clear." He pointed at the juice on the counter. "Is that for me?"

She tossed him the bottle. "Are you changing the subject?"

He drank the entire bottle in one smooth motion. "Blume's not a fool. He wouldn't poison you on his own property. I think Gianni is playing Alfrey and Blume against each other. Besides, I recognized the clan tattoos of the Inverni who attacked you in the SUV. He's from a subclan of the Alfreys."

She showed him a slight smile. "Terryn, my friend, you forget whom you're talking to. I'm sensing a subtle evasion in your voice modulations."

He nodded, staring down at the floor. "Simon Alfrey and his father Skene manipulate the lesser Inverni clans to no good end. Simon's involvement makes me uncomfortable."

"Yeah, well, uncomfortable doesn't quite cover how I feel about someone who's tried to kill me," Laura sent.

Terryn sighed and looked up. "It would not be an exaggeration to say I blame the Alfreys for the death of my father."

Laura's eyebrows shot up. "You know I want to hear why."

He shrugged. "The Alfreys stirred the Invernis to challenge the Danann leadership. The Dananns tried to make us slaves—at least that is the story the Alfreys told. As High Chief of the Clans, my father confronted Maeve. Then the Alfreys submitted to Maeve, destroying my father's support. He died in Maeve's prison."

Laura crossed her arms as she leaned against the counter. She knew Terryn was heir to the rule of the Inverni clan but that he refused to take the underKing title to which he was entitled. For years, she had thought it was because he wanted to keep peace with Maeve. Without an invested Inverni leader, the Dananns had no one to rally support against. "You won't take the title because you don't want Maeve to say she gave it to you."

Terryn nodded. "I cannot let her undermine my authority by claiming I rule because she removed my father. The Alfreys think they will take over with her blessing someday, so they do her bidding. Simon Alfrey would not have been involved in a drug raid unless it was really something much bigger."

She pushed away from the counter and placed a hand on his shoulder. "Simon Alfrey screwed up, Terryn. I can identify him at the scene. Let me do that, and you'll have one less Alfrey to deal with."

He placed his hand on hers. "You were glamoured, Laura. The only confirmation you have of that is the mac-Cullen heir and a *leanansidhe*. That presents a credibility problem."

She dropped her hand. "And Sinclair."

Terryn walked to the door. "A second-generation fire giant masquerading as a human also has little weight in a fairy court, even if he were willing. No, we will have to catch Alfrey with stronger evidence."

"We'll think of something," she said.

He bowed as he left. "I appreciate that. Now get the rest that Cress ordered. We have much to do in the days ahead."

Tired didn't cover how she felt. Whenever she heard that someone had been admitted to a hospital for exhaustion, the concept baffled her. She tried to imagine feeling more exhausted than she did at that moment and couldn't. Laura put water on to boil as she pulled down the Murphy bed. She steeped some tea and curled into the corner of the couch.

Staring at her hand, she thought about the raid. She tried to force lines on her palm into a pattern that might trigger a memory. From one angle, the three lines radiating across the palm could be the Celtic ogham rune *gort* or the German *ansuz*. A single rune could mean anything, though, never mind the question of why Sanchez—who wasn't fey—would use a rune to convey a message. Maybe an "F," she thought. Foyle?

She let her hand fall to her lap. Aaron Foyle was right about one thing: Last words were important. She remembered the look in Sanchez's face. He'd known he was dying. He didn't pray or speak a lover's name. He used his last breath to tell her something—something important enough to use his final moments of life. And she couldn't remember.

She left the tea on the counter and turned the shower on in the bathroom. She watched herself undress in the full-length mirror. Humans would kill for the body she had at her age, but not the rest. Her hair hung lank. Darkness shadowed the skin under her eyes. Her lips, wiped clean of lipstick, looked thin and colorless. Her eyes unsettled her. She saw the small signs—the faint traces of crystallization forming, the slight recession into the skull, the uncanny depth that intimidated people. Age was catching up with her. Fey age. It appeared in the eyes first with the fey, eyes that had seen much. Sometimes too much.

The hot water beat down on her face. She stood, motionless, letting the heat seep into her, letting it reach deep beneath the skin where she could feel. Drying off, she felt better, physically anyway. The steam from the shower fogged the mirror, blurring her image. For a moment, she remembered what she'd looked like in her youth.

She slipped into bed, feeling the cool, crisp, white cotton sheets, noting the designer bedcover, and taking in the room meticulously styled in tones of soft creams and beige with splashes of maroon and bright yellow. Perfect.

Something had to change.

She turned out the light. With the drapes closed, the studio apartment plunged into darkness punctuated by the phosphorescent glow of the alarm clock. She wondered what she would have done in Sanchez's position. What would her last words be? A cry of pain? For love? She murmured a sad laugh in the dark. She didn't know Sanchez or his life, but she knew hers. She was lying alone in the dark in an empty, sterile apartment with no one. She would have done what he had done, tried to complete a mission. It was all she had, pathetic as it was.

The years piled up, the missions, the plans, and, every

time, she stepped forward. Every time, she did her duty. For the Guild. For InterSec. Sometimes she had provided the means for great things to happen, only a very few knowing about it. Sometimes she had done those great things herself, with even fewer people knowing. Her life had become a cycle of stress, endless games of subterfuge, and feints. Nothing ever truly resolved. Things got worse. Things got better. It didn't matter which, because there was always something more to do.

And she never said no. Not during undercover operations. Not during armed conflicts. Not when the Guild wanted one thing, and InterSec wanted another. Whatever the request, she managed to satisfy everyone else.

Everyone ended up satisfied but her. She had people she trusted with her life, who weren't actually her friends. She had friends to whom she couldn't talk about her life. At the end of the day, she lay down on many different beds, and home had become not the comfort of an apartment, but a windowless room that everyone else thought was a closet in an office building.

Something had to change. She picked up the phone and dialed.

"Hello?" Sinclair answered.

"It's me. Are you okay?" she asked.

He chuckled in her ear. "Yeah, I'm okay. I'm bunking in an examining room at the Guildhouse until Terryn can decide if I'll see the light of day again."

"I didn't get a chance to see you before I left," she said.

"You should be glad you're alive and asleep after what you went through."

"I am," she said.

"You're asleep?" he teased.

She laughed. "No, you jerk. I'm glad I'm alive."

He lowered his voice. "Me, too."

She closed her eyes and listened to his slow steady breathing on the other end of the phone.

"You there?" he asked.

"Yes. I just wanted to say good night, Jono."

"Thanks. I'll see you tomorrow, babe."

She replaced the phone on the cradle. As she slid deeper under the covers, she realized she was smiling and realized it was for herself.

For a change, she thought.

30
CHAPTER

LAURA STRODE TOWARD the Anacostia station house. A formidable Mariel Tate reflected back at her from the windowed doors—sharp heels, streamlined jumpsuit, large sunglasses, all black. Two Danann security agents flanked her. They walked in sync, people on the sidewalk edging out of their way. She was there on business and meant it to be apparent.

She started the day in the Mariel Tate apartment, going through the motions of making breakfast, straightening the apartment, and getting dressed. She moved without thinking, focusing on the routine of preparing for the day. The closer she got to leaving the apartment, the more her thoughts shifted to the day's agenda. As the events of the previous night replayed in her mind, anger grew, a low simmer that rose until she found herself pacing the floor, ready for a fight.

People knew things they weren't telling. For all the suspicions in the D.C. SWAT squad, no one pressed their issues, no one questioned people's actions. Everyone did what she was doing: waiting for someone else to make the next move, waiting for an excuse to take action. By the time she left the apartment, she'd decided enough was enough.

She was not waiting for the next incident to happen or for new information to be handed to her. She wanted answers, and she was going to get them. Captain Aaron Foyle was the place to start, whether he liked it or not.

Inside the doors to the station house, she held her Inter-Sec badge out to the desk duty sergeant. "Mariel Tate, InterSec. I'm here to see Captain Foyle. Immediately."

The desk sergeant's neutral face hid resentment at her tone. "I'll see if he's in."

"I'm not waiting," Laura said. She walked past the desk, grasped the secured door and shot a burst of essence into it. The lock cycled and opened.

"Hey!" the sergeant shouted. He jumped from his seat, reaching for his gun.

Ignoring him, Laura continued inside, holding her Inter-Sec badge high enough for the surrounding officers to see. Behind her, a Danann gestured and ball of white essence sprang from his palm toward the desk sergeant. The light wrapped itself around the gun. The sergeant swore as the gun became too hot to handle, and he dropped it on the floor.

The Dananns followed Laura as she marched through the open desk area into the hallway at the back. Their body shields hardened as police officers drew their weapons. Two patrol officers blocked the hall.

"InterSec, stand down," Laura said. The perimeter of her shield hit them from five feet away and thrust them to the side, pressing them against the walls as she passed.

Foyle stood at the door to his office, hands on his hips. "What seems to be the problem, Agent Tate?"

"We need to talk," she said, backing him toward his desk.

No one comes in, she sent to the Dananns, and, with a gust of essence, she slammed the door shut. Foyle stepped back until his thighs bumped against the desk. "What the hell do you think you're doing?" he said.

"Salvatore Gianni. Where is he?" she asked.

"He didn't show for roll call this morning," said Foyle.

"That doesn't answer my question," she said.

"I don't know where he is. This is my office, Tate. Cut the bullshit before I have to explain why I had an entire squad room open fire on you," he said.

Truth resonated in his voice. He didn't know where Gianni was. "Let's sit then," she said, taking the guest chair. She released her body shield.

Foyle looked confused as he moved behind his desk. "What's going on?"

Relaxed, Laura crossed her legs. "Gianni is wanted by InterSec in connection with an attempt on the life of Agent Janice Crawford. We're considering him armed and dangerous and will take him down without hesitation if he resists arrest."

"What's your evidence?"

Laura shook her head. "Need-to-know. You're not on that list. I want some answers from you, though. You had an undercover agent on your team. Who knew and when?"

Foyle grabbed his phone. "This conversation is over."

Without moving, Laura sent a burst of essence at the phone and knocked it across the room. "I asked you a question, Captain. We can do this here or I can take you in under suspicion of aiding and abetting."

Foyle went slack-jawed. "Are you crazy?"

Laura gave him a cold smile. "Don't make this difficult."

Fear finally started to register with him. "You're serious."

"Dead serious. Answer my question," she said.

"I received information that Janice Crawford was sent to infiltrate my team," he said.

"You requested her," Laura said.

He nodded. "I received the information after Sanchez died."

"From?"

He stared and compressed his lips.

"I am not playing with you, Foyle. Answer the question."

"Gianni had an informant," he said.

"Who was the informant?"

"A fairy named Simon Alfrey," said Foyle.

"Also wanted by InterSec. You believed the word of the worst member of your team?" she said.

"I confirmed it through another channel," he said.

Laura nodded. "Hornbeck's office."

It was a logical conclusion, but Foyle seemed surprised she knew. "Yes."

"We know you have a professional relationship with the senator. Did Gianni?" she asked.

Foyle shook his head. "Not that I'm aware of."

"Did Gianni work with you on the Archives ceremony?"

"No. I am a liaison for the senator. Tylo Blume's people handled everything with the Capitol police."

"What about Simon Alfrey?"

Foyle's clenched his jaw. "He's a consultant to the senator."

"Details, Captain Foyle, I want details," she said.

"Why don't you ask the senator?" he asked.

Laura tilted her chin down. "Captain Foyle, I and the two agents with me have broad legal authority. You can answer my questions here and now, or they will drag you down to the InterSec facilities at the D.C. Guildhouse. Once there, you may have one phone call. Do not think that if you call the senator, you will enjoy sleeping in your own bed tonight, or tomorrow, or the foreseeable future. I can and will make your life absolutely miserable within the confines of my authority. This is your final warning. Now, what is Alfrey consulting on?"

"I don't know. The senator meets with him occasionally," he said.

"What was Alfrey doing at the house fire in Anacostia?"

Foyle looked genuinely startled. "How do you know he was there?"

Laura smiled. "You were sloppy, Foyle. We picked up an open video feed from the site."

Laura stared at him while he considered his answer. He wouldn't meet her eyes. "He volunteered to search the house," he said.

"You didn't find that odd?" she asked.

Foyle shrugged. "Not until this moment. I was at a meeting with the senator when the call came in. Alfrey was there. He offered to help."

"Why the secrecy?"

Foyle frowned. "I needed help I couldn't get. He had security clearance through the senator. I made the call."

"And you didn't find it odd that Janice Crawford and Jonathan Sinclair almost died in an explosion?" she asked.

Foyle ran his hand over his head. "Alfrey said the place was clear. Afterward, he told me Crawford must have created the explosion."

"Has Alfrey been involved with anything related to the upcoming Archives ceremony?" she asked.

He shook his head. "Not that I know. He used to work with Blume, but not anymore."

Relief swept over Laura. The Archives ceremony security, at least, wasn't compromised. She decided to muddy the water for Foyle. "What about Sinclair? We know he acts as your driver. Have you ever seen him with Alfrey or Gianni?"

"Obviously, he works with Gianni here. They do detail work together at Blume's club. Sinclair didn't show up for roll call today either."

"We know where he is," said Laura. She stood. "You've been played for a fool, Captain. Count yourself lucky that that is my belief at the moment. Simon Alfrey is now considered a terrorist. If Gianni or Alfrey contacts you in any way, I want to know ten seconds later."

Foyle glared at her. "You know I'll be on the phone as soon as you leave here."

Laura opened the door. "I said ten seconds later, Foyle. Do not make me come back," she said without turning.

She stalked back through the station house, with the Dananns in her wake. Officers lined the hallways or took position behind desks and cabinets. Most had their guns drawn. When she reached the lobby, over a dozen more officers blocked the door, guns trained on her.

Shields only, unless they fire, she sent to her escorts.

She didn't break her stride as she approached. "My name is Mariel Tate of InterSec. My appointment with Captain Foyle is over. I'm leaving."

She heard clicks as a few officers cocked their weapons. Like a ship breaking through waves, the hardened body shields pressed them back in confusion until the way to the exit was clear. No one fired.

In the bright sunlight outside, squad cars and police vans blocked the street and sidewalk. Laura stopped. "Danu's blood," she muttered. More officers scrambled into view at the end of the block. She cocked her head at the Dananns. "Looks like someone blocked my car in. Would you guys mind giving me a lift?"

She heard the distinctly hollow sound of someone chuckling inside a metal helmet. "Anytime, Agent Tate."

Her security escort grasped the reinforced straps on her jumpsuit sewn in over her shoulder blades. They leaned forward, shifted the position of their wings, and drew essence from the air. With no effort, they shot into the sky.

Despite the enormous rush, Laura kept the grin off her face. It had been ages since anyone had taken her for a flight. The Anacostia neighborhood fell away. The seemingly fragile Danann's wings hummed with energy as they shifted on currents of essence, not so high as to trigger government defense measures but high enough to give a glorious view of the seat of government. With the wide vista below her, she remembered why she had come to the city.

As they approached the Guildhouse, they swooped in lower, and the downside to staying in the city so long became visible. Too many cars and too many people. Lost hopes and dreams were evident in the surrounding neighborhoods that clustered around the Capitol like desperate moths to an indifferent flame. The Dananns set her gently on the sidewalk in front of the Guildhouse. No one paid attention. Fairies landing passengers in front of the Guildhouse were hardly a unique sight. She entered the building, hoping Terryn had had better luck finding Gianni.

31
CHAPTER

TERRYN GLARED AT Laura from behind his desk. The voice on the other end of his phone was audible.

"I thought Mariel Tate was supposed to be a diplomat," Sinclair whispered loud enough for Terryn to hear.

Laura gazed at him from under her brow. "Not helping, Jono."

"I understand," Terryn said for the fourth or fifth time. "I'll talk to her . . . yes, thank you."

He hung up. "What got into you?"

Laura tried to look contrite. "I'm sorry, Terryn. I walked in with my black suit and two Dananns and . . . got a little carried away."

"Carried away? They mobilized practically an entire battalion," said Terryn.

"I had to know that the Archives ceremony wasn't compromised."

"Foyle says you threatened him," he said.

She shrugged dismissively. "Oh, please. It was a veiled threat at best."

Sinclair twisted his lips to keep from smiling. A series of emotions crossed Terryn's face—uncertainty and frustration. Laura couldn't blame him. She liked to exert authority as Mariel once in a while to get results. It worked. It was nice to have an ID that let her stomp her feet anywhere she wanted sometimes. Admittedly, though, she didn't usually cause a police response. Waking up angry hadn't helped.

By the expression on his face, Terryn knew he wasn't going to get anywhere berating her. "We'll deal with this later. Gianni was not at home or at the Vault," he said.

While she went to Anacostia, an auxiliary team had hit Gianni's apartment and another had gone with Terryn to the Vault. "Did you talk to Blume?" she asked.

Terryn nodded. "We had no problems. Once he learned that Alfrey had been in the building, he let us search the premises."

"The entire place?" Sinclair said. "I practically couldn't go to the bathroom without an escort."

"Just a few offices and public areas," said Terryn. "His cooperation did not extend to risking his offices being searched unattended."

"What did Alfrey want with him the other day?" Laura asked.

"He wasn't specific. They were partners in various business ventures but had a falling-out," Terryn said.

"Can we confirm that?" asked Laura.

Terryn nodded. "Already in motion. Preliminary results confirm they went their separate ways two years ago. Alfrey had decided to take his politics in a more radical direction."

"Are you comfortable taking Blume off the table?" asked Laura.

Terryn spread his hands. "No, but he's cooperated. We're not finding any connections that are unusual for someone of his level of influence. And he broke off connections with a partner when the guy went radical. I don't see anything to pin on him."

Laura paced around the side of the office. "I don't like Blume. He was afraid of something last night. There's a connection."

"When we find it, we will deal with it," Terryn said.

Laura sat again and leaned forward. "We have another

problem. InterSec has a leak. Gianni knew Janice Crawford was a plant, and so did Hornbeck."

Terryn nodded. "Nothing is one hundred percent secure, not even the Guild."

She looked away from Terryn. "Do you think it was Liam?"

"Who's Liam?" asked Sinclair.

Laura ignored him. Terryn paused, his eyes shifting to Sinclair. "It's possible. Other possibilities exist."

Sinclair jutted his jaw out in annoyance. "It wasn't me. I've had more than one opportunity to put her down, flutterboy."

"Jono!" Laura said.

He glared at her. "He can imply that I'm trying to kill you, and you get mad I called him a name?"

"It's not that, it's . . ." She fumbled for words. "It's not very nice."

Sinclair laughed. "Good. I got my point across."

"Anyway," Terryn interrupted, "the good news, if we can call it that, is that only a low-level agent was exposed. I'll have Cress start pulling files to check on everyone you interacted with as Janice Crawford inside and out. We may find someone who knows too much about her."

"I'm retiring her," said Laura.

"You know I wanted that, and now she's too compromised to keep in play any longer," Terryn agreed.

"Retire? For good?" asked Sinclair.

Laura leaned back with a mixture of disappointment and resignation. "I've done it before. When a persona has outlived its usefulness, there's no point in keeping it."

"Does this mean we can't live together anymore?" Sinclair asked in mock sadness.

Laura glowered but didn't answer him. "Do we have anything new on the drug-raid data?" Laura asked Terryn.

He slid a folder across the desk. "The raid did, in fact, disrupt a drug operation. There's been chatter about its being a front. It looks like you were right. The evidence and underground chatter strongly point to an assassination plot, with Senator Hornbeck or the president as the likely targets."

Laura shook her head. "Who will both be at the Archives tomorrow. That puts the ceremony back in play as a target. We have to get it canceled, Terryn."

Terryn frowned and nodded. "We've informed both offices of the information and received the standard reply."

Laura knew what that meant. "Dammit! Someone needs to tell those idiots they won't need to bow down to terrorists if they get their legs shot out from under them," she snapped.

"They have full confidence in our ability to protect them," said Terryn.

Laura scoffed. "And if something goes wrong, we'll get hung out to dry because they didn't listen to us."

Terryn sighed. "This is Washington."

"I have an idea," said Sinclair. They both stared at him as if they had forgotten he was in the room. "What? I can't have an idea? I thought you wanted me on the team?"

Laura glanced at Terryn. "Go on," he said.

"We flush them out. You said you weren't going to use Crawford anymore. They're trying to kill her because they think she knows something. Use her to flush them out," Sinclair said.

Terryn shook his head. "Too risky."

"I like it," said Laura. Sinclair nodded a flattered smile at her.

"Laura, you've done enough. I'm putting other agents on this. You and I will focus on Archives security," Terryn said.

"Agreed. Tomorrow. Today, I want Alfrey or Gianni or both."

"No."

She tapped a finger on his desktop. "I'm demanding the right to do this, Terryn. They've tried to kill Janice three times. I deserve the chance to get them before this goes any further."

"What do you have in mind?" he asked.

With a sly look, Laura leaned back in her chair. "I'm going to be terrorist bait."

32
CHAPTER

LAURA STOOD OUTSIDE Sinclair's apartment, running their plan over in her mind one last time. The wards inside the apartment remained active, and it was time to make Alfrey think, whatever his greater plans were, that they were in true danger. She hoped he would take the bait. With a deep breath, she knocked on the door.

Sinclair opened it immediately. "What happened?"

She rushed in and stopped short of the dampening field near the armchair. "I had to talk to you."

Sinclair closed the door. "They told me you were in protective custody."

"I was. I had to talk to you. I remembered something, Jono, and I don't know what to do."

He stepped close and brought his hands up to hold her. She slipped away, remaining outside the field and giving him a warning look. "First, tell me what happened. I got a call last night that you needed me outside the Vault. When I went out, four guys jumped me and took me to a house outside the city. They wouldn't tell me anything, then let me go about an hour ago."

"Someone tried to kill me last night," she said.

"What!" he said.

They stepped into the dampening field. Laura spread sheets of paper on Sinclair's coffee table with large text and plenty of white space. "That's a good start," she said.

Identical sheets were on the dining-room table and another set on the kitchen counter. Laura had written dialogue as well as movement directions, a flow designed to weave in and out of the fields of the listening wards throughout the apartment.

Sinclair sat next to her. Sinclair's knee touched the side of her thigh, grazing it, not firmly enough for her to call him on it. It took several heartbeats before Laura noticed she hadn't automatically moved away. "You think this will work?" he asked.

She pursed her lips, tilting her head from side to side. "It was your idea."

Sinclair sighed. "I know. If they were trying to kill us before, they'll definitely try after this."

She turned an intentionally enthusiastic smile at him. "Isn't knowing it's going to happen better than wondering?"

He looked amused. "You're odd, you know that?"

She stood and adjusted her T-shirt. "Just stick to the dialogue. Ready?"

He checked the pages. "Here goes . . ."

He stepped out of the field of the living-room dampening ward. "I'm getting a beer. You want one?" he asked.

He waited near the dining-room table while Laura stepped away from the dampening field.

"Yeah."

Sinclair moved into the kitchen. Laura had placed masking tape around the listening-ward field to show him when his medallion was too close and blocked transmission. Laura leaned against the dining-room table. "Someone tried to poison me last night. InterSec got it out of me in time."

Sinclair came to the kitchen door. "Gods, are you okay?"

"I'm fine. Really. But here's the weird part. When I woke up, I remembered the raid. All of it, Jono."

He went back in the kitchen. "That's great, isn't it?"

"I'm a little freaked out by it."

Sinclair retrieved two beers from the refrigerator and handed her one. "Are you going to keep me in suspense, or are you going to tell me what you remember?"

"What do you think of Gianni?" she asked.

Sinclair sipped his beer and checked the printed dialogue. "Okay, change the subject. He's okay. A little rough around the edges, but I don't have a problem with him."

"No, I mean compared to me," Laura said.

Sinclair smiled and moved in close. He straddled her as she leaned against the table, but didn't touch her. *Just read the dialogue, Sinclair. We're not on camera,* she sent him.

He smirked. "You're way hotter."

"Oh, and how hot do you think Gianni is?"

Amused, he jerked his head back. "Don't worry about that. He doesn't even register."

Jerk. Stick to the dialogue, she sent. She poked her finger against his chest and pushed him away. "Seriously, you've known him a lot longer than you've known me. If I told you something bad about him, what would you think?"

Sinclair took a swig of beer. "I'd think he was an ass. Why are we talking about Gianni?"

She led him into the living room. "He shot me, Jono."

"What!" Sinclair said.

They stepped back into the jamming field.

She shoved him in the shoulder. "I am going to kill you if you don't take this seriously."

"If someone's going to kill me, I'd rather it be you," he said.

She sighed in exasperation. "How did I get into this?"

Sinclair grinned. "By lying."

She pushed him out of the dampening field. "Keep moving."

He darted back in to check his dialogue, then out again. "No, I believe you. I just don't get it. Why the hell would he try to kill you?"

She followed him out of the field. ". . . worse. Sanchez said something to me. I think I should go to the FBI or InterSec."

They returned to the dining room, close enough for the kitchen ward to pick them up. "What did he say?" Sinclair asked.

"Maybe I shouldn't tell you," Laura said.

Sinclair picked up the page of dialogue they were on. "What the hell, Crawford? You just told me Gianni shot you. What the hell did Sanchez say that can be worse than that?"

"I'm afraid, Jono. Someone's tried to kill me three times since the warehouse," she said.

Sinclair lifted the script, his brow furrowing as he read. "Wait a minute . . . three? You told me about the bridge and last night. What else happened?"

She paused in surprise. She hadn't told him about what happened at the FBI building—which had happened to Mariel, not Janice. She improvised, not wanting to dwell on the slip-up. "Someone tried to run me off the road, just like what happened to you. I thought it was a drunk driver until now."

Get back to the script, Jono! she sent.

His eyes searched her face. "Why do you play things so dangerously?"

She waved the script in front of him. "I didn't ask for this, Jono. That's why I'm afraid. If I tell you everything, you'll be in danger, too."

He held her arms. "Maybe this isn't a good idea after all."

Jono, please! We can't mess this up. They're listening, she sent.

"So you think I should keep quiet?" she asked.

He ran a finger along the line of her jaw. "I think I want you to be safe. Let's just go away, get away from all this."

Angry, she grabbed his hand. "Jono . . ."

He tilted her chin up, leaned down, and kissed her. She closed her eyes and found herself surrendering to the moment, the warm and full pressure of his lips against hers. It had been so long since she had let a man touch her. So long since she had even wanted to be touched. She didn't move. Sinclair broke the kiss. She savored the moment, knowing that when she opened her eyes, it would end. But it had to end. She didn't want to risk allowing something to happen between them that would only end badly.

She looked up at him, not angry or annoyed, but regretful. "I can't do this."

"Neither can I. Not if it means losing you before things have even started," he said. He twined his fingers into hers and led her into the bedroom. She let him lead her, let him hold her hand like that, and told herself it was part of the plan to continue the fake dialogue in the bedroom.

Sinclair sat on the side of the bed, and the listening ward faded as his medallion interacted with it. Laura tugged her hands away and placed them on his shoulders. He held her hips and pulled her closer.

She shook her head. "This isn't going to happen, Jono."

He slid his hands higher and drew her down with him as he fell back on the bed. She lay on top of him, refusing to straddle him. With his fingers in the belt loops of her jeans, he wiggled her back and forth. "We could always drink more beer so you can tell me how drunk you were and how you don't remember a thing."

She rolled off him. "Stop. We can't. I told you I don't date colleagues."

He stretched on his side. "Oh, but you can kiss them, huh? Besides, we're not technically colleagues until Terryn decides I'm good enough."

She snorted. "Oh, you're good all right. Just not the kind of good I think Terryn had in mind."

With light touches, he walked his fingers up her arm. "Someone's making excuses," he sang softly.

Laura grabbed his hand when it reached her shoulder. "Jono, we don't have time for this." He relaxed his hand to lie flat on her shoulder. She slipped off the bed. "We have to get out of here."

Sinclair leaned his elbows on his knees, thinking through what she said. "Where do we go?"

"Stick to the plan. The Guildhouse, then the safe house. When the listening ward reactivates, we get back to the script and talk about going out for more beer. Got it?" she said.

"Got it," he said. The listening ward reactivated as he rolled off the bed and pulled a pair of shoes from the closet.

"Now? You want to go for more beer now?" Laura said, putting a note of surprise in her voice.

Sinclair slipped on his running shoes. "Sure, we've got the whole night, babe, and, trust me, you're going to get thirsty."

She walked out to the dining room. "I'm going to hold you to that."

Sinclair appeared in the doorway as she gathered up the dialogue sheets from the table. He retrieved the script from the counter while she gathered the rest from the coffee table. Turning, Sinclair was behind her. He handed her the rest of the pages. "All set?" she asked.

She shoved the papers in her duffel bag and tossed it to Sinclair. He looked down at it, then retreated to the bedroom. "Wait a sec, I need some cash."

"I've got cash," she said pointedly.

Sinclair reappeared waving a leather shaving kit at her, and Laura rolled her eyes. "I'm ready," he said.

They hit the sidewalk. "You went back for deodorant and shaving cream?" Laura said in disbelief.

"And a toothbrush," Sinclair said in mock self-defense. "I believe in good oral hygiene even when I'm on the run from shadowy assassins."

They reached her SUV and separated to the opposite sides. "There's a tooth-fairy joke in there somewhere," she said.

She called Terryn as she pulled in to traffic. "We're on our way. We should be in the safe zone in about three blocks."

"Agents are in place. Drive safely," Terryn said.

She made a mental map of their planned route from Sinclair's apartment to the Guildhouse. If Alfrey or Gianni had planted listening wards, they sure as hell had people watching the apartment. To keep suspicion down, Terry would hold off backup for the first few blocks. After that, they would drive a protective gauntlet, watched by Guildhouse agents.

When she reached the corner, a black car blocked the street. Laura skipped the intended turn. "Do you think that's them already?"

Sinclair adjusted his line of sight in the visor mirror. "Definitely. That was the wrong way on a one-way street. Turn two blocks up, and we should be fine."

Laura goosed the accelerator. Behind them, four black cars appeared in formation in pairs. Perfectly normal black-car behavior in D.C., except for the fact that they weren't escorting anyone and were speeding up.

Laura checked her mirrors. "They took the bait."

Sinclair twisted in his seat to look out the rear window. The cars had no insignia, and the license plates displayed consecutive numbers. Not a good sign. Laura gunned the SUV through a yellow light. All four cars ran the red. Definitely not a good sign. The cars moved to pass on either side. When the lead cars reached the SUV, they paced it.

"Hang on," Laura said. She slammed on the brakes. All four cars shot past the SUV. As they braked, Laura gunned the engine and spun the steering wheel. The SUV rocked savagely side to side in a tight turn. Laura slapped the police light onto the roof and hit the gas pedal. Oncoming traffic careened to either side as she tore up the one-way street.

"We're cops now?" Sinclair said.

"Whatever it takes, Jono. If we can't get to our backup, maybe we can draw them to us," she said.

Two black cars followed. Laura skidded the turn at the next corner. Cars pulled over as her police light warned them off. The SUV flew through an intersection as Laura hit the dashboard phone. Static crackled over her speakers. She fumbled in her pocket for her cell and flipped it open. More static. "They're jamming the phones," she said.

A third black car joined them. Laura yanked the wheel as the car sideswiped against her, fishtailed, and swung down the next street. "Do you see the fourth car?"

Sinclair checked the rear window again. "No sign."

Gathering a burst of essence in her mind, she wrapped it

around the memory template of Terryn's signature and threw a sending. *Being pursued off route. Logan Circle heading to the Guildhouse.*

She accelerated and made a U-turn at speed. Two cars swept past, but the third came straight on. Stomping on the accelerator, she burned rubber into the pavement. As the SUV pivoted, she veered into the black car and slammed it with her real panel. Skidding sideways, the car danced on its right tires and flipped in a shower of sparks.

"Nice move. One down," Sinclair said.

Laura checked her mirrors. "Where the hell is that fourth car?"

"I don't see it either. We're five blocks off route. You've got to make a turn if we're going to get any help," Sinclair said.

Traffic blocked their path ahead. Laura shot a look at the rearview mirror. The two remaining cars drew closer. As they careened toward the stopped cars, Sinclair braced himself against the dashboard, and Laura held her breath. With a deft spin of the steering wheel, Laura ran a narrow gap in the jam.

Sinclair whooped. "You can drive!"

One of the black cars made the gap. Laura powered down her window and thrust her arm out. She released a scattered fan of essence, white lighting erupting from her fingertips so fast it made her arm jump. The bolts sizzled across the lane, and one of the other car's tires blew. It swerved wildly, its momentum fighting the dead wheel, and lurched to a stop against parked cars. The third black car tore past it.

"That's two," Sinclair said.

"Four blocks," Laura said.

A metropolitan police squad car leaped out of a side street. It shuddered left as Laura swerved right. The black car shot past it and gained on the SUV, while the squad car recovered and turned.

"Two more blocks," Sinclair said.

White streaks of essence flared across the night sky. A sending hit them both. *Aerial backup behind you.*

The squad car and the black car jostled for space in the narrow street.

Hit your brakes now! Laura sent to the officer. She slammed on her own. The black car swerved to avoid her, jumped the curb, and sailed through a windowed storefront.

"And that's three," Sinclair said.

A black blur pierced by blazing headlights sped out of a side street and smashed into their passenger side. The SUV spun. Laura fought the motion, the world smearing in flashes of white-and-red light, cars and buildings spinning past the windshield. She hit a car, then another. Sinclair shouted as the air bags deployed. Blinded, they crashed into something solid. The abrupt stop flung Laura forward into the air bag, the seat belt biting her shoulder and wrenching her back against the seat.

Laura batted against the air bags. "Jono? Jono? Answer me!"

His limp frame hung forward, the seat belt straining to hold him upright. Laura grappled with her belt and wrenched it free. The door was jammed. Furious, she hit it with essence and it flew off with a metallic shriek. She jumped out.

The last black car gunned toward her. She held both arms straight out, fingers clasped, index fingers pointing, and aimed at the oncoming car. From her fingers, a sharp line of essence burned like a spear through the air and splintered on the car's grill.

Laura swore as the essence flowed around a protection ward on the car. She dragged essence out of the pavement, the asphalt rippling around her with the strain. With a scream, she released it all in a yellow streak like lightning. The ward on the car splintered into fragments of green light, as Laura's bolt shattered the windshield and detonated inside with a white flash. Glass shards hurtled toward Laura, and she staggered under the onslaught against her shield. The glass hung for a moment, glittering in the headlight glare, then fell to the ground.

Laura swayed on her feet. The Janice glamour wavered, weakened from her dissipated essence. She reached out one more time to the ground beneath her feet, drawing essence out of the earth and into her body. The emerald necklace flared beneath her shirt, a glow that lit her stark features. Panting, she stared at the smoldering black car.

"That's four," Sinclair said.

Laura spun. Sinclair leaned against the back of the SUV, an arm wrapped against his ribs. Blood smeared across the side of his head. He cocked a smile. Laura took two long strides and hugged him. "Ouch," he said.

She let go. She pulled his head down and kissed him with a passion that surprised both of them. When she broke the kiss, he grinned. He lifted his gaze. On the next block, the officers from the squad car approached the gaping hole of the storefront where the other black car had vanished. "There is no way anyone's going to believe you're a low-powered druidess after this," Sinclair said.

Laura surveyed the wreckage. Sinclair was right. If the ripped-open black car wasn't bad enough, the fragmented asphalt she'd left behind was confirmation that Janice Crawford was more than what she claimed.

Time for another change in plans. "Showtime, Jono. We'll get people in position as soon as possible, but here's where you prove you can pull your weight. Play scared and get Foyle on your side."

"What's the plan?"

She pushed aside the SUV's air bag and found her cell phone. Terryn picked up instantly.

"I'm killing Janice Crawford right now. Send a wagon with a body, ASAP," she said.

Terryn didn't argue. "Anything else?"

She glanced at what was left of her car. "Yeah. I wrecked another SUV."

33
CHAPTER

POLICE AND FIRE cordoned off the street at either end. The SUV sat like an exhausted beast, its air bags hanging out the doors like ruptured organs. In the surreal flicker of blue, red, and yellow emergency lights, Sinclair stood over Laura's prone body, which was still glamoured as Janice Crawford. Two EMTs jumped out of a van with a gurney. They looked human, but their appearance didn't match the essence fields Sinclair sensed. He recognized the shape of Cress's essence.

Cress made no indication she knew him. "Step aside, sir."

He moved back as they shifted Laura from the ground to the gurney. "Where are you taking her?"

They moved with a controlled urgency. "GW. You need attention?"

"No."

Cress climbed in the emergency wagon, and the driver closed her in with Laura's body. The van rocked as it pulled away. Cress stared at Sinclair's dwindling figure through the rear door windows. "Is this wise?"

At the sound of Cress's voice, Laura's self-induced

trance broke. She breathed deeply, stimulating her heart-beat. "Nothing is. Can I sit up?"

Cress checked Laura's pulse. "Wait a few blocks. What happened?"

Laura rolled her head to stretch. "They came faster than expected and forced us out of the safe zone."

Cress's essence feathered over Laura's body, tendrils curling along the edges of her body signature, sensing its strengths and weaknesses. As always, Laura felt the desire in the touch, the need for essence that Cress fought against. "You have some bruising. Do you want me to take care of it?"

Laura sat up, Cress helping her with gentle hands. "No. I'll keep them unless I can't function."

On the other side of the van, a draped figure lay on a gurney. Laura removed her emerald stone, the Janice glamour blurring and shifting as it slid off her. She handed the necklace to Cress. "Can you charge it? I'm bone-dry."

Cress pushed essence into the persona template in the stone. Folding down the sheet on the other gurney, she exposed the Inverni from Laura's poison attack and slipped the chain around his neck. The glamour field spread over him, interacting with the almost vanished body signature of the dead body. His residual fairy essence shifted and faded beneath the druid signature on the stone, and his physical appearance warped and changed. Laura stared at an apparently dead Janice Crawford.

Cress caught her. "What's wrong?"

Laura shook her head dismissively. "It's always odd to see a glamour I've worn on someone else."

Cress folded the sheet back over the Inverni. "Do you think Sinclair is up for this?"

Laura stared out the window as if she could see back to the accident site. "He'll have to be."

The van pulled to a stop, and Cress handed Laura a set of car keys. "Terryn's waiting at the Guildhouse."

"Thanks for everything, Cress."

Laura hopped out, and the van resumed its trip to the hospital. Her Mercedes was parked at the curb. The music came on loudly when she started the engine. She leaned her head back. The plan had failed. Whoever had been in the black cars, it wasn't Alfrey. The power levels would have been higher. He had help, that much was clear. He wouldn't have sent Gianni after her, even if he thought she was minor league. If he'd come at her himself, he wouldn't have used a car. No, she thought, he sent henchmen, which meant he had an organization. She reminded herself that the Inverni had threatened Blume in front of a government building. He had balls. Which made him more dangerous. At least no civilians had been injured, she thought. That would mitigate some repercussions.

She drove to the Guildhouse at normal speed. The lights of emergency vehicles up the street flickered in her rearview mirror as she pulled in to the garage. Between the attempted bombing and the mess out front, the Guildhouse was on high alert. It was indirectly her fault, her failure to prevent it. And now, another failed attempt. Doubt worried at her as she took the elevator. She didn't like losing.

In the public-relations office, she walked through the closet to her private room. She spared a moment to wash her face before activating the Mariel glamour. The tepid water was insufficiently refreshing, but it helped her feel better. When she lifted her head, the calm, cool beauty of Mariel faced her in the mirror, with no sign of Laura's underlying stress. This is my life, she thought, this is what I do. Hide my face to find comfort and hide myself to avoid problems.

She shook off the melancholy and returned to InterSec. She found Terryn monitoring the news on three stations in his office.

"I'm sorry," she said.

He closed his laptop. "You tried. It was worth the effort."

"Can we protect Sinclair?" she asked.

He turned away from the screens. "I think so. We have inside help with the Capitol police. They've been alerted. He's already making a convincing case to the responders that he has no idea why you were pursued."

She dropped into the guest chair. "They were on us instantly, Terryn. They forced us away from the safe zone. We have a leak."

He rubbed his eyes. "I know, but that has to go on the back burner. We have the assassination target."

He handed her printouts, Homeland Security dispatches summarizing reports from various agencies. She skimmed them. Confirmation was coming in from several fronts.

Dropping the papers on her lap, she laughed in disbelief. "Hornbeck? It's Hornbeck? I could kill him myself right now."

34
CHAPTER

THE NATIONAL ARCHIVES sat between Seventh and Ninth Streets like a monolith—because it was a monolith. Big, dramatic, solid, the limestone-and-granite building was constructed to impress and to last. Layers of security protected precious documents inside, second only to that granted to the president. The archivists tended and preserved government records—both grand and mundane—so that researchers and citizens could access their history and understand their country. Except, of course, if their government didn't want them to, Laura thought.

The Guildhouse monitored the U.S. government's actions as much as any foreign entity's. The disappearance of strategic documents from public view did not go unnoticed. U.S. citizens had no idea of the daily minutiae of their government—the signing statements and policy procedures that affected their way of life and over time eroded their rights. The American government gazed with envy as Maeve ran the Seelie Court as only an absolute monarch could—perhaps the only true monarchy left in the world that functioned. Slowly, as the papers and records vanished into the bowels of the National Archives, their access restricted, the rule of law changed, tightening its hold on an unwitting populace.

Laura mingled with dignitaries making their way around the Archives to the entrance. On the Pennsylvania Avenue side, she noted a statue—a seated woman staring into the distance, an open book on her lap. The figure seemed caught in a moment of realization, as if something she'd read had prompted her to wonder about its implications. She didn't look happy about it. The engraving on the pedestal read WHAT IS PAST IS PROLOGUE.

A chill swept over Laura in the warm night air. The phrase echoed in her mind, a line from Shakespeare. A sense of dread touched her, the truth of the statement burning like a firebrand of warning in her inner vision. The future was a mystery, but its course could be seen. A few fey had the ability to see the future—or at least possible futures, but the final outcome always surprised. Laura shook off the feeling, determined not to let omens tease her fears for the evening.

Sinclair waited for her at the main-entrance security checkpoint on Constitution Avenue. She admired his tailored black suit and expensive tie, which he wore as comfortably as his day-job wardrobe of fatigues. He hid more than one weapon under his jacket. Other security officers working undercover for the event had guns as well. The fey sensed iron content, so the undercover status of anyone in the room carrying a weapon was undercut by sensing abilities. Laura gave Sinclair an advantage by adding a glamour to his medallion that masked the metal presence.

Flashing her badge, she skipped the queue and went through the metal detectors. The guest list for the opening included high-level officials from domestic and foreign governments. Secret Service agents patrolled the perimeter, and a more obvious metropolitan police presence directed traffic to the surrounding streets. Those who kept note of such things recognized that security was higher than usual for such a gathering. Even given the list of senators and House members and the high-level fey from both the Guildhouse and the Teutonic Consortium, security was tight.

"The president still insists on coming?" Laura asked quietly.

Sinclair scanned the crowd. "And Hornbeck. Not bowing down to terrorists and all that."

"And when someone dies, we get blamed for their ignoring us," she said.

A small smile flashed across Sinclair's face. "I love my new job."

They climbed the stairs to the main level of the building. "Foyle's on board now?" she asked.

"Completely. If anything, he's more on top of this than the Secret Service," Sinclair said.

Laura watched people filing into the Rotunda. "The passion of the converted. I'm worried you told him too much."

"It was unavoidable. He knew about the threat to Hornbeck. Once Secret Service muscled in on Triad, he had to know what was up," said Sinclair.

The reports of Alfrey's former association with Blume's firm had set off too many alarms for the Secret Service. An immediate review of Triad staff ensued. Whatever his motivations were, Hornbeck retained enough clout to keep the security firm at the event. With Blume's presumed innocence in the matter and his staunch defense of the integrity of his firm, political considerations came into play, and Triad was allowed to retain a role in security. As an alternative to an outright firing, no Triad staff were allowed inside the building. "Secret·Service is confident?" she asked.

Sinclair nodded again. "They booted everyone who had less than five years with the company or a known association with Alfrey off the Triad team. Backgrounds were rechecked. Triad stays outside," he said.

She made a point of not looking at him. "And you were assigned to me. What a lucky coincidence for you."

He grinned. "When opportunity knocks, I tend to answer."

Amused, she glanced at him. "Let's find my assistant, Saffin. She's been here all afternoon running the final checklist."

Sinclair took her arm, but Laura slipped out of it.

"You're security, Jono. Not my date. Two paces behind, please."

He smirked. "Yes, ma'am."

A string quartet played in the loge while across the way guests milled around the expansive floor of the Rotunda. The Declaration of Independence and the U.S. Constitution remained on display for the evening, though the Bill of Rights was secured in the vault below. Normally when visiting hours were over, the documents were electronically lowered in their sealed casements to a basement vault. Rumor had it that in addition to being fireproof and bombproof, the vault two stories below was nuclear bombproof. Laura once asked the chief archivist if it were true, but the woman changed the subject.

Waitstaff circulated through the crowd offering appetizers, champagne, and seltzer. Between the volume of people and lack of space, a formal dinner had been nixed early in the planning. No one on the Washington event circuit went hungry, though. On any given night, back-to-back fund-raisers or parties provided enough food to qualify as an evening meal. Not particularly healthy food, but no one starved.

Laura spotted Saffin listening politely to an older man and woman. When they made eye contact, Saffin gave her a subtle look of pleading. Laura pretended not to notice the older couple and pulled Saffin away.

"Thank you. I didn't know who they were and didn't want to insult someone important," she said.

"You look amazing," Laura said.

Saffin preened. Her maroon designer dress highlighted her mocha skin. "I used my entire last bonus check for it."

"And well spent. Is everything under control?"

She nodded vigorously as she looked around. "It was a little crazy this morning with all the security changes, but it's good now. Oh! I should warn you. Once the speeches start, they're dropping an *airbe druad* on the whole Rotunda. No one will be allowed through the essence barrier for about thirty minutes, so go to the bathroom now if you have to."

Laura chuckled. Saffin had thought of everything. "I want to check the security on the Treaty before things start."

Saffin touched her arm. "I'll do it. We're keeping it in the vault until Guildmaster Rhys makes his speech. You stay and mingle." She leaned closer and whispered. "And there is a very handsome man behind you watching your every move. You should talk to him." Saffin hurried off.

"My assistant thinks you're handsome," she muttered to Sinclair.

"You have an excellent assistant," he said.

Near the Declaration of Independence, Hornbeck held court, with Tylo Blume at his side. Blume didn't look like someone who had ever been denied a place at the table. In fact, he seemed pleased and relaxed as he laughed and talked with a Supreme Court justice. He should be happy, she thought. He got what he wanted.

On the opposite side of the room, Guildmaster Orrin ap Rhys moved through the gathering, oblivious to the Archives staffers and security personnel who scurried around him. For all their tendencies to vanity and superiority, most Dananns dimmed their essence and hid their wings from sight. It made dealing with humans easier—and enhanced the intimidation factor tenfold when they flashed their full power. Not Rhys. He was never shy about his normal appearance and more than happy to attract attention. He had been a negotiator of the Treaty of London and took pride in the achievement. To have another opportunity in the spotlight pleased him enormously.

Resha Dunne spoke with a group of fairies, mostly Dananns. A twinge of pity struck Laura at the sight of the glazed look on their faces. Resha's social skills needed serious overhauling. Her desire to help him warred with her preference for his ineffectualness. A stronger leader in the public-relations area would make her job harder.

Sinclair followed her as she slipped back to the entrance. "I want to talk to Foyle."

"He's in the Public Vault," said Sinclair.

The area behind the Rotunda served as an interactive

display area. The exhibit of fey documents took up the entire space by special arrangement. Foyle waited near the entrance in full-dress uniform. Many people knew him as a police officer, either for his work on the force or with the Fey Relations Committee, so there was no point in trying to pretend he wasn't security.

"Is everything going smoothly, Captain Foyle?" she asked.

He made a slight courtesy bow. "Fine, Ms. Blackstone. Is there anything you need?" he asked.

She was surprised he remembered her name. As Laura Blackstone, she had little interaction with him since the Archives handled security, especially with the president involved. "I'm just doing a last-minute walk-through."

She passed into the exhibit area. On impulse, she stopped and turned back. "Captain Foyle, has anyone else been inside yet?"

"Just staff, ma'am," he said.

She nodded. "Archives?"

He nodded as well. "And security. General entrance is scheduled for after the speeches."

She smiled. "Yes, of course. Thank you."

She entered the exhibit. Computer screens lined the walls. Convergence and its mystery were presented first, a series of theories outlining recent thought as to how the event occurred. When the fey first arrived, they'd kept themselves hidden from the general public. They didn't understand the world they found themselves in and tried to understand what had happened and where they were. Eventually, the Celtic and Teutonic factions revealed themselves to major governments in order to form alliances.

Original documents were on display within glass frames. The earliest documents showed High Queen Maeve's diplomatic efforts with President Wilson. History was on her side. Wilson was keen on the unity of nations. Laura recognized Maeve's hand in the subtle manipulations that played on Wilson's fears of war—and especially his growing concerns with Germany. The Elvenking's aggressive efforts to ally with the German government gave him pause, and the alliance with Maeve was inevitable. Maeve pushed for a series of stunning concessions from both the U.S. and Britain. The Seelie Court at Tara became officially recognized as a nation by treaty, and the rest of Europe fell in with their dominant allies.

Laura checked her watch. The speeches would start soon. *Saffin?* she sent. With the extra security wards in place, she allowed the sending a few moments to find its destination, but no response came. She retraced her path to the entrance, where Sinclair waited with Foyle. "Have you seen Saffin?" she asked.

Foyle craned his neck about the crowd. "Your assistant? She went down to the basement vault."

Laura tapped him politely on the arm. "Ah, thank you. She said she would be checking that area. We should return to the Rotunda, Officer Sinclair. I think things are about to begin."

They paused on the threshold of the Rotunda. The guest speakers had moved toward the podium next to the empty case where the Bill of Rights was usually displayed. Saffin should have been back upstairs at that point, but Laura still didn't see her. She called Saffin's cell, but it went to voicemail.

"She's not answering her phone or my sendings, Jono. Saffin wouldn't cut things this close. Something's wrong."

35
CHAPTER

LAURA LOOKED TO see if Saffin was among the Archives staff. She should have been with them near the podium. "I'm going down to the basement vault. If there's a problem, Saffin should have called or found me," Laura said.

"I'm going with you," Sinclair said.

She placed a gentle hand on his chest. "No. You'll slow me down. Your clearance isn't as high as mine. It's probably nothing. I'll be quick," she said.

"At least let me escort you to the elevator. If Foyle sees me without you, I'll get a bad mark in my file." His playful expression amused her, so she decided not to pull rank and let him go with her.

Terryn, have you seen Saffin? she sent.

Negative, he replied. His instant reply increased her concern. Terryn was supervising grounds security outside. If he heard her, Saffin should have. They cut across the loge. Security officers flanked the elevators. She flashed her Guildhouse badge at the nearest guard. "I need to go downstairs."

He spoke briefly into the two-way on his wrist, and an elevator opened a moment later. As she stepped in, he started to follow. She held her badge up again. "Thank you, Officer, but I'm attending a private meeting."

He checked her badge security level, then backed away. The doors closed. As the car descended, Laura sent a surge of her body essence into the perfect stone around her neck, and the Mariel persona enveloped her. The illusion of a long evening gown vanished to reveal a form-fitting jumpsuit.

The lower level was closed to the public for the evening. Security staffers challenged her as soon as she stepped into the theater lobby. She lifted her Mariel Tate ID. "I need to do a last-minute review in the vault."

Two guards confirmed the ID badge before letting her approach the locked area. She slid the ID through a scanner and entered the hallway leading to the vault. She sensed a residual trail of Saffin's essence, but there was no way to tell which direction she had gone. At a T-shaped intersection, she met two Capitol police officers. The badge went up again. "Last-minute review."

They let her through without question. Turning right, she reached the vault area beneath the Rotunda. The open round room held the mechanism that raised the documents for display upstairs. The Bill of Rights was off the mechanism and secured to one side, flanked by two guards. The Treaty of London had taken its place on the mechanical system to be raised at the moment Guildmaster Rhys gave the formal unveiling speech.

"I was told a Guild staffer named Saffin Corril was down here," she said to the nearest guard.

"She reviewed security on the Treaty about an hour ago." His voice spoke truth to her.

Laura sensed a residual echo of Saffin's essence on the document casement. Within the elaborate bronze frame, the black text of the Treaty stood out from the pristine white parchment as if it had been written yesterday. At the end of the second page, crisp signatures finalized the agreement— Wilson's tidy, slanted hand first, Asquith's sinuous swirl lower and to the right, and Maeve's elaborate spider scrawl to the left on the bottom. She wondered if the progressively chaotic signature styles reflected the progressively complex issues for each of the signing parties.

Three original copies existed, held by the governments of the original signatories. The American copy had been preserved the same way as the founding documents of the U.S. and resided in its original helium-filled casement. Given its more recent vintage, the encasement had not been upgraded during the renovation of the Archive, a subject of controversy in some quarters. It didn't need to be. Fey craftsmen had assisted with the Treaty and applied several layers of spelled preservation. Active druidic and fairy spells vibrated against Laura's sensing ability.

Satisfied that the Treaty was secure, she turned to leave. A flicker of essence in the casement caught her eye. She looked back but saw nothing amiss. Taking care not to arouse interest from the guards, she focused her ability on the casement. Essence lit in her vision, swirls of red, yellow, and green in tangled protection patterns. Nothing unexpected or unusual. She moved slightly, and the flicker came again.

She held still, waiting, as essence trembled on the edge of a blank space in the document. She pushed more body essence into her sensing ability and a subtle change rippled across the white space in a dull blue haze.

Terryn, I need you to see something in the basement vault. Bring Cress, she sent.

On our way, he sent back.

She roamed away from the Treaty to look at the mechanism that raised and lowered it. If the electronic system failed, it had a manual override. The guards watched her in a bored way.

When Terryn and Cress arrived, she muttered a sleep spell in Gaelic. A curtain of essence fluttered across the room and settled over the four guards. They froze, eyes staring forward with no sign of awareness.

Laura waved Terryn and Cress over to the Treaty. She pointed to the blank space. "Cress, there's something here. It feels like a fairy spell, but I don't recognize its type."

Cress directed her black, dark stare at the Treaty. Laura

watched her probe the case gently with delicate tendrils of essence. The strands twined their way through the security bindings without touching or triggering them. Apparently, whoever had created the spells had not taken into account the refined skills of a *leanansidhe*.

"It's a masking spell," she said, her voice low and flat.

"Can you get through it without stripping it?" Laura asked.

She extended more tendrils from her body essence. "It maintains itself with ambient essence, making it likely a Danann spell. A newer security spell is layered over it and causing interference. I can absorb the essence from the casing without altering the template of the security spells. I won't be able to hold it long without the template degrading and the alarms triggering."

"Do it," said Laura.

Cress closed her eyes and breathed deeply. The essence in the surrounding air changed, fading from sight as it flowed into Cress. The patterns of the protection spells glistened as they bled off, Cress absorbing each spark of their essence. The ghost of the spell framework remained behind. She burrowed through the spells, moving faster as if each step relieved pressure on the next. She reached the final, strange blue haze. As essence leached off the spell, words materialized in the blank white space.

A sharp intake of breath from Terryn grabbed Laura's attention. She didn't know what surprised her more—the hidden paragraph or Terryn's reaction. "That wasn't supposed to happen," he said.

Laura scanned the new paragraph. "Aid against Seditious Elements . . ." she read aloud. She finished the rest in silence. "Danu's blood, Terryn, does that mean what I think it means?"

"The spell's degrading," Cress interrupted.

Terryn recovered from his surprise. "Release the essence, Cress. We don't want attention."

Cress exhaled with a soft rasp, the violet tendrils of her essence expelling softer red-lit essence as it retreated. As she withdrew, the spell on the casement glowed with renewed energy. Cress swayed at the final disengaging of her essence. Terryn wrapped his hand around her waist. Laura averted her eyes as she siphoned some of his fairy essence.

"What the hell is going on, Terryn?" Laura asked.

"Wake the guards before they realize how much time has passed," he said. Terryn and Cress moved to where they were when Laura had executed the binding spell, while she took position again by the manual override. With the muttering of a cantrip, the binding released. The guards shifted in place, their muscles reacting to the sudden freedom.

Will you please tell me what this means, Terryn? Laura sent.

She shuddered at the wave of anger that preceded his response.

War.

36
CHAPTER

TERRYN AND CRESS followed Laura down the long hall, mental sendings flying among them. They passed the two Capitol police guards at the turn in the hall and went out to the theater lobby.

What do you mean, war? Laura asked.

The Seditious Acts targeted the Inverni opposition to Maeve. It makes us criminals if we object to Maeve's rule. That is what my father died to prevent. Maeve did it anyway. They all lied, Laura. The Inverni will declare war over this.

Laura considered the implications, her mind racing as she tried to understand how the hidden agreement factored into an assassination threat against Hornbeck. She couldn't see a connection. Her thoughts jumped to Blume. Triad had added security spells to the Treaty casement. They had to have noticed the interference between their security spell and the Treaty's masking spell like she did. She grabbed Terryn's arm. "He knows about the clause."

"Who does?"

"Blume," she said. She remembered the nearby guards in the lobby and switched to sendings. *Hornbeck's not the target, Terryn. Orrin ap Rhys helped write the Treaty. He's the real target. Blume's going to try to provoke war be-tween the Inverni and Dananns. It's the only thing that makes sense. He wants to weaken the Celtic fey with a fairy war. We need to shift the alert to Rhys and detain Blume.*

She felt several strong flutterings from Terryn. *I agree with the assessment. I've shifted security. I'll deal with Blume personally.*

I'll join you in a moment, she sent.

Where are you going? Terryn asked.

Saffin's down here, and she better not be dead, Laura sent back. She opened the door to the theater lobby, and Terryn and Cress slipped through. Laura returned to the junction in the hallway. In the brief space of time, the guards had changed. The Capitol police had been replaced by In-vernis in dark green fatigues. She didn't recognize them until they turned toward her. She stopped. The Triad logo emblazoned their breast pockets—block capital letters ex-cept for the "A," which was replaced with a bright red tri-angle.

A memory thrust itself into her awareness: Sanchez scraping lines in the blood on her hand, turning the hand so Laura could see it. One of her guesses about the lines in his blood was right—it had been an "A," but not for Aaron. The "A" in a logo replaced by a red triangle. Sanchez hadn't said "stop" and "try." He'd said "Stop Triad."

Terryn, Triad's down here. Repeat: Triad has infiltrated the Archives. We need Guild agents here immediately, she sent.

On my way, he sent back. He didn't ask her to elaborate.

She walked toward the guards as if nothing were wrong. "I'm looking for a brownie from the Guildhouse. I was told she was down here."

The two guards exchanged glances.

"She was here earlier, but she left," one of them said.

"How long ago?" she asked.

"Over an hour," the same one said.

She tilted her head. "That long? Did you see which way she went?"

He shrugged. "Upstairs."

Laura didn't need any ability to see he was lying. They hadn't been there five minutes earlier, so they definitely weren't there an hour earlier. She was about to challenge them when she heard a door close. Another Triad guard appeared at the end of the hall. He disappeared around a far corner in the opposite direction of the basement vault.

Laura stepped away from the guards to follow the other. "Maybe he saw her."

The guard who spoke moved into her path, his hands flickering with indigo light. "Ma'am, that's a restricted area."

Laura arched an eyebrow at his primed essence. "I have all access."

The other guard joined the first. "Not down here."

Laura glanced up the hall, then back to the guards. "The most sensitive material is in the vault. What could possibly be down there?"

His face set with determination, the first guard stepped closer. "You have to leave now, ma'am."

They drew in more essence, their hands burning brighter. In a blur of motion, sparks of essence flew from Laura's hands. "Sleep," she said. They crumpled to the floor.

She rushed down the hall. Outside a locked door, she found a concentration of Saffin's essence. Laura grasped the doorknob and sent a surge of essence into it, the metal resisting. She pushed back, the tumblers inside moving grudgingly as she forced them with essence. The door swung open.

The musty odor of old cleaning materials wafted out. Saffin's essence blazed in green flames on the floor. Laura hit the light switch and gasped. Bound with rope, gagged, and blindfolded, Saffin huddled. Her body trembled in spasmodic pulses as she screamed against the gag. Long claws flexed at the ends of even longer fingers. She had gone boggart.

Laura crouched in front of her, holding her hands wide to cast a soothing spell. "Shhh. It's okay, Saffin. You're safe now."

She stroked the air, chanting essence into the spell.

Saffin shimmied back with a growl. Laura darted her hand in and pulled off the filthy gag. Saffin threw her head back and shrieked.

She struggled against the ropes. "Bomb, bomb, bomb," she chanted.

Laura interrupted the spell. "A bomb?"

Saffin's face suffused with anger. "Bomb, bomb, bomb."

Laura activated her body shield. In her boggart state, Saffin could be extremely dangerous. "My name is Mariel. I'm going to take off the blindfold, Saffin. You are safe. Safe. Do you understand me?"

Laura feared she was too buried in the boggart shape to understand, but, amazingly, Saffin nodded. Laura grabbed the blindfold and lifted. As soon as her eyes were freed, Saffin lunged at Laura. Laura leaned away and brought her hands up again with the soothing spell. "Safe, Saffin. You are safe. You need to relax. If you relax, I can get these ropes off you."

Saffin's eyes bulged as her jaw dropped open to reveal long, jagged teeth. As the soothing spell took effect, some of the fierce green light in Saffin's eyes dimmed. Her swollen skin remained, the ropes biting her flesh. "Bomb spell," she rasped.

"Where, Saffin?"

"Stop. Stop. Bomb," she said.

Laura held her shoulders. "Where is it, Saffin?"

"Stop. Stop," she said.

Laura wanted to shake her, but knew it would make things worse. Saffin had come to check security, and someone had not only stopped her but prevented her from doing her job, which triggered her boggart mania. She wouldn't revert to her normal state until she completed her task.

"I will help you, Saffin. Tell me where the bomb is," she said.

"Treaty. Treaty. Bomb," she said.

"I'm going to get the ropes off, Saffin. You have to tell me where the bomb is," said Laura.

She nodded. "Treaty. Laura. Treaty."

Laura struggled with the intricate knotting on the ropes. "Yes, Saffin. We will find Laura and tell her about the bomb. Tell me where the bomb is. Tell Mariel."

"Treaty. Treaty. Treaty," she said. Her frustration rose, and her skin pulsed.

Laura paused. "It's the Treaty, Saffin? Is that what you're saying? The bomb spell is on the Treaty?"

Excitement lit Saffin's face. "Yesyesyesyesyesyes. Stop. Stop."

Laura pulled at the rope knots. Saffin bent her arm at an unnatural angle and yanked it free. She shoved Laura away and slashed the remaining rope to shreds. She loomed over Laura with a feral grin, her limbs long and flexible. "Bomb. Bomb. Bomb."

Laura backed away. Cornering a boggart was never a good idea. She backed into the hallway. Saffin's eyes bulged wider. *Behind you, Laura!* she sent.

Laura dropped and spun, kicking out behind her. She struck someone—a man—who fell, then rolled away. Laura jumped to her feet. Gianni lay faceup on the floor. He pointed his gun in her face. "You weren't supposed to be here, Agent Tate."

Laura raised her hands and gave him a winsome smile. "I don't recommend you fire, Gianni. You shoot, the woman behind me will be on you before you feel the recoil."

He stood, keeping the gun on Mariel. He tapped his headset. "Breach at Position 12."

Saffin growled and surged forward. Gianni lost the cocky attitude as his aim drifted toward Saffin. Laura shot a burst of essence in his face. He staggered back, clutching at his eyes. With an essence-hardened fist, she laid him out with a roundhouse punch to the head. He hit the wall and slid to the floor.

"That was for Janice Crawford." She kicked him for good measure. Moving quickly, she spun a binding spell on him that functioned with razorlike ribbons of essence. The more he struggled, the more the binding would burn into his flesh.

Saffin tackled her from behind. Laura scrambled beneath her in panic, expecting sharp claws to pierce her skin. Essence raked the air above them. She twisted her head to look down the hall. Three Inverni fairies in Triad uniforms came toward them.

"Stay!" Saffin growled. She bound down the hall on all fours, jumping from floor to wall and back again, evading essence-fire with an astounding agility. She launched at the lead Inverni, arms and legs forward. He screamed as she landed, the claws on her hands and feet ripping into his torso.

The other two Inverni fell back in terror, firing wildly. Panicked, one of them took to the air, but in the close quarters, he hit the wall and careened against his partner.

Saffin evaded their fire with every leap and turn. She sprang from the wall, flipped across the ceiling, and swiped her claws. An Inverni shrieked as her hands tangled in his wings, sparks of white essence bleeding from the tears she made. Saffin lifted him and flung him at his retreating partner. Their bodies met with a sickening crack, and they fell motionless.

Saffin whirled to face Laura. "Bomb, bomb, bomb." She raced toward the basement vault.

Laura pulled herself to her feet. *Terryn, the Treaty's primed with a spell bomb. I need Cress back down here,* she sent. She ran after Saffin. As she neared the vault, she heard Saffin's raging howl punctuated with essence-fires and screams.

Laura skidded to a stop. *Terryn?* She pumped more essence into the sending to give it the effect of a shout. Still no response. *Cress?* she tried. Nothing. Laura doubted both of them could have been taken out without warning. Her sendings were being jammed.

Another scream from the vault grabbed her attention. She hardened her body shield and charged into a bloodbath. Two guards lay dead near the entrance. Saffin sprang among the columns and ceiling beams, slashing at a retreating Inverni, his uniform shredded and bloodied. She evaded his essence-fire, but her blows landed, opening wounds on his face. Another Inverni worked behind him, sending the Treaty on its way through the ceiling to the Rotunda above.

Laura threw a jagged spear of light that hissed and crackled as it flew. The shot hit the lift mechanism and reacted with the metal. The odor of ozone filled the air, the scent of essence-fire and burned electronics. The Treaty ground to a halt.

The Inverni fired at her as he leaped to the manual controls, gears grinding with the speed and strength of the fey. The Treaty rose and disappeared into a ceiling shaft.

Saffin knocked Laura aside and jumped. She landed on the Inverni's back and wrenched her hands down. He screamed and convulsed as Saffin stood over him, the shredded remains of his wings dangling from her hands.

Laura ran to the manual controls and pulled on the gearshift. It wouldn't move. She couldn't reverse its direction. Saffin howled and scrabbled at the grease-slick hydraulic system.

"Saffin! Stop!" Laura shouted. Saffin ignored her. "Saffin! Listen to me! You did it. You found the bomb. You did it, Saffin. Calm down. You finished your job."

Saffin hesitated, uncertainty glimmering in her eyes. Laura stepped closer and lowered her voice. "You did it, Saffin. Good job. You can stop now. Mariel will take care of it."

"Laura?" she rasped.

"I will tell Laura," Laura said.

Saffin thrust a hand at her. "Laura!"

Laura did a double take. Was this something about boggarts she didn't know? Could Saffin see through her glamour? She pushed the thought aside. Time enough later to learn about it. She hoped.

"It's okay, Saffin. Yes, Laura knows about the bomb. Come with me," she said.

Tension drained out of Saffin, and she slumped against Laura. Her mania subsided. Even as Laura guided her across the room, she felt the woman's body shifting beneath her hands, the limbs retracting to their normal length, the elongated features smoothing out. Laura wanted her out of the area before she fully recovered. Extreme boggart mania resulted in blackouts. She didn't want Saffin to know what she had done until she was prepared to hear it.

More Inverni waited for them in the hallway. Laura extended her body shield. Saffin clung to her sleeve as they staggered under essence shots. Laura counted five attackers, highly trained and focused. She had power, but she needed to tap organic essence to take on that many alone, and so far underground, there was little available. Saffin growled deep in her throat as her mania returned.

Laura bit her lip. She had to get upstairs. She hugged Saffin from behind, words freezing in her throat. She took a deep breath. "Saffin, we need to get past them. Do you understand me? We have to stop the bomb. Will you do this for me?"

Saffin broke from her embrace in a blur of hair and claws. She bounded down the hallway toward the Inverni, her passage a spiral of acrobatics as she avoided essence-fire. Laura forced herself to watch as the screaming started.

37
CHAPTER

LAURA RAN UP the stairs, Saffin's raspy breath in her ears. She did not want to think about what she had seen. What had happened. What she had caused to happen. She did not want to think about what she would say to Saffin when it was over. If she lived long enough to give explanations. They left bloody footprints on the marble steps.

Saffin growled deep in her throat. Laura put a soothing hand on her head. She had never seen a brownie so deep in a boggart mania. "Stay with me, Saffin. It will be okay."

They reached an unguarded landing on the ground level. Above, essence-fire and fighting echoed down from the main floor. Laura grabbed Saffin by the arm. "You need to get out, Saf. Find Terryn macCullen. Tell him about the bomb in the Rotunda. Can you do that for me, Saf?"

Panting, Saffin stared with a crazed light in her eyes. She trembled and made a sound between a cough and a bark. Laura fought tears at the sight of her twisted and bloody face. Saffin touched Laura's cheek, using the flat of her palm to keep her claws from scratching. "Go, Saf. Hurry."

The boggart burst into motion. Laura fought back her emotions as she watched Saffin leap from side to side toward the entrance lobby. With a deep breath, she ran up the last flight. As she made the final turn to the main level, a stray shot of essence ricocheted down at her. She flattened herself against the wall and called up her body shield. After fighting through the basement hallway, no one was left to pursue her up the stairs. That wouldn't last long. Once the bodies in the basement were found, more fighters would be coming up behind her.

Where are you, Jono? she sent.

Public Vault. His sending came through rough and faint.

She breathed a short-lived sigh of relief. The Public Vault was on the opposite side of the Rotunda from her. *Any fey support with you?*

Foyle, he responded. The sending sounded forced and broken. Either she was too far away from Sinclair or his weak ability was failing. She was losing time. A short flight of steps separated her from the Rotunda. She bowed her head and said a prayer of protection. Tightening her body shield, she sank to the floor and crawled up the stairs. Another essence-bolt sparked around her. Laura screamed in panicked alarm, holding her hands out.

"Help! I've been shot!" she shouted.

Keeping her head down, she sensed an Inverni above her. She hunched forward, gathered essence in her chest, and released it in a single burst. She ran as it struck, and the Inverni fell. At the top of the stairs, she yanked him out of sight behind her.

On the opposite side of the loge, a door led to the Public Vault. She peered around the corner. Inverni fairies lined the loge area, powering an essence barrier across the entrance gate to the Rotunda. The barrier sizzled and crackled with light as the fey trapped inside fired at it. She leaped into a roll across the floor, wildly firing as she came up onto her feet. The Inverni returned fire, but their shots went astray.

She leaped over two prone humans at the entrance to the Public Vault, Capitol police officers who hadn't even drawn their weapons. She didn't stop to check if they were alive. Racing through the documents exhibit, she weaved in and out of display cases and room dividers to the back. Sinclair's head rose from behind a bank of computer displays and waved her in.

"Get down!" she said. He ducked as she joined him behind a panel. Foyle lay on the ground, his uniform coat and open shirt soaked in blood. His gun was on the floor beside him. "Is he alive?"

Foyle's eyelids fluttered open. "Yeah, he is. What's the situation?"

"Unknown number of hostages in the Rotunda. What's back here?" she asked.

"They made a sweep and took everyone down. We're the only two left," said Sinclair.

"Is the president inside?" she asked.

Foyle shook his head. "We aborted in time."

Laura exhaled in relief. The fallout from the attack was going to be bad enough without the added nightmare of a trapped sitting president. She threw out her hand for silence. A faint whir carried on the air, the sound of gossamer wings in flight as they shunted essence. A wave of Inverni essence swept over them and passed on.

Laura waited until she no longer felt them. "They'll be back. Can you move, Foyle?"

He shook his head. "Two hits. Leg and chest."

Laura looked up at Sinclair. "We've got to get into the Rotunda. There's a bomb."

"Where the hell is our backup?" Sinclair said.

"Fighting to get in through the entrance," she said. She leaned out to check the area. "Give Foyle your gun," she said to Sinclair. Sinclair checked the clip and handed it over.

Laura crouched in front of the downed officer. "Hero time, Foyle. You up for it?"

He gave her a crooked grin. "If I recall, you don't like hearing no."

She smiled back. "Good man. I'll do everything I can to come back for you. Do not let those Invernis come in behind us."

He grabbed Laura's arm. She and Sinclair helped him into a better vantage point. Foyle placed both his and Sinclair's guns in his lap. "For what it's worth, Agent Tate. I'm sorry I listened to the wrong people."

She squeezed his shoulder. "Apologize later. Good luck."

She grabbed Sinclair by the arm and pulled him into the open. Halfway to the exit, shots rang out behind them. No one followed them.

They stopped at the loge. "What's the plan?" asked Sinclair.

"Unbutton your shirt," she said.

He smirked. "Danger turn you on?"

She lowered her brow at him. "We need to get through that essence shield. Make sure I can get at that medallion of yours."

He started to lift the chain. "Just take it."

She stopped him with a hand on his arm. "We'll keep your fey nature secret if I can salvage that. If not, don't worry. I'll rip it off your neck."

He smiled. "I love it when you talk like that."

She thumped him on the chest. "Stop it. We're going to charge the barrier. The moment we're through it, hit the ground."

He peered out the door. "Isn't the point of the barrier to keep us out?"

She nodded grimly. "Gambling time. I'm betting on your grandfather for help. Come on. And don't get hit."

They charged the Rotunda gate, streaks of essence leaping from Laura's hands. More Inverni opened fire on them from the far end of the loge. Laura picked out essence waves from at least six Inverni maintaining their barrier. Laura shoved Sinclair toward the entrance gate. He stumbled in surprise as he hit the barrier and froze in place.

Spinning away, Laura hardened her shield and focused an essence shot on the Inverni directly above her. His head snapped back, and he fell hard inside the Rotunda. Without him, a thin spot formed in the essence barrier.

Laura lunged at Sinclair. He hugged her to his chest as they collided. She screamed as essence raked across her back. The barrier resisted them, slowing their momentum. Essence-fire burned through her body shield, and Laura screamed again. She clutched Sinclair's medallion and fired essence directly into it. Its field exploded in size. The essence barrier thinned. She hit the medallion again. Its field ripped a hole in the barrier, and they fell through. Laura landed on top of Sinclair with a gasp as the wind left her.

Sinclair's eyes went wide. He rolled and wrenched her with him as a bolt of indigo lightning scorched the floor. An Inverni had followed them through the barrier. Laura scrambled up, dazed. She thrust out her hand. A gunshot exploded in the air. The Inverni's cheekbone shattered in a spray of blood. Laura looked down at the gun in Sinclair's hand. "I thought you gave your gun to Foyle."

"You didn't say both guns," he said.

Fanned around Sinclair and Laura, fey of every stripe ranged in an arc and fired at the barrier. Behind them, human and fey diplomats huddled against the wall, a riot of body shields creating layers of protection. Laura picked out Hornbeck near the back of the crowd under a distorted layer of essence generated by Resha Dunne. Blume was nowhere in sight.

At the back wall, the emergency alarms had activated, and the display cases were empty. Except one. The Treaty had reached the Rotunda. Cress stood in front of it, gripping the edges of the casement.

"Can you stop it?" Laura whispered.

Cress held up a hand for silence. A complex maze of essence enclosed the Treaty, an intricate web of layers within layers. Security and preservation charms and bindings pulsed and vibrated in rainbow hues of essence. Beneath them all, a deep green orb radiated with a force that burned against Laura's skin.

"Helhound, is that thing the bomb?" asked Sinclair from behind her.

Laura nodded. "It's enough pressured essence to vaporize everyone in here."

Protection spells wrapped around the core of the bomb. Cress's deep violet essence threaded its way through the levels, sorting out the purpose of the spells. Her tendrils danced along a green grid, wrapped around it, and tugged.

The essence leached away, pulsing back up the strands into Cress. The grid faded. She started on the next one.

"Too many," Cress whispered, her stark, black eyes wide.

"What is it?" Laura asked softly.

Cress paused. "They're all trigger spells. I have to sort each one to find its purpose. I can't identify which one triggers the bomb or how."

"Can Sinclair's medallion help?"

Cress shook her head. "Weakening the protection essence is a fail-safe on some of the triggers." Without a word, Sinclair moved back.

"What can I do?" Laura asked.

Cress focused on the document. "Power. If I can tap someone's Power, I can move faster."

Body essence. Cress wanted body essence. Laura trembled as she took a deep breath. "Take mine, Cress. As much as you need. All of it, if necessary."

Cress moved her head slightly. "It won't be enough. I need more than one person."

Laura swallowed hard. If Cress needed more than one person, she meant at least one would die as she drained them. Laura looked around the room. She didn't know what to do. Pick someone, she thought. Hit them with a binding spell and let Cress work. Her eyes came to rest on Orrin ap Rhys. "What about the Guildmaster? He's Danann. Does he have enough?"

Cress absorbed another spell layer. "He's the strongest fey here."

Guildmaster, you're needed by the Treaty, Laura sent.

The barrier is weakening. We will be through in minutes, he sent back.

Laura appealed to his vanity. *We do not have minutes, sir. There's a bomb. Only you can stop it.*

Rhys dropped his hands. He gave one last look at the essence barrier and started toward them. As he drew near, Laura saw his body signature towering around him like a storm cloud. Powerful was an understatement.

Cress gasped. "Something's happening."

Laura looked down at the Treaty. A wheel-shaped layer of yellow essence glowed in a pattern, bolts of light arcing along its radial spokes. The arcing grew, jumping from one part of the pattern to the next. They bent and swirled, twisting together and leaping out in the same direction. Laura followed the line of their path to Rhys. The bolts grew larger.

"Rhys, stop!" she shouted. He froze. The bolts stabilized but didn't dissipate. Laura looked at the strange essence leaning toward Rhys, and she saw it for what it was. "The Treaty was supposed to rise during Rhys's speech, Cress. The bomb is keyed to his body signature. He's the trigger."

Cress swayed. Black spider fractures appeared on the orb. "I think . . . I think it's too late."

The orb pulsed and expanded, white light burning in the fractures. Cress's essence plunged into the cracks. Her violet essence became thick ropy strands as they sucked greedily at the orb.

"Cress, you can't contain that!" Laura shouted. She tried to pull her away. Cress screamed. The orb bulged and burned brighter. Laura threw out her body shield. "Everybody down!" she screamed.

A shock wave of white essence exploded. It slammed against Laura and threw her off her feet. The white light enveloped her, and she stopped motionlessly in the air. Bodies hung in suspension surrounded her, trapped in the frozen explosion of a brilliant white haze. Within its center, Cress glowed in black-and-purple silhouette. The light collapsed. Laura hit the floor, blinded by the afterimage. Dazed, she forced herself to stand.

Cress hovered like a lavender flame above the floor, scorching the stone beneath her feet. Her head fell back, and darkness oozed from her lips. Essence convulsed and radiated outward in waves. Laura staggered into Sinclair's arms.

"She can't hold it, Jono," Laura said.

He dragged Laura away, shouting. "Get everyone back! Shields! We need as many shields as possible."

Everyone retreated from Cress's burning figure. Hemmed in by bodies, Laura joined the other fey on the far side of the Rotunda. They extended their body shields, the human guests tangled against the wall behind them.

Light shivered off Cress and struck the body shields. They warped, and people fell. Another burst released. The shields shifted again, pressing against the crowd. A third burst pulsed, stronger than the last. The shields shuddered, leaving little room between them and the wall. Laura fought to retain her balance.

Get against the wall, Jono. Your medallion's fighting the shields, Laura sent. She didn't wait to see if he complied. Another pulse of essence burst from Cress. The body shields retreated, tightening the gap. Screams went up as some collapsed. The odor of burnt flesh filled the air. People spread out to cover the breach.

Laura cast a broadcast sending. *She's trying to do a controlled release. Time your energy to the waves!* Another burst and the entire line of fey stumbled back. The screams behind her were deafening as Laura fought to hold herself up. Again, and half the line fell. Laura bowed her head under the strain.

Cress floated like a brilliant mauve star beneath the Rotunda ceiling dome. The skylight in the center of the dome shattered under the pressure, shards of glass disintegrating as they fell into her burning field. She rose higher, her body cycling to a deep lavender as the energies within her fought for release. Tears sprang to Laura's eyes. The essence was too much. Cress was burning out. She was dying.

The damaged skylight framed her body like a broken eye, the top edge of the Inverni barrier rippling just below. Laura's skin prickled as she watched essence escape through the skylight.

Up, Cress! Release the essence up! Cress didn't acknowledge.

Blow the roof, Cress! Straight up! No response. Cress burned brighter. The next wave mounted in Laura's vision. Body shields were no match for what was coming.

Dammit, Cress! Go up!

Cress's arms moved. Laura bit her lip as she willed the *leanansidhe* to hear her. Cress's arms floated out, then lifted. Laura almost laughed. She had heard. Cress's mind was still in there. Clasping her hands over her head, Cress pointed up as the essence crested within her, burning with power.

She let go.

White essence geysered in a violent surge from her chest. Laura shouted as the torrent hit the dome and blasted it off its base. Chunks of masonry showered down, pummeling her body shield. Laura poured the last of her energy into her shield and prayed to whatever goddess would listen to her lost voice. Wild wind tore through the Rotunda as the raging column of light lit the night sky.

In the rumble of stone and bodies, Laura collapsed.

38
CHAPTER

LAURA SPIT SEDIMENT out of her mouth. Cries and moaning filled the air. A cool breeze swirled through the gaping hole in the roof. She staggered to the center of the floor. Cress lay on her side, eyes closed, hiding those disturbing dark eyes. Laura laid a gentle hand on her, as Cress had done for her so many times. Her essence was faint, but there. She was alive. Instinctively, fine purple filaments waved up from Cress's skin to suck greedily at Laura's body essence. Relieved and revolted, Laura withdrew her hand.

A phalanx of Danann security agents swarmed through the dome, a brilliant indigo light plunging through their ranks. The edges of Terryn's indigo wings burned white with speed. He landed and gathered Cress in his arms. Laura met his eyes for a fraction of second, saw pain and fear before he leaped into the air and vanished in a smear of blue light.

"Laura!" Sinclair swept her into his arms and kissed her. Kissed her lips, her cheeks, her eyes. She laughed, kissing him back, running her hands up behind his head. He hugged her, and she let him, tucking her face into the side of his neck.

Slowly, the memory of where they were—and who she was—came back to her. She still wore the Mariel glamour. She released him and adjusted her jumpsuit with an embarrassed smile. She cleared her throat. "It's good to see you, too, Officer Sinclair."

He laughed and shook his head. "My apologies, Agent Tate. I don't know what came over me."

The smile faded from her face as she took in the scene behind him. Bodies lay everywhere amid the debris. She sensed pain and horror and relief. Orrin ap Rhys stood among the worst injured, directing the security forces. Laura's heart skipped a beat as she recognized Resha Dunne lying facedown on the floor. She hurried to his side, relieved to see the spark of life in him as she neared. He stirred, lifting his head off the floor. She helped him up.

He rubbed at his mouth. "I need a drink of water."

Laura straightened his tie. "This is nice. Hermès?" she asked.

He gave her look of utter bafflement as she walked away.

Sinclair grabbed her arm. "We have a problem."

She followed the direction of his nod. Foyle stood near the gate entrance to the main floor. "That's not Foyle."

Laura narrowed her eyes at the man. He was too far away for her sensing field. "What do you mean?"

"I know Foyle's shape. That's not him. Besides, he was too wounded to stand," Sinclair said.

Laura moved closer, saw there was no blood on Foyle anymore. Sinclair was right. Foyle's essence hummed with power. Not human. It wasn't Foyle. The man turned away from the scene and walked toward the exit. Laura ran after him and grabbed his shoulder. "Hold it!"

Foyle yanked away from her. "Unhand me!"

She blocked his way. "I don't think so."

He drew himself up. "I am Captain Aaron Foyle. Get out of my way."

Laura wrenched the man's shirt open to reveal a small gem on a gold chain. She tore the glamour off him. Foyle's face shifted and blurred away as narrow, indigo wings swept upward. Laura fashioned a blade of essence in her hand.

"You're not getting away this time, asshole."

She plunged the blade into Alfrey's head, and he dropped like a stone.

39
CHAPTER

LAURA WATCHED ALFREY through the glass window. He remained poised as he reclined in his chair surrounded by tall obelisks of quartz that dampened his fey abilities. Terryn sat outside the wards, equally calm, as if they were discussing the weather. She searched Alfrey's face for some remorse for the twenty-seven deaths at the Archives. She saw none. She felt a small satisfaction at the swollen bruise from his left ear to his chin and the way he forced air through the wired jaw.

"You are not like your father," Alfrey said.

Indifference flitted across Terryn's brow. "Unfortunately, you are much like yours."

"Your father would be disappointed to see you now," he said.

"Do not speak of my father again, Alfrey. I may forget myself," said Terryn.

Alfrey snorted. "You forgot yourself a long time ago when you aligned yourself with the Danann scum."

"I will not be distracted. Who are your allies?" asked Terryn.

Alfrey smirked. "My allies? My allies are who they've

always been. The fey who resist the domination of the Danann usurpers. The Elvenking's slaves. The humans who do not fear us." He leaned forward. "And the true Inverni whose leaders failed them. Those are my allies, macCullen, and they grow in number with each passing day."

Terryn stood. "I see we are done for another day."

Alfrey chuckled. "Pray, do me a favor macCullen? When you see Tylo, tell him he, too, has fallen from the path of redemption. Tell him Triad was never his, and we shall prevail where he fails."

Terryn didn't respond. Laura fell in step with him as he left the room and walked to the elevator.

"How's Cress?" she asked.

"Better. Recovering. She will survive," he said.

They stepped into an empty elevator. "She was amazing, Terryn. She saved us."

He nodded. "Yes. I've read the reports."

"Is Blume cooperating?" she asked.

Terryn hit two buttons on the elevator panel. "At the moment, yes. I am playing on his gratitude for pulling him out of the Rotunda before Alfrey's men trapped everyone else. He has been quite instrumental in identifying people for us."

Laura stopped the elevator. Terryn arched a single eyebrow at her. "What's going on with Alfrey is more than bad, isn't it?"

"It will get worse," he said.

"Can this really cause a war between the Dananns and the Inverni?"

He crossed his arms and stared at the floor. "The Seelie Court lied. The Treaty says what it says. Maeve has much to answer for, as do the U.S. and Britain. It may lead to something more than a civil war among the fairy clans."

"What are you going to do?" she asked.

He wouldn't meet her eyes. "I don't know. I walked away from all that years ago."

Laura reached out and held his arm, a familiar gesture that felt awkward. "I will stand by you, Terryn. Whatever you need. Just ask."

He started the elevator. "Thank you."

At the seventh floor, she left him and returned to the public-relations department. Laura sat down to a stack of pink message slips. Hornbeck had called twice. She stared at the number, then dialed. He startled her by picking up himself. She didn't realize it was his personal cell.

"How are you, Senator?" she asked.

"Better than some. I was happy to hear you made it out of there all right," he said.

"Thank you. How can I help you?" she asked.

He chuckled. "After what happened last time I asked you for something, I'm surprised you would offer. No, I called to apologize personally for my role in the recent affair. If I hadn't insisted on using Blume's people, none of this would have happened."

"There's no need to apologize, Senator. The Triad sleeper agents were deeply embedded. Alfrey was planning this for years. If not the Archives ceremony, it would have been something else."

He sighed on the other end of the line. "I can't help feeling somewhat responsible. If there is anything I can do for you, let me know."

Laura smiled. "I wouldn't mind a little support in the Senate now and then."

Hornbeck chuckled again. "Yes, well, wouldn't we all. Keep in touch." He hung up.

Saffin entered with another stack of mail. Laura winced at the sight of the healing cuts and bruises on her face and arms. Saffin, however, smiled as she filled the in-box. "I sorted these by priority as best I could."

Laura looked up at her with a grateful smile. "Thanks. Could you close the door and have a seat?" Curious, Saffin tilted her head and did as asked. "Are you all right?" Laura asked.

Saffin nodded, self-consciously holding her hand over bandaged fingers. "My healer sent me home with an amazing potion. I slept for three days. I'm fine."

"No—I mean, good, of course—what I meant, though, is, how are you about what happened?"

Saffin met her eyes with a frank stare. "I'm a brownie, Laura. I become a boggart. They're both who and what I am."

Laura looked away. "I wish I could be so comfortable with myself."

"It's my nature," Saffin said. "There's no sense in fighting it. I came to terms with it a long time ago. I have faith that when I go boggart, the Wheel of the World has a purpose that makes sense for me."

Laura fidgeted with a pen. "How long have you known?"

Saffin frowned. "Known what?"

Laura met her eyes. "At the Archives, when Mariel Tate found you, you called her Laura. Me. You called me Laura. How long have you known?"

Guilt crept across Saffin's face. "A few years."

Laura dropped back in her chair, letting her surprise show for once. "Years! How did you find out?"

The guilt turned to amused embarrassment. "Your brown suede Gucci pumps were scuffed."

"What?"

Saffin smiled pertly. "Mariel Tate wore the same pair with the same scuffs."

Laura leaned back. "That's it? You concluded I was wearing a glamour because of a pair of shoes?"

Saffin rocked her head back and forth. "Well, that was the first clue. Then I noticed Audra Henley had the same loose stitch on a jacket, Sylva Wentworth had the same ink stain on her Prada jeans, and whenever you sent me to Candace Burke, I found Terryn macCullen's number on the caller ID, then you would disappear."

"I have an ink stain on my Prada jeans?"

Saffin held her index finger and thumb about a quarter inch apart. "Just a little one outside the right knee."

Laura covered her face with her hands and laughed. "I can't believe I was that sloppy."

Saffin shook her head. "Well, unless you have other assistants like me, I doubt it. I love your wardrobe."

Laura regained control of herself. "Who have you told?"

Saffin's eyes went wide. "No one! I figured if you didn't tell me, it had to be heavy-duty undercover work."

Laura shook her head. "I can't believe this."

Saffin nervously rubbed at her bandaged hand. "Am I in trouble?"

Laura considered the ramifications. Saffin had known for years and never said a word. "Of course not. In fact, it's a relief. Tell you what: Let's keep this between us. No one has to know."

Relief swept over Saffin's face. "That sounds easy."

"Good. Now, I have a ton of stuff to get off my desk before my flight tonight. Don't put any more calls through," said Laura.

Saffin opened the door. "That reminds me, I got you upgraded on the final leg to St. Barts."

"Thanks, Saf. I can never thank you enough for everything."

Laura shook her head in disbelief. Shoes. Outside the door, she heard Saffin gasp. A moment later, she scurried in carrying a vase of long-stemmed red roses. "I bet I know who these are from!" she said.

Laura opened the note card. The message was a phone number with "Jono" written under it.

"The big guy from the Archives?" Saffin asked.

"The big guy from the Archives," Laura said. Saffin strutted out with a smug look.

Laura called the number.

"Hey, I haven't heard from you in a few days," Sinclair said.

"It's been crazy," she said.

"I thought since you still have the key to my apartment, you should probably have my new cell number."

"I'm sorry. I'll return the key," she said.

"You don't have to. I trust you. Are you free for dinner tonight?" he asked.

She rubbed the card between her fingers. "I told you, Jono. I don't date colleagues."

"What colleague? I met this woman at an exhibit the

other night. It was like fireworks. I don't work with anyone like that," he said.

Laura allowed herself a grudging smile. He wasn't going to stop. "What do you think of Caribbean food?"

Look for the next Connor Grey novel

UNPERFECT SOULS

by Mark Del Franco

In the Weird, the bad stuff went down at night. People fought. They screwed up. They died—sometimes by accident, sometimes by their own hands. And murder happened, too, more frequently in this end of town than in any other . . .

In the Boston neighborhood known as the Weird, the Dead of TirNaNog stalk the streets. When a decapitated body floats out of the sewer, former Guild investigator Connor Grey uncovers a conspiracy that may bring down the city's most powerful elite.

As the violence escalates, Connor is determined to stop it—with help from one of the most dangerous beings of Faerie. To save his friends and allies, Connor realizes, a sacrifice must be made—one that will bring about the destruction of everything he holds true. And this time, Connor doesn't care what it takes—even if it means unleashing the darkness that burns within him.

Coming February 2010
from Ace Books